--- ★ ---

The beam of Thomson's flashlight swept back and forth, from the rocky hillside with its thin skin of turf across the beach to the waves rolling forward, falling back, rolling forward again. "The tide's coming in. How far above… Ah. There he is, poor chap."

Three rays of light converged on a long shape, inert as driftwood. The man lay diagonally across the pebbles, feet to the land, head to the sea, one arm flung out as though reaching for something that exceeded its grasp. Just beyond his fingertips lay the flashlight Alasdair had given him, glass broken, bulb extinguished.

His face was turned away from the probing lights. That, as far as Jean was concerned, was a very good thing. And yet even her shrinking gaze discerned that below the red cloth of his jacket glistened a smear of crimson, and a crimson thread wove its way between the pebbles toward the lick of the waves.

Thomson set aside his first-aid kit and squatted down to inspect the body, the physical shell of a human soul.

---   ---

The BLUE HACKLE

LILLIAN STEWART CARL

W❁RLDWIDE®

TORONTO • NEW YORK • LONDON
AMSTERDAM • PARIS • SYDNEY • HAMBURG
STOCKHOLM • ATHENS • TOKYO • MILAN
MADRID • WARSAW • BUDAPEST • AUCKLAND

Recycling programs for this product may not exist in your area.

THE BLUE HACKLE

A Worldwide Mystery/September 2013

First published by Five Star Publishing in conjunction with Tekno Books and Ed Gorman.

ISBN-13: 978-0-373-26864-1

Copyright © 2010 by Lillian Stewart Carl

Printed in U.S.A.

For Anjali Ravi Carl.
The last but far from least book of the series for the last but far from least member of the next generation.

In a stately home, no one can hear you scream...

Alasdair Cameron and Fergus MacDonald were childhood friends. Their fathers' caps carried a blue hackle, the badge-feather of a distinguished Scottish regiment. Now the feather in Fergie's cap is the decaying Dunasheen Estate on the Isle of Skye. His desperate schemes to save his home depend on a collection of historic artifacts, a handful of paying guests expecting a traditional Scottish New Year celebration, and the help of Alasdair and Jean Fairbairn.

For Jean and Alasdair, the bells of the new year are also wedding bells—their rings are ready, their guests are invited, and the Gothic folly of Fergie's chapel is waiting.

Then a guest is found murdered, the police crash the party, and Alasdair and Jean find themselves juggling knowledge, belief, and a list of suspects whose secret agendas raise more than a few hackles.

Is that the icy winter wind, or the banshee-wail of a long-dead MacDonald chatelaine affirming that only Fergie's motives are true-blue? Or is he hiding a secret agenda beneath his fool's cap and bells?

Ring out the old, ring in the new. But if Alasdair and Jean can't untangle the threads of the past and net a present-day killer, then they and their wedding rings won't get to the church on time—and more blood will flow for the sake of Auld Lang Syne.

ONE

Jean Fairbairn peered over the railing of the footbridge. If sufficiently motivated—chased by bloodthirsty swordsmen, for example—she could have dangled by her hands from the walkway and dropped into the rocky, muddy gully that had once been a moat. She'd be skewered anyway, but giving up and going quietly had never been part of her vocabulary.

Nor was it part of the vocabulary of Scotland, where the past had played out in scenes of blood and thunder, fire and sword. Now popular memory and the Scottish Tourist Board elided here, revised there, and edited fierce bloody-mindedness into high Romance. Though history could still be perilous, as the thud and blunder of Jean's own, lowercase, romance had proved.

Alasdair Cameron, the object of her romantic inclinations, inspected the ruined castle that rose above the far end of the narrow walkway even as he said, "No need to go chucking yourself over the edge just yet, the wedding's not 'til the third."

"Thank you, light of my life," Jean returned. "Was it this Dunasheen Castle or the other one where Rory MacLeod tried to jump from wall to tower to see his lady love?"

"This one, I'm thinking, it being a medieval tale. Though it goes that he reached his lady love via the stairs, her husband came breaking in, sword in hand, and he made the leap from tower to wall, meaning to escape."

"Both versions are variations on a theme, the lover's leap, fatal or otherwise." That brought Jean back around to the choice she did not, thank goodness, have to make, between a sharp edge and a hard place—her imminent matrimonial plunge notwithstanding.

She hadn't intended to fall for anyone, let alone a Scottish detective inspector. And now-ex-policeman Alasdair hadn't meant to fall for a part-time historian, part-time journalist, full-time inquiring mind wanting to know. But their hearts had led, leaving their heads to play catch-up, and here they were, on a bridge both literal and symbolic.

Smiling, Jean also considered the snaggle-toothed battlements of the ancient castle keep. Outside the tower, lichened blocks of dark gray stone imperceptibly became lichened bedrock, knitted together with tussocks of grass and tufted by saplings springing from crevices. Inside the tower, seabirds nested in empty windows and in hollow fireplaces now suspended from sheer walls. The wooden floors where people had stood warming their chillblains, cooking their food, and thanking goodness for strong defenses atop a small, craggy islet—moats and drawbridges making good neighbors—had decayed into nothingness long ago.

The old castle was dignified in its desolation, and yet Jean also sensed an air of sadness for times past and regret for lives spent. She wouldn't be surprised if it was also haunted, but she hadn't lingered long enough for her spectral early warning system to activate.

Alasdair raised his camera, took several photos, then jotted something on a notepad.

"Now what? Secret passages? Buried treasure?" Jean pulled her hands up into her sleeves in an attempt to warm them up.

"That path running outside the enceinte, the boundary wall," he replied. "It's partially eroded, right dangerous, and wants blocking off. Or rebuilding with a railing, but Fergie's saying he can afford only what will keep the place standing."

"Structural faults aren't really in your line of work."

"Oh aye, here's Fergie—and wee Diana as well—thinking I'll be advising him on locks and the like for the new castle, not on shoring up the old one, but it's something I can be doing to help. This bridge, now, is likely no more than thirty years old. A bit damp, mind. It wants checking for rot." He stamped on the walkway, sending a reverberation through the wooden slats beneath Jean's feet.

A good thing she wasn't acrophobic. Claustrophobic, yes, and dubious about darkness. She'd declined a visit to the dungeon in the foundations of the old tower, more like a cave than a cellar, never mind Alasdair and his flashlight. The issue wasn't only its impenetrable shadow and low, vaulted ceiling, but its smell; dead fish, defunct rats, decaying seaweed, mold and mildew.

She inhaled deeply of the cold wind and vaporized Atlantic that scoured her cheeks—out with the bad air, in with the good—and looked up at the sullen gray sky. Seagulls spiraled like flecks of white confetti, their harsh squawks piercing the thrum and seethe of the waves against the far side of the islet. "What isn't damp? This is the Isle of Skye. It's a giant soggy sponge. Look at those clouds, it's going to rain again any minute. Sleet. Snow."

"It's not cold enough to sleet or snow."

"Coulda fooled me."

Alasdair glanced at his watch. "It's getting on for half past three. Sunset, this time of year."

"Tell me about it. I moved to Edinburgh from Texas last January. That was a shock. It wasn't until it was still light at midnight in June that I thawed out and dried up." Not least because it was in June that she and Alasdair stopped circling each other like duelists and surrendered to their mutual attraction.

If he caught her reference, he showed no sign of it. Grasping her gloved but cold hand in his, he pulled her toward the mainland—or main island—side of the bridge. "Skye can have positively brilliant days in December and January. We'll be seeing one yet. Just now, though, we could do with a cuppa."

"No kidding." *Tea,* Jean thought. *Chocolate biscuits.* Caffeine and cocoa, two of the basic food groups.

Their rubber wellie boots clumping, they scrambled up the mud-and-gravel path to the top of the brae. This hill might not be nearly as tall as the towering cliffs propping up other stretches of the Skye coastline, but still it commanded a view. Or would, when one of those brilliant days came along. Fergie promised a panorama, from the islands of the Outer Hebrides across several miles of open sea to the north to the peaks of the Black Cuillins to the south, beyond the end of Loch Roy, a narrow inlet of the ocean that formed the eastern boundary of Dunasheen Estate.

Now, though, either sinking clouds or rising mist blotted the horizon, and the waves where loch met sea, below the ramparts of old Dunasheen, gleamed gunmetal gray. The terrain resembled a tattered crazy quilt laid over the bones of the earth. Patches of olive drab, rusty brown, and more gray were lumped around weathered boulders and pocked by reed-fringed pools scummed by ice. A few blots of light in the murk were all Jean could see of the village of Kinlochroy, at the far end of the loch.

But she and Alasdair weren't walking to the village, not when the magnificent Scots Baronial pile of new Dunasheen Castle lay just ahead. The warm glow of its windows and the red and green fairy lights edging its eaves made the building into a humongous Christmas card. All it needed to complete the effect was snow softening the stark, black limbs of the trees tucked in behind garden walls.

"All right!" Jean pulled Alasdair to a halt. "Take some

photos to go with Fergie's interview. Look, there's even a guy in a red jacket walking out of the courtyard—perfect timing, very photogenic."

Muttering something about electricity rates and Fergie not knowing when to stop, Alasdair raised his camera. "The interview's covering the estate, the renovations, the paying guests and all. You're not meaning to encourage his fancies and odd notions."

"Define your terms. You think not putting milk in your tea is an odd notion."

His slate-blue eyes that could be chill as the North Sea sparkled like a tropical lagoon. A wry crumple only deepened the graceful curve of his lips.

Jean ignored his silent retort. "Sure, that's the deal, your security expertise and my journalistic skills in return for a New Year's Eve party and a wedding. The weird stuff is off the record. It would hardly scare away the customers, though. A lot of people love weird stuff. *I* love weird stuff. But Fergie's your friend, so he gets a free pass. Especially now, during the Daft Days between Christmas and New Year's Eve."

"Especially as we're all a bit daft, in our own ways."

That was one concession, Jean thought, he would not have made even a few months ago.

Either rain or sea spray drifted across her face and glasses, making her squint at the suddenly blurry landscape. But the welcoming windows and cheerful lights still shone, and with Alasdair at her side she walked toward them.

It wasn't her step that was springy, it was the ground she walked on—water, peat, layers of cultivation both literal and cultural. Skye, *An t-Eilean Sgitheanach,* the wing-shaped isle, a name to conjure history, legend, and the dubious shores between. She could create multiple articles for *Great Scot,* the magazine that was partly her investment and fully her employment, without getting too close to Fergie's more marginal notions, although his notion of making a self-sustaining business of a Scots Baronial white elephant was the point of the exercise.

"New" being relative in this part of the world—new Dunasheen dated to the early 1600s, when the local MacDonald laird had, after years of conflict, at last dispossessed the local MacLeod laird. He'd then abandoned the old castle and proclaimed his wealth and sophistication by erecting a manor house à la mode. Since then, generations of Lords Dunasheen, MacDonalds all, had renovated, rebuilt, and re-created. Annexes and towers encrusted the original building. Bow windows sprouted from walls, and dormer windows from moss-lined slate roofs edged by crow-stepped gables. Conical turrets called bartizans seemed to hang onto corners by sheer will power but were actually supported on corbels, protruding stones set in decorative tiers. Chimneys both tall and short capped the exuberant, if time-stained, structure like exclamation points.

Even in the dull light, the stucco-like lime harling that protected the stone walls from the uncompromising elements reflected a sheen of pink. The original had been colored by the bull's blood used as a gelling agent, Fergie had said, just as the mortar holding together the bare stones of old—eight hundred years and more old—Dunasheen had been coagulated by the eggs of sea birds. You used what resources you had here at the outer rim of civilization, thought Jean. You called in favors from old friends. You promoted your white elephant as a fairy-tale castle.

The man in the red jacket marching along the footpath toward her and Alasdair must be a product of Fergie's marketing scheme, moats and drawbridges now making good customers. They met up with him just where the path twisted between fissured, lichen-encrusted boulders, half-concealed by unblooming heather.

His bulbous nose was red, too, and his square, blunt face was burnished by the wind. Sandy hair streaked with gray fluttered back from his wide forehead. Hunkered down into his thickly padded jacket, his hands thrust into his pockets, he was still taller than Alasdair, who in turn was taller than Jean. But then, most people who were not children or hobbits were taller than Jean.

The man's face creased into a triangular grin, wider on one side than on the other, filled with uneven teeth. His oddly pale gray eyes gleamed with humor. "If this was a golf course, it'd be all rough and no fairway."

"Oh aye," Alasdair replied. He and Jean turned sideways, giving the man passing room.

He maneuvered past, saying, "'Scuse me, mate," in a twang squeezed against the roof of his mouth. "You too, Missus. Is this the way to the church?"

He was either Aussie or Kiwi, Jean deduced, her ear for Down Under accents not tuned finely enough to detect the difference. She'd have to ask.

Alasdair answered, "The old church or the new one?"

"The one with the crusader tombstones that was burned down by the MacLeods in 1645."

Who had surrounded the building, Jean added silently, swords drawn, as the congregation of MacDonalds perished inside—clan conflict fed on religious conflict and vice versa. But the delectable odor of smoke teasing her nostrils this afternoon was that of smoldering peat, implying warmth and sanctuary.

"Then, no, you've gone the wrong way," said Alasdair. "That path runs from the garden at the western side of the house. The new castle. But you can follow the beach below the old castle round to the left, past the wee promontory, and then climb the brae to the church."

Jean assessed the slight pucker between Alasdair's eyebrows as a mental note: *Tell Fergie to lay on directions to the local sights.*

Her own mental note was a selfish one. The horrific events at the old church trumped its historical interest, and she was just as glad the wedding was scheduled for the new one, a charming Gothic Revival folly. Not that she'd sensed more than a melancholy chill at the old church—churches, plural, walls layered atop more walls layered atop ancient foundations—when she and Alasdair had stopped there on their tour of inspection.

She tried luring the stranger into conversation with, "You're already familiar with the history of the area, then."

"Yeah, I've been tracing the family tree. I'm a MacLeod myself. Greg MacLeod, Townsville, Queensland, Oz. You're at the castle, too?" He extended his right hand.

"Aye," Alasdair said, without introducing the topic of weddings. "Alasdair Cameron, Edinburgh." He exchanged a firm handshake and passed the friendly hand on to Jean.

To her cold fingers, Greg's hand seemed almost feverishly warm, slightly damp, and linty from his pocket. "Jean Fairbairn, also Edinburgh, though I started in Texas. But you've come a lot further than I have, all the way from Australia."

"Not so far, not these days. My multiple-great-grandfather, though, came out on a leaky ship. Transported near two centuries ago, and not for nicking a loaf of bread. For murder." Despite his words, Greg's grin evened into a rectangle, revealing a few more teeth—Jean wondered if they were issuing extra ones in the southern hemisphere.

"Murder," Alasdair repeated, if not amused, then not alarmed, either.

Abruptly the light wasn't dull at all. A gleam of sunlight pierced the cloud, glanced off the sea, and swelled like a scarlet wound along the southwestern horizon. Every puddle, pool, and trickle of water in the surrounding moorland glittered.

Dazzled, Jean said, "After two hundred years, having a murderer in the family seems more exotic than shameful. In fact, I hear having ancestors among the convicts in the First Fleet provides a bit of cachet in Australia these days, when for years it was something you hid beneath the antimacassars. Or was your ancestor in the First Fleet?"

"Not at all, no. Tormod MacLeod left Skye in 1822. He wouldn't have had an easy go Down Under, but he missed out the worst days of Botany Bay. Though I'm starting to think the old guy crossed up the law to get himself a ticket to a warmer climate." Greg returned his hands to his pockets and his shoulders to a crouch. "But here I am. Blood is thicker than water."

"You've not chosen the friendliest time of year," said Alasdair.

"Christmas in London, though! Lights, music, food, grand museums, galleries. And Harrods, Debenham's, and Burlington Arcade for the wife. Now my credit card needs resuscitation. I'll have to take out a second one to pay the overweight luggage fees."

Jean smiled. Alasdair nodded agreement.

"Now for Fergus MacDonald's New Year's package, a traditional Hogmanay here on the old home ground." Greg stamped his athletic shoes against the black dirt of the path, producing a slight squish and runnel of brown water. "Bloodstained ground. The MacDonalds and the MacLeods went at it like billy-o, once."

"Putting rings on each other's fingers and daggers in each other's hearts, to quote some old historian." And Jean added to herself, oh yes, Skye was conjuring magazine articles. She'd have to ask Greg for more details of his rogue ancestor. In her previous life, she'd learned that putting a personal face on history added entire minutes to her students' attention spans. The same ploy worked with readers. "Did Tormod MacLeod murder a MacDonald?"

"It's not so clear in the old family story just what happened. That's why I'm here, to get the facts, if there are any facts to get. Our local clan group and the genealogy sites on the Internet only go so far. I found Dunasheen's website, though. *Dun na sithein,* fortress of the fairies. I could hardly resist following up on that."

"*Sithein* can mean fairies," allowed Alasdair. He'd already expressed caution at Fergie's take on the subject, not to mention Fergie's promise of a private showing of the famous Fairy Flagon and the unveiling of yet another notion.

Jean, though, was sharpening her pencil for the revelation. "But what are fairies? The little people who lived here before the Celts arrived? Nature spirits? Lingering ghosts of the dead?"

"The old Celts remind me of our aboriginal people, seeing spirits in the landscape. You think any of my old MacLeod rellies are still hanging about to answer my questions, give me the good oil now?" Greg laughed, a peal of unaffected merriment. The wind snatched the sound from his lips and whisked it away.

Jean and Alasdair shared a glance. If Greg was allergic to the paranormal like they were, then his old MacLeod relatives might well answer his questions. Or not. No one knew the capriciousness of ghosts better than the team of Fairbairn and Cameron.

White gulls sailed overhead, stained pink by the ray of sunlight. Of sunset. "My old granny," said Alasdair, "she was fond of saying that gulls carried the not-yet-departed spirits of the dead."

"Hopefully my old rellies are well and truly departed. I'd rather read ghost stories than end up in one." Greg raised his arm to inspect his watch, a massive number that probably displayed stock quotes as well as time and date. "Well then, I've got time for a squint at the old castle first. It's straight on, is it?"

"That it is." Alasdair pulled the small flashlight from his jacket pocket. "Have a care, the paths are rough and narrow, and there's no artificial light. You'd best be using this torch. Just bring it back to the house when you've finished. It's Fergie's."

"Ta. See you later, then." Greg squished away toward the old castle.

Alasdair squelched away toward the new one. Jean fell into step beside him, not without a cautionary glance at his rosy face. "When did Fergie get nicknamed that, anyway?"

"My dad was calling him Fergie Beg before I was born. That's what his own dad called him, himself being Fergie Mor."

"Little Fergus and Big Fergus. But your dad wasn't Alasdair Mor."

"No, he was one of dozens of Allan Camerons. Likely there were more than a few murderers amongst the old ones. Raiders, robbers, rapists. Rum crew." He spoke casually, just stating a fact.

"I've wondered if your choice of profession was overcompensation for a colorful family tree."

"Mind that my own dad went for a soldier. And his dad as well."

"That, too. Being born to a middle-aged, retired officer would shape your worldview. I'm sorry I never met your dad."

"He was right tolerant of colonials such as Americans and Australians." Alasdair glanced back at the old castle, then stopped and turned. Jean followed his gaze.

There was Greg, like Jean herself, an outlander called back to the dark and bloody ground of his forebears. Maybe he was a policeman, too, or a chartered accountant, or another mild-mannered academic-cum-journalist.

He worked his way up the path outside the enceinte and disappeared into the keep. A few moments later the red jacket appeared atop the tower, gleaming like a tiny flame.

The clouds thickened, the sun sank, and land and sea, loch and castle, fell into shadow. A patch of pale light sparked on the ruined battlements—Greg had switched on a flashlight. The spill of light over the rough and tumbled stones, part man's work, part nature's, seemed brighter than the indistinct human shape. Then both man-shape and light eased down behind the wall and were gone.

TWO

WITH A SLIGHT SHRUG, Alasdair turned from the old castle toward the new. "Old Tormod was transported rather than hanged, and in those days judges and juries weren't likely to split hairs. He may have killed the man in self-defense. Or else the jury was packed with MacLeods. At any rate, Greg's right, there's more to that story. Eighteen twenty-two's a bit late for a clan feud. And for religious conflict, come to that."

"I wouldn't think even your fine-tuned instinct for the criminal could do much about a two-centuries-old case," Jean told him.

"Does anything need doing about it? Other than you writing it up for *Great Scot?*"

"Well, no," conceded Jean. Several raindrops raked her face.

They walked on toward the welcoming, if expensive, glow of Dunasheen's windows and what had to be a mile and a half of fairy lights. Her ears and nose felt brittle as ice, and her hair waved so wildly around her wool scarf that the chill wind penetrated to her scalp. A flock of black and white birds whorled upward from the moor, their cries eerier than those of the gulls. Gulls sounded like rusty screen doors. The cry of the oystercatchers, though, carried a trailing bittersweet that made Jean think not of soon-to-depart souls, but of lost ones.

The call of the birds faded into the silence. Or, rather, into the absence of human noise—no car engines, no voices, none of the constant electronic hum of modern life. All Jean heard was their own footsteps, the sigh of the wind and the unceasing rise and fall of the sea, like distant thunder. The snap and flap of the blue-and-white Scottish flag flying from Dunasheen's highest tower. And the ring of a telephone.

Hiking up his coat, Alasdair dug into the pocket of his jeans and eyed the glowing screen of his cell phone. "Ian said he'd phone before the office closes down for Hogmanay. Half a tick, Jean."

Typical Alasdair, to set the ring tone of his mobile to the ordinary double bleat of a British telephone. Typical Alasdair, to double-check with his provider before leaving Edinburgh and make sure his mobile would work here in this remote northwestern corner of Skye. He'd been dependent on her phone when they were in the United States in November. Now she was the one restricted to Fergie's land lines. Funny, Jean thought, how even a portable phone on a base unit looked like an antique while a rotary dial seemed antediluvian.

Beyond Alasdair and his electronic umbilical, the faintest of blushes still tinted the waves of the loch. Loch Roy probably meant Red Lake, from *ruadh,* red. Although the stones here weren't red, not like those on the far side of Skye. Had the waters of the loch been tinted red with blood from various clan battles? More likely, the name came from a person's name—Rory, also from *ruadh,* as in red hair. Or, considering the climate, red face, red from the cold or red from the reaction to that bright yellow globe in the sky when it condescended to appear.

Did he have red hair, the ill-fated Rory MacLeod who had chosen the hard place below old Dunasheen over the sharp edge at his back? How about Greg's ancestor Tormod, of dubious but intriguing memory?

Alasdair said, "It's by way of being a fake, is it? Well then, the Duke has no call claiming a large insurance settlement."

Cold as they were, Jean's ears twitched, and she abandoned her wordsmith's reverie.

A pause while Ian, whose virtues lay in method rather than imagination, spoke. Then Alasdair replied, "No, it's not at all surprising. Crusaders, soldiers, toffs on their Grand Tours, they'd bring back loads of art, antiques, artifacts, holy relics—not all of it legally, mind you. And half the time not knowing what they had, nor caring, come to that, so long as they put on a good show. There's a trait's not yet died out, not by a long chalk."

No, it hadn't, Jean thought, with another look at the castle. But she couldn't criticize Fergie and his daughter and business partner—who, despite Alasdair's "wee," was almost thirty years old—for trying to present a good enough show to hang onto their house, the physical representation of their own family tree.

"Cheers, Ian. Enjoy your holiday." Tucking the phone into his pocket, Alasdair turned to Jean.

Her feet in their wellies were so cold she felt as though she was wearing ice buckets, and shuffled rather than stepped. "Tea," she reminded him. "Coffee. Maybe a wee dram, even. A warm fire. One of Fergie's dogs or our own cat, whatever, as long as it's got fur. I'll get my notebook and lie in wait for Greg and his murder story. Or Fergie and his plans for saving the estate, whoever crosses my bow first."

"Right," Alasdair said. Once again, they started off toward the house, this time walking even more briskly.

Ahead of them, the courtyard gate opened and shut with a clang. A woman hurried across the gravel terrace and up the path, arms knotted across the chest of her fake-leopard-skin coat. One hand held Fergie's largest flashlight tucked below her elbow like a semi-concealed weapon. Luxuriant golden-blond curls bounced around her pert, tanned face. Her tight red mouth loosened far enough to say, "Hello there. Have you seen a bloke in a red jacket?"

"Greg MacLeod?" Alasdair returned. "He walked down to the old cas—"

"Stupid sod! I told him he could wait 'til tomorrow, we've just arrived, not even unpacked, but no, we've come halfway round the world, he said, what's a few more yards, dark or no flipping dark?"

This was "the wife." At first glance, Jean thought she was twenty years younger than Greg. At second glance, Jean realized that she wasn't at all younger, she was simply fighting gleaming tooth, painted nail, and hair color a shade too bright for her complexion, against the forces of entropy.

"I'm Tina MacLeod, Greg's, well, Greg's been going on for years about this godforsaken place, imagine that!"

God had phoned it in a few times out here, thought Jean, but you could say that of Sydney or Brisbane, too.

Alasdair's expression remained neutral.

"London was good, lights, a hotel, nightclubs, but no, that's not enough, he's stuck on the flipping family tree, been rattling on about it for flipping years. Here we could be sitting at the C Bar back home, having a cold one beneath the palms—do you know Townsville, that's in the tropical part of Queensland—I read a brilliant story about a miniature dinosaur in the back garden, made perfect sense."

Alasdair managed to get a word in. "He's gone down to the beach and round to the left."

"I'd better yank in his lead, then, it's almost time for tea. Or drinks, more likely. Anti-freeze. Ta." She picked her way past, the wellies she, too, had liberated from the stash by the back door slapping along the path. A few paces away, she switched on the flashlight. A bubble of luminescence danced before her like a will o' the wisp leading unwary travelers to their doom.

"Have a care," Alasdair shouted after her. "The path's right slippy."

"Ta!" Tina said again, without turning around.

They waited while the light disappeared down the slope to the bridge, reappeared at the hulking shadow of the ruined castle, vanished behind the wall. Faintly, Tina's voice called, "Cooeee, Greg!"

It was back luck for a woman or a blond or red-headed man to be first across the threshold at the new year, although whether Fergie's Hogmanay package included that old custom, Jean didn't yet know. He could have a twofer with Tina MacLeod.

Exchanging dubious smiles, she and Alasdair turned away from the old castle, a dark shadow against the clouds. Great minds thought alike, but his was less likely to be visualizing will o' the wisps and doom than pondering how dangerous ruins could be, and not from anything paranormal… It was the sky that was ominous, Jean told herself, not Skye. A year ago she'd learned that seasonal affective disorder was a real threat in the depths of a Scottish winter. It said something about the national temperament.

As long as the free-range Aussies made it past the castle, they'd be okay. Even Jean, whose middle name was not "Grace," had managed to get from church to castle along the pebbled beach without mishap.

She and Alasdair pressed on across the gravel and stepped through the gate into the courtyard. The damp cobblestones inside glistened with streaks of gold, red, and green. The arched door in the angle of the wall displayed a wreath of holly and ivy tied with MacDonald tartan ribbons, hung so that the Green Man knocker—one of Fergie's artistic endeavors—peeked mischievously from its center.

They walked up the three steps to the door. Alasdair set his hand on the iron handle. From inside came a barely perceptible strain of music.

Then a long, wavering, shriek, pulsing with anguish,

echoed across land and water and set the gulls to screeching and flapping upward like winged ghosts.

Jean spun around, her heart lurching. "That's got to be Tina!"

Instead of leaping back down the steps, Alasdair threw the door open. Sweeping Jean with him, he lunged inside and shouted, "Fergie! Diana!"

She blinked at what seemed like a flood of light, although it was only the contrast—the aging ceiling fixtures weren't emitting more than a yellow glow. This was the back door, the postern gate, where old and mismatched boots, limp hats, and a couple of tall vases bristling with umbrellas, walking sticks, and fishing rods had come to roost.

"Fergie!" Alasdair bellowed, drowning out the music Jean could now identify as the CD she had given Fergie, the latest from her friend and neighbor Hugh Munro, who was singing lustily about heaving away and hauling away, bound for South Australia.

From the open door behind her came a cold draft and an ominous—no, not silence, a distant sobbing, wailing sound that was neither wind nor sea. And Jean doubted it was a banshee, although on Skye, you never knew.

What had happened? A path given way, a stone turned beneath an unwary foot, slippery mud, the force of the wind, the darkness—it was Greg, wasn't it? He'd been wearing athletic shoes, not wellies, not that wearing wellies was a guarantee of traction. Or had Tina herself fallen?

Jean ran back out onto the stone step, but heard nothing. Funny how her face was now hot, so that the wind felt like a slap with a wet fish.

Two shapes rushed at her through the kaleidoscope of light and shadow and with a gasp she jerked back against the door frame.

A big black Lab and a little white terrier swarmed around

her legs, leaving mud and damp on her jeans and the aroma of wet dog in her nostrils, then stampeded into the house. The last time Jean had seen them, they'd been dozing in front of the fire in the drawing room, inert as hassocks.

She reeled back through the doorway to find Alasdair pulling out his notepad and wallet—there was the phone. He punched three numbers. "We're needing an ambulance, someone's injured at old Dunasheen Castle—Alasdair Cameron, at the new castle—Kinlochroy, aye—very good then."

He clicked his phone shut, jammed it into his pocket, and bellowed, "Fergie!"

A wet yellow raincoat fell off its hook, crinkling to the floor. Hugh sang the old sea chantey about South Australia full of rocks, and fleas, and thieves, and sand. The dogs had vanished, leaving only a trail of muddy paw prints across the tile floor.

In a stately home, no one could hear you scream.

"No one heard you. No one heard Tina, either." Jean jittered to the door and the darkness outside, then to the row of coat hooks, where she replaced the raincoat, then back across the tile floor to the cabinet where Fergie kept the flashlights. She grabbed two and handed one of them to Alasdair. "There's a bell pull in the drawing room, Fergie used it this afternoon."

"Give it tug then, see if it rouses Fergie or Diana, or one of the Finlays. If not them, then the manager's cottage is next the garden. The constable at Kinlochroy's been alerted. I'm away back down to the old castle."

No point trying to convince him to stay put and wait for help. The roses in his cheeks had perished under a drift of snow, and his features tautened into his *I'm in charge here* expression. When he paused on the doorstep to throw her a crisp, ice-blue glance, she forced her chin up and lifted her left hand in a wave. "I'll catch up with you. Be careful!"

And he was gone. The rapid crunch of the gravel beneath his boots faded. The gate clanged.

Her hand was still extended toward the darkness. The diamond on her ring finger glinted, a micro-prism clarifying the brassy ceiling light.

Don't think about it. Find Diana. Find Fergie.

Jean spun around, spun back again, shut the door, and realized she'd tracked mud across the scratched tile floor—well, who hadn't, the dogs' paw prints were only part of what looked like a child's finger painting project.

Dumping the flashlight on the nearest surface and stuffing her scarf and gloves into her pocket, she pulled off her wellies. Where were the shoes she'd left here earlier? No time to search.

In her thick wool socks, she skated rather than ran down the dimly lighted corridor, around a corner, and up a short flight of steps beneath a moth-eaten stag's head sporting a Santa Claus cap. The doors of the Great Hall, the door of the library… She threw open the door of the drawing room, zig-zagged around the furniture to the Gothic Revival fireplace, and yanked the tasseled end of the bell pull—to no discernible effect. Whether some distant jangle would attract the attention of a MacDonald, or one of the Finlays, resident caretakers and chief bottle washers, she had no way of knowing. Come to think of it, this afternoon Fergie had supplemented his yank at the bell pull by shouting down the hallway.

Alasdair should have phoned Fergie, too. Where the hell was everyone?

A movement in the corner of her eye jerked her around toward the tall windows. But it was only her own reflection wavering in their black, mirrored depths, her crown of auburn hair turned inside out, her shoulders up around her ears, her stance that of a prizefighter in a corner of the ring.

What she punched was the "Stop" button on the CD player.

Sorry, Hugh. His voice halted between one beat and the next. Were those footsteps? Jean spun toward the door. No. She was hearing the tick of a clock.

Dunasheen wasn't one of those stately marble-halled homes tricked out with gilt cherubs, the sort of place that made Jean feel as though she was dragging the knuckles of all ten thumbs on the floor. This drawing room was friendly and functional with a Persian rug, needlepoint chair covers, a piano. The holly jolly crimson and tinsel of the season decorated mantelpiece and chandelier, while odds and ends from Chinese snuff bottles to Roman coins to prehistoric fish hooks were installed on every horizontal surface. An antique screen decoupaged with flowers, fairies, and saccharine Victorian angels almost managed to conceal a flat-screen TV set the size of a coffee table.

Jean wondered how many of Fergie's family antiques, artifacts, and holy relics had been sacrificed to fund Dunasheen's upkeep. But he had enough left to make that good show, spiced with his own paintings and sculptures.

Was that low murmuring wail, almost a voice but not quite, the wind in the chimney? Was it Tina screaming again? Alasdair might not have reached her yet. Maybe he'd slipped himself, and fallen, and lay broken and bloodied on the rocks… A chill puckered the back of Jean's neck.

Come on, come on! She yanked the bell pull again, then jogged to the door, looked down the hall, and shouted, "Fergie! Diana! Mrs. Finlay!" Her voice died away into silence.

Dozens of painted and photographed eyes gazed accusingly down from the Pompeiian red walls, not least those of Fergus Mor and Allan Cameron. Fergie's and Alasdair's fathers wore the kilts, tunics, and bonnets or tam o'shanters—stiffened berets with wool pompoms—of the Queen's Own Cameron Highlanders, an old and greatly honored regiment. Each bonnet, adorned with a badge and the colored feath-

ers of a blue hackle, was bent toward the other. Or Fergus
Mor's, rather, was bent down toward Allan's, demonstrat-
ing the maximum allowable versus the minimum allowable
regimental heights.

Breathe, Jean told herself. In with the good air, out with
the bad.

The embers piled in the grate emitted more of an ashy
breath than warmth, and the castle's scents of baking and
furniture polish were tinged with mildew. Perhaps the house
had become the terrestrial version of the *Marie Celeste,* abandoned to its ghosts.

Although if new Dunasheen had any ghosts, neither Alasdair's nor Jean's sixth sense had picked up on them in the few
hours since their arrival. It was her five ordinary senses that
at last detected footsteps in the hall. She wouldn't have to run
down to the manager's cottage after all.

Jean popped out of the drawing room to see Fergie am-
bling toward her, round face and round glasses gleaming with
good will. With his lavender sweater and slippers and bulky
physique, he looked ready to host a children's television program, welcoming them to a neighborhood where he played
the part of a purple dinosaur. "Ah, it's yourself, is it, Jean?
No worries, we're making the tea, though you're good for a
dram as well, I should think."

"Tina MacLeod's down by the castle, she was screaming,
Greg must have fallen, Alasdair's already called 999 and he's
gone back down there."

Fergie gaped at her, pale blue eyes bulging, mouth working. "The old castle? But he went round the back—"

"One of the Aussies may be hurt!"

His lips snapping shut on a four-letter word, Fergie ges-
ticulated frustration to heaven and the gods of the historic
homes business—rising damp, mounting bills, and now this.
And then with a grimace of contrition, for, after all, the wel-

fare of the guests came first, he said, "I'll organize the men-folk, if her, him needs carrying—though if there's a broken limb involved, we shouldn't—blankets, tea—if you could ask Diana to find the first-aid kit…" Mumbling beneath his breath, pirouetting so swiftly his long gray ponytail swung in an arc behind him, Fergie loped back the way he'd come.

"Where's Diana?" Jean called after him, but he didn't hear.

If she remembered their arrival tour, and there was no guarantee she did, then he was heading for the new and pricey commercial kitchen and his command center at the garden end of the house.

Jean started after him, only to stop dead in the center of the antechamber, foyer, lobby—she couldn't remember what Fergie called the room that was the formal entrance hall. She'd sounded the alarm. Now she needed to get back down to the castle.

In the distance, a door opened. A gust of canned laughter blew down the hall and was then choked off as the door shut again. Aha, the Finlays were in the kitchen watching a TV show or listening to the radio or doing something that, along with the thick stone walls, had muffled Alasdair's shouts. That's why Fergie himself had finally answered the bell. As for Diana, who knew?

I'm coming, Alasdair! She made a U-turn. Flashlight. Boots.

The massive wooden front door at the far side of the room vibrated beneath a rain of blows. A muffled voice shouted, "Hey! Anyone home? Answer the door, already!"

THREE

ALL RIGHT! THE cavalry had arrived!

Looking right and left—Fergie had disappeared and no one else was in sight, not even a dog—Jean skidded across these considerably cleaner tiles, raised the latch, and opened the door.

Three people, tall, not-so-tall, and shorter-than-Jean, stood in the tiny porch. As one, they pushed past her into the house and stood huddled together while she shut the door.

"I pushed the freaking doorbell five times," said the man with the razor-cut black hair, closely trimmed goatee, and mountaineer's parka.

"I told you, Scott," said the brunette in the stylish narrow glasses and belted trench coat, "these places are big, it takes a while for the servants to answer the door."

The girl wore a red-and-gold-striped knitted muffler looped around her neck and shoulders. Above it, dark eyes in a pale, pinched face grew larger and larger, taking in the guns and swords arranged on the walls, the vaulted ceiling with its colorful clan shield bosses, the massive turnpike stair spiraling upward into shadow.

"The luggage is in the car," Scott told Jean. "Is there valet parking here?"

The woman looked down from her superior height. "You need to get someone to help you. We don't travel light."

Regaining traction, Jean's brain recognized the accent of her own country people. More or less—she guessed North-east Corridor. The appended "already" from the other side of the door should have tipped her off. "Um, yeah, I'll call Fergus MacDonald, the owner."

Realization swept the man's face. "She's not a servant, Heather."

Heather's face knotted in suspicion. "Who is she, then?"

Jean bit back a tart, *Someone who can hear you just fine,* and said only, "I'm Jean Fairbairn, I'm a guest here, but we've got kind of a situation so I answered the door. The doorbell doesn't work, by the way. We found that out this aft—"

"A situation?" Scott demanded.

Heather placed her hand protectively on the child's wool-encased shoulder.

"Someone's had a fall down at the old castle. I need to—"

"I'm sorry to hear that. How about we just let ourselves in, okay?" Scott threw the door open and headed back outside. His hiking boots, so new they squeaked, were already muddy—black smudges traced his path in and out.

I've already let you in. But that didn't matter. Taking two steps backward, sweat trickling down her back beneath her shirt, Jean said, "Great. Fergus or his daughter Diana will be along any min—"

"We booked a suite," said Heather. "A king-size for us, a single for Dakota here."

The child spoke up. "Please tell me the bathroom's not down the hall. One of my girlfriends stayed in a B and B and said the bathroom was down the hall and you had to share with strangers."

"It's all en suite. That is, the bathroom and toilet's attached to the bedroom."

Two pairs of eyes stared at her.

"Here, a bathroom can be just that, a room with a bath, it doesn't automatically come with a toilet."

Through the doorway Jean saw Scott pulling bag after bag from the trunk of an SUV. Beyond him, headlights jounced over the ribbon of tarmac that passed for a driveway. Was that the constable from Kinlochroy? It seemed like twenty hours since Alasdair called, but it was probably only twenty minutes.

Yes, the reflective stripe on the side of a small, square all-terrain vehicle caught the lights of the house as it drove by. Would the local arm of the law reach as far as the old castle? The designation "all-terrain" was more hope than fact when it came to this rough ground.

"Nice meeting you," Jean said, "I've got to—oh!"

A woman swanned down the helix of the staircase, her feet in their chaste low-heeled pumps skimming the stone treads, her body swaying like a willow wand in black pants and white Aran sweater, her blond hair flowing in satin waves away from the red roses blooming in her cheeks. An angel descending Jacob's ladder would look like a chimpanzee in comparison. "Did I hear… Oh, hello here! You're the Krum family, I expect. I'm Diana MacDonald. *Ceud mille failte!*"

"Say what?" Heather's lipstick had worn off, leaving only the darker red of the liner tracing her lips, so that her grimace was that of a cartoon character.

"A thousand million welcomes," said Dakota. "That's Gaelic. They speak Gaelic here."

"Aren't you a clever lass!" Diana's smile cast sunshine throughout the room. "Thank you, Jean, for playing hostess. I apologize for the broken doorbell."

"No problem," Jean said, backpedaling even more rapidly. She hated to miss Diana in action, but she hated even more to leave Alasdair alone in the dark with a—situation.

"Is that Mr. Krum?" Diana asked.

Scott tramped in, juggling a matched set of leather-trimmed bags and suitcases. "Oh, hi."

"Leave the luggage," said Diana. "We'll organize it. Your accommodations are in the William Wallace suite, a double bedroom and a foldaway bed in the sitting room. Drinks are at half-past-six in the library, and dinner at half-past-seven. This way, please."

"I could use a drink after those roads. Jeez, our driveway's wider than the one marked as two-lane." Scott dumped the luggage and Heather guided Dakota to the stairs.

"Would you care for tea and biscuits just now?" Diana asked, already several steps up.

"Biscuits?" repeated Heather.

"She means cookies," Dakota said.

"Tea," said Scott. "Yeah, whatever."

Free at last, Jean skated back down the hall. Would Miss Dakota point out that William Wallace had probably never set foot on Skye? No matter, his name was marketable, and if Diana understood anything, it was her market. How odd, then, that she'd missed the Krums' arrival, especially when she'd been expecting them.

Diana's delicate Scottish complexion was always rose-pink, but now it was positively crimson. She must have been embarrassed at missing her cue or in a rush or both. Maybe she'd been in her office, tied hand and foot with tape the color of her cheeks, the kind spooled out in vast quantities by both heritage watchdogs with their lists of permissible changes and heritage advocates with their lists of grants-in-aid—well no, Diana ran the house, Fergie wrestled with red tape.

The sound of multiple footsteps on stone treads and Diana's soothing voice faded into the upper reaches of the house. "The weather's been dreadful but we're expecting it to clear tomorrow, just in time for our New Year's Eve celebration."

What the lady of the house hadn't been expecting was an accident at the old castle. But Fergie could tell her about that. Jean slid to a stop in the cloak room, where she managed to pull on her wellies and button her coat, wrap her wool scarf around her head, and thrust her hands into her gloves, some-how all at the same time.

A flashlight clutched to her chest, she shut the door and raced across the courtyard. *Alasdair, I'm coming!* The lights reflecting from the damp-sheened cobblestones created an optical illusion and she stumbled, then righted herself. The crash of the ironwork gate behind her reverberated into the distance. The very silent distance.

Jean's light-adapted eyes found the night doubly dark. At the far side of the gravel perimeter, the interior light of a small square car looked like a klieg light illuminating a human shape in a peaked police cap. She homed in on the— Well, not the cavalry. Its scout.

"Hi. I'm Jean Fairbairn. I'll show you down to the old castle."

"P.C. Thomson here," the constable replied, not at all star-tled by her appearance. But then, the slam of the gate would have waked the inhabitants of the graves at the old church. Settling his fluorescent yellow jacket over his chest, he turned toward her. As far as she could tell in the gloom, he was about fifteen, and a foot taller than she was. If police work didn't pan out, he could get a job selling toothpaste—his smile shone with a light of its own. "No worries," he went on, "I'm a local lad, I've visited the old castle many a time. What's happened?"

"A guest, Greg MacLeod, walked down to the old castle at sunset. He wanted to go to the ruined church. We—my fi-ancé, Alasdair Cameron, and me—we told him how to get there by going along the beach. Then we met his wife. She was looking for him. She went down to the castle and we heard her scream. Alasdair went right back down there. That was twenty, maybe even thirty minutes ago." Jean danced backward across the gravel, toward the path.

Thomson seized a bag from his car, slammed the door,

fired up his flashlight, and headed out. "The ruins are dangerous, right enough. Kinlochroy Council and Lord Dunasheen have been going at it for years now, who's responsible for shoring up the place, planting danger signs, and the like. The old laird, he let the place go rather than spend on its upkeep, squeezing his pounds so tight you could hear the Queen's picture squealing."

Good lad. He could walk, talk, and even make jokes simultaneously. Whether she could was another matter—she had to adopt a part jog, part forward stumble to keep up with him. "Entropy tends to outrun good intentions. And clumsy tourists, though I don't know that either Greg or Tina was clumsy. Alasdair's with them now."

A clang behind them was the gate. The walrus-like shape trotting toward them was Fergie's, laden with a folded blanket and a carrier bag. "Jean! Wait up! Is that Sanjay with you?"

"Sanjay?" Jean repeated, sure she'd misheard some Gaelic expression.

"My granny's folk are from India," the constable explained.

"Cool," said Jean, remembering Hugh's song about the Scots as rovers, as swords for hire and missionaries, as transported criminals like Greg's ancestor Tormod.

Thomson turned to Fergie. "Sorry to be called out on business, Fergus."

With the Highlander's fine disregard for titles, "Fergus" instead of "Fergie" counted as respectful address. Jean said, "I never did get the first-aid kit from Diana. I couldn't find, er, an American family arrived and she's dealing with them."

Fergie nodded. If he knew Diana had been AWOL, however temporarily, he didn't show it. "Rab Finlay's on his way as well, but Lionel, the manager, it's his day out."

"I've got my kit." Even Thomson had to shorten his steps on the twisting and bumpy path. At his heels, Jean followed not only his flashlight but his reflecting coat, and

Fergie trudged along behind her, his breath rasping louder and louder.

Mist was gathering, shimmering strands drifting across the circles of light from their flashlights like homeless phantoms. Beyond the rocks, pools, and scrubby bits of heather, Jean made out nothing more than a muted shimmer on the underside of the clouds, the reflected glows of Dunasheen and Kinlochroy. A similar shimmer played across the water of first the loch and then, as they approached the castle, the sea. She felt as though she was trailing along with her little lantern, looking for an honest man…well, she was. She was looking for Alasdair.

Down the hill they went, and across the bridge, first Thomson, then Jean, then Fergie. Thomson went up the enceinte path like a mountain goat, then turned to offer Jean his hand. Putting her feminist pride in her pocket—one casualty was enough—she took it. But instead of steadying her up the slope, he heaved her upward so forcefully her feet almost left the ground. With a scramble she retrieved first her footing and then her hand, and managed a breathless, "Thanks."

She turned to take the blanket from Fergie, the beam of her flashlight spattering down the craggy drop-off to one side, her shoulder brushing the damp cold of the ancient stone wall to the other. A shudder raised the hair on the back of her neck. The night had stripped the old castle of its dignity. Now the broken barricades seemed more sinister than sad, concealing icy eyes that watched the living souls clambering past and hating them for their warmth.

The faint blip on her paranormal radar faded so fast she suspected it might merely have been imagination, the dark, the scene getting to her. No time to analyze, not now.

Fergie, too, hauled himself up the path and stopped at its summit, catching his breath. Ahead, the yellow blur that was Thomson dropped sedately down what might have once been stone steps, but was just as likely to be stacked bedrock. Balancing their burdens, Jean and Fergie levered each other down six or seven levels and across a muddy, weedy patch onto level ground.

There was Alasdair! Or there were two circles of light, rather, meeting, blending, parting again, emanating from a shambling lump. Jean thought for a moment that Alasdair and Tina were supporting Greg between them. But no, the clump wasn't wide enough for three. As the double figure resolved itself from the darkness, she saw Alasdair holding flashlights in each hand, and his right arm locked around a staggering Tina.

The last memory of warmth and light drained through Jean's cold feet into the unforgiving ground. There was only one reason Alasdair, and Tina with him, would have left Greg alone.

FOUR

THE FLASHLIGHT BEAMS flared and clashed. Jean squinted. Then they settled, and she saw Tina's face. Illuminated from beneath, it resembled a mask of tragedy, mouth hanging open, mascara smeared beneath empty eyes, skin like clay.

Every line of Alasdair's features was carved in Skye basalt. The vapor of his breath rose and blended into mist. "Jean, Fergus, P.C.—"

"Thomson, sir. Sanjay Thomson, Kinlochroy." And, before Alasdair could react as Jean had to his first name, "Where's the injured party?"

Tina let out a moan like a collapsing accordion and buckled. Thomson grabbed her other arm. Spasms rippled through her body and her curls trembled.

Fergie took the blanket, threw it around her shoulders, and pulled her into his own arms. "Come along, dear. Let's get you back to the house. A cup of tea will go down a treat. Maybe a wee drop of brandy as well."

"Greg," Tina said in a tiny voice.

Greg. Jean felt shivery, sick, numb, and she'd barely met the man. She could imagine—but didn't want to—how Tina felt.

With a quickly suppressed gulp, she took one of Alasdair's flashlights from his bare and therefore icy hand and exchanged it for Fergie's carrier bag. A thermos bottle sloshed at its bottom, next to several plastic cups. Of course. Any emergency situation in the British Isles could be mitigated by tea—warmth, caffeine, and sugar. But no amount of tea was going to bring Greg MacLeod back.

Fergie guided Tina's stumbling feet toward the gantlet of the enceinte path, and beyond it the oasis of new Dunasheen. His voice, murmuring sympathies, faded into the rhythm of the wind and waves, a rhythm much slower than Jean's own heart.

Alasdair introduced himself to the constable and shook his hand. "Sanjay."

"My grandad was stationed in India and my granny's from Delhi." The constable replied just as patiently as he had with Jean—no doubt he'd had lots of practice—and in a return-of-serve asked, "That's *the* Alasdair Cameron, ex-D.C.I. at Inverness?"

"Aye, one and the same," Alasdair replied cautiously.

"I've swotted up on the Loch Arkaig and Loch Ness investigations. Brilliant detective work, Chief Inspect—Mr. Cameron."

"Thank you, constable, but I was no more than part of a team." Alasdair's face remained stony, although a glint in his eye, directed toward Jean, acknowledged her role as partner and gadfly in both of those cases as well as two others. "Let's be getting on with this investigation, shall we?"

"Yes, sir." Thomson started off, his feet creaking across the small stones of the shingle beach. "This way, sir?"

"Aye, straight on." Even as he spoke, Alasdair's gaze tarried on Jean's, and the glint in his eye wavered like a candle in a draft.

"What happened?" she asked. "Did he lose his footing, or did a stone turn beneath his shoe, or what?"

"I'm thinking *or what*."

Jean's heart slumped downwards. "But how…" She'd find out soon enough.

Alasdair pulled his gloves from his pocket and onto his

hands, but not before Jean glimpsed the mottled rust-red on his fingertips. *Bloodstained ground. The MacDonalds and the MacLeods went at it like billy-o.*

She glanced back to see the glow of Fergie's flashlight moving across the bridge and up the hill and then fading away, a MacDonald now giving aid and succor to a MacLeod.

Alasdair was off after the pale shiny blur of Thomson's coat, so fast Jean had to hustle to keep up. No telling what was lurking out here to pick off stragglers. And she'd be thinking that even without Alasdair's dire *or what*.

The beam of Thomson's flashlight swept back and forth, from the rocky hillside with its thin skin of turf across the beach to the waves rolling forward, falling back, rolling forward again. "The tides coming in. How far above…ah. There he is, poor chap."

Three rays of light converged on a long shape, inert as driftwood. Greg lay diagonally across the pebbles, feet to the land, head to the sea, one arm flung out as though reaching for something that exceeded its grasp. Just beyond his fingertips lay the flashlight Alasdair had given him, glass broken, bulb extinguished.

His face was turned away from the probing lights. That, as far as Jean was concerned, was a very good thing. And yet even her shrinking gaze discerned that below the red cloth of his jacket glistened a smear of crimson, and a crimson thread wove its way between the pebbles toward the lick of the waves.

Thomson set aside his first-aid kit and squatted down to inspect the body, the physical shell of a human soul. Alasdair hunkered down beside Thomson. Jean tucked her arms as close to her body as she could and still train her flashlight on the scene, but she was cold with more than the temperature. The wind tugged at the scarf around her head and its soft wool tickled her cheek.

"I've phoned Doctor Irvine," said Thomson. "He'll be here soon as may be."

"Good," Alasdair replied. "He can do the preliminaries. Me, I've phoned D.C.I. Gilnockie at Inverness C.I.D."

"Criminal investigation? But he fell."

"If he fell, what did he go falling from?"

The young man shone his flashlight right and left, back and forth. "Oh. There's nothing high enough just here, is there? Did he go falling from the castle wall and crawling away— away from the house, though, I'd be expecting him to crawl toward it, looking out help. And if he'd died from a fall, his head would likely be cracked open or his neck twisted round."

Alasdair said, "Very good."

Jean wondered if Thomson realized what high praise he was getting, Alasdair suffering idiots and fools just about as gladly as he suffered biting insects like the infamous West Highland midge. She flexed her knees and took a step back, then forward again, so as not to miss anything. So as not to show disrespect to the dead.

"The shingle," Alasdair went on, "is less likely to show marks of him crawling than sand, aye, but I had me a good look-round whilst Tina, well, whilst Tina ran to and fro, and saw nothing. Gilnockie will order a full work-up. I've likely missed a scuff mark or two in the dark, or, if we're lucky, footprints. In any event, I'm thinking he died where he fell— or fell where he died, rather, just here."

Thomson considered that a moment. Then, gingerly, he knelt down and placed his flashlight and his cheek almost on the pebbles, all the better to sight along the trickle of red. "The blood's coming from his chest. His jacket's torn."

"Oh aye. The wound's in his chest, or as near as I can tell save rolling him over. And his jacket's not torn but sliced."

"A slice, is it? Could he have fallen on a bit of flotsam or…

He didna fall. It was no accident." Thomson's eyes sparked and abruptly he sat up and back.

Alasdair waited.

"He was stabbed and the weapon carried away."

As superfluous as Thomson's kit, Jean offered no comments aloud. Silently, though, she said to the constable, *Go ahead, change that passive voice to active—someone stabbed him, someone carried away the weapon. It was...*

"A murder? Here? On my patch?" Thomson's voice swooped to a higher register. Then his body seemed to grow heavier and more compact, and his voice sank again, finding its specific gravity. "Well then. Visitor or local makes never mind, we canna have murders, now, can we? What are you thinking happened, sir?"

Jean read Alasdair's nod as a repeat of her own. *Good lad.* Tucking her flashlight beneath her arm, she reached into the carrier bag for the thermos.

"He was alone no more than twenty minutes," Alasdair said. "From the time we saw him on the battlement—and he did not fall, he let himself down carefully—to the time we met Tina was no more than fifteen. And it was perhaps five more minutes before we heard her scream."

"How long did you talk to Ian at the office?" Jean poured tea into a plastic cup, the warmth searing through her gloves, and handed it to Alasdair.

"Ah, ta. Twelve minutes, according to my phone."

Jean poured Thomson a cup as well. Steam coiled upward in the glow of the flashlight.

"Thank you kindly, madam. Mr. MacLeod here, he was after seeing the old ruined church, you were saying?"

"So he was telling us," Alasdair answered over the edge of the cup. "He had no time to get there, though. Likely he never even reached the wee promontory. He met up with someone else and they did not stand about talking. One, maybe two thrusts, and the killer was off along the beach and past the church. Whether he then circled round the estate to Kinlochroy or went on along the coastline—well, we'll leave the evidence-gathering for the C.I.D."

Thomson was looking more starstruck by the moment, his tea forgotten, steam dissipating, in his hand. He dragged his gaze away from Alasdair's face to his surroundings. "If the killer had come away along the path, you'd have seen him. By sea, well, it's a rough night."

You could tell, Jean thought, what a landlubber she was. The concept of water as highway hadn't occurred to her. And yet there was a reason the formal entrance of the new castle faced the loch. Passable roads were late coming, here. The early peoples of this area hadn't felt they were on the rim of civilization at all, when such a broad highway connected them to the world.

"What's further up the coastline to the north?" Jean asked. "More beaches? Or cliffs?"

"Cliffs," replied Thomson. "No proper beaches, and no proper roads save the one leading to Keppoch Point and the lighthouse. The works are automated, but there's a hermit lives there. Or so folk are saying of him. I'm thinking he just prefers the company of the birds and the sea creatures. No harm in that."

"Usually not, no." Alasdair drained his cup.

Jean envisioned the beautifully drawn map of Dunasheen Estate posted on the website. The house or new castle and its dependent buildings lay to the west of Loch Roy, south of the old castle on its islet. The extensive garden with its smaller segments lay on the sheltered southwest side of the house, otherwise there would have been nothing but gorse and heather lining the forest walk leading to the new—newer, newish—church. Whereas the old church was outside the walls, almost outside the estate entirely, northwest of the house.

Light flashed in the corner of Jean's eye and she looked around. Two beams of radiance preceded two humanoid blobs down the hill and onto the bridge. They didn't indicate the Scene of Crimes Officer, unfortunately—more likely the blobs were Rab Finlay and the doctor. Instead of pouring herself a cup of tea, she screwed the top back on the thermos.

What had Greg said? Oh yes. "He said something about having time for a squint at the old castle. I thought he meant having time before it got dark."

"But what if he had an appointment with someone at the church?" asked Alasdair.

Two minds, one thought. Go figure. "If that person wasn't the murderer, then maybe he or she saw something."

"Aye," said Thomson.

"And look here," Alasdair went on. "He fell with his head a wee bit closer to the castle, as though he was turning and going back to it. Or as though he was trying to escape his killer. And yet he was stabbed in front, not in back. Could be he turned about to strike out with his torch."

Thomson nodded, remembered his tea, and swallowed it in one audible gulp. Jean collected the cups. Yeah, the female ran the refreshment services, but it wasn't as though she had anything more to contribute, not right now, anyway.

"Hullo!" called a man's voice, and the two dim shapes squeaked across the shingle, the occasional raindrop like a nanocomet streaking down through the beacons of their flashlights.

Yes, the man in the lead was burly Rab Finlay. His tweed cap was pulled down low and his gray-shot black beard bristled upward, so that his cheeks reddened by weather and nose reddened by the weather's antidote—anti-freeze, Tina had said—seemed squashed between. He tucked his flashlight beneath his arm, thrust his hands deep into his pockets, and bellowed, "Can a man not sit at peace by his own fireside without being called out in the cauld and wet?"

"The man's hardly got himself murdered just to be troubling your evening," Thomson said.

"Murder?" repeated Rab, the r's rolling into the darkness like cannonballs down a staircase. "No guid will come of that."

Young Dakota Krum, thought Jean, would probably have added *"duh."*

She less than cleverly deduced that the other man was Dr. Irvine. But she could make out very little of him beyond a wizened form wrapped in a raincoat, with two bright eyes and a nose sharp as a hatchet beneath a floppy-brimmed hat.

"What have we here?" he asked. "A corpse, is it? And an Aussie corpse at that, Rab's telling me. You're thinking it's foul play? Well now, let's have a look." He knelt down, positioned his flashlight, and opened his bag.

Again Jean stepped back, and this time stayed back and partially turned aside while Alasdair introduced himself, gave Irvine her name without designating her as partner, intended, or thorn in the side, and proceeded with as much chapter and verse as was available.

"Well," said Irvine, "the man's dead, I'll testify to that—and will, I expect—and I agree that a stab wound's the likely cause. But under these conditions even the pathologist would be hard put to tell you more."

"Right." Alasdair began issuing orders. "Fetch a tarpaulin to cover the body, if you please, Rab," the *even if you don't please* implicit in his tone. "Doctor, I'd be obliged if you'd take as many photos as possible, allowing for conditions."

"I've got no cam—" Irvine began.

Alasdair pulled his own small camera from his pocket. "Here you are."

"Very good then." The doctor trained his flashlight on the camera, assessing the buttons.

"P.C. Thomson, stay with the doctor just now, please. A team from Portree's on its way, but they'll not be here soon. Sooner than Gilnockie and his team from Inverness, though, lest they come by helicopter, and in this murk… Well, in any event, we're in for a long night."

Momentarily, Jean flashed back to Glendessary House, how she'd spent an eternity waiting for the police to come. Waiting for Alasdair to walk into her life, had she but known, and so forth.

"Aye, sir." Thomson peered into the heaving shadow that was the ocean. "There might be marks at the waterline, the scrape of a boat, footprints, or the like. I'll have a keek, shall I?"

"Good idea," said Alasdair. "Well done."

Thomson grinned, then quickly reversed his expression back to somber.

"Oh, and Thomson," Alasdair added, "we've got no time for a lesson in public relations. Suffice it to say, the media will be following the police like the night the day. Mind how you go."

"The media," repeated Thomson, and despite the dim light, Jean could swear he paled. "Aye, sir. Just the facts. Courteous but firm. No worries." He started slowly off across the shingle, illuminating each step.

Alasdair rubbed his hands together, perhaps less to warm them than in pleasure at finding a disciple. Turning away from the sea, he spotted Rab still contemplating the body, his breath a vapor of steam and beer. "Rab, the tarpaulin?"

Wordlessly, grasping his flashlight in a gnarled hand, Rab turned back toward the castle. His profile in the gloom was that of a troll searching for a bridge to live under. But his little light went on across the footbridge without establishing residence and vanished over the hill.

The flash of the camera seemed like an explosion. Jean stepped back even further and tucked the thermos up against her chest, but its exterior was no more than lukewarm. That's why it was a thermos.

If she felt cold, Alasdair was half-frozen. He'd been out here all this time. But then, he was Highland-born and bred, unfazed by chill. And he was a cop, unfazed by—or at least, undemonstrative at—sudden death.

That she'd seen too much sudden death over the last year wasn't his fault. Together they had dealt with criminals exploiting the romance of Bonnie Prince Charlie, the pseudo-science of the Loch Ness monster, the claims made by a bestselling novel about Scotland's Rosslyn Chapel, and tales of witchcraft in colonial Virginia.

The mist thickened into a mizzle, droplets gathering on Irvine's and Alasdair's shoulders to glint in the lights the way the diamond in her ring had glinted.

She supposed Tina had a diamond ring, too. And a wedding band. Maybe she and Greg had matching ones, engraved like the ones waiting for Jean and Alasdair with their initials and the date of their wedding.

To wed. To join. To espouse. To unite in a knot that could be cut abruptly asunder.

An hour ago Greg had been laughing, complaining about his wife's shopping, asking about a two-centuries-old murder and anticipating exploring the ancestral ground. Now he was a cold slab of meat lying on that ancestral ground, pawed over by hands that would infinitely rather be holding cup and glasses of holiday cheer.

An hour ago Tina had been anticipating a drink and a Hogmanay party. Now she was alone and bereft, an entire planet between her and home.

To fall in love was to risk everything.

"Jean."

She jumped, jerked back to the scene, lights puny against a dark sky and a dark land joined by a dark sea, Alasdair's voice in her ear and his presence at her shoulder.

"Let's you and me be getting ourselves back to the house," he said.

"Yeah," she said. "It's going to be a long night."

FIVE

JEAN PACED UP and down in front of the fireplace in the sitting room of the Bonnie Prince Charlie suite, the best in the house, Fergie had assured them.

At least Charlie really had set foot on Skye, conducted by the intrepid Flora MacDonald. Who was probably no relation to Fergie—MacDonalds were thick on the ground here. But, with the other interesting ancestries turning up this evening, why not?

Taken together, the suite's rooms—living, bed, dressing, and bath complete with tub, shower, and toilet—had almost the square footage of Jean's flat in Edinburgh. Since August she'd been sharing that space not just with her cat but with Alasdair. None of them had particularly sharp elbows, but still, independent spirits demanded room of their own. Hence their purchase of the recently vacated flat next door. Add the expense to that of combining the two dwellings into one, and neither Alasdair nor Jean had any grounds to criticize Fergie's spending habits.

He might be investing in his estate, but we're investing in the state of our matrimony.

Fergie and Diana hadn't gone overboard fixing up this suite. While the fabrics were fresh and cheery and a brand-new clock radio sat by the bed, every surface and wall was decorated with the sort of flea-market stuff dealers called collectibles—vases and figurines, a peeling set of Walter Scott novels, stuffed birds, horse brasses, and wicker baskets.

Likewise, the furniture was a miscellany gleaned from

the recesses of the house. It ranged from a curlicued Georgian desk to a heavy Victorian wardrobe that—Jean had checked—did not open onto Narnia, to a single Louis someteenth chair spun out of sugar and gilt that had been claimed by Dougie since neither of the humans dared sit on it.

The little gray cat was now disguised as a tea cozy, paws and tail tucked, whiskers furled. His iridescent golden eyes watched Jean. *Another criminal investigation?*

"Don't ask," Jean told him. She'd already answered Alasdair's questions on the way back from the beach, despite nothing much having happened at the house in his absence. But then, like the non-barking dog in the Sherlock Holmes story, even absence was evidence.

Feeling every year of her accumulated forty, Jean turned the back of her lap toward the electric fire whose three glowing bars were giving their all. The appliance looked like an alien crouching in the interior of the four-hundred-year-old stone fireplace. But places like Dunasheen no longer housed more servants than guests, including maids whose purpose in life was to lay coal fires and set them alight when the gentry returned from gallivanting across the moor.

Her hands and feet tingled in the heat. Her head fizzed, thoughts rising and popping like bubbles in a flat soda—motive unknown, opportunity a very narrow window, means a knife in the dark.

When Alasdair walked through the doorway from the bedroom, she could tell from the vertical furrow between his eyebrows that he was ticking off the same list.

She knew his expressions, his face, and his form as well as her own. His short-cropped hair, a ripple of golden grain tipped by frost. His regular, unremarkable features, planes and angles assembled like a geometry proof, rational and elegant. His armor of reserve, claiming privacy rather than secrecy, that had once fooled her into thinking he felt no emotion. His broad shoulders, slender hips, strong hands, compacted into a relatively small frame. The angle of his head, tilted in consideration of a Fergus MacDonald painting over the mantel, and the solidity of his tread. Some men sagged into middle age. Alasdair stood all the straighter, especially when facing trouble.

"Well," she said.

"Well," he returned.

"I've almost had a feeling of foreboding all day, although I thought it was just the darkness. Or even wedding nerves."

"You're having second thoughts, are you now?" He spoke more wearily than warily.

"You know me. I'm down to twentieth thoughts, maybe thirtieth, not that any of them are going to make me back out. We've not only reserved a priest, we've filled out all the paperwork!"

That drew a smile from his taut lips, restoring their curve.

"I just want, well, dang it, I want to live happily ever after. Even though that's an aspiration based more on hope than experience."

"We'll muddle through this one, too, Jean."

"This one. Yeah. It's like together we make some sort of critical mass and generate sudden death. Not just sudden death. Murders."

"We met because of a murder."

"Sure, but it's hardly fair that someone had to die for us to meet."

"We've beaten the odds a bit, oh aye. But maybe the odds are turning the other way and we'll soon be getting that 'ever after,' 'happily' to be defined later."

That drew a smile from her. She wrapped her arms around his chest and nestled her face into the angle of his shoulder. Sparring partner, best friend, lover. Betrothed.

He held her close, the slight prickle of his jaw against her cheek, his hands still radiating cold through her sweater and into her flesh, his body humming with subtle electricity that was anything but cold.

The chill lingered in his sweater and jeans, and the scent of soap with which he'd washed his hands of blood and dirt. And something else, a whiff of a rich, tropical fragrance, gardenia or lotus, maybe. "What's that…oh. Tina's perfume. You had your arm around her."

Gently, with a light kiss on her cheek, he extricated himself from the embrace and extended his hands toward the fire. Personal interlude over, time for work. "It took some doing convincing her to leave the scene, 'til I thought to tell her that every step she took—and she was taking more than a few, trotting to and fro wringing her hands and moaning, poor woman—was destroying a bit of the crime scene."

Yeah, Jean thought, *I'd be moaning, too.* "Could she answer any questions? Did she say anything about Greg meeting with someone at the church?"

"She blethered on about his genealogy studies, and how foolish they were, a waste of time, energy, money. And she was saying how they'd made a gamble coming here."

"A gamble?"

He shook his head. "She was not giving me context. Their holiday has likely overextended their budget."

"He blamed that on her shopping spree in London." Jean's idea of a shopping spree was a bookstore crawl from the glossy covers at Waterstone's to the dusty, cracked bindings at an antiquarian's. "Do they have children? Other relatives back in Australia?"

"A son, I got that much, how he'd not be coming here to help, not with two small children. And there's a brother as well, though I could not make out if he's hers or Greg's. 'How can I tell Kenneth?' she kept saying."

"Well, there's someone who needs to be notified. Is she up to making a call?"

"Fergie's saying no, not just now. He's asked Irvine to see to her. Kenneth will be hearing the bad news soon enough, I reckon."

As though certain the matter was well in hand, Dougie lay down his head and dozed off. Jean strolled over to her favorite feature of the room, a bay window with a padded seat running along its length. That would be a great place to sit and read on a sunny afternoon, assuming they had sunny afternoons. Now Jean could see nothing but, again, her own reflection in the glass-covered night.

No. Through her own image, she saw the lights not of Kinlochroy but of a set of headlamps coming up Dunasheen's driveway, past the garden wall. "They made good time."

"Who?" Alasdair joined her at the window.

"The team from Portree, that's less than an hour away, but…oh. Wait."

The headlamps slowed, made a right-angle turn, and stopped, illuminating the facade of a stone cottage. Then the lights went out. A shadowy figure moved from car to cottage, a door opened, and a window lit up.

"That's Lionel Pritchard, Fergie's manager," Alasdair said. "Leastways, that's his cottage."

"Fergie said it was his day out. I guess he hasn't heard the news or he'd come up to the house."

Leaving the curtains open—only a human fly would be able to see in a third-story window—Jean stepped back into the warm aura of the heater. "Greg went down to the beach right after he and Tina got here, and was alone for only twenty minutes. There's not much chance he just happened to run into a mortal enemy. And why would a total stranger kill him? He must have known his murderer."

"Or his murderer knew him."

"Whatever. How many people could he have known so far away from home?"

"Dozens. More. Maybe he's traveled here again and again. Maybe he's in constant contact with half the folk on Skye. And just now our list of suspects includes all of them."

"Surely you'll be able to eliminate most of them."

"I'll not be doing it, that's Gilnockie's job."

"Sure it is." Jean knew full well that once a detective, always a detective."

Alasdair's lopsided smile registered her point. "I'll be dialing back the territorial imperative, all right?"

"It's not up to me," she told him. "Patrick Gilnockie, isn't it? He took your position when you retired last August."

"Oh aye. You've never met him."

"No, I haven't. You said he was older than you, which made me wonder why he was lagging behind you in promotions. If he isn't as bright as you, though, he wouldn't have taken over for you."

"He's sharp as a tack, no worries there, a grand detective. He was not as committed as me to the police work is all, but then, he did not burn himself out." Alasdair didn't have to add, *like I did.* Jean had been there at the slow fizzle and sudden flare of the embers.

She murmured, "He wasn't as likely to be committed as you. You know, institutionalized?"

Doing her the courtesy of ignoring the bad joke, Alasdair peered out into the gloom.

"The murder had to have been premeditated," she told his back. "It wasn't suicide—knives don't get up and walk away. It wasn't an accident—oops, I didn't mean to kill him, I was just cleaning my knife and it went off. And I don't see how twenty minutes could be long enough to generate a crime of passion, you know, the argument, the shoving match, the weapon drawn."

His reflected expression was both bemused and amused. "You're making bricks without straw, Jean. Mind you, I'm agreeing with you, for the most part. Greg meant to meet someone at the church. Whether that someone is the murderer, or knows who the murderer is, we'll be seeing. It's possible he killed himself and the someone took away the knife, but without further evidence, I'm thinking there's no need to go complicating matters any further than they already are. As for an argument, well, some arguments fester for centuries."

Putting rings on each other's fingers and daggers in each other's hearts. Yeah, she'd had to say that, hadn't she? But free association was her specialty. So was color commentary. "There aren't too many arguments festering on this side of the Irish Sea, not fatal ones, anyway, not any more."

"When we know the why," said Alasdair, "then we'll know the who."

She smiled at him saying "when" rather than "if." "And when we know the who, then we'll know the why."

"Oh aye." He looked around and up. At first Jean thought he was again considering Fergie's painting, an interpretation of the legend of St. Michael and the dragon. Archangel and beast were entwined in mortal and gaudy combat, silver lance against green scales, both splashed with crimson. Michael's helmeted face might look like a canned potato and his lance like a ray gun, but Fergie's figures had a blocky integrity, and his design was quite nice, dragon and man resembling a knotwork figure from the Book of Kells.

But Alasdair hadn't turned art critic; he was looking at the small, ornate clock. "It's going on for five. Portree should be arriving soon. Gilnockie, though, he's got a long road."

"Only a Brit would think that less than a hundred and fifty miles was a long road." Jean visualized the route south along Loch Ness, then west past Eilean Donan Castle of a million postcards and calendars, over the Skye Bridge and across almost the entire island. "The roads are all two-lane, no single-tracks until you're past Dunvegan, and the odds of getting behind a caravan/camper trailer or tour bus are next to nothing this time of year."

"In daylight and fine weather," he replied, "you could be driving the route in maybe three, three and a half hours. In the dark and wet, well, he'll likely be here by nine, depending on how long he's spent assembling his team."

As though summoned by his words, another set of headlights flashed beyond the window. Alasdair spun around like a cat spotting a canary and Jean trotted to his side. Two vehicles materialized in the glow of lights from the house and stopped beside the Krums' SUV that still sat in the middle of the gravel parking area.

A patrol car and a small panel van disgorged assorted human figures, which donned reflective canary-colored jackets and fired up flashlights. The cavalry might be arriving, but from here it looked more like the circus.

The clock on the mantel emitted a tinny, tinkly version of the Westminster chimes and struck five times. From somewhere in the house a deeper version of the same was followed by the two sonorous notes of a doorbell. "Now it's decided to start working again," Jean said.

"You're not in the hall playing footman just now." Alasdair picked up his coat and gloves. "Portree wants guiding to the scene. You're coming out as well, are you?"

A spousal point to the man for asking. She replied, "Thanks, but no. I'll see if there's something I can do to help Fergie and Diana. Poor Fergie, the last thing he needed was a fatality. And yes, I know, the situation is a lot harder on the MacLeods."

Dougie was sleeping soundly. Food, drink, and sanitary facilities were available in the dressing room—he could spend his holiday in the suite, no need to get closer acquainted with

the household dogs. Switching off first the electric fire and
then the overhead light, Jean joined Alasdair in the hall and
waited while he locked the door, then handed her an extra key.
He didn't need to point out that half the people in the house
would have keys. There was a murderer afoot.

Jean and Alasdair didn't need a trail of breadcrumbs or a
ball of string to find their way. In the course of their heritage-
industry duties, they'd learned how to navigate this sort of
pile, from artifact to artwork to antique. You passed the tapestry depicting the Irish myth of Grainne, Fionn, and Diarmuid—faded threads telling a soap-operatic tale of passion,
jealousy, and death. You turned left at the sculpture of a gob-
lin holding a functioning if dim light bulb. You turned right
at the suit of armor with a pink handbag slung over one steel
gauntlet and a pink feather boa looped across its breastplate.
You went straight ahead past the mock-Tiffany stained-glass
window depicting a mermaid that Fergie had rescued from a
biscuit factory scheduled for demolition.

On their arrival yesterday, he had given Jean and Alasdair a more comprehensive tour than usual, since they were
friends—and prospective sponsors—of the family. Despite
its faint smell of mildew, Dunasheen was indeed a fairy-tale
castle, a fabulous warren of a place. Some areas were beautifully fitted out, fabrics brushed, wood gleaming. Others were
still works in progress or works never undertaken. The place
was romantic, oh yes, and mysterious, although "mysterious"
was not a word Jean planned to use in her article for *Great
Scot*. Assuming an article was still viable, now.

Alasdair strode on ahead, the floor emitting a series of
squeaks and creaks beneath his tread, and stopped beneath
the arch leading onto the turnpike stair. He cast a jaundiced
look at the sprig of mistletoe dangling from the light fix-
ture. No, it wasn't a good time to put the provocative vegetation to use.

Voices echoed up the spiral staircase, Diana's dulcet tones saying, "...I don't believe we should be doing that, in the circumstances."

"We've got no choice. It's part and parcel of the plan," Fergie said, his mild tones whetted.

Alasdair looked at Jean. Jean looked at Alasdair. Plan? Fergie's ploy to exchange security advice and favorable publicity in return for a wedding? Or his plan to reveal another marketing gambit along with their private viewing of Dunasheen's most famous artifact, the Fairy Flagon?

"As you wish—" began Diana.

"It's not my wish, we agreed—"

"Very good," she stated, her voice sharpened to a ginger-snap. Light steps went down the stairs to the first floor and faded away.

No need to point out to either Diana or Fergie that a murder on the doorstep did have a tendency to make the best-laid plans gang agley. No need to let them know they'd been overheard.

After a discreet pause, Jean and Alasdair started down the staircase. "Mind the tripping stane halfway along," he reminded her, "the one Fergie was going on about."

Oops. Jean grabbed for the handrail, a stiffened rope strung through giant metal eyelets, and placed her feet even more carefully on the long, slightly dished steps like misshapen slices of stone pie. There it was. One of the treads was half the height of the others, designed to trip up a charging attacker and let a defender get the drop on him.

Just as they had the first times she'd gone up and down and up again, her five-and-a-half senses detected a chill gathered in that spot, a different sort of chill than that of the draft sliding invisibly up the shaft. This time, instead of pushing through the spot, she stopped.

The back of her neck puckered at a ripple of emotional energy, at the catch between her shoulder blades and the weight on her shoulders that signaled a leak from the next dimension. "Do you feel that?"

"Oh aye," said Alasdair, his presence at her back mitigating the chilly creep of her flesh. "There's a wee bit ghostie just here, not near as strong as some, though."

"Fergie said a guest told him he was pushed by invisible hands here."

"He tripped himself up. I've never yet sensed a ghost could push. As I've told Fergie..."

Fergie looked around the curve of the stair, ponytail lank, brow corrugated. Reseating his glasses on his nose and forcing his sagging jowls into a smile, he completed Alasdair's statement. "Ghosts are no more than recordings, not quite video, not quite audio, another sense entirely."

Oops again. Unlike Diana, Fergie hadn't gone on his way. As for his words—Jean rounded on Alasdair. "You told him you're allergic to ghosts? I thought that was your best-kept secret."

"Kept from most folk," said Alasdair. "I've told you."

"No, you showed me."

"I was no more than twelve at the time I showed Fergie," Alasdair explained. "I was not aiming to show anyone anything, but I'd not yet learned what you're calling the great stone face routine."

Fergie's face slipped into a reminiscent smile. "We were standing in a passageway at Stirling Castle, Alasdair watching someone walk by who wasn't there, half buckled with the weight of his own sight. That was my reward for agreeing to look after such a young lad, and me graduated from university and engaged to be married. Not the first time Alasdair's knocked me back a step or two."

Alasdair's expression was far from stony, if less than enthusiastic.

"But I never picked up a thing," Fergie went on. "When

it comes to the supernatural, I'm tone-deaf, color-blind, and numb, more's the pity. There are some say that Dunasheen has a guardian spirit, the ghost of my ancestress, Seonaid MacDonald, the Green Lady. Some say Rory MacLeod falls from the old castle tower, again and again. You couldn't prove either by me."

Jean wasn't sure whether to boggle more over the image of Alasdair as a child or of Fergie actually wanting to sense ghosts.

Fergie's smile reversed back into a worried frown. "I was coming to tell you that the cops from Portree have gone round the back and are waiting at the courtyard gate."

"Thank you kindly, Fergie. I'll try getting back for dinner." With a stylized salute, two fingers to the end of his eyebrow, Alasdair walked on down.

Skipping the issue of whether Alasdair had told Fergie about her own allergy, she offered their host a consolatory smile—*I know how you feel, believe me, I know*—and plowed ahead. "Do you happen to know what Greg MacLeod's occupation was?"

"He told me he'd recently sold a factory manufacturing tourist paraphernalia, soft toy kangaroos, T-shirts, didgeri-doos. He said something about investments in property, and how he's dealing in art and starting up a museum of religion, an antipodean version of the one by Glasgow Cathedral. There're brochures from the Glasgow museum in his and Tina's room, I saw them when I brought her back to the house."

"The St. Mungo Museum of Religious Life and Art. I love the place, and not just because it was one of my first articles for *Great Scot*… Hold that thought. Be right back. Alasdair! Wait up!" Jean galloped on down the stairs and into the entrance hall.

He was just heading into the back corridor, and made a U-turn at her shout. "Eh?"

"Can I have the phone, please? I need to ask Miranda whether she's ever heard of Greg. He's an art dealer and was opening a museum."

"He's one of her lot, is he then? Was, rather. Sounds to me they're not traveling on a shoestring." Alasdair pulled out the cell phone and handed it over. "I've programmed it with Thomson's number, if you're needing me whilst I'm at the scene."

"Thanks," she replied, and as he turned again toward the postern gate, "Mind your step. There are a lot of rocks out there that could work as tripping stones. As for ghosts…"

"Aye, I saw and heard Rory MacLeod plunging into the keep half a dozen times whilst I waited with Tina. It's that sort of night." A nod, a flash of a smile, and his steps faded away down the back hall.

SIX

Oh yeah. It was that sort of night. The next knock on the door would be Count Dracula collecting blood samples.

The phone clutched to her breast, Jean turned back to the staircase. Funny how twitchy she could get without her communications slaves, not just her cell phone but her laptop computer, when she'd managed to spend the first half of her life without either.

No, she'd told Alasdair back in Edinburgh, she didn't need to haul along her computer. All she needed was her paper notebook to jot down odds and ends. She wasn't going to write the article about Dunasheen on the spot. This was the time for a celebration of the year's end and their own beginnings, not for web surfing or e-mailing.

There was never a good time for researching the extinguished life of a murder victim.

Meeting Fergie at the foot of the steps, she asked him, "Can I borrow your computer sometime? If I'd brought mine along I wouldn't have wanted it, but since I didn't..."

"Any time. You know where my office is." His shoulders turned one way and his stomach the other, trying to be two places at once. "Drinks for the guests—the Krums and you and Alasdair—dinner—we'll organize food for the policemen in the old servant's hall beyond the kitchens, that's now the staff sitting room in the summer, when we have folk in from the village to help Nancy and Rab."

"That's nice of you."

"Seems the least we can do, in the circumstances."

Hosting the police, then, wasn't what Diana had been arguing against. "Can I help organize anything? Or I'd be glad to sit with Tina. I promise I won't give her any third degrees." *Not yet, anyway,* Jean added to herself.

"She's in a bad way. Doctor Irvine is seeing to her, I expect with sedatives."

Knowing that the Krums were settling into the Wallace suite, Jean asked, "She's in the Mary, Queen of Scots suite?"

"That she is, yes. I hope she'll not think that's in bad taste, with Mary being widowed twice and all. Poor woman."

Tina, he meant, not Mary. Jean couldn't resist a quick, one-third degree. "Greg took off right after he arrived, right?"

"Yes, he left just after arriving, didn't even stay for his tea—Tina wasn't half upset with him for that. He stopped just long enough to get his hat, I expect. I heard him walking down the stairs as I went round the corner to my office. I was there listening to a CD when you rang the bell and called out."

Greg hadn't even waited long enough to get a hat. Jean asked, "Did he say anything about knowing anyone here? Did he ask directions to the old church?"

"If he knows anyone here, he didn't tell me, other than saying he'd never visited the old country before. And no, he didn't ask directions. I indicated the rooms in the house as I took them up the stairs is all. You met him on the castle path and he told you he was going to the church?"

"Yes. We think he had an appointment with someone there."

"That's odd, then, I mean, him going by the castle path." Frowning, Fergie took a couple of steps toward the back hall. "But the place is confusing."

"You took the MacLeod's to their room? Where was Diana?"

"Sorry, Jean, can't stop any longer—there's work needs doing." He strode off toward the kitchen, but not before she saw the shadow that lay on his normally affable expression deepen to a thundercloud. What was up with him and his daughter? What had they been, if not arguing, then having words about? And where had she been right before sunset, anyway?

Jean looked suspiciously down the hall toward the back door. When she and Alasdair came back to the house, the dogs had been outside. And there'd been a wet raincoat hanging in the cloak room. It had fallen off its hook, as though it had been tossed there just moments earlier.

What was she trying to do, pin something on Diana?

Jean turned toward the staircase and jumped. Diana stood on the bottom step, her complexion no longer flushed but a dewy ivory-pink. "Hullo, Jean," she said, but her cornflower-blue eyes were fixed on something over Jean's shoulder.

They'd heard her go down the turnpike stair. She must have gone back up one of the secondary flights while making her appointed rounds. "Hi," Jean said, and to head off the flush she felt mounting into her own cheeks, "Sorry about everything that's happened today. That's still happening."

"No need to apologize," Diana told her. "None of it's your doing."

"Well no, it isn't."

"Do you mean to join in tonight? None of this is the Krums' doing, either, and they're expecting their Hogmanay activities as per the posted schedule."

"Yes, I'll join in. Alasdair's going to try and make it to dinner."

"Perhaps you could assist Father in entertaining the Krums, then?"

As in, divert their attention from the murder? "Sure," Jean said, "assuming anyone will think my blathering is entertaining."

She hadn't been fishing for a compliment, and sure enough

she didn't reel one in. "Thank you. Drinks in the library at half-past-six, dinner at half-past-seven. Also, I'm sure we'll soon be getting more attention from the media than we'd like, and to that end I've asked our manager, Mr. Pritchard, to close the main gates. You're media yourself, now…" Diana paused delicately, her porcelain brow creased ever so slightly.

"I've never yet written about one of the investigations I've been involved in. I do history, travel, legends. Seeing is believing and believing is seeing—you know, how people act on what they perceive, not on what actually exists. The Loch Ness monster, the Bible imagery at Rosslyn chapel, that sort of thing."

"Your articles are—illuminating. We appreciate your doing one about Dunasheen." Diana didn't need to add anything along the lines of, *As long as it doesn't mention the murder.* "And Alasdair's attention to security matters as well, most helpful."

"Alasdair and I appreciate the holiday and the wedding."

Only now did Diana's gaze focus on Jean, if less on her face than on her apparel. Her full, soft lips stretched in a pained smile, she said, "There's no need to dress for dinner," and she wafted away down the back hall.

Jean glanced down at her oversized sweater and wilted jeans, getting the message, and started toward the stairs thinking that in order to produce Diana, Fergie must have crossed himself with a Dresden figurine. She'd have to ask Alasdair for the particulars of the late Mrs. MacDonald. All Jean knew was that she had been an Englishwoman, and that Diana had been raised in the Home Counties while Fergie manufactured soap bubbles in the advertising and public relations industries. An English childhood explained a lot…

Wait a minute. Jean made a quick about-face. Why had Diana been looking so intently at the wall opposite the staircase? Had she seen a mouse?

Jean saw a large brass-bound wooden chest, like a treasure chest, what the Scots called a kist. On it sat a small cast of Michelangelo's *David,* loinclothed with a paisley-pattern silk tie, and a scarlet poinsettia dusted with glitter.

On the wall hung a couple of targes, small studded shields, set atop crossed claymores like the skulls and bones on a pirate flag. The leather sheaths of two officer's regimental dirks, complete with tiny pockets for a small knife and fork. A fatbladed Gurkha knife. A tier of basket-hilted swords and a wheel of pistols.

Jean had once read that an oath made on the hilt of a dirk was as binding as one made on a Bible. But she doubted if any of the displayed weapons were genuine—they more likely came from the Scottish equivalent of the factory Greg had owned in Australia, and had rolled off an assembly line beside plush Nessies and plastic bagpipes.

However—she stepped closer, the better to see in the less-than-glaring light—the swords did have a certain patina, the targes had been battered around, and the sheath of the dirk on the right was...

Empty.

No. Oh no.

Her breath turned to feathers, like those of a dove caught by a hawk, and lodged in her throat. Leaping forward, she seized the sheath between thumb and forefinger and shook it, as though the eighteen-inch blade had somehow become invisible.

The carved pommel of the remaining knife was topped with a cairngorm, the smoky quartz glowing sullenly below a fine web of scratches. The silver fittings of both sheaths were discolored by tarnish, and the leather was worn. Had one dirk belonged to Fergie Mor and the other to Allan Cameron?

It didn't matter where the blades had been. What mattered was where one had gone.

Jean managed to suck first one, then another fuzzy breath into her chest. Alasdair had programmed Thomson's number into the phone. But he wouldn't yet have made it to where Thomson was standing guard. And if he had, what good would it do telling him about a missing knife, when he already knew that a knife had killed Greg MacLeod? When the first thing he'd do upon arriving at the scene was set Portree—handy collective noun, that—to searching for the murder weapon?

If the murder weapon had come from inside the castle, that would cut Alasdair's list of suspects down to just a few names.

Not, Jean assured herself, that the missing dirk was the murder weapon. The sheath could have been empty for years—she sure couldn't testify one way or the other. Fergie, though, would know all about it. He would have a perfectly logical explanation.

So why, asked the nagging little voice of the devil's advocate in Jean's head, *had Diana been staring at the vacancy?* Coolly, unflappably, keeping up appearances very nicely, yes, but taking note of something off, something wrong, when already things had gone badly wrong.

She'd tell Alasdair about the missing weapon—and missing Diana—at dinner, before Gilnockie arrived with a full scene-of-crimes team. A team that could search for fingerprints on the silver fittings and on the leather itself. Where she'd just left her own.

Stamping irritably at first the tile floor and then the stone treads, Jean trekked back up the stairs. She plunged through the chilly ripple of sensation without stopping to analyze whether it was malice or melancholy, those being two emotions often attached to lingering souls.

Greg hadn't wanted to play a character in a ghost story himself, and he wasn't necessarily doing so. Still, spirits often lingered hoping for justice, even vengeance. And that, Jean thought, was where she and Alasdair came in. Not just as seekers of truth, justice, and the legal way, but also as layers of ghosts. Normally she loathed the excuse, "Because we can." But when it came to laying ghosts, both real and figurative, those that could, had a responsibility to do.

Real ghosts. Maybe that was an oxymoron.

She stepped back into the Charlie suite, switched on a cute but faint table lamp, and sat down on the tartan cushion lining the window seat.

The tiny screen of the phone displayed a Missed Call notification. Ah, Rebecca Campbell-Reid, the distaff half of good friends in Edinburgh, had left a message just about the time Alasdair was dealing with a distraught Tina. Either he hadn't heard the phone ring or he'd ignored it. Good for him. There were times Jean wondered just who was the slave, the phone or its owner.

Rebecca's voice mail was delivered in a good-natured American voice whose accent had been moving eastward ever since she'd married Michael, Scot and proud of it. "We're still on for the wedding, bagpipes and all, no worries there. We'll be obliged to bring Linda, though. The child minder's got the flu, drat and double drat. So much for that child-free interlude. Can you ask the MacDonalds if they've got a cot? If not, we'll rig something up. At least the bairn's not crawling yet. Gotta go, emergency meeting over a collar that's turned out to be a fake."

Jean eyed the now mute face of the phone. She'd have to tell Michael and Rebecca about the death at Dunasheen, although she could spare them the ramifications until the official team had sifted through them.

The Campbell-Reids had been, if not helping hands, then peripheral nerves at all four of team Cameron and Fairbairn's earlier cases. Investigations. Things. As historians and employees of the National Museum of Scotland and Holyrood

Palace, respectively, their knowledge of and connections to the art, artifacts, and antiquities business had proved invaluable.

They'd given Jean and Alasdair a hard time about Fergie and his Flagon, no matter how much she insisted it had been old Lord Dunasheen, Fergie's uncle, who claimed the alabaster cup was an artifact of the world beneath, or beyond, or even inside, wherever supernatural beings came from. And now…well, Alasdair was right, she was operating with only a wisp or two of straw. She'd check with the Campbell-Reids once she had a brick or two, not to mention a crib for the baby.

On the gilded chair, Dougie's ears pricked forward, then back again. Jean, too, heard a faint crunch of gravel. She looked through the window to see a figure muffled in a yellow raincoat walking swiftly away from Lionel Pritchard's cottage and down the drive. Shutting the gates, as Diana had directed, would discourage the reporters. But with the pleasant village of Kinlochroy providing food, drink, and sanitary facilities, they would roost for a while, if only to justify being called way from their Hogmanay celebrations.

Jean reminded herself just as she had reminded Diana that she was a journalist, not a reporter. Either way, she needed to check with bas camp. Michael and Rebecca were valuable references and moral support, but Miranda Capaldi was both Jean's partner and her employer in the travel-and-history magazine, roles that Miranda balanced as gracefully as a fine Royal Doulton cup in its translucent saucer.

Jean pressed a number and was momentarily startled when the call was answered by a male voice: *"Great Scot."*

It only seemed like midnight. In real time, the office was still open and receptionist Gavin was duly minding reception. "Hi," Jean said. "It's me. You mean Miranda's making you work all the way to six P.M.?"

"Oh aye," the lad returned. "My filing wants sorting before

I'm allowed away on holiday. How are you getting on at the Misty Isle?"

"It's misty," Jean said. "Downright murky, even. Put me through to Miranda, please, and she can tell you all about it."

"Righty-ho."

A click and a buzz and Miranda's smoke-and-honey voice answered. "Miranda Capaldi."

"Hi. It's me," Jean said again.

"You're supposed to be honeymooning, Jean."

"No, I'm supposed to be writing a puff piece about Fergus MacDonald, advertising executive turned stately homeowner. The honeymoon doesn't come until after the wedding."

"Tell Alasdair that," Miranda said with a laugh, and then her laugh trailing away into caution. "Please tell me you're not phoning because there's been criminal activity."

Really, Jean thought, Miranda's ESP was uncannier than her own, and much more useful. "I'm afraid so. An Australian visitor's been stabbed to death on Dunasheen Beach, mere minutes after getting here. Alasdair's in full police mode and the troops are assembling."

"Ah," Miranda said. "Well then. Pity." After a suitable moment of silence, she asked, "Australian, you're saying?"

Jean told her everything she knew, little as that was, of Greg MacLeod's artificially shortened life: Townsville, Queensland. Clan societies and genealogy. A souvenir factory. Property. The art market. A museum of religion a la St. Mungo's. "Although," she concluded, "I bet his museum has another attribution, since St. Mungo is peculiar to Glasgow."

"There's something to be said for, say, the Woolloomooloo Museum of Religious Life and Art."

Jean surprised herself by laughing, if shortly. "You went Down Under year before last."

"Aye, that I did, attending a benefit in Sydney for the descendants of the Scottish masons who built the harbor bridge.

Whilst I was there I spoke to several clan societies, including the MacLeods, and made the round of galleries and museums as well. The Ozzies lay on lovely receptions, all in the interest of British/Australian business and cultural relations, of course."

"Of course," said Jean, with a knowing nod. She heard either the soft chatter of Miranda's keyboard or the discreet jingle of her jewelry.

"No Greg MacLeods are named in my notes, nor have I a business card on file. You've tried an Internet search on the man, have you?"

"If you'll look in the next office, you'll see my laptop sitting on my desk."

"Oh aye. And here's me, saying, no, you'll not be wanting your computer, being a blushing bride and all. Half a tick."

Jean refrained from pointing out that she and Alasdair were past the blushing stage, even though, with Jean's fair to fishbelly-white skin, flushing was always an option.

"There's more than a few Greg MacLeods in the world," Miranda announced. "Here's yours, though, in a newspaper article from last year. He sold Waltzing Matilda Gifts to Gung Hay Fat Choy International for a tidy sum, however you're defining tidy."

"That confirms what he told Fergie, though I don't know why he'd lead Fergie on."

"Here's another bit in the same newspaper, last March. MacLeod gave a donation—another tidy sum, I reckon, or it would not be in the papers—to the Bible History Research Society for excavations in Israel."

"That connects him with the museum." Jean frowned—somewhere in the storage closet of her brain, the name Bible History Research Society rattled like a skeleton shifting uneasily.

"Just coming, Gavin!" called Miranda. And, back into the telephone, "Sorry, Jean, must run."

"Fergie says I can borrow his computer," Jean told her. "And maybe Tina MacLeod will be up to answering questions when D.C.I. Gilnockie gets here. The guy who replaced Alasdair at Inverness."

"You'll soon be hearing the bellow of the alpha males, then."

This time Jean's laugh was more of a snort, the skeptical retort of the alpha female. "Alasdair promises no territorial disputes this time around. I think he's finally accepting he's in another business now. And he told me Gilnockie's a good cop."

"You'll be keeping me up on events, then. I'll try asking about among my Ozzie contacts, but with the holiday and all, they're more likely hanging about Bondi Beach than answering e-mail."

It always seemed odd to Jean that Christmas and New Year's were mid-summer events Down Under. But that was her own cultural bias. "Thanks. I'll talk to you again before I see you on the second."

"You're still holding the wedding, then?"

"Oh." Jean looked around the room, from the painted dragon above the mantel to the sleeping moggie on the posh chair, but neither was offering any advice.

Maybe she and Alasdair should cancel the festivities. Maybe holding a wedding under the shadow of an unsolved crime would taint their marriage. Or maybe she and her equally stubborn beloved shouldn't let some bloody-minded person control their destiny any more than various bloody-minded people had already done.

"Jean?" Miranda asked.

"Yeah, we're still holding the wedding."

"That's the spirit! Keep your pecker up, eh?"

"I should hope so."

"It's not too late to be organizing a release of doves. Saw

it done once at a wedding in Hampshire, just lovely, off they flew into the blue sky…"

"…and were probably picked off by hawks. Thanks anyway, Miranda." Jean shook her head, round-filing Miranda's dove idea with her other ones: arriving at Dunasheen chapel in a horse-drawn carriage draped with roses, exiting while military re-enactors formed an arch of swords, champagne fountains and a cake shaped like Edinburgh Castle at the reception.

"You've got no taste for bells and whistles, do you now?" Miranda said sadly.

"No. And neither does Alasdair. Talk to you again soon." Jean hit *End* and leaned against the stone bar separating two windows. It felt like a cold finger tracing down her back.

Her smile ebbed. Her ears echoed with the absence of Miranda's familiar voice. With the absence of any sound at all except for the eerie whistle of the wind in the chimney. The shadowed room in front of her seemed to fade away, and she saw the lights of Edinburgh and the crowds jostling along the sidewalks, fireworks over the Castle and rock bands playing.

No lonely beaches there, just the occasional lonely alley, and all the agitations of the city. There was something— there was a lot—to be said for mountains, sea, and sky, even a clouded one. Caledonia, stern and wild, harsh and beautiful. She'd committed herself to Scotland before she'd committed herself to Alasdair.

Sitting up, she looked into the darkness, at the lights of the village blurred by the mist and rain, at the fluorescent stripes on the police cars shining in the lights of the house, at the man standing—

The chill on her back surged through her body, tightening every follicle. A human shape stood below the window, so still she'd have thought he was one of Fergie's sculptures, if there'd been a sculpture in the parking area. The posture, feet planted wide apart, hands thrust into pockets, indicated a man. But it wasn't Pritchard, the manager. He'd been wearing a yellow raincoat. And why would he stand there when he had a nice warm cottage or even nicer, if cooler, castle to go to?

This man wore mottled black, boots, pants, a long jacket with a hood. A hood pulled so well forward that it encompassed only shadow, like one of Tolkien's ringwraiths or a specter of Death.

Then he moved, tilting his head back so that the light revealed his face, white as old bone. He spotted Jean in her window, outlined against the dim light, and his body straightened from a merely cautious pose to an alert one.

She didn't move. She didn't breathe. She returned stare for stare with those hollow eyes.

Did he slump slightly? Or did he hear the front door opening? Just as light gushed outward and ran off his jacket like water, a yellow-coated figure ran up the driveway and a male voice shouted, "You there!"

The dark figure faded into the night.

SEVEN

JEAN EXHALED BETWEEN teeth clenched so tightly her jaw hurt.

Yellow-coat ran into the parking area, still yelling, "Here! You there!" Which seemed a bit contradictory, but she was hardly in a position to criticize. She didn't recognize the voice, and the figure was too slender to be either Fergie or Rab Finlay. Pritchard, probably.

Below Jean, presumably from the front porch, Diana's cool voice cut the heat of the male's. "Mr. Pritchard, Lionel, if you please, there's no need to shout."

"Diana, we can't have the man hanging about. Your own father…"

"No harm done. Someone in the village likely told him about—the unfortunate event—and he stopped by on his way home to have a look at the police vehicles."

His gait as smooth as a hobby horse's, Pritchard strode to the door. Jean had to lean forward and press her ear to the icy glass in order to hear him say, "We're hardly on his way, the path runs beyond the garden wall. He had no call…"

The slam of the front door echoed upward, vibrating as subtly in Jean's ear as distant thunder. She sat back on the window seat. Who was "he"? Where was "home"? And was Pritchard's accent English rather than Scottish?

Well, so was Diana's. And Fergie himself had been infused with a "proper" accent, as befit the nephew of a baronet, never mind his thistle-strewn Highland ancestry. Although with Fergie, the infusion hadn't quite taken.

The clock on the mantelpiece chimed six times. She'd

promised to be in the library at six-thirty. With one last searching glance out the window—no mysterious figures, no irascible managers, no police people—she pulled herself to her feet and headed into the bathroom.

Her cosmetics bag was wedged between a ceramic lizard studded with fake gems and Alasdair's nylon shaving kit, which in turn sat next to a Chinese vase holding fresh if odorless flowers. Maybe instead of donning the cap, bells, and motley of a court jester, she should don war paint. She applied eye shadow and mascara, chose a colorful tapestry vest over a basic skirt-and-turtleneck combo, added necklace and earrings, and traded her walking shoes for decorative flats, all the while pondering what Diana had called the unfortunate event.

It was too much to expect the mysterious man in the parking area to be the murderer. Murderers, in Jean's thankfully limited experience, didn't stand around looking sinister. Besides, Diana and Pritchard both knew him, or of him, at least. He must be some local character.

If one of the two military dirks in the entrance hall was the murder weapon, then the murderer must have come from inside the house. Or passed through it. Or known someone with access to it. Did that mean the murder had been a collaborative effort, and that there were two killers to apprehend? *Great.*

In the bedroom, the telephone lay where she'd left it, on one of the tasseled pillows piled on the four-poster bed. Its little screen gazed up at her blankly. *No, he doesn't need you right now.*

She tried a telepathic message instead: *Alasdair, let everyone else deal with the crime scene. Come get dinner.*

Her summons produced only Dougie, who trotted out of the dressing room licking his lips, leaped onto the bed, and snuggled down amidst the pillows. Jean regarded him with a touch of envy. Not so long ago she'd been proud of her hard-earned self-sufficiency, the sort of pride that went before falling in love. Now she was incomplete without a man, if far from just any man.

They had been through more together in less than a year than she and her first husband had experienced in two decades. Alasdair had never met her ex, a man who was all ground and no imagination, but she'd met his, a woman who was all imagination and no ground. All four had promised to have and to hold until death did them part. But it wasn't death that had parted them, although divorce was a sort of death.

Fergie had lost his wife to disease. And Tina had lost Greg to murder.

Jean jerked to attention as the clock struck six-thirty. Places to go, people to see, clues to ferret out. Tucking the phone into her second-best evening bag, a small leather pouch on a long strap, she gave her engagement ring a quick polish against her skirt and charged out into the hall.

She almost caromed off Scott Krum, who was lifting the lid of an ivory-inlaid chest opposite the door of the Charlie suite. He dropped it with a thud and whoosh that made the Grainne tapestry ripple. His teeth gleamed in a fixed smile framed by his dark—no, what Rab Finlay had was a beard. Scott's goatee looked like it had been traced on his face by a black marker.

"Oh," he said. "Hi. I forgot the camera, the girls want snapshots, I came back upstairs—this is your room, huh?"

"Mine and my fiancé's, yes."

"Your fiancé is here, too?" He sidled away.

With a suspicious glance at the chest—Fergie probably wasn't keeping the family silver in there—and another at Scott—she didn't see any cameras about his person, but a digital one would fit in a pocket—Jean locked the door and allowed herself to be led toward the staircase. "We're getting married at St. Columcille's, the Dunasheen chapel, on the third."

"Great, great. After you." Averting his eyes from the bedizened suit of armor, to say nothing of the mistletoe, Scott waved her onto the turnpike stair.

Jean stepped past the tripping stane and the chill spot, and at the second-floor landing asked, "So are y'all enjoying the Wallace suite?"

"Heather hasn't found much to complain about yet, and that's saying something."

They walked down the first flight in silence, Jean breathing in the odors of roasting meat and baking pastry. Her stomach's pitiful grumble reminded her she'd missed tea and Nancy Finlay's superior baked goods, but then, she'd feasted on them yesterday, so it averaged out.

Safely in the entrance hall, Scott said, "I guess you're wondering why I was on the third floor."

"The question had crossed my mind." Jean turned around to face him.

He'd abandoned the smile for an embarrassed grimace, but his eyes were guarded. "I work for an auction house in Maryland, doing appraisals, estate sales, that kind of thing. You know, *Antiques Roadshow* stuff. I was curious about what the MacDonalds have tucked away here. The older the house, the greater the chance of something really cool lying forgotten in a closet."

No kidding, Jean thought, but what she said was, "Something that could be bought cheap and then sold on for a lot of money?"

"I don't cheat anyone. Reselling is part of the business." He dropped the grimace as well. "So what do you and your fiancé do for a living?"

"I'm a journalist and part owner of *Great Scot* magazine in Edinburgh."

"I've heard of that. Pretty good worldwide circulation, right? Both paper and electronic?"

"Yes, we're blanketing the world with dead trees and pixels both."

"You think you could cut me a deal on advertising rates?"

"You'd have to check with my partner, Miranda Capaldi. She's the boss." And the various departments such as Advertising, Circulation, Editorial, Printing, and Web Design were scattered from Leith to Dalkeith, hardly out of Miranda's sight, but pretty much out of Jean's mind. "Alasdair—Alasdair Cameron—is the head of Protect and Survive, the security agency."

Scott nodded. "Oh yeah, they've got a good reputation. I'd like to touch bases with him. Where is he?"

"He's…" She redirected her statement in midstream. "He should be here for dinner."

"Great. We've got drinks first, huh? The library, Diana said. Down this way?" Smile restored, he bowed Jean toward the hallway.

"Yep, this way." She glanced back at the two black sheaths, establishing that the one on the right was still empty. Scottish regimental dirks were collectible items, but if Scott had decided to help himself, he'd have taken the sheath with its silver fittings and diminutive knife and fork as well.

Just because he was checking the place out didn't mean he was a thief. Just because Jean's curious nature had developed a suspicious streak didn't mean there was anything suspect in an art dealer like Greg and an antiques dealer like Scott turning up in the same place at the same time. They'd both been attracted by the house itself. And Fergie certainly had things to sell, if not actively for sale.

Like books. Passing beneath another stag's head, this one wearing a Sherlock Holmes-style deerstalker hat complete with an eagle feather, Jean led Scott into the library.

Glass-doored cabinets lined the room, rank after rank of books old and new glimmering behind polished panes like treasure at the sea bottom. The cabinet holding the Fairy Flagon was closed—Fergie was understandably protective of his family talisman. A peat fire burned in the fireplace, with both of the dogs, the Lab and the terrier, lying broadside to it and absorbing most of the warmth. New Age interpretations of Christmas classics emanated from hidden speakers. In front of the center window sparkled a Christmas tree, every light reflected in the glass.

Jean tasted the air like she would a fine wine—a trace of smoke, a soupçon of old paper and leather, the sharp odor of evergreen, the silken hint of spices. No wet dog, though. The animals looked as though they'd been blow-dried.

Had they reacted at all to the black-clad man standing alone, wet, and cold in the parking area, looking not at the police vehicles but up at the lighted windows of the house? Or did they know him?

Heather Krum waited in the middle of the room, her arms folded across a beaded and embroidered jacket, her narrow glasses perched below a heavy fall of bangs letterboxing her eyes. "There you are," she snapped to Scott. "I thought you'd met up with that Diana woman."

"Our hostess?" he retorted. "I ran into Jane on the staircase, okay?"

"Jean," Jean corrected, without continuing on to correct Scott's geographical ambiguity.

Heather's slitted eyes looked Jean up and down. "Are you here alone?"

"No, I'm here with my fiancé for our wedding on January third."

"Oh." Despite her tight ski pants, Heather flounced into a chair.

Jean wasn't sure whether her soon-to-be married status or

her age had absolved her of threatening the Krums' relationship. She hesitated between being insulted and laughing, but
neither seemed appropriate.

Dakota was methodically working her way along the
shelves, her head tilted as she considered Fergie's impressive array of books, not just peeling and yellowed ones dating to generations past, but also contemporary titles ranging
from astronomy to crypto-zoology, from archaeology to geo-
mancy, from history to frenzied fringe tomes claiming that
alien astronauts had not only built ancient structures from
Stonehenge to Angkor Wat to Teotihuacan, but also that alien
astronauts were humanity's primeval gods.

Odd notions, yes, and Alasdair was justified in questioning Fergie's taste for them, but then, like all odd notions, they
were thought-provoking, horizon-expanding, and downright
entertaining.

Atta girl, Jean thought at Dakota, and, at the same time,
Watch out, you'll end up like me. Although there were a lot
worse places to end up.

"So," Scott said to Jean, just a bit too loudly, "what about
the guy—it's a guy, right?—who fell down at the old castle?
Is he okay?"

"I told you," said Heather, "we didn't hear any sirens, so
he must be all right."

Jean was intended to be counselor as well as jester, then.
Thanks, Diana. "Ah, um." She looked down at her feet planted
solidly on the faded rug. "I'm afraid there was no need for
sirens. No rush. He, ah, didn't make it."

"You mean he died?" Heather's nostrils flared as though
someone had just handed her a bucket of muck.

"That's what 'didn't make it' usually means," Scott informed her.

Dakota looked around, smooth features crumpled.

"The police are here," Jean said quickly, "and they're taking care of everything, and the local doctor's with his wife. Greg's wife, that is. The man who—didn't make it."

"Good," said Heather. "I mean, bad. I mean, I'm sorry."

Dakota turned one way and Scott the other. He stared up at the painting over the mantelpiece. This one depicted Calanais stone circle on the island of Lewis. The glow of a small fire at the base of the tallest, square-shouldered, megalith diffused upward and met a similar glow in the lowering sky, probably the rising moon. Over the fire crouched a figure that would have been human except for wings catching both light and dark in subtle grades of color, like a pigeon's breast.

Beneath it, on the mantel, stood an olivewood nativity scene, presented straight up. At least, Fergie had tucked the E.T. action figure behind one corner of the stable, not substituted it for baby Jesus in the manger.

Scott made no remarks—or photographs, either, never mind his expedition to retrieve the family camera. Heather inspected a fingernail the same color as the painted sky. Dakota looked at the bookcase, but Jean could see her expressionless face in the glass, while the peppy features of the teen idol on her sweatshirt floated ghostlike below.

She considered injecting the sudden silence with something artificially cheery, such as the suggestion they could all consider the unfortunate event as a real-life mystery weekend. But over and beyond having to expand "he died" into "he was murdered," this was no game.

A musical rattle from the corridor, like glass wind chimes, fell joyfully on her ears. "The drinks are here!" she announced, probably giving the Krums the impression she was an alcoholic needing a fix.

The door opened, admitting Fergie. He now wore a beautifully cut dark suit over a tartan waistcoat—somewhere a Savile Row tailor was weeping—and pushed a serving cart laden with bottles, glasses, and steaming punch bowl. Not,

Jean thought, that the red liquid splashing behind the cut glass had to be particularly hot to steam. Beyond the fire's aura, the room was cold. The two dogs looked up but didn't get to their feet.

"Good evening, how are we getting on?" Fergie said with a grin. If St. Patrick had had such an affable grin, he could have charmed the snakes out of Ireland instead of ordering them to go.

Scott essayed a smile. Heather did not. Dakota stared.

"I'm Fergus MacDonald, the poor chap responsible for this castle. And you're the Krums, from the U.S., like Jean here. Scott, Heather, Dakota. Welcome, welcome." He was working uphill, but, trouper that he was, went gamely on, "Are the dogs all right for you? No allergies?"

"We're fine, thanks," said Scott. "Heather's got a poodle at home."

"The Lab is Bruce," Fergie said, "and the terrier is Somerled. Good lads, aren't you?"

The dogs fluttered their tails against the tile of the hearth and with grunts of satisfaction let their heads fall back down.

"We have several fine single malts, a continental aperitif or two, or—'tis the season and all—we have wassail. My special recipe. And lemon squash for the lass."

Dakota crept forward. Squashed lemon?"

"It's kind of like Seven-Up or Sprite with lemon," Jean explained. And to Fergie, with a deep inhalation of cinnamon and nutmeg, "I'd love a cup of wassail. Do you make yours with cider?"

"Oh yes, and with wine, fruit, and spices. The latter two used to be quite special, mind you, in these northern climates." Delicately Fergie pushed aside several clove-studded lemon and orange slices and ladled out a cupful. "Here you are. And you, Mrs. Krum?"

"I guess you don't do cosmopolitans," Heather said.

"If that's what you'd prefer," began Fergie, "I'm sure I can…"

"Let it go, Heather." Scott extended both hands. "We'll take wassail, thanks."

"Very good." Fergie placed two more cups in his hands, the small, smooth hands of someone who'd only worked with his mind, then gave Dakota a tall glass adorned with mint and a cherry.

Scott drank deeply. After a tentative sip over her protruding lower lip, Heather allowed, "It's good," and retracted the pout.

Reminding herself that the drink was full of alcohol and her stomach was full of air, Jean let one swallow of insidious sweetness slide down her throat. Then she cradled the warm cup between her cool hands and pushed aside any comparison of the crimson drink to crimson blood. Nor did she ask if Thomson or Portree had taken Fergie up on his offer of sandwiches in the staff sitting room…no, wait, was that a door opening far down the hall and a couple of male voices?

"What's that burning in the fireplace?" asked Dakota.

"Peat," Fergie answered, and launched a soliloquy about peat bogs, and wood as a precious resource, and the Yule log in the Great Hall among other observances planned for tomorrow night—his smile was that of a child anticipating Santa Claus—and how the Log represented the Yule bonfire, which was a major observance along the outer rim of Scotland and its islands, the areas heavily influenced by the Norse, as evidenced by the fire festival Up-Helly-Aa in the Shetlands every January.

None of the Krums blinked. Jean edged closer to the door. Yes, her internal sonar detected Alasdair's voice.

"This is the time of year," Fergie went on, "when trows or trolls come out form the underworld and carry mortals away. Not to worry, though, we're protected here at Dunasheen by our Green Lady."

Not necessarily, Jean thought.

"The Green Lady's our resident ghost or fairy, a *glaistig,* green being the fairy color. The story goes that you can hear her singing, in a fashion, when something either bad or good is going to happen. Or you can see her gliding silently toward the house…"

The glass wobbled in Dakota's hand and her eyes expanded to fill half her face. Heather reached out a protective hand, but her slice of a gaze turned toward Fergie. "You're scaring the kid, Mr. MacDonald."

"Fergus, please," he replied, and, "Oh. I'm sorry. Mind you, it's just a story."

That wasn't what he said a little while ago, but Jean had learned with her nieces and nephews to soften the edges a bit. Storyteller discretion advised.

Fergie added, "I've never seen or heard a thing."

Oh. With the slightest of prickles between her shoulder blades, like invisible fingertips tracing her spine, Jean realized that she had heard a thing. That low murmuring wail in the drawing room hadn't been Tina's voice carried over the moor. The Green Lady had been announcing Greg's death.

"I'm not scared," Dakota said. "I saw a ghost while we were driving up to the house, a ghost closing the gate in that tall wall."

"Did you now? In the garden, was she?" Fergie caught himself. "Erm, likely you saw our manager making a round of the premises."

Jean doubted that. Pritchard hadn't been on the premises.

"Dakota," said Scott, "what did we tell you about saying things like that?"

"I don't know whether it was a man or a woman," she insisted. "But it was a ghost. I saw it in the light of the headlights."

Jean had to bite her tongue to keep from blurting questions. Did the child see someone in a yellow raincoat or even a reflective coat like those worn by the police? Had she seen the man in mottled black, whose jacket had had some sort of shiny, water-repellant coating? Or was the poor child, like Jean and Alasdair, allergic to ghosts? She'd have been better off allergic to the dogs. Her parents would have sympathized with that.

Standing up, Heather seized the girl's arm and pulled her toward a corner of the room, Scott following. "Dakota, we wouldn't be here if it wasn't for you. This is your grade school graduation trip, remember?" Her *sotto voce* hiss wasn't sotto enough, and carried over the jazzed-up, dumbed-down version of "Silent Night" that jangled from the speakers.

Dakota's lower lip, shining with pale pink lip gloss, trembled. "The counselor told you to take a trip together to make up for Dad having to travel so much on business. You brought me along to kill two birds with one stone, you said."

"We could have gone to Cozumel by ourselves," Scott told her. "But you wanted ghosts and castles, so we came to Scotland." And, to Heather, "No wonder she's seeing things."

"We bought you a book to read while we had our happy hour at the pub," Heather said, and to Scott, "She was looking at the ghost stories there at the bookshop. There was a rack of them by the front desk, below the Dunasheen guidebooks."

One of Jean's ears twitched backward, dropping an eave or two. An intriguing café-and-bookshop stood across the street from the pub, the Flora MacDonald, in Kinlochroy. The Krums had stopped there, then, to wait until check-in time—a formality that the MacLeods had skipped.

"Dakota, you said if we went on this trip you'd show a better attitude." Now Heather played the guilt card.

"Never mind," said Dakota. "Just forget it."

"We'll overlook it this time," Scott told her. "But if this trip is going to work, you need to straighten up and fly right."

No fair, Jean thought. It wasn't the girl's responsibility to see that the trip went well, any more than it was her responsibility to fix her parents' marriage.

And she thought, so the Krums had been on the premises, more or less, at the time of Greg's death.

Fergie stirred the punch, pretending he wasn't hearing the Krums' mutters, but his crestfallen gaze crossed Jean's. She sent him an encouraging smile. *It's not your fault. They've got issues. We've all got issues.*

Her other ear twitched forward, hearing soft-soled shoes padding along the corridor from one direction and heels clicking along from the other. With a jingle of tags, the dogs got to their paws and stretched.

The heels arrived first, and turned out to be Diana's virtuous pumps. Above them she now wore wide-legged white pants and a basic black top set off by a stunning Egyptian collar necklace of lapis lazuli and turquoise beads, the shades of the sea around Skye. An aura not just of class but of perfume hung around her, something fresh, woodsy, and understated. With her own polished version of the MacDonald smile, she announced, "Dinner will be served in ten minutes. I've set out place cards and menus."

And had probably calligraphed each one personally, Jean thought with more humor than envy. Still, she couldn't help a second look at the white, raw silk pants. She'd never owned a pair of even denim white pants, not with all the hazards of tomato sauce, blueberries, and plain old dirt.

Scott turned toward Diana with a slightly snockered grin. "That's a great necklace. Have you ever had it appraised?"

"It's a family heirloom," Diana told him, which didn't answer his question.

Heather bristled but said nothing. Dakota looked from parental expression to parental expression and rolled her eyes. After a brief pause, the room filled with classically trained voices singing, *"Gaudete, gaudete, Christus est natus, ex Maria virgine..."*

A man appeared in the door behind Diana and Heather deflated into a snockered smile of her own. Even Jean stared. Skin like milk and honey, large, rich, brown eyes, black hair in thick waves, smoothly rounded cheeks and solid jaw topping a tall, slender body...oh. He was wearing a uniform and carried a peaked cap beneath his arm. P.C. Sanjay Thomson, revealed in all his glory.

"Hullo, Di, Fergus," he said, white teeth shining in a crescent of a smile that showed not the least trace of self-consciousness. But then, he'd probably been causing hearts to flutter all his life. He aimed the smile at the Krums and said, "Hullo again. Saw you at the pub, didn't I?"

"Oh yeah," said Heather.

Stepping up beside Thomson, if not exactly basking in reflected glory, Alasdair offered a polite nod to all and sundry. Jean was the sundry, she supposed, since the nod warmed to a half-smile by the time it reached her.

She ran a quick assessment of Alasdair's face, its pallor beneath the weather-burnished scarlet and the set of each wrinkle, like crevasses in a glacier. His posture was neither more or less erect than usual. If the investigation had made any headway—finding the murder weapon, for example—she saw no evidence of it in his stern expression. He'd been able to do no more than set Portree to work securing the scene and checking out the vicinity.

The dogs tail-wagged their way to Sanjay's black-clad legs. He squatted down, perhaps warming his hands in their fur as much as petting them. "Hullo there, Somerled, Bruce. Good lads, aren't you now?"

"P.C. Thomson," said Diana, with a slight shooing gesture. "We've laid on sandwiches and tea in the staff sitting room."

"Righty-ho, Di. Come along, lads." The young man and his furry friends headed off toward the kitchen.

Alasdair eyed Diana, head tilted, waiting to see if she designated him fish or fowl.

"Dinner in ten minutes, Mr. Cameron," she said, and wafted away.

Fergus rubbed his hands together, only the slightest of edges to his smile. "Dinner! Steak pie!"

"Say what?" asked Heather.

"Look at it as a kind of beef Wellington," Jean said. "Bits of meat beneath a crust."

"Yes, yes," Fergie said. "Nancy's food is to die for, as you Americans would say. Let's get on down the hall, shall we? Hospitality being a fine Highland tradition and all."

Yeah, Jean thought with a glance at Alasdair, *hospitality, and treachery and betrayal.*

A spark in his return glance showed that he was thinking the same thing.

EIGHT

JEAN FINALLY FELT warm again. Nothing like a good meal cooked and then served by Nancy Finlay to reset the internal thermostat.

She folded her napkin and smoothed it down next to her dessert plate, empty except for a strawberry stem. Maybe it was a sign of desensitization, but murder or no grisly murder, child or no put-upon child, she'd consumed the delicious soup, fish, meat and veg, trifle and fruit, with good appetite and moderate sips of a less than sophisticated but good-natured Burgundy.

So had Alasdair, no doubt needing fuel after his outdoor vigil. Now he, too lingered at the table, toying not with his napkin but his watch. Surely it was eight-thirty by now. Waiting for Gilnockie was like waiting for Godot.

Diana's elegantly lettered cards had placed Fergie at the head of the table—if you defined "head" as the seat closest to the door—and Diana at the foot, with Jean next to Scott, Alasdair next to Heather, and Dakota between, close enough to her mother that Heather could indicate the proper fork and insist on the child eating at least one Brussels sprout.

Each patch of dining territory was generous enough to make Jean acutely aware two places were missing, one for Tina, one for Greg. But even their chairs had been whisked away, out of sight.

Alasdair had greeted the Krums with his usual grave courtesy, answered some of Scott's questions about security issues, and held up his end of mostly Fergie's conversation about history, language, myth, and culture. In the spirit of sol-diering on, Jean had contributed anecdotes along the lines of the past being another country, one that you probably wouldn't want to visit. But mostly she watched her thoughts playing billiards, clacking from who, to where, to when, to why. Even Fergie's genial expression occasionally grew vacant and his face turned to the windows, blank sheets of black ice facing the coastline and the man lying cold if not neglected below the even blanker windows of the old castle.

Now Diana rose from her chair, initiating a general move-ment upward. "We have a library of films available in the drawing room, and satellite television as well. I'll be serv-ing coffee or cocoa."

"Is the single-malt still on tap?" asked Scott.

"Yes, it is," Diana said.

Heather said, "Scotch isn't on tap. Beer, that's on tap."

"It's just an expression," Scott retorted, adding in an au-dible mutter, "Jeez."

As Diana eased the Krums toward the hall door, the door of the butler's pantry and back passage to the kitchen swung open. Inside stood a youngish man with a wiry frame who had to be Lionel Pritchard, Dunasheen's manager. His small head, eyes like buttons, sleek brown hair edging a receding hairline, and sleek brown moustache edging an almost lipless mouth reminded Jean—unjustly, she informed herself—of a snake.

His beckoning finger drew Fergie from the table to the doorway, where he said in a rasp of a whisper Jean could barely overhear, "The phone's going again and again, report-ers asking questions."

Shaking his head, Fergie replied in a hoarse whisper of his own, "Tell them we don't know anything and refer them to the police."

In the front of the room, Scott asked Diana, "Does the satellite feed include football? Not your soccer, American football. It's that time of year, the college bowls, the pro play-offs..."

"Only you," said Heather, "would come all the way to Scotland to watch football. Let it go, already."

"This way," Diana said, her gesture that of a traffic cop—*move along, move along*.

In the back of the room, Pritchard hissed, "I'm sure the police are saying what they can. But the reporters are making a meal of it, talking about 'the stately home murder.' I expect Dunasheen will be on Page One of the *Sunburn* tomorrow morning. Although there's no such thing as bad publicity. Just as long as they spell 'Dunasheen' correctly, eh?"

What? Jean thought. Was he clueless or did he just have a crass sense of humor?

Fergie neither corrected Pritchard nor laughed. He wilted, covering his face with his hand. Alasdair took a step toward him, then, apparently thinking twice about offering hollow platitudes he might have to recant, sat back down in his chair.

Pritchard oozed back into the pantry and Fergie stumbled behind, leaving the door swinging.

Dakota made her way to the hall door, inspecting every photo and print she passed on the way. Jean smiled, remembering the words of one of her own cousins: "I bet you read cereal boxes, too."

Why yes, she did.

She had to talk to the child about ghosts in general and what she'd seen tonight in particular, without going behind her parents' backs. Although if Gilnockie decided Dakota needed to help the police with their inquiries, all bets were off.

With a last look at the portrait hanging at the head of the table, and a last glance over her shoulder at Jean—did she sense a kindred spirit, or was she just wondering why the older woman kept smiling at her—Dakota followed the others into the hallway, and that door shut, too.

Alone at last, but this was no time for billing and cooing. Just one thing…

Jean had been looking at the portrait all evening. It depicted a blond woman wearing a moss-green dress with a satin shawl collar, a locket at her exposed throat. Her features were clumsily drawn, but with such affection that her smile beamed from the painted canvas like the glowing fire in the Calanais fantasy. "Is that Fergie's portrait of his wife—what was her name?"

Alasdair looked up at it. "Oh aye. That's Emma MacDonald. Mind you, I only met up with her two, maybe three times, having nearly lost touch with Fergie during those years."

"I see the resemblance to Diana," Jean said, without employing any adjectives such as "cool" or "smooth." "He hung the portrait at the head of the table so she could still be the lady of the house. Although I don't suppose she was ever the lady of this house."

"No, he inherited Dunasheen—and the title, come to that—three years ago, and she's been gone four, I'm thinking. Breast cancer. Pity, that."

"Oh yes, it is." Jean sat back down and leaned her elbows on the table, a casual, even sloppy, pose she'd hesitated to assume in front of Diana. "Fergie was talking about his Green Lady, as in a household chatelaine returning after death to continue her domestic duties. But Dunasheen isn't haunted by his wife."

"Got it in one. Dunasheen's haunted, Fergie's not." Alasdair inclined his head toward the portrait. "I'm thinking that's why he's so keen on seeing ghosts."

"On believing in the supernatural. He wants to know that Emma's not really gone." The room fell silent, the dense wooden doors and stone walls muffling any sounds. Still, Jean lowered her voice. "I'm pretty sure I heard Seonaid Mac-Donald, the Green Lady, in the drawing room, right after you went after Tina. A kind of murmuring wail, just like in the stories."

Alasdair nodded. "So she's real, then, it's that Fergie cannot sense her. Nothing peculiar about that, not to us, leastways."

"But what is peculiar is that Dakota, the little girl, was insisting she saw a ghost when they drove up the driveway, which would have been about the same time."

"Maybe she's got the allergy, poor lass."

"Or maybe she saw a person. There was a man in black standing in the parking area about six. Pritchard yelled at him to go away."

"Thomson was going on about a hermit living nearby. Sounds to be the local character. Maybe it was him."

"Then he's not a hermit in the traditional sense, like the Egyptian holy men who'd take up residence on top of a pillar in the desert, or the Celtic ones on their little islands."

"That's all you heard, Pritchard seeing him off?"

"Diana defended him, said he wasn't causing any harm, that he'd probably been in the village—I guess even a monk or a misanthrope would need more food than shellfish and seaweed—and he heard about Greg and stopped on his way home to see the police cars. Although it seemed to me he was looking at the house. He saw me sitting in the window and had himself a good hard stare."

Again Alasdair nodded, the equivalent of clicking "save" in a computer program. "Likely the man's the equivalent of the village idiot, a bit of an embarrassment."

"Mentally-challenged," Jean corrected, albeit with a smile.

"Aye." Alasdair leaned on the table, too. Between them, down the expanse of snowy linen, paraded six small sculptures of tree trunks. Eyes, noses, and mouths were sunk deep into the wrinkles of the bark, and branches bearing the leaves of different kinds of trees made stylized crowns, reminding

Jean of Tolkien's tree-people, the ents. Except hollows in these sculptures held tea lights, still flaming, if somewhat wanly in their puddles of wax.

Jean wondered if Diana would have preferred classical silver or brass candlesticks, whether Fergie's taste for fantasy was a source of conflict.

"Still," Alasdair said, "he might could have seen or heard something near the beach. I'll have a word with Thomson and Fergie as well."

Who? Oh. The man in black watching the house. Jean dropped her voice into a harsh whisper of her own. "There's something else. Alasdair, did you notice that one of those regimental dirks hanging in the entrance hall is missing? Just the knife, not the sheath."

"Is it now?" Whatever trace of post-prandial satisfaction had softened his expression vanished like sunlit sky behind a thunderstorm, and his eyes and mouth hardened with the implications. He looked at his watch again.

A familiar brittle jingle echoed from the pantry. Through the door came Nancy Finlay pushing the serving cart, now furnished with several bottles and a coffee carafe emitting a delectable vapor. Her gray hair was set in waves solid as cement curbs, revealing rhinestone earrings. Her watery gray eyes were edged with blue shadow and her lips gleamed with red lipstick that, Jean saw as she spoke, also edged her front teeth. "Fergus bid me bring your coffee and drinks here. He said you'd be having yourselves a wee bit blether about the murdered man, may he rest in peace. Though that's not likely, not with him being done to death afore his time. We had no such goings-on in the old laird's day. It's like being transported back in time, no stranger safe and families going at it…"

Like billy-o, Greg had said.

"Thank you, Nancy." Fergie reappeared on her heels and

took possession of the cart. "An excellent dinner, despite the distractions."

"Ah, it's nowt but plain food with a bit extra." She wiped her hands on the ruffled apron she wore over a flour-dusted doubleknit pantsuit. "I made a plate for young Sanjay. A scraggy lad like him needs more than sandwiches. Di could do with building up as well, and both American lasses, mother and daughter. Good to see you're not after slimming yourself to a skeleton, Jean."

Jean managed to squeak, "Thank you." Nancy meant that as a compliment.

"I've sent Rab with a tray for that poor Mrs. MacLeod," Nancy went on. "The doctor's saying she's agreed to try a wee bit dinner. She's not half demented, puir lass, but then, so we'd all be."

"Quite right," said Fergie. And, as the hall door opened, "Ah, here's the doctor just now."

Nancy stood like a Hebridean Colossus of Rhodes while Irvine greeted everyone. Half a head taller and twice as broad, she made him look like a leprechaun. "Sit yourself down, Doctor," she said at last. "I'll be along straightaway with your dinner."

"Thank you kindly," Irvine replied, "but no need. I'd just had myself tea and a sandwich when Sanjay rang."

"Your loss, then." Nancy strode back toward the pantry and into the swinging door, which didn't swing.

From its other side came Rab's bellow. "Have a care, woman."

"Have a care yourself," retorted Nancy, and this time managed to push her way through the door. Their competing voices dwindled into the kitchen.

Sitting himself down in what had been Dakota's chair, next to Alasdair, Irvine ran his hand up his high forehead and across his hair. It was white as thistledown and the same texture—he succeeded not in smoothing it down but in fluffing it up.

"How is Tina getting on?" Alasdair asked. "Gilnockie and his team will have questions that need answering soon as may be."

"She's responding well to a mild dose of sedative," replied Irvine. "I'm hoping she's eating Nancy's lovely meal, but when I left her she was making phone calls."

"To Australia? On my phone?" Fergie asked. And, quickly, "She's welcome to do so."

"No, she's got herself a phone. Here's your camera back again, Alasdair, was it? Young Sanjay's telling me you're by way of being a famous detective."

"Alasdair, aye," was all he would admit to. Ducking Jean's acerbic glance, he accepted the camera, switched it on, and started viewing the photos on the playing card-sized screen. His face frosted over as Irvine made brief but explicit remarks about body parts.

Fergie turned one way and busied himself with bone china cups and crystal glasses. Jean turned the other way and busied herself by inspecting the pictures lining the walls. The chandelier suspended from a gorgeous knotwork plaster ceiling made this the brightest room in the house, except for the kitchen with its industrial lighting, and she could easily make out a theme.

Perhaps building on the adage that an army marched on its stomach, Fergie had chosen to line the dining room with the history of the Scottish fighting man. Prints and etchings in various stages of dilapidation portrayed Norse berserkers, medieval crusaders, swords for hire in myriad countries including Russia, while red-jacketed and bekilted soldiers plied their business in Revolutionary Virginia, below the Sphinx, beside the walls of Lucknow. Black and white photographs showed soldiers swathed in the uniforms of Victorian empire, wearing bearskin hats, pith helmets, or—Jean turned completely around—the flat metal helmets of World Wars I and II. Above the sideboard, the photos tapered away, just as the Scottish regiments had recently been trimmed down and consolidated to much gnashing of teeth and clashing of verbal claymores. And yet they were still serving, as a small color snapshot of several men in modern desert gear testified.

Jean leaned sideways to better see a black and white photo beside the sideboard. There, again, were Allan Cameron and Fergus Mor, this time with a third uniformed man. The hackle on his tam o'shanter appeared to be white, indicating a different regiment.

Fergie dealt out the coffee. "Liqueur as well?"

"Sure, thanks," Jean told him, adding to herself, *maybe the alcohol will cancel out the caffeine.* Although she was expecting to get no sleep tonight anyway—and not for the reason she'd originally anticipated. "Fergie, who's the third man in that photo?"

"A chap my father was at school with. I don't know his name. They met again during or after the war, I believe. Suffice it to say, whilst my father and Alasdair's enlisted in the Cameron Highlanders, this chap signed on with the Royal Scots."

"The oldest of the Scottish regiments."

"It is that. They claim they were Pontius Pilate's guard, appropriately enough, and say they'd never have fallen asleep whilst guarding Jesus's tomb."

"I always thought the way the Roman guards fell asleep was divine intervention," said Jean. "Why 'appropriately enough'?"

"Because Pontius Pilate was born in Scotland, at Fortingall in Perthshire. Pilate's father was sent out as an ambassador after Caesar's invasion of Britain and married a Pictish chief's daughter."

"That's a great story, but as history, the dates don't add up."

"That's as may be," Fergie conceded, "but then, history's all in the interpretation."

Jean didn't try to deny that—she made her living affirming it.

Fergie set a small glass brimming with golden liquid in front of her, then doled out the same to Alasdair and Irvine. "Supposedly there was an inscription with Pilate's name here at Dunasheen some years ago, brought back by a crusader or a soldier, who knows? But it's long gone."

"That's a shame. The only other inscription with his name on it only turned up in the 1960s, I think it was, and that's not complete."

"Ta." Alasdair arranged cup and glass in formation—by the right, drink!—and sent Fergie a sharp look from beneath his brows. "My dad's regimental dirk's hanging in my mum's sitting room in Fort William. The two dirks in your entrance hall, are those the ones belonging to your dad and the other chap?"

"Yes, they are. A fine set, aren't they now, two regimental dirks, complete to the last detail. The fittings need a polish, I'm afraid, but running Dunasheen's a rear-guard action against decay. What's a bit of tarnish when…" Fergie let his sentence trail off.

Jean could fill in several possible endings, but assumed that "…when one of the dirks murdered a man" wasn't among them. So then, either Fergie didn't know one was missing, or he was covering up its loss. *Great.*

She stirred cream into her coffee, turning the black liquid into brown, and caught a black look from Alasdair that cream wouldn't mitigate. She bounced his look back. *I don't want Fergie to be implicated, either!*

And she hadn't even mentioned Diana being late on the scene to greet the Krums.

Irvine was still manipulating the camera. "Grand photos of the old castle."

"Those are for Jean's magazine article about Dunasheen." With a shrug in her direction, Alasdair turned back to the camera. He didn't speculate whether the article was still on track. It had probably never occurred to him to speculate if the wedding was still on track. His blond shot with gray head almost bumped into the cumulous cloud of Irvine's. "Well now, that's interesting."

"What?" Jean asked.

"Greg MacLeod," said Alasdair. "Jean, did you notice him having his hand to his ear as he stepped out the gate?"

"No." She half-rose from her chair, leaned across the table, grasped Alasdair's cold hand, and angled it so that the pattern of smudges on the camera display resolved themselves into an image. Dusk, Dunasheen, and a man in a red jacket, with, yes, his hand to his ear. "I bet he's talking on a cell phone. No reason we'd notice that."

Alasdair pulled the camera back and peered at the picture, but even though there were times Jean suspected he had x-ray vision, he wasn't capable of blowing up the photo.

"I don't understand," said Fergie, "why the man talking on the phone is important."

"You never know what's important," Jean told him.

"This may not be important at all," Alasdair said. "But Thomson was telling me and Portree that he turned out Greg's every pocket and found the usual, a wallet, money—proving robbery's not the motive, by the way—but no phone."

"Tina must have taken it while she was alone with him," Jean said. "That's no big deal, maybe they had only the one— heck, we only have the one—and she knew she'd have to call home with the news. That's what she's doing now, didn't you say, Doctor?"

Alasdair overrode Irvine's mumble of agreement. "When

I reached her, she was trotting to and fro wringing her hands, as near to incoherent as makes no difference. All I could make out was something about having to tell Kenneth."

Irvine added, "Kenneth is Greg's brother, I caught that much. Every time she started to calm herself, she'd work back round to his name and off she'd go again."

"Kenneth MacLeod," Fergie repeated.

"I reckon she's phoning him or the son just now," said Alasdair. "The question is, who was Greg phoning—or who phoned him?"

"The someone he intended to meet at the church?" Jean guessed. "Although it might not have been anything more than a computerized call advertising a holiday in Australia."

The hall door opened and Diana sailed into the room. "Are you finished with the drinks trolley, Father?"

"Oh yes, yes, we are. Sorry, we got to talking about the, erm…"

With a gracious smile directed at no one in particular, she neatened the remaining cups and glasses and took up a position behind the cart.

"Diana," Alasdair said, his voice part velvet, part grit. "Who was the man standing in the parking area, looking up at the house, at six P.M. or thereabouts? The one Pritchard saw off?"

Her hands on the push-rail contracted so fiercely her knuckles glinted like pearls. But the only change in her expression was a flutter of her lashes, as though someone had shone a light into her eyes. Her voice preternaturally calm, she replied, "I have no idea."

Jean sensed Alasdair's police-whiskers stiffening. Diana had a very good idea where the man lived. She knew—or felt, at least—that he was harmless.

His plump cheeks flushing, Fergie said only too loudly, "It

was Colin Urquhart, I expect. He daren't show his face to me, I'd see him off, and right smartly, too. Layabout. Toe rag."

"Now, now…" began Irvine.

Diana's pink lips parted, revealing her set teeth. "This is hardly the time or place…"

Fergie backed off, his hands raised in surrender. No, whatever was staining the family linen, this was not the place to air it out.

Jean looked at Alasdair. *Fergie, angry?* Alasdair looked at Jean. *Diana, lying?*

A series of thuds reverberated through the house, and the doorbell whirred and then rang.

NINE

JEAN COMPARED PATRICK GILNOCKIE to Alasdair while the two
men conferred in the entrance hall.

Gilnockie was substantially taller, somewhat leaner, and so
much paler of complexion and eye he seemed almost colorless.
Even his hair, cut above his high forehead in a military-style
short back and sides, was a neutral gray. His face seemed to
be carved of stone, not craggy but austere, a patrician arch to
his nose like the flying buttress of a medieval cathedral. He
listened to Alasdair's accounts of events while peeling off his
black gloves, loosening his navy blue muffler, and turning
his level gaze to the two sheaths and one dirk hanging on a
wall no less stone-built than his expression.

Jean knew only too well that Alasdair's stony expression
was a pose, a wall like old Dunasheen's enceinte, not only
defending against invaders but also confining a molten core.
With Gilnockie, though, she suspected the stone was fathoms
deep, any magma pools at its root since cooled.

Alasdair would say she was leaping to conclusions. She
preferred to think she was following her intuitions.

"…and Irvine has gone home, asking us to phone if Tina
MacLeod needs looking after." Alasdair took a half-step back
indicating the passing of the torch. He'd done his bit. He was
entitled to step down now, not that he'd exit the picture, being
expert advice and curious as a cat to boot.

Gilnockie nodded. "Thank you."

The sound of recorded voices echoed from the drawing
room. From the other direction came the murmur of live

voices, Thomson chatting with Rab, and the clash of dishes as Nancy cleared away dinner and anticipated the arrival of Portree, the next shift in her scheduled feeding of the multitudes.

Fergie peered around the corner and caught Jean's eye, but couldn't quite manage a smile. She sent one to him instead. "It's an invasion, isn't it?"

"I suppose you're accustomed to it."

"You never get accustomed to it. Not if you're bystander, anyway, and even the cops will burn out eventually. Like Alasdair."

Alasdair heard his name and looked around. Spotting Fergie, he waved him over and made introductions.

"Anything I can do to help matters along…" Fergie said, leaving the end of his sentence open to interpretation.

"A map of the property would be right helpful," returned Gilnockie, his voice still hushed. "We'll be needing an incident room. A lumber room would work a treat, so long as there's electricity."

"There's the old kitchen, behind the new one. It's got a door into the courtyard, near the old laundries and shops. Make it easier for the lot of you to come and go."

And keep the lot of them out of the house? Jean queried silently.

"The telephone connection will hardly be up to the needs of your computers," Fergie added.

"No worries," said Gilnockie. "If necessary we can stop by the police house in Kinlochroy or even return to Portree. I'll have a word with my sergeant, start setting up so we can begin taking statements and collecting evidence. Alasdair, you'll be showing me to the scene, eh?"

Alasdair took a full step back. "The local constable is—"

"I'd appreciate your opinion. Round the back, is it? I'll not be a minute." Replacing his gloves, Gilnockie turned toward the door. "I'd be obliged if you'd set the constable to guarding the knives," he added, and the door shut with a thump.

Fergie looked at the display of dirks, his brows drawn down in puzzlement. Then his eyebrows shot up his forehead, his mouth fell open, and he stopped breathing.

"You did not know the dirk had gone missing?" Alasdair asked, more in the sense of fair play, Jean estimated, than to gather information.

With an inhalation that was almost a moan, Fergie turned his bulging eyes on Alasdair. "Greg was killed with a knife, Sanjay was saying. Was it that one? The dirk belonging to my father's school friend?"

"No one knows that, not just yet," Alasdair said. "When did you last see it?"

"Several days ago. Several weeks ago. I don't know. There are so many things to keep track of, I've never had time for a proper inventory. And you know how you see what you expect to see."

No kidding. Jean waded in. "Fergie, how come you have the second dirk, too?"

For a fraction he stared as though he didn't recognize her. "Ah, erm, the man was killed in the war and my dad kept his dirk and his bonnet. He had no relations, or my father couldn't find them, or something to that effect…" He turned back to Alasdair, his face taking on a grayish tint. "Am I a suspect?"

Alasdair could have said, "No." Instead, he said, "It's early days yet. Gilnockie's a good cop. He'll sort it. And, as your security advisor, I'd suggest you not hanging valuable or dangerous items just inside the front door, leastways, not without bolting them to the wall like the other weaponry."

"Ah," said Fergie. "Quite right."

A tattoo of footsteps and Scott Krum shot around the corner. "You know something, Fergus, there's a hell of a lot of policemen milling around outside for an accidental death. What aren't you telling us?"

Fergie turned his ghastly complexion toward Scott, stared at him, too, then managed to stammer, "The man was murdered, Mr. Krum. The police are investigating."

"Okaaaay." Scott looked from Fergie to Jean to Alasdair. Apparently finding nothing inspirational in their faces either, he vanished down the hall.

"I'll—the old kitchen—things stored away…" Fergie headed toward the back hall, then, clumsily, spun around and came back again, expression firmer but still whey-colored. "Was it you who saw Urquhart hanging about, Jean?"

"I saw a man dressed in black looking up at the house. Pritchard told him to go away, but Diana said he wasn't causing any harm."

Fergie shook his head so vehemently his ponytail swished back and forth, either disagreeing with Diana's opinion or shuddering that she'd have that particular one.

"Who is Colin Urquhart?" asked Alasdair.

"A loony. A nutter. He's squatting in the old keeper's cottage at Keppoch Point lighthouse, studying the wildlife, he claims. In November, he went berserk in the pub, broke some bottles and glassware before Sanjay calmed him down. He's threatened me to my face, offered me a death threat, if you can imagine."

"A death threat?" Alasdair repeated.

"I caught him messing about the new church and asked him to move on. He got right up my nose, said I'd best have a care, men in his vicinity died nasty deaths. I looked about for something to defend myself with, but he went on his way without making good on his threat. Pritchard does his best, but Diana, well—it's not that she's encouraging him, don't get me wrong, it's that she has a kind heart."

One half of Alasdair's mouth quirked upward. *Aha.*

At least they now had the answer to one imponderable, why Diana had lied about Urquhart. But, like most answers, this one only created new questions. Jean hazarded, "You're trying to protect her from him, but she doesn't understand, and thinks you're stifling her?"

"Yes. Odd how much more sympathetic to my own parents I am now." Fergie summoned a shaky smile. "She's all I've got. Dunasheen, well, the balance sheets, they're a problem— who knows how much longer I'll have it, but Diana, now, I know I'll be walking her down the aisle sooner rather than later, and I can't really blame Urquhart for hanging about her, even as a child my uncle called her Diana Ban, fair Diana, but damn it, he's just not..."

"He's not good enough for her," Alasdair finished.

"No, he's not good for her, full stop. Oh, I know, nowa-days we talk about psychological disorders and the like, and the man's been to war, I hear. And we're told to do unto oth-ers and show mercy. Still, he frightens me. I only wish he frightened Diana as well, or, failing that, went away." Fergie's voice died into a pained sigh.

So Diana had taken on a reclamation project. Or perhaps the goddess of the hearth, the vestal virgin of Dunasheen, the proper British rose, had allied herself with a suspect character as a way of acting out. Jean's inner bad girl was tempted to pump a fist in the air. But her inner schoolmarm—much the stronger of the two—pointed out that playing with matches could burn more than a girl's fingers.

Look who Jean herself had ended up with, about the least suspect character in the British Isles.

Alasdair's eyes met hers, reserving judgment and remind-ing her to do the same. To Fergie he said, "Gilnockie will be taking a statement from Urquhart as well."

"He's a violent man," insisted Fergie, and then, grudgingly,

"But just because I've taken against him doesn't mean he's your murderer. Our murderer."

P.C. Thomson came strolling around the corner without his canine entourage. "Thank you for the grand meal, Fergus. Am I needed on the beach, Mr. Cameron?"

"You're needed here," Alasdair answered. "Have an eye for these dirks, see that no one messes them about 'til D.C.I. Gilnockie's people come for them."

"The dirks?" Thomson leaned forward to look. "A blade's turned up missing, has it? You're not thinking..." His dark eyes swiveled toward Fergie's pasty face. With admirable restraint, he said only, "Aye, sir," and took up a stance beside the massive chest. His firm nod was leavened by a satisfied tilt to his mouth, evidence of the good dinner and now duty indoors.

Around the other corner came the Krums, Scott and Heather looking right and left like Custer's scouts scanning the horizon. Scott turned a faux grin on Fergie, Alasdair, Jean, and Thomson, but didn't focus on any of them. "We're pretty jet-lagged. We're going upstairs."

Dakota grumbled, "We were just getting to the part where the spaceships..."

"Read some of those books you brought along," said Heather. "We were this far from paying excess baggage fees."

"Good night, then," said Fergie.

Jean tried, "If Dakota would like to stay downstairs a while longer, I'd be glad to sit with her. I like science fiction, too." *And we might find we have more than that in common,* she concluded silently.

Dakota opened her mouth. Scott said, "No, really, you don't want to watch a movie with her, she asks questions the entire time."

"Good for her," Jean said under her breath, but the family was already on the staircase and climbing.

Heather said, as though footnoting a previous statement,

"It's not as though there's another hotel close by, just a tacky little place or two in the village."

"This isn't a hotel," Scott said. "Diana corrected you on that already."

Heather tossed her head. "Oh yeah, she made quite an impression on you, didn't she?"

Alasdair refrained from pointing out that even if the Krums packed up and left tonight, they'd still have to give statements to Gilnockie, and they disappeared around the curve of the staircase.

Muttering beneath his breath, Fergie started for the back hall, then less spun than floundered back around. "Jean, Alasdair, I promised to show you the Fairy Flagon and, well, there's something else, something special for your article, but I'm afraid it will have to wait until tomorrow."

"No worries," Alasdair told him, overriding Jean's, "What something else is that?"

Fergie vanished down the back hall while Alasdair himself started off in the other direction, toward the cloak room. Jean clung to his heels. "You might just as well get on upstairs," he told her.

"You're not getting rid of me that easily," she replied. "I'll see you to the path. Get some fresh air."

"Right."

No need to explain that despite the size of the house, the tall ceilings and the large rooms, she was feeling a bit claustrophobic. A grandfather clock beneath a back stairway struck nine-thirty as they passed, its notes echoed in a syncopated rhythm by other clocks scattered throughout the house. Surely there had been enough hours since sunset and crisis to make up a complete night, but almost twelve more hours of darkness lay ahead, stretching out to infinity. At least they were past the solstice and the nights were getting shorter.

In the cloak room, Alasdair once again pulled off his shoes

and chose a set of wellies. "I'll get Patrick settled quick as I can. I know we were having a bit of a busman's holiday to begin, and we're not honeymooning just yet, but still…"

"But still." She exchanged her own shoes for wellies, then remembered she'd taken her coat upstairs. She grabbed the yellow raincoat hanging by the door, the one she'd replaced on its hook after their headlong entrance. One of the sleeves was partially inside out and when she poked it back into alignment it emitted a pleasant woodsy smell.

It was better to just come out and say what needed to be said. "Fergie didn't kill Greg. If nothing else, he wasn't at all winded when I caught up with him in the back hall and told him there's been an accident—which is what I thought it was, then—but he was breathing really heavily when we walked out to the old castle, so he couldn't have run from the beach all the way around by the church and back here."

The wellies were ice cold and stiff as bricks, but more accommodating than Alasdair's face. "Whyever would I be suspecting Fergie?"

"Because you're a good cop. The same reason you need to know that I played footman and opened the door for the Krums because Diana missed her cue. You remember, the dogs were outside and this raincoat was wet? I think she got back to the house right before we did. But Fergie didn't seem to know she'd gone anywhere."

Alasdair didn't react. He made a conscious effort not to react, Jean estimated, slamming a portcullis, raising a drawbridge, mortaring a few more blocks onto his patented frost-and-stone face. He turned away, lifted his coat off the hook, slipped it on, and only then said, "I'd be hurting Fergie even worse by suspecting Diana."

"No, she'd be hurting him by getting involved in something underhanded. She's already hurting him, even if all she's got going with Colin Urquhart is leaving a basket of scones on the gatepost."

"But what motive could she have? What motive could Colin Urquhart have, come to that?"

"Why was Greg murdered, period?"

With an incoherent growl, Alasdair plunged out into the glimmering darkness and across the courtyard, leaving her—the nettling but necessary voice of his conscience—to play catch-up.

She'd thought the house was cold. The salt sea wind was so much colder it sucked her breath from her lungs. She braced herself, expecting rain or even sleet, but no. In fact, the clouds seemed to have lightened a bit, in texture as well as color.

The police vehicles were set out in a tidy rank. Doors opened and shut, reflective jackets formed into knots and parted again, flashlights flashed. Two moved purposefully away toward the old castle, its tower a straight-sided shadow against the fitful gleam of Portree's invisible flashlights beyond.

Jean recognized Gilnockie's murmur, and held herself to a half-step behind Alasdair as he homed in on it.

"There you are, then." Gilnockie's gesture included the woman who stood beside him. "Detective Sergeant Lesley Young. Alasdair Cameron, ex-C.I.D. His wife, Jean Fairbairn."

Close enough. "Hello," Jean said to Young's compact shape.

Someone's beam of light raked the sergeant from top to toe. Beneath her bulky fluorescent jacket, she stood with chin up, chest out, shoulders back. Her ordinary, even bland, cosmetic-free features were set with the nervous intensity of a mongoose. Jean almost ducked aside, but all Young offered was a brusque "Hullo" before she turned back to the others.

Now there, Jean thought, was an odd couple, even odder than Alasdair and his former and unlamented sergeant.

Whatever. Thrusting her hands into the pockets of the raincoat—she'd been too intent on keeping up with Alasdair to think of gloves or a scarf—Jean shifted anxiously and coldly from foot to foot while Gilnockie rounded up his troops and headed them out.

"I'll be back straightaway," Alasdair told her, not pushing his luck by instructing her to wait inside. He fell into step beside his erstwhile colleague, telling him, "We're speculating—aye, we, that's Jean and me—that MacLeod was meaning to meet someone at the old church…"

Jean smiled at that. They'd been a long time getting to that automatic "we." But they weren't, and never would be, joined at the hip, just at the heart.

Reflective jackets, white coveralls, flashlights, a stretcher, light stanchions. The cavalcade moved off down the path, was partially obstructed by the hillside, reappeared in individual blips at the castle, then fell into shadow. A few moments later the faint thrum of a generator added a new note to the thrum of the waves. Lights sprang up behind the ancient walls as though a flying saucer was strafing the beach.

Jean was reminded of a sound and light show at a tourist attraction. She imagined portentous music and a plummy voice narrating the story of Rory MacLeod, who had leaped from Dunasheen's tower to escape a wronged and therefore wrathful husband. The lover's leap, the maiden's leap, soldier's leap, Leap Year, when women were entitled to propose marriage instead of enticing the object of hr affections into initiating the marital leap of faith. She couldn't remember now which of them, she or Alasdair, had brought up the subject of marriage.

Her thoughts wobbled to a stop. She heard no music, no voices, only a scrape of gravel as a lone constable patrolled the parking area. Her hands, clenched in the pockets of the heavy coat, were chilled to the bone—except for the spot at the root of her thumb poked by something sharp. She shifted her hand away from the annoyance.

Standing around here waiting for Alasdair was sheer masochism. His "straightaway" could be hours, depending on how many of his opinions Gilnockie demanded. One more time she trekked across the courtyard and into the cloak room, to find Fergie donning hat, coat, and gloves, and the two dogs straining at their leashes.

"Ah, Jean. Just taking the lads here for their last run of the night. Nothing like a dog to get you up and moving, eh?" If his face hadn't yet defaulted to its usual affability, at least it was no longer rumpled like an unmade bed. "Rab and Nancy are clearing things out of the old kitchen. Will the police be wanting chairs and tables, do you think?"

"Usually they bring their own." So now she was the expert on incident rooms. "Alasdair's gone down to the crime scene. I'm going upstairs."

"Diana's gone up as well. She's got a headache, understandably enough. Things didn't exactly go to plan this evening."

Jean didn't blame Diana for keeping her head down, out of the line of fire. "Sorry," she said, having nothing better to offer than sympathy. "Good night."

"Good night. Off we go, Somerled, Bruce, time to check your p-mail." Fergie maneuvered the dogs into the night and shut the door with a very quiet click, rather like Gilnockie's whispery voice.

She would have slammed the door. Jean took off the raincoat, hung it on the hook, slipped off the wellies and on her shoes. She started for the corridor, then reversed course. What had been sticking her hand, anyway?

From the pocket of the raincoat she pulled a white business

card, its thick, high-quality paper water-stained on one corner but still relatively crisp. "Fergus MacDonald and Diana MacDonald" read the raised lettering. "Dunasheen Castle, Kinlochroy, Isle of Skye. Weddings and quality holidays." The phone number, website URL, and e-mail address were printed discreetly in the corner.

Fergie had blanketed the world with identical cards. There was a silver tray filled with them in the suite upstairs, and Jean had left several with assorted friends in Edinburgh—darn it, she hadn't asked about the baby crib.

She turned the card over. On the back, in jagged black letters, was written, "Meet me at the church at 3. CU."

CU? Colin Urquhart? Was that three P.M. today? Which church, old or new? Well, technically the new one was a chapel, but not everyone was as pedantic as Jean.

Was that Colin Urquhart's handwriting? Was that where Diana had been this afternoon, meeting with a violent man just as a visiting Australian met with a violent end?

Jean folded the card so tightly in her hand that all four corners pricked her palm. She hurried along the halls, distractedly returned P.C. Thomson's "good night" and bolted up the shadowy staircase past the suites where Tina MacLeod was—eating, weeping, phoning—and the Krums were probably looking out over the courtyard toward the real-life *C.S.I.* episode.

Halfway up the next flight, Jean stubbed her toe on the tripping stane and scrabbled frantically for the rope handrail. But what she grasped was a cold hand.

Or the hand grasped hers, rather, steadying her onto the next step and sending a bolt of ice through her body, from the sixth-sense receptor on the back of her neck down her spine to her toes.

The spectral hand moved her shrinking flesh and blood hand to the rope and released it, leaving Jean clinging like a mountaineer over an abyss. Clinging like a householder in an earthquake, except this was a temblor in the space-time continuum, the strongest she'd ever felt. And she'd felt quite a few.

As quickly as she could with the lead coat of perception weighting her shoulders and buckling her knees, she looked around, up, down, sideways…there! A woman stood on the third-floor landing, her form sketched in shade upon shadow.

She wore a high-waisted, low-necked, straight-skirted gown of the early 1800s, frilled at breast and sleeves and ornamented with rich embroidery around the hem. A shawl with a paisley-patterned border hung loosely from her lower arms. Her hair was pulled into a knot on the top of her head, except for the ringlets cascading past either side of a face colorless—not Gilnockie's pale, but colorless—except for cornflower-blue eyes. The full lips were parted as though on a sigh, even though no breath passed between them. The eyes looked both at Jean and through her, into a dimension so alien it couldn't even be named the Otherworld.

And then she was gone.

Every tendon quivering like a rubber band, Jean straightened from her crouch and caught her breath. Had the ghost's clothing been tinted a faded and weathered green, or had Jean simply filled in the color? No matter. She'd just met the Green Lady, up close and personal. Very personal.

So much for Alasdair and his, "I've never yet sensed a ghost could push."

This one hadn't pushed. She'd pulled. She'd saved Jean from a nasty fall. And she'd… Jean looked down at her hand, still cold as ice. The business card was gone. No. The ghost couldn't have taken it. Whatever emotion, whatever desire, caused her to linger at Dunasheen couldn't extend far enough to palming evidence incriminating her multiple-great-granddaughter Diana Ban…

There was the card, on the step where she'd dropped it.

Jean picked it up and scanned it suspiciously. *Fergus Mac-Donald and Diana MacDonald. Meet me at the church at 3.*

Much more cautiously, she climbed the rest of the stairs and made her way down the hall and into the Charlie suite. Once inside, she slammed the door and stood with her back against it.

I'm going to have to tell Alasdair.

TEN

ALASDAIR REAPPEARED JUST as the fluorescent letters on the bedside clock confirmed the sitting room clock's twelve tinkling strokes. Midnight wasn't necessarily the witching hour.

Jean peered out from the heaped bedclothes like a mummy from her wrappings while he paced into the bathroom, face taut, lips tight. So things hadn't gone well at the crime scene.

Closing the academic journal she hadn't been reading, she put it and her glasses on the bedside table. Dougie was curled up beside her leg, doing his imitation of an anchor. But Alasdair didn't try to evict the cat when he slipped into the bed and switched off the light.

Jean blinked at the surrounding darkness—ah, good, a glow leaked between the window curtains—and turned to her beloved. It was like snuggling up to a marble statue and she broke out in gooseflesh. Served him right for all his cracks about her cold feet. "You're frozen."

"Oh aye," he replied on toothpaste-scented breath. "I was not meaning to stay so long at the scene, but Patrick…"

She waited.

I do not know what's come over the man. He's gone distant, in a way. His wife left him a decade ago, before I ever met him, so it's not that."

Ouch, Jean thought. "Maybe he's burned out, like you were."

"When I was burning out, I worked all the harder."

"I noticed," Jean said. "What happened at the scene?"

"Nothing's happened, that's the problem. Patrick's waiting

for daylight and the pathologist's reports, forensics, and all. And Tina needs questioning. For all we're knowing, Greg's been getting death threats more direct than the one Urquhart made Fergie. I stopped outside the Queen suite just now, and put my ear to the door like the worst sort of sneak, and heard Tina's voice but could not hear the words. She was speaking on the phone, I reckon. It's by way of being morning Down Under." He was starting to warm up, becoming flesh and blood once again.

Speaking of which… "A couple of things have happened here. I met the Green Lady on the staircase, and she's no wee bit ghostie. It must be true what they say about Skye, it's half in the Otherworld. Plus I found a note in the pocket of Diana's—I think it's Diana's—raincoat." Jean filled in the details, cooperated with Alasdair's interrogation, and finally lay silently while the mills of his intelligence and experience ground exceedingly fine, but, as yet, produced nothing.

Dougie stood up, yawned, and moved to a spot at the foot of the bed. He kneaded the duvet, plucking it with his claws, and settled down again.

Last night he'd found himself shut into the sitting room listening to the rhythmic squeaks of the ancient four-poster. Jean and Alasdair hadn't accomplished their purpose without pausing half a dozen times to laugh—no matter what arrangement they'd attempted, the bed squeaked. That left the room something to be desired as a honeymoon suite, although with those same thick walls, neither squeaks nor ensuing laughter would dampen the honeymooners' enthusiasm.

A murder, now, that was a damper.

Tonight Jean dozed off yet again in Alasdair's arms, this time fully clothed and chilled rather than sweaty, and woke repeatedly with images of hackled bonnets, cornflower-blue eyes, and bloodstained shingle clinging to her mind. When she at last fell soundly asleep, she dreamed the same images and more, struggling through faceless shapes holding flashlights.

The beam of one flashlight pierced her eyelids, sending a flare of crimson across her vision—blood, fire, and swords gleaming… She opened her eyes to see a thin ray of sun stretching from the gap between the curtains and hitting her in the face.

Not just morning, but also sunlight, what a concept. And either the ambrosial aroma of coffee hung on the still, cold air, or her caffeine receptors were going into withdrawal.

With an insistent meow, Dougie hopped up onto the bed. At least he hadn't waked her with a claw in one nostril, as he'd once done. She crawled to her feet and dispensed cat comestibles.

Alasdair rolled out of the bed, saying, "It's gone nine" with resignation rather than disapproval. There were nights when quantity of sleep had to make up for quality.

They walked warily down the turnpike stair, finding no Green Ladies in residence. Nor was Sanjay Thomson still guarding the entrance hall—only the hooks showed where the two dirks had hung. Jean hoped that Gilnockie's forensics team had worked late rather than started early, allowing the constable to go home for the night.

Chafing dishes lined the sideboard in the dining room, steaming with sausage, bacon, eggs, kippers, baked beans, grilled mushrooms, and tomatoes. Racks held crispy if cold pieces of toast beside bowls mounded with butter, jam, and marmalade. It was all insulation against the cold, like the sumptuous dinners, Jean supposed, although considering those dinners, she'd just as soon have had a bowl of porridge this morning.

A tea pot and a coffeepot sat on the table beneath cozies shaped like a chicken and a pumpkin, respectively. As befit their national origins, Jean took coffee and Alasdair tea.

They didn't eat alone, not with all the eagle-eyed soldiers looking down from the surrounding photos—especially the third man with Allan and Fergie Mor, whose bunched eyebrows indicated that he was either facing the sun or he had sensed his dirk would one day serve as a murder weapon.

Jean shifted her gaze to the tall windows, which now revealed a shimmering vista of gold and green land, gray stone, and blue sky with clouds like smears of whipped cream. Her feet twitched eagerly. No surprise that a trio of empty plates occupied one end of the table, along with the dregs of two coffees and one cocoa. The Krums were already up and about.

Jean was draining her second cup of life-affirming liquid into a grease-lined stomach when Nancy Finlay bustled through the swinging door, Rab at her heels less bustling than dawdling with broom and dustpan. "Good morning," she said. "I'll be clearing away now."

"We've got the polis in the old kitchen," said Rab, in such a dark tone Jean expected him to add, "and we're phoning the exterminator."

"That puir Mrs. MacLeod," Nancy said, "putting up such a brave front, coming down for breakfast and then not eating more than a bittie toast, and here's me making her up a nice plate of bacon and sausages and sitting down to keep her company."

Jean's gaze glanced off Alasdair's. No surprise Tina might find sausage, bacon, and small talk a little hard to stomach. Although, once again, Nancy meant well.

"Fancy," Nancy went on, "paying guests and now the polis at Dunasheen, poking and prying. I'm afeart it canna be helped."

"The old laird, Fergus's uncle, he's likely birling in his grave," concluded Rab.

At least Jean and Alasdair weren't paying guests them-

selves, although their raison d'être was to create more of the
same. "Where is the old laird's grave?" she asked.

"In the graveyard at Kinlochroy." Nancy stacked plates so
briskly they pealed like bells.

"No one's buried at St. Columcille's? The new—newish—
chapel?"

"Not a bit of it, no." Rab seized coffee and tea pots. "Not
a proper church, is it now? Never consecrated, not after the
murder and all, though it's registered for weddings, no worries there."

Jean and Alasdair had chosen the chapel and an Episcopal
priest for a religious ceremony not only to reflect their own
family traditions, but because a civil wedding lacked any
resonance of the history, mystery, and myth that had drawn
them together to begin with… "What murder?" she asked,
just as Alasdair asked, "What murder?"

Rab answered with a scowl. "That was a right scandal, the
laird ordering all the pernickety, papish, carved bits for his
church, and the apprentice stone mason outdoing his master,
and the master that jealous he stitched him up for the murder
of the laird's wife, or so it's said."

"There's a similar legend associated with Rosslyn Chapel in the Borders," Jean replied. "Was she murdered in the
chapel?"

"No, no, they found her here at the house, on the staircase,
strangled by a strong pair of hands, like those of a stonemason."

"Or those of someone with a right good temper." Alasdair
cocked an eyebrow at Jean, daring her to guess just which
staircase had seen the dreadful deed.

"That story's not half fancies and lies," Nancy stated, and
headed for the pantry. "Off we go, Rab. It's the last day of the
year and the house is wanting a thorough clean."

Making a face at her back, Rab followed. The door swayed back and forth and stopped.

"Oh boy." Jean met the flare in Alasdair's eye with a flash of her own. "The chapel is Gothic Revival, meant to evoke a medieval Catholic church, what the good Presbyterians of Skye would call 'papish.' It had to have been built in the early 1800s. The Green Lady's wearing clothes from the early 1800s. Greg said his ancestor Tormod was transported in 1822."

"You're thinking Seonaid MacDonald, the Green Lady, was murdered? And that Tormod was the apprentice? But if it's known he was framed…" He pushed back from the table. "No need to go manufacturing a case from whole cloth. We've already got one. Let's have ourselves a visit to the incident room."

He led the way down the back hall, past the new kitchen with its contemporary stainless steel, to the old with its soot-stained stone vault. Jean kept herself from ducking—the ceiling wasn't that low—as she stepped down a short staircase onto linoleum that a century or so ago had been stylish and trendy.

Two electric bulbs dangled like spiders from the ribs of the vault, emitting a tentative glow. No surprise a couple of police people were setting up not only tables, chairs, and computers, but also lamps. An electric kettle stood amid a collection of mugs and tea bags beside a stone sink big enough for Dakota Krum to bathe in. On the far side of the room, looking very small and lost, Fergie inspected a bulletin board set in the maw of a vast fireplace. Alasdair made a deliberate right-face away from Fergie, picking his way over cables and cords toward two windows like super-sized arrow slits.

Below them, Gilnockie and his sergeant, Lesley Young, sat across from Tina MacLeod. They'd obviously tried to make her as comfortable as possible, with a cushion on her folding chair and a cup and saucer on the plastic tabletop before her. Still, she sat in a nervous huddle, limbs knotted, curls springing in all direction, leopard-skin coat draped over her swaying shoulders like a gutted pelt hung out to dry. "...no threats," she was saying, her voice featureless as the Nullarbor Plain. "No problems at all. He had the museum, meetings with planning commissions, receptions, golf holidays—loads of exciting things. Even the genealogy was exciting to him. He was a happy man."

Gilnockie acknowledged Alasdair's presence with a grave nod, then leaned back in his chair, at ease. An old briar pipe would have completed his image, except Gilnockie's lips were too thin, too ascetic, to grasp something so self-indulgent. "You arrived here at a quarter past three. Then what?"

Tina didn't seem to notice the newcomers. "Greg took himself off to the church."

"Was he meeting someone there?"

"Not so he told me, no."

"Did he seem to be in a rush, as though he had an appointment?"

"He was driving too fast for those roads. They're no more than bitumen laid over sheep paths. But then, he's, he always drove too fast. Ken used to say—Ken, he..." Tina stopped, and pressed her pale, almost gray, lips so tightly together her chin looked like a prune.

After a moment, Gilnockie asked, "What did Ken say?"

After another moment, Tina replied, "No matter, not anymore."

Young's limp dishwater-brown hair was scooped carelessly back, ends straggling beside her lean, keen face with its pointed chin. Her hand and arm close to the torso of her button-down blouse and jacket, as though defending herself, she held up Greg's cell phone. It was one of those so sophisticated it probably brushed teeth. "You took the phone from Greg's pocket whilst he was lying dead on the beach."

"I don't remember picking it up, but there it was in my pocket."

"Bits of the phone's memory have been erased," said Young. "There's no record of activity before the three calls made late last night to Australian numbers."

"It's Greg's phone. He could take photos and text and the lot. All I can do is make calls."

"There are no texts here," Young pointed out. "Only photos of your relations."

"Who did you phone last night, Mrs. MacLeod?" Alasdair asked.

Young sent a sharp, almost hostile glance up at him. Gilnockie said nothing, his calm gaze remaining on Tina's face.

Her red, swollen eyes, embedded in dark pouches, large enough for koala embryos, looked up at Alasdair, then back at Gilnockie. "I phoned the family in Townsville. A friend in Sydney. And Kenneth, Greg's brother. I had to tell him myself. I couldn't let him read it in the papers." Tina picked up her cup, stared at it, then let it crash down to the tabletop. Her face twisted. "I'm sorry. I'm so sorry."

"Thank you, Mrs. MacLeod. Lesley, escort her back upstairs, please." Gilnockie stood up, leaving Young to grasp Tina's shoulders and maneuver her to the door as though she was loading furniture on a truck. As soon as she was out of earshot he added, "Poor woman. Dreadful state she's in."

Alasdair's eyebrows tightened, creating the vertical cogitational crease that Jean knew only too well. But he offered no opinions about Tina, Young, or Gilnockie himself, who gestured toward the bulletin board where Fergie still stood. "We've downloaded the photos from your camera and printed them out. The others are coming in. There's nothing from forensics just yet. Mrs. Finlay's saying she doesn't have enough hands to be dusting the weapons in the front hall every few moments, and she's got no idea when the dirk disappeared, and not to trouble her when she has cleaning and cooking to see to. Rab was saying the same thing, if more, ah, assertively."

Jean could hear them, muttering about the good old days when assisting the police in their inquiries wasn't part of their job description. "What did Diana say?"

"We haven't interviewed Diana yet. She's running errands."

"But you're thinking the dirk's the murder weapon?" asked Alasdair.

"That's my theory just now. The postmortem shows that Greg was stabbed twice by a blade eighteen inches long, a right-handed person striking from below. He died instantly." Pulling a pen from his pocket, Gilnockie mimed two thrusts into Alasdair's chest.

"None of this clumsy overhand business like you see in the cinema, then," said Alasdair. "That's flashy, but not as quick or as effective."

Visualizing the famous shower scene in *Psycho,* Jean nodded. "So the killer was very efficient. Someone who'd had military training, maybe?"

"I beg your pardon?" Gilnockie turned a puzzled glance toward her.

But Alasdair had learned to follow—not her train, her carnival ride—of thought. With something between a grimace and a grin, both quickly suppressed, he produced from his own pocket the small white square of a business card. "Jean found this bittie paper in a raincoat hanging by the back door. It looks to be someone was making an appointment for the time and near the place of the murder. The 'CU' might be a chap named Colin Urquhart, who supposedly's an ex-soldier."

Fergie was turning away from the bulletin board, too far

away to hear Alasdair's "supposedly" which was ordinary police-speak but which did cast doubt on Fergie's information. Jean moved to intercept him, hoping to keep him too far away to hear Diana's name. "Good morning."

"Good morning, Jean. Lovely day, isn't it? I told you we'd be seeing the sun yet." His amiable smile lit only the bottom half of his face. His eyes still reflected the photos, the harsh, cold light of camera flashes illuminating a harsh, cold scene.

"Yes, you did. Beautiful day. Have the Krums gone out already?"

"They're having a look round, yes. And Diana's away to Kinlochroy for a few last-minute items for the old-fashioned Hogmanay festivities tonight."

He didn't have to market to her. Jean knew that "old-fashioned" was relative—the Scottish tourist industry was creating tradition as fast as it could—but he was just defaulting to his usual spiel. "When was St. Columcille's built?"

"It was completed in 1822. The designer meant to leave it unfinished, all the better to suggest a medieval ruin, but the laird at the time, Norman MacDonald—Norman the Red, he was called—he had it completed, if not quite to his original scheme. That was seen locally as too Catholic. I suppose it's not a proper folly, even if we do hold weddings there." Fergie's smile seeped upward.

Jean seemed to hear the whir of spinning wheels and the clank of looms. They might not be manufacturing a second case at all. "Rab was telling us…"

"Fergus!" called a peremptory male voice.

Jean and Fergie looked around to see Pritchard gesticulating from the door.

"Now what?" Fergie asked the air. "If you'll excuse me, Jean…"

"Oh!" she exclaimed as a neuron fired, stinging her memory. "I've been meaning to ask you if you've got a baby crib.

A baby cot. My friends from Edinburgh have to bring their little girl. She's just six months old, so they don't need anything elaborate."

"A little girl?" Fergie's smile swept over his face and down his body, so that he wriggled like a delighted puppy. "Wonderful! Tell them the lass is welcome to the family cradle. And you, Jean, you're welcome to my computer—it's switched on and booted up."

"Fergus!" called Pritchard. "The reporters have got at the Americans."

With a glance toward Gilnockie and Alasdair, Fergie started toward the door. "Thanks," Jean called after him, and wondered what was up with Scott and Heather, not to mention Dakota, another little girl. It wasn't as though they knew anything about the case. All they knew was the laird and his daughter.

The stately home murder. Stately homicide. Great.

The blip and whir of electronics contrasted with the voices echoing off the vaulted ceiling and from the void of the fireplace. The hearth still held traces of ash and bits of charcoal from fires long dead. Supposedly ashes cleaned out of the household fireplaces on New Year's Eve could be read like tea leaves, foreseeing the future. But Jean saw nothing—unless the future was dark.

She tried visualizing Alasdair's charcoal gray Argyll jacket, the one he wore with his kilt for special occasions. Like the dinner party where they'd first connected. Like his upcoming wedding.

He took a step away from Gilnockie. "Well then, Patrick…"

"I'm just joining the team at the beach—the sunlight's a blessing, no doubt of it—I'd be obliged if you'd come along as well. At the back gate in five minutes, eh?" He ambled toward the coat rack beside the outside door, stopping en route to inspect and approve each assembled work station.

Alasdair stared after him, his expression no doubt intended to be inscrutable. Jean drifted toward him. "For once you're trying to give up the police work and you can't get rid of it. And I was worried you'd be clashing antlers with him."

Alasdair's eyes narrowed in irritation, but they were still turned toward Gilnockie.

"If you're at the beach you can avoid Fergie. And Diana—she's gone to Kinlochroy, cutting through the reporters like an icebreaker. You heard what Pritchard said about the Krums, right?"

"I'm afraid so." His irritated gleam shifted to the door leading to the main house. So many fires to put out, so little time. And his hoses and axes mothballed. Decisively, he headed up the flight of steps, Jean matching him stride for stride.

In the hallway, she said, "I'm going to check out some things on Fergie's computer. And I'll take the phone, please, so I can check in with the reserve troops in Edinburgh. I'll meet you at the old church in what? An hour? We can walk back by the new one—which, by the way, *was* built in 1822."

"I'm not surprised." Alasdair pulled the phone from his pocket and handed it over. "Half past eleven at the old church," he said, and almost managed to get away before she caught his shake of the head and roll of the eye. But she did catch them, and indulged in her own shake and roll at his disappearing back.

Then a crash and a woman's harsh shout sliced through the silence.

ELEVEN

PELTING INTO THE entrance hall, Jean almost collided with Alasdair. He stood just inside the open front door—that was the crash, the heavy wooden panels hitting the wall.

Beyond the tunnel of the tiny porch, on the sun-drenched gravel of the parking area, Tina MacLeod stood braced between two suitcases. Her spotted coat was buttoned to the throat. Her sunglasses hid half her face, while her red lips looked like a bloody slash across the other half. Prying them apart, she said, "I'm leaving."

"No, you're not." Lesley Young stood between Tina and the three cars parked along the garden wall in the stance of a soccer goalie.

"I can't stay here. I have to leave. I have to get away." Tina yanked on her suitcases, but the wheels snagged on the gravel and they topped over.

Young seized one of the handles. "Have you no police in Austria? Don't you know you can't be leaving the scene of a crime?"

Tina pulled back. "That's Australia, you stupid cow."

"Had your bags all packed, did you? Why are you running? What are you hiding?"

Alasdair's nostrils flared and his lips clamped. Jean dodged as he strode out the door, then tiptoed behind him into the brilliant light of day.

His large, capable hands grasped one leopard-skin shoulder and one drab cloth-coated shoulder, stopping the spontaneous tug-of-war. "That's enough, the pair of you. Mrs. MacLeod, if you're wanting to see your husband, he's in Portree. Inspector Gilnockie can arrange transport."

Tina threw herself away from Alasdair's hand, only to droop over the remaining suitcase. "That's just it—I mean, no, I don't, I can't—you don't understand, I can't stay here."

"You're guilty, are you now?" demanded Young.

Guilty of what? Jean asked herself. Then she felt the heel of an imaginary hand hit her in the forehead. *Oh*. Tina had gone looking for Greg. Maybe he'd been alive when she found him.

Alasdair wrenched the second suitcase away from Young, throwing her off balance. Even as she lurched backward, gravel spattering, he snapped, "Sergeant, I'd recommend you remembering police procedure. Inspector Gilnockie is expecting you at the beach. Get on with it."

Young stared at him, eyes blazing and then cooling in his arctic blast. *Don't say it,* Jean beamed telepathically at her. *Don't tell him he has no authority here.*

Contracting to a defensive crouch, Young scuttled around the far end of the house just as Sanjay Thomson came loping up the driveway, a woman constable keeping pace with him. Both were sending dubious glances over their shoulders.

Jean squinted toward the mass of color seething around the wrought-iron gates at the end of the drive. That's right, the Krums were holding an impromptu press conference. But Fergie and Pritchard were dealing with it. They didn't need her help. They didn't even need her shivering, tooth-chattering presence—the air was calm but so cold that the thin, liquid sunshine barely registered on her shrinking flesh. She crossed her arms around her sweater-clad midriff and tucked her hands into her armpits.

"You'd not be getting away without passing the reporters," Alasdair told Tina. She turned, looked, and wilted even further. He clasped her elbow, steadying her. "You, W.P.C.— what's you name, please?"

The female constable goggled at him from beneath the brim of her hat, the ends of her short-cut carrot-red hair waving at her freckled temples like antennae. "Orla McCrummin, sir. Portree."

She seemed to expect Alasdair to rip open the front of his sweater and reveal red-and-yellow, rampant-lion-of-Scotland initial monogrammed on superhero spandex. His reputation preceded him, thanks probably to Thomson.

His expression that of someone ignoring a bad smell, Alasdair said, "W.P.C. McCrummin, escort Mrs. MacLeod to her room and sit down with her."

"Yes, sir." McCrummin took possession of Tina's arm as Thomson claimed the suitcases with that usual male grimace of, *What's in here, bricks?*

"P.C. Thomson," said Alasdair. The youth hung back while McCrummin gently guided Tina to the door. "Get on with the luggage, then collect Colin Urquhart at the lighthouse and bring him to the incident room."

"Sir, Inspector Gilnockie was sending me to collect Colin not an hour since, but he was not home."

"Ah," said Alasdair, with such a subtle release of tension in his head and shoulders that Jean was sure only she saw it. So the investigation was proceeding, if by steam rather than bullet train.

"What were you saying about Colin Urquhart?" she asked Thomson. "He's a hermit?"

"Of a sort. He comes into the village now and again, but mostly keeps to himself. Some folk say he's a layabout, a toe rag, that he's squatting in the lighthouse keeper's cottage. But he's paying rent to the lighthouse board, so Kinlochroy council's got no reason to move him on. And he's not asking anyone for money, he's got some sort of assistance, being ex-military."

"Ex-military," Alasdair repeated. "Fergie was saying he's got a tendency to violence."

"Post-traumatic stress disorder, Doctor Irvine's saying. Aye, Colin caused a wee bit stramash at the pub in November. Rab Finlay and Lionel Pritchard and two of the older chaps, pensioners, they were taking the mickey by saying soldiers nowadays have it easy, hot meals and the like. He's not a bad sort. He had a rum go in Iraq is all."

"What's his relationship with Diana MacDonald?" asked Jean.

"She's kind to him. She's always had a good heart, has Diana."

"What's your relationship with Diana?" Alasdair asked.

"Friends," Thomson said with a quick smile. "We played together when she visited here as a child."

Yes, Jean thought, the local constable was the best source of information on a community. The trouble was, the local constable was still a member of the community.

"Inspector Gilnockie has not yet interviewed her, has he?" asked Alasdair.

"She's not had time to sit herself down with him, no."

"Thank you. Mrs. MacLeod's in the Queen of Scots suite." Alasdair stood still, very still, as Thomson walked into the house and hung a left toward the stairs.

Jean considered the glacial ridges in Alasdair's face, all the thicker for the frustration bubbling beneath. She ventured, "Well?"

"Aye?" asked Alasdair, and then, "You'll catch your death, Jean, outside without a coat."

"You're not wearing one either," she said, and led the way back into the house. She shut the door, asking, "Who threw the door open? D.S. Young?"

Alasdair was halfway to the back hall. "Aye. Tina closed it carefully, I reckon. She almost got away."

"But you're right, she wouldn't have made it past the reporters. They'd have alerted Thomson and McCrummin, like the geese that alerted the sentries in Rome, whenever it was. I'd say poor Tina, but, damn it, Young has a point, no matter how clumsily she expressed it."

His smile was thin as a blade but vanished before it was fully drawn. "It's only now occurred to you that Tina might have killed Greg herself?"

That figured, it had never occurred to Alasdair that their own wedding might be in jeopardy, just that spouses killed spouses. "Yes, it's only now occurred to me. Cynicism is *your* occupational hazard."

"And rose-colored glasses are yours."

"Right," she said, expelling the "t" like a micro-missile. "Someone erased the phone's memory. Yeah, Gilnockie can get records from Greg's provider, but that will take time, and doesn't change the fact that if it wasn't Greg who altered the memory, it was Tina, and she lied about it. If Tina killed him herself, she would have had the knife with her when we saw her, but…"

"Why? Oh aye, why?" Alasdair stepped back. "Jean, I'd better be getting onto Gilnockie."

"Yeah, you go on." Of all the places where Jean would have liked to be a fly on the wall, Alasdair's next conversation with Gilnockie just went to the top of the list. Nevertheless, she could only see ghosts, not practice astral projection.

Around the corner and back down the hall beneath a plush toy moose's head, and she was in Fergie's office. She was tempted to lock the door, but this wasn't her sanctuary, it was his. Who else's could it be, with its collection of books, artwork, and gimcracks jumbled together like the contents of Ali Baba's den and scented with potpourri and mildew?

An orange Ganesh, the mutli-armed Hindu elephant god, sat atop a bookshelf stacked two and three deep with books and magazines. A tooled-leather copy of *Gulliver's Travels* supported a framed illustration from *Peter Pan* and a paperback on the Shroud of Turin. From a crystal block sprouted a letter opener shaped like Excalibur. A copy of the Kildalton Cross from Islay, ancient homeland of the MacDonalds, hung above a CD changer stacked with albums of New Age music, Bollywood scores, and chanting monks. Next to that sat a portable telephone on its base, one dating all the way back to the last century—ancient, in electronic years.

Several of Fergie's own works-in-progress were propped in a corner, the top piece a sketch of the old castle as it had once been, smoke eddying and flags flying above a medieval galley pulled up on the beach.

A triptych of photos—Emma in her wedding gown, Emma holding infant Diana, child Diana mounted on a pony—was half-obscured by the papers drifting across a Victorian slab of a desk. The red tape was getting ahead of Fergie, it seemed.

The desk was stationed in front of tall windows draped with lush but frayed brocade. Jean looked through the wavery glass to see a part-flagstone, part-gravel yard below. To one side sat a cement-block building, no doubt storehouse and garage, its brutal lines accented by the empty flower pots, plastic bins, and broken sculptures piled against it.

On the far side of the yard, though, rose the lovely lichen-encrusted stones of the garden wall, breached by a wooden gate and topped by bare tree limbs. A sign beside the gate might read, "To Old Dunasheen Church"—it was small and weathered and Jean couldn't quite make it out. Yesterday she and Alasdair had made their way to new and old churches alike via the main garden gate, past the trees and dormant flowerbeds. This looked like an alternate route.

A spark floated across her memory and winked out the moment she tried to grab it. Someone, somewhere, had said something about walking to the church. But then, who hadn't said something about walking to the church? She was on the way there herself.

"Don't you dare cloud up," she told the sky, a dome of radiant Celtic blue—the Scottish flag, the sea around the Highlands and Islands, Alasdair's eyes, ever changing, always profound.

She eyed the desk and a filing cabinet, and her palms itched. This was her chance to snoop. But Fergie wasn't a suspect. Over and beyond his non-heavy breathing, she found it hard to believe his transparent face could hide any plot deeper than the next day's menu.

As for who was a suspect, well, it was a matter of who had an opportunity—or seemed to, right now. Diana. Nancy. Rab. Lionel Pritchard. Colin Urquhart. Any or all of them might prove to have an alibi, something that Tina herself lacked. Scott and Heather were long shots. They were in the area when Greg was killed, but how could one of them have gotten the dirk from the front hall before they'd ever set foot in it?

Or the deed could have been done by someone from the village or elsewhere on Skye, or even by some sort of Australian mafia hit man working not under the sign of the Black Hand but of the Red Kangaroo.

Since Alasdair wasn't there to snort at that one, Jean snorted at herself and sat down at the plywood computer desk in the corner. When she started to type "Greg MacLeod" into the blank box of the search engine, she barely got as far as "Greg MacL" before a second box appeared, holding the complete name plus the word "Townsville." *Whoa*. That meant, didn't it, that Fergie had already done the same search?

Yes. Of the list of hits, laboriously summoned over Dunasheen's phone line, several were tinted a been-there, done-that purple.

Maybe Fergie checked out all his potential guests. Why? Out of curiosity? Caution? Cupidity, with those balance sheets not adding up? Maybe it was Diana who'd checked. But then, her office was at the other end of the house, near the postern gate cloak room. Yesterday Fergie had made a joke about how they e-mailed each other.

Jean skimmed the hits, finding a few words about the MacLeod Art and Artifact Gallery, which was, as yet, an empty storefront near Townsville's famous aquarium. She found a few more words about St. Columba's Museum of Religious Life and Art, ditto. Greg had intended the two places to share the same roof, then. He'd evoked a saint beloved by his ancestors, Columba, known as Columcille in the holy man's own Celtic language, rather than choosing an internationally known one like St. Andrew.

Jean clicked on the "images" button and drummed her fingers while the molasses-like connection delivered photos of Greg's broad, blunt face and rectangular smile. In one shot, he had his tuxedoed arm around an elegantly dressed woman who was not Tina. Not that there was anything wrong with that—the photo was linked to an article about the opening of a posh resort in Cairns.

Still, Jean couldn't help but wonder if, like the Krums' holiday, the MacLeods' was intended to repair a faltering relationship. If so, well, jealousy was a time-honored motive for murder. Although if Jean had wanted to murder her spouse—and she'd had her moments with both prior and anticipated spouses—she wouldn't have gone to all the trouble and expense of doing so on the other side of the world. The fact that Tina had effectively trapped herself at the scene implied her innocence.

Jean moved on to the same factoids Miranda had already turned up, the Waltzing Matilda sale and the donation to the Bible History Research Society. That name made another bony rattle in the overstuffed cupboard of her brain. So, since she had a world of reminders at her fingertips…

Well, look at that. The Bible History Research Society was also already in the search queue. Its website trumpeted its support of archaeological digs exploring not just the historical roots of the Bible, but intending to prove its literal reality. And good luck to them, Jean thought. Stories didn't have to be literally real to be profoundly true.

That was where she'd heard of the BHRS, at an academic conference she'd attended in her former, pre-*Great Scot,* pre-Alasdair life. One speaker, an archaeologist, had been incensed by the rise of the BHRS and similar organizations, no matter whether they were earnest amateurs or predatory con men. Their rejection of rigorous scientific method detracted from genuine archeological studies of the Holy Land and encouraged the trade in illegally dug, to say nothing of faked, antiquities.

Just as the human mind always wanted to believe, Jean thought with a polite nod toward Ganesh, the human mind always came up with ways of exploiting belief.

Stealing a piece of paper and a pencil from Fergie's desk, Jean jotted down the URLs and several notes about gallery, museum, and BHRS. Police minions would turn up the same evidence. Whether Alasdair and his pro-MacDonald sensibilities heard it from her or from them didn't matter. Facts were facts, especially when they pointed to Greg's interests coinciding with Fergie's. And then there was Scott Krum and his auction house.

She ran a quick search on "Scott Krum + auction + Maryland" and established not only that he was who he said he was, but also that Fergie had looked him up as well.

Surely Fergie wasn't planning to sell the Fairy Flagon. Things couldn't be that bad, financially…wait. He was going to show her and Alasdair something else, something special for her article. Scott was right, valuable collectibles could be tucked away in the corners of an old house like Dunasheen.

Was Fergie sitting on something so valuable it would over-write the red on those balance sheets with black?

Jean slumped down in the chair. Yes, she believed in syn-chronicity, the way coincidences happened with what seemed like intention aforethought. But when it came to murder, when did coincidence become enemy action? While she sure didn't want to think of Fergie as the enemy, maybe he *was* capable of hiding dark schemes and devious plots. Or maybe it just hadn't occurred to him that whatever he was up to was dark and devious—not, at least, until Greg died.

Fergie's e-mail program probably wasn't password-protected, but she wasn't going to snoop or sneak or slink around any further than she already had. Let the pros do that. Even so, maybe, just maybe, she'd finally grasped the end of a thread—threads, plural—leading to that elusive motive.

She set the computer to standby, folded the paper into her pocket, stood up—and noticed the portrait hanging beside the door. In three steps she was across the room and look-ing up at it.

The plaque on the frame read, "Seonaid, Lady Dunasheen, 1799-1822. Beloved wife of Norman MacDonald." And yes, oh yes, the painted face was that of the Green Lady. Ex-cept in life, roses bloomed in Seonaid's cheeks, the light of a summer's afternoon shone in her smile, and the fabric of her gown glowed a rich emerald green. This painting wasn't one of Fergie's. The touch was both more precise and more spirited, the colors subdued, the drape of the gown and the shawl expertly rendered, and the shadows subtly realistic. It had been painted from life, by a professional.

Odd to find an aristocratic woman in that time period with a Gaelic name. Jean sounded out the word beneath her breath. Sho-NADE, the Scottish version of Irish Sinead. Janet, in other words. Almost her own name.

She was not surprised to see that Seonaid had died, rela-

tively youthfully, the same year the church was completed
and Tormod was transported for murdering the laird's wife.
For murdering Seonaid MacDonald. No wonder her spirit lingered, if not actively seeking revenge, then at least not finished with this plane of existence. And yet, as Alasdair had
pointed out—twice, now that she thought about it—there was
something irregular about Tormod's fate. Perhaps his trial had
ended in that peculiar Scots verdict of "Not Proven," the sort
of ambiguity that had shaped much of Scotland's turbulent
history. The sort of ambiguity that shaped real life.

"Thank you," Jean said to the image, "you know, for the
stairs." She heard a distant voice or three, but none of them
issued from Seonaid's painted lips.

Onwards.

Jean didn't always learn from experience, but last night's
encounter had taught her where the tripping stane was lo-
cated. She breezed on past it and into the Charlie suite, where
she found Dougie hiding beneath a chair looking like a pin-
cushion with eyes. "What's wrong?" she asked, with a trem-
ble of her own hackles.

The bedroom door was shut. She'd probably left it open.
That was something she was still learning, to shut doors.
After all, she'd lived most of her life in a climate where air
movement was something to be encouraged, not stopped.

One step, two, three…she threw open the bedroom door.

Oh. The bed had been made, fresh towels laid out in the
bathroom, and the wastebaskets emptied—not to mention
Dougie's litter box. Now that was service. "Nancy or Rab,
Diana or Fergie, somebody made you get off the bed, is that
it? Poor little guy."

Petting and crooning eased the serrated edge of Dougie's
backbone and produced a rumbling purr. That was no doubt
soothing to the moggie, but did little for Jean's own nerves.
They felt like telegraph wires humming with a torrent of dots

and dashes, signals hiding a message she didn't know how to read. Or had Morse code been supplanted with emoticons and text-speak?

Like, she thought, CU. *See you.*

It wasn't only young people who texted. Anyone could have used that abbreviation. Just because the handwriting on the card looked like a man's didn't mean it was Colin's. There was another question for Gilnockie to grind through his mill.

Still sitting on the floor, Jean checked the phone. There was no message from Miranda, not that she expected one. No need to rattle her gilded cage. Jean punched Michael and Rebecca's number, and the man of the house answered almost before the phone had rung.

"Hey, it's me," said Jean. "Would you believe the sun is shining in Skye?"

"I'm having it on good authority that it does from time to time," Michael replied. "I'm also having it on good authority—as in the morning *Scotsman*—that you've had a murder at Dunasheen."

The Scotsman had probably not indulged in "stately homicide," but you never knew. "Yes, I'm afraid so. And as these things go, the skies may be clear but the case is murky. Heck, even the cops are a bit murky." She gave him the abstract but omitted her conclusions, such as they were so far. "And Fergie says Linda's welcome to the MacDonald family cradle."

"Ta for that, then. Rebecca's saying something about buying a baby pen, as we'll be needing one in any event, but just now she's had to go in to work."

"Another meeting about a fake collar? What's all that about?"

"Holyrood Palace was by way of paying a small fortune for a collar, one of those elaborate neck ruffs, supposedly worn by Mary, Queen of Scots. Then one final test showed that it's a genuine sixteenth-century piece, but Mary's mono-gram was sewn onto it recently."

"Didn't they check what the thread was made of?"

"Oh aye, no fools they. But the villain's worn down the thread and the needle holes, then smeared the lot with dust from a medieval dig or artifact. He'd have his money if Rebecca hadn't questioned the style of the monogram. That's when they sent the piece to us, we set it beneath a high-resolution microscope, and abracadabra, there's polyester molecules beneath the dirt, likely picked up when the faker's thread was stored next to the polyester sort."

"Well done!" Jean said. "You see that a lot these days, a perfectly respectable artifact tarted up with an inscription or something linking it to a famous person or event, whatever."

"Tarting up the price," said Michael.

"Speaking of museums and artifacts, our murder victim, Greg MacLeod, was starting up a museum of religion and an art and antiquities gallery in Townsville, Australia. Have you heard of him?"

"No, not a word, though I can ask about if you like."

"Yes, please. I bet you're familiar with the Bible History Research Society, though."

"Oh aye. Well-intentioned folk, unlike some in the business, but you're minding what that road to hell is paved with... There's the baby waking from her nap. We'll be seeing you for the wedding, Jean, unless you and Alasdair go losing your nerve and elope. Or are put off by the murder."

"No, we're committed, to the wedding and the investigation as well. Happy New Year!"

"A good one to you when it comes," he returned, "in spite of it all."

Committed. Yeah, that was about it, no matter which meaning you attached to the word.

With a groan, Jean regained her feet and punched the number of Hugh Munro, musician extraordinaire and her next door neighbor. Alasdair's neighbor, too, now.

"Forward into Scotland's past!" answered Hugh's voice, like a shot of single malt, brisk with a subtle sweetness.

"Hi Hugh, it's me. And yes, *The Scotsman* is right, we've had another murder."

"I hadn't seen the paper this morning, Jean, I've just now tuned up my fiddle and rosined my bow for Hogmanay. A murder, you're saying? Ah, bad luck."

Again Jean delivered the abstract, this time finishing, "You've toured Australia, haven't you?"

"Oh aye, the lads and I played in Sydney, Melbourne, Brisbane, and Perth. No Townsville, though I did meet a grand fiddler with a group named Kilbeggan based there. We exchange e-mails from time to time, bits of music and the like."

"Could you ask him—her—a couple of questions about Greg MacLeod and his gallery and everything?"

"Her," said Hugh. "Trying to work round Inspector Gilnockie, are you? I was thinking that was Alasdair's role."

"No, I'm trying everything I can think of to get this case settled, solved, whatever, before the wedding."

"I'll be doing what I can, then. Sorry this had to happen." Hugh went on, "You're also phoning to ask about the work at your flat, I reckon."

"Well yes, except I bet no one's working today."

"No one's there the day, no, but last night they punched through the wall between the two sitting rooms and began clearing away the older kitchen. Loads of grease round the cooker, the old lady must have been frying up every night."

"She was. I could always smell it. Better than eating it, I guess. Thanks, Hugh. I know your concert tonight will bring in the new year properly."

"I'll be obliged to play the newer tune for 'Auld Lang Syne,' not Burns's own, if I want a singsong. A good year to you and Alasdair when it comes, and I'll be there with my clarsach to play you down the aisle on Sunday."

"Happy New Year." Jean plumped down on the window seat. Okay, she'd set her partners in crime to asking questions—and she hoped to heaven they and the official crew found some answers by Sunday. If she'd thought about it, she could even have had Michael contact his opposite number at the Scottish Services Museum…

No. How could they identify the owner of the missing dirk when they didn't know his name? Just because a few threads in this tapestry of an investigation were starting to form warp and weft, if hardly pattern, she had no way of knowing if the Royal Scot dirk-owner was one of them.

She'd been hearing voices for a minute or two, she realized, and swiveled to look out the window. If she'd been a painter like Fergie, she'd have reached for her brush and colors.

The black peaks of the Cuillins pierced the far horizon, the only sharp angles in the entire landscape. Coppery, rust-gold-green hills, dozens of little waterfalls making shining stripes down their flanks, rose behind the white-painted houses of Kinlochroy. The village clustered between the hills, the deep blue of the loch, and the stone wall marking the boundary of Dunasheen Estate. A pitted asphalt driveway looped between the garden wall and the grass sloping down to the loch, avoiding several large if windblown trees.

Jean imagined a coach-and-four rolling up an earlier incarnation of the drive and decanting Queen Victoria and her tartan-swathed ghillie, or marching redcoats searching for Bonnie Prince Charlie, a royal on the lam, or Vikings pulling boats up onto the shore.

Today's equivalent of Viking berserkers, reporters with cameras and microphones, were still clustered outside the front gate. Halfway along the drive, just past the manager's cottage, Fergie, Pritchard, and both the dogs herded the

Krums toward the house. As they drew closer, Jean could make out their expressions, Fergie bewildered, Pritchard angry, Heather resentful. Scott looked as though he'd been sucking on a pickle. Dakota darted up to the main garden gate, pushed it open, and was brought to heel by her father with the same gesture Pritchard used with the dogs.

No rest for the curious. Jean grabbed coat, scarf, gloves, and phone, made her apologies to Dougie, and charged out of the room.

TWELVE

DOWN THE STAIRS she went, passing the tripping stane with neither physical stumble or psychic ripple, and emerged onto the porch just as the motley crew arrived.

"Why can't I walk in the garden?" asked Dakota, her high-pitched voice less whiny than simply weary.

No one replied.

"Mrs. Krum," Fergie said, his bewilderment puckering into hurt, "I really don't think it's necessary to…"

"What? You have something against freedom of speech? You've got that here, too, don't you? Don't you think honesty is a virtue?" Heather shot a glance at Scott that was obviously intended to be the equivalent of a dirk between the ribs. "I mean, we're setting an example for the kid here."

Yes, thought Jean, trying to hover invisibly beside the protuberance of the porch, *you're setting an example for the kid.* And right now the kid was looking from face to face but finding nothing for her there.

"You have to consider," Pritchard explained, "whether your honesty is going to have a detrimental effect on others. Telling the reporters that Dunasheen serves poor food, which is, after all, your opinion—"

"That steak pie thing last night, the meat was overcooked and the dough was heavy, that's all I said. And the house is cold and the bed lumpy. I'm just saying."

"Heather," said Scott, "Lionel here's got a point. What if the reporters go off and repeat—"

"People need frank and open criticism so they can learn

to do better. That's what I teach in my getting ahead in business classes, that's what I practice in real life."

"Oh yeah," Scott said beneath his breath, "that's what you practice in real life."

"What's that supposed to mean?" demanded Heather.

Fergie made a double down-boy gesture, and not to the dogs, who were sitting quietly, tongues lolling, tails beating. "Mr. Krum, Mrs. Krum, we're getting on for elevenses. I'll have Nancy make us up a pot of tea and some biscuits—something to warm ourselves with, eh?" His expression reminded Jean of medieval jesters who would slice open the corners of their mouths, carving a permanent smile.

"Fine, fine," said Heather, and swept past Jean into the house.

Fergie turned his ghastly smile on Jean. "Elevenses?"

"No, thanks, I'm going for a walk through the garden and out to the old church." She turned toward Scott, intending to make one more attempt to separate child from parents—if this didn't work, she'd have to give it up before they took her for a pedophile.

Scott spoke first. "If you're going to the garden, well, last night you said you'd keep an eye on Dakota…"

The child looked up, even her fuzzy earmuffs perking.

"I'd be glad to take her with me." Jean suited action to word by giving Dakota's slight shoulder a gentle shove. Set in motion, the girl scampered toward the gate, her striped muffler flying behind her.

"See you at lunch, then," called Fergie, and disappeared inside, presumably not to tell Nancy about Heather's criticisms lest Nancy spike Heather's tea with arsenic.

Jean started after Dakota. Behind her, Scott hissed sarcastically, "Thanks, pal."

"I didn't know you hadn't told the old trouble and strife,"

replied Pritchard, "you know, the wife, that you were here in September, did I now?"

Whoa. Dakota was already out of earshot. Jean stopped and pretended to tie her shoe.

"No," conceded Scott. "It's my own damn fault for thinking Heather and the kid would enjoy the place while I did some business. No good deed, and all that bull. Neither of the MacDonalds was even here in September, but now Heather's convinced I've been getting it on with Diana. Not that I'd have a problem getting it on with Diana. Once those icy ones melt, it's the ride of your life."

Well, yes, Jean thought, Alasdair being a case in point. Still, when Pritchard replied with a suggestive snigger, she looked indignantly around and made her worst Medusa face at both men. They were facing the other way, which was just as well.

So Pritchard was up to something behind his employers' backs. Had he sold Scott the dirk in September? Probably not—a dealer would have wanted the sheath, too. Scott could have stolen just the knife, but then, he would have had to either take it home with him and bring it back, or leave it somewhere in the U.K., both options arguing that he had planned in September to murder a man in December.

And yet, what if Scott had had an appointment with Greg, a fellow traveler in the art and antiquities trade, yesterday afternoon? Or with Diana, all protestations to the contrary? But he'd been with Heather in Kinlochroy then. Hadn't he?

And then there was Pritchard—he could have been dealing with Greg MacLeod...

"Mrs. Fairbairn?" Dakota was holding the gate open.

Jean smiled. "Coming. Sorry. And call me Jean." Technically she was Ms. or Miss Fairbairn—and this time around she was sticking with that name, considering how she'd spent the last year reclaiming it. No way, though, did that imply this marriage would break down, too.

"Thanks for letting me come with you," Dakota said. "They keep having the same argument over and over, it's just the names that are different. So Diana's pretty. That doesn't mean, you know."

Jean stepped into the garden, devoutly hoping that a ten-year-old didn't know, except in broad outline. And as the gate clanged shut behind her, she thought, speaking of Diana, that made two incidents on the chatelaine's front doorstep this morning that she'd missed. Had she really gone shopping, searching for, say, a potato with just the right number of eyes? Or had she lied to Fergie—again—and gone somewhere else entirely?

The sunshine held little heat, although the light itself was warm. Soaking in the tentative rays, Jean let Dakota lead the way along the labyrinthine paths. The child pointed out the sculptures hidden in the shrubbery—a faun here, eyes downcast demurely, a Virgin Mary there, eyes cutting upward coquettishly. The vivid colors of a totem pole leaped out of a clearing. Some of the larger trees sported little gnome doors at their bases or eyes, noses, and lips on the trunks.

She should volunteer to do a guidebook for Fergie. He must have interesting stories about where these things were obtained or why he created them. With that thought, Jean straightened, shifting the metaphorical monkey on her back, and enjoyed the scene.

Even in winter, the garden had a derelict beauty. The beds were mostly empty, sleeping beneath a layer of wood chippings, but berries and bits of foliage clung to some of the shrubs and small trees, and the bare twigs of others traced delicate patterns. The shadows of the larger, leafless trees lay across the gravel walks, so that the sun seemed to wink in and out as woman and child strolled along.

The air didn't seem nearly so cold here, and was scented by leaf and loam with an elusive promise of spring. Beyond their own footsteps and Dakota's voice, Jean heard birds squawking and singing, the rustle of branches and—was that another set of footsteps?

She looked back, thinking perhaps Scott had ducked his confrontation with Heather and followed them. But she saw no one. *Paranoid, moi?* You'd think she'd been involved in several murder investigations or something.

Dakota darted past the tree-lined alley leading to the new church and Jean didn't divert her. She wanted to have her second look at the place with Alasdair, so she could voice her thoughts about Seonaid, and Tormod, and the events of 1822. None of them might have relevance beyond Greg's genealogical quest, but still, no story should be left unturned.

After fifteen minutes of Jean strolling and Dakota zigzagging from sight to sight, the main garden gate rose before them once again. They'd missed the path leading to the old church. What Fergie needed to sculpt next was a Minotaur.

Now, though… "Is this where you saw the ghost?" Jean asked, as casually as she could.

Dakota scuffed through the sodden leaves. "You heard that, huh?"

"It was a little hard not to hear it. But that's okay, I like ghost stories."

"It's no story. We were driving up the driveway and my mom was bawling out my dad for leaving her alone in the pub—"

"Leaving her alone?"

"Yeah, he was like, doing some deal at the office back home but couldn't get cell phone reception. So he went outside and walked down to the harbor, took him forever, she said. Not so long, he said. If she'd just sat tight in the pub he wouldn't have had to wander around town looking for her."

"He had to look for her? You mean, she left you in the pub and went looking for him?"

"Yeah, he was mad she left me alone, but she said it was his own fault and I wasn't alone anyway, that nice-looking policeman was talking to the bartender. Though she didn't say 'nice-looking' to Dad, just to me."

She did, did she? Jean thought.

"There were a lot of people there, like the guy with the beard, you know, who was bringing out the breakfast stuff..."

"Rab Finlay?"

"Yeah, him. Mom says he can't speak English but Dad says he's just got a thick accent. I mean, you can, like, pick out most of it if you pay attention."

She said. He said. Jean recognized the head-butting dialog of a tense relationship. But that wasn't her business. What was her business was Greg MacLeod with a phone to his ear. Means, opportunity, the competitive nature of the antiquities trade as motive. Not that she wanted to finger Dakota's father—or mother, wandering around town—for murder any more than she wanted to finger one of Alasdair's friends. "I'm sorry I interrupted. You were driving up the driveway..."

"Yeah." Dakota considered the gate's decorative scroll-work, a bit rusty in spots but still graceful, like an aging ballerina. "As we went by the gate here, someone, like, stepped through it, out of the light, and shut it behind him."

"What made you think it was a ghost?"

"He was all shiny, from the lights of the house and from the car lights, too. In dark clothes, but shiny."

Jean remembered Colin Urquhart standing beneath her window. Had he been on the estate earlier that evening, too? "Could you see his face?"

"No, he had a hat or something pulled down low."

A hood, Jean thought. "He was going into the garden, not coming out of it?"

"Into the garden, yeah."

"You're sure it was a man?"

"Well, no, not really. But he hugged the woman standing inside the gate."

Jean stopped in her tracks. "Woman? Inside the gate?"

"I just caught a real quick look as we drove by, you know? The man stepped through the gate, shut it, and walked right up to a woman with long skirts and funny little curls hanging down beside her face. I saw her face, it was white as a sheet. Do you think she was a ghost, too?"

Jean went giddy, as though the path beneath her feet had whisked away and she'd dropped into free fall. *Seonaid.* The man—if it was a man—had seemed to hug her because he walked right through her. He hadn't seen her. But Dakota had. Dakota was allergic to ghosts.

"I always get, like, a creepy feeling when I see a ghost." Hesitantly, Dakota's mitten-covered hand indicated the back of her neck.

Jean closed her eyes, grasped her equilibrium, and prayed for the right words—honesty wasn't always the best policy, as Heather had proved. She looked down to see the child's small gamin face turned upward.

"I'm sorry, I'm not suppose to tell stories like that." Dakota's hand fell back to her side and she looked down, waiting for the ruler of logic to rap her knuckles.

"But it's no story, you just said. Sometimes," Jean went on, "people see things that aren't really there, like thinking the wake of a boat is the Loch Ness monster. Optical illusions, wishful thinking, whatever. It happens. But sometimes we—and I do it, too—sometimes we see things that other people can't see. That creepy feeling on the back of your neck. I know exactly what you mean."

Dakota looked up. Sparks flared in the depths of her big, dark eyes.

"I think the man you saw was just that, a man. A living one. I might have seen the same man standing outside the house later on. He was probably on the way to the village and stepped out of the driveway when he saw your car coming. The woman, though, yes, she was a ghost. I saw her on the staircase last night. She's Seonaid MacDonald, who died in 1822."

"Oh wow," said Dakota, the sparks exploding into fireworks. "Cool!"

Jean bit back, *No, it's not cool, you've already seen how your parents reacted.* "It's like an allergy. Some people have it, some people don't, and it's hard for the people who don't to understand."

"And they don't want to hear about it. Yeah, I know. My grandmother has to be real careful with Chinese food because MSG gives her a headache, but my mom says it's all in her head, that why aren't the people in China walking around with headaches, then?"

Jean started to say, "A headache is definitely in your head," but this was no joking matter. "I call being able to sense ghosts an allergy, but it's not a medical condition, a situation science can recognize and explain. Yet, anyway. It's weird, and it's very personal. I know some people who get, well, vibes off things, which is similar, but you're only the second person I've ever met who actually sees ghosts."

"Who's the first?"

For asking that, Jean awarded her another *atta girl.* "My, er, husband, Alasdair Cameron."

"Oh. Him. He doesn't say much, does he?"

"He gets his point across," Jean said with a grin.

Grinning back, Dakota did a dance step through the leaves.

Jean's grin wobbled into a squirm. She'd just picked up her own disciple.

Time to move on, and without laying *this is our secret,*

okay? on the child's already burdened shoulders. If Dakota told her parents what Jean had told her, well then, they'd deal with it. The child was going to spend her life dealing with it. Jean remembered her own youth, the impatient sighs, the indulgent nods, the teasing and, worse, the sincere offers of psychiatric help. And then there were the people who assumed she must share their own weirdnesses.

Reticence, edging into Alasdair's taciturnity, worked real well.

Briskly, Jean pushed open the garden gate and sent a suspicious glare toward Pritchard's picturesque cottage. In the summer it would even have roses growing around the door, but now the gray stone facade glowered behind a few thorny twigs. "I saw another gate around the side of the house," she told Dakota. "It might be a more direct route to the old church."

"Sure," Dakota said, all weariness evaporated. Absolved, maybe.

Side-by-side, they walked past the three parked cars and around the corner of the house to the flagstone and gravel yard. From this side of Fergie's office window, Jean saw the door of the new kitchen, flanked by garbage bins. The garage filled in the entire space between the house and the wall. If you wanted to reach the sea from here, you'd have to go into the house and out the far side, or back around the front of the house, or through the small wooden gate, where, yes, the hand-lettered sign read, *To Old Dunasheen Church.*

Just as Jean lifted the latch and pushed the gate open, she caught a movement in the corner of her eye. Fergie stood in his window, the telephone to his ear, a cup of tea in his hand. He lifted the tea in salute.

Jean waved, thinking, baronet under glass. Castle under siege.

"He's a nice guy, isn't he?" asked Dakota.

"Yes." Jean closed the gate, hoping that "yes" was an honest answer.

The child bounded up a narrow path between an evergreen hedge and the bare ruined choirs of a vegetable garden, her shoes squelching. Here, too, a few stubborn leaves quivered in the still air, gulls squawked overhead, and a low booming resonance that flowed through Jean's ears to fill her heart was the surge of the sea.

What she heard with her head was a small but distinctive *snick* from behind. Was that the gate shutting, the latch falling into place, her paranoia becoming flesh? She looked over her shoulder but saw nothing around the curve of the hedge except a small brown bird flapping frantically across the path, fleeing... She walked into Dakota's back. "Oops. Sorry."

"That's okay. I wasn't sure where to go. This way?"

The main path bent off to the left, running into the streaked shadow beneath the trees. A thinner path skewed suddenly to the right, up a low hill, and around and over several boulders. "The church should be that way, yes. Beyond the trees."

They picked their way to the boulders, and past them, and emerged onto a hillside shelf above the sea. "Whoa," Dakota said on a long whistling breath.

Jean didn't say anything. She breathed in the cold, sweet-salt air, and shaded her eyes with her gloved hand. Sure enough, beyond the brilliant dark blue billows of the water, the horizon was closed by an undulating rim of land tinted violet-blue by distance and melting into the cobalt blue of the sky. Even though she knew she was looking at two of the Outer Hebrides, Harris and Uist, she felt she could see clear to Ireland. And beyond, to Tir nan Og, the Celtic version of heaven. No wonder the early Celtic saints had braved that sea to share their beliefs. No wonder generations of residents had built places of worship here, in this place that proved "earthly nirvana" was no oxymoron. No wonder generations of emigrants were called to return. *Blood is thicker than water.*

To the left rose the remains of the church, broken walls and pointed gable ends of dark gray stone, cracks still black with soot. Beyond it the ground fell away, and then rose again into a line of cliffs, mounting higher and higher until the topmost hillock was crowned by the white block-and-spire of Keppoch Point lighthouse. No more than half a mile separated it from Dunasheen Castle.

There was the exit from the path Jean and Alasdair had taken yesterday, beneath the eaves of the trees at the far end of the grassy shelf. Could the murderer have run from the beach, via one or the other garden path, to the driveway in time for Dakota to see him? Yes, with knowledge of the landscape, a flashlight, and a strong pair of legs.

Urquhart must know his way around Dunasheen Estate. Would Dakota recognize him if she saw him again? If she'd seen him to begin with.

Remembering her brief as educator, Jean turned back to her. "Fergus MacDonald has found 'fairy houses' here, ancient stone walls hidden in the heather and covered with lichen. They could go back thousands of years. And his grandfather found some Roman coins, although whether they were left by the Roman fleet that may have reached here, or whether they were brought back by some tourist, is open to debate. No context, you see."

"They should get archaeologists out here."

"Yes, they should. There are too many interesting sites to dig them all, though. And once you dig a site, you've destroyed it forever."

"Oh. Yeah. I hadn't thought of that."

Jean and Dakota swished through the tall, reddish-gold grass toward the latest and last church. Even at midday, the sun hung at half-mast, so low that the shadows of the walls reached toward the sea. "A hermit may have lived here ages ago. The original church was built around the first millennium. At least one since then was sacked by Vikings."

"Cool."

"Not to the sackees," said Jean. "This church was built by a notorious cattle-thief and raider in the fifteenth century to atone for his crimes. There's no way of knowing if it worked."

That went past the child's head.

"This church was burned down in 1645," Jean concluded, without providing details, let alone mentioning how barbecuing the neighbors was a fine old human tradition. That dreadful act of violence seemed to have destroyed the spirit that had drawn people to this place—at least, no one else had built here. And yet, while the memory lingered in men's minds, it did not seem to linger in the eternities of the land, the sea, and the sky.

She listened with every sense she possessed, then, so quietly her voice blended with the sound of the sea, asked, "Are you picking up anything?"

That didn't go past Dakota's head at all. "No. There aren't any ghosts here. It's just kind of cold and sad and yet there's something else."

"The melancholy of age and the consolation of beauty," Jean murmured. Hey, that was a good phrase. She should use it in her article.

Beyond a low wall lay the graveyard. What slabs and knobs of tombstones were not swallowed by grass were weathered out of true, so that they resembled natural boulders inscribed with frost and lichen rather than the names of the dead. Here and there trembled a white feather, shed by a gull, not an angel.

"So there are some really old dead bodies in there," said Dakota.

"In acid soil like this, they're all gone, not even bones left."

"Oh."

"The special gravestones are over here." Jean walked the child over to a shed topped by a sheet of green corrugated plastic better suited to protect cows or sheep than rare artifacts. But then, in Scotland, artifacts like these weren't all that rare.

Beneath the roof lay a row of fissured gray slabs, patched with moss, lichen, and the occasional strip of concrete. Hands long gone to dust or mud had carved them with armored men holding spears or swords, or, in a couple of cases, just the sword itself, surrounded by raised cords and knotwork like a medieval fetish. Several other slabs were graced by a cross, a skull, or both. A few patches of moss had recently been peeled away from one, revealing damp, corroded stone.

Dakota eyed the gravestones, soldiers on parade, and said, "That guy's helmet looks like a chocolate kiss." So it did, the metal curving around the roughed-in face and coming to a point on top. "They weren't all buried in a row here, were they? Did they all die at the same time?"

"No, the stones are from different time periods, and even though some people—" *Like Greg MacLeod,* Jean thought "—say they're the graves of crusaders, they probably don't go back that far. Though there were a lot of Crusades."

"What are Crusades?" Dakota asked.

Jean had no short answer for that, or one that wouldn't force her own beliefs on Dakota—there being a fine line between sharing your beliefs and ramming them down someone's throat. A shame how often the former was perceived to be wimping out and the latter to be stirring and inspirational. How would Greg MacLeod's museum have presented such issues—contemporary happy-clappy, traditional smells and bells, prescriptive fire and sword?

"The Crusades were wars," she said. "The original graves were scattered around the church yard. Fergus's uncle collected the best gravestones here, to protect them, although the finest one, of a priest or bishop holding a chalice, is in the National Museum in Edinburgh."

"That guy there's holding a really nice sword," said Dakota, pointing.

Jean peered into the green-tinged shadow of the shed, following the direction indicated by the girl's mitten. A broken stone lay on its side behind two of the upright ones, as a prop rather than as part of the display—its carved figure was no more than a clumsy bashed-out sketch of a human being. Or maybe the original mason had intended the figure to be a skeleton, in which case its position, sinking into dark peaty muck, was appropriate…

A straight edge lay next to the figure's rudimentary hand, half concealed by a tuft of grass. A straight edge reflecting a watery gleam of light and ending in what might have been a chess piece, black and knobbly, and beside that round glow like a cat's eye in smoky gray.

The shapes spun through Jean's vision like those in a video game, assembling themselves into a whole. Her breath burst out of her lungs in a couple of four-letter words, hastily edited for tender ears. "Holy shi-moley."

"What?" Dakota asked.

Grasping the girl's shoulders, Jean pulled her back. "Don't touch anything. Don't make any more footprints. Stand still. I've got to make a phone call."

THIRTEEN

DAKOTA STOOD STILL, her expression swinging between puzzlement and alarm.

Her folks are gonna love this. Jean whipped out the phone and punched Thomson's number. Kudos to Alasdair for thinking of programming the phone with that, otherwise they'd have to run down to the beach looking for him—and for Gilnockie, okay, it was still his case.

The readout displayed the time. 11:45. Where was Alasdair, anyway?

"P.C. Thomson."

"This is Jean Fairbairn. Are you with Alasdair and Inspector Gilnockie?"

"Oh aye, that I am, if you'd like…"

"I've found the—well, the missing regimental dirk, not necessarily the murd—" She saw Dakota's ears growing like Dumbo's beneath her earmuffs. "It's with the grave slabs in that shed next to the old church. Y'all need to get up here ASAP."

"Aye, madam, I'll spread the…"

Word, Jean concluded, when Thomson ended the call a bit too quickly. *News.* Stuffing the phone back into her pocket, she peered once again into the shed. Was that mud on the knife blade or the dark rust-red of blood?

Now Dakota's eyes were growing larger, the mind behind them evaluating acceptable responses. Jean told her, "Let's go around to the other side of the church, okay?"

"Okay."

"Are you getting cold?"

"A little."

A minute ago, Jean would have said the same thing. Now, if she unbuttoned her coat a cloud of steam would escape. "We'll go back to the house as soon as the others get here."

"Okay." And, after a moment punctuated by the brush of grass against denim, Dakota said rather than asked, "The man who died, he was killed."

"Yes."

"Maybe with that knife. That's what the police have to find out. Okay?"

Well, no, it wasn't, but…a shadow ran swiftly over Jean's face. She looked up, but saw nothing. A bird must have come between her and the sun. It wasn't a blip in reality.

Dakota was looking not up but down. Jean followed the direction of her gaze.

From this side of the church, they could see into the ravine separating the hillside shelf from the steep slope leading to the lighthouse. The bridge spanning the rocky stream at the ravine's bottom was identical to the one spanning the moat at the old castle, as though Fergie's uncle, the old laird, had found them at a two-for-one sale.

And just as Jean and Alasdair had stood on the one bridge yesterday evening, this morning Diana and Colin Urquhart stood on the other. Except this couple wasn't sharing a joke but a passionate kiss, the silk scarf tied around her blond hair tucked in close to his dark tam o'shanter. They couldn't have been entwined any more closely if they'd been wearing the same coat.

But they weren't. Diana's coat was a beautiful lilac tweed. Colin's was a bulky camouflage jacket…that's what he'd been wearing when Jean saw him last night, a black hooded sweatshirt beneath a military jacket treated with waterproofing and fire retardant chemicals that shimmered in the light.

Clasped together, they swayed back and forth as if to silent music, oblivious to their audience. Colin, Jean saw, knew his way around Dunasheen's daughter as well. She was going to have to reassess that "vestal virgin."

Dakota asked, "Are they having sex?"

"No, they aren't!" Jean grasped the child's narrow shoulders and this time spun her quickly toward the church wall with its empty, bird-nested windows. "Look there, see how the stones in the wall aren't too well dressed, they're still kind of lumpy, except for the ones at the corners, which are squared off, they're called quoins."

"Dressed? Coins?"

From the corner of her eye, Jean saw a human figure duck back into the exit of the smaller garden path, the one leading from the kitchen yard. Pritchard? The shape was masculine, and too slender to be Rab's. Had he been afraid she and Dakota would steal the totem pole? Or was he keeping an eye out for Diana?

Here came the cops up the brae from the beach, Gilnockie and Alasdair at point. Here came Diana and Colin up from the bridge, walking a demure three feet apart. Maybe no one had been home at the lighthouse when Thomson knocked on the door this morning. Maybe no one had answered the knock. Or maybe…surely the constable hadn't lied, but then, he was Diana's childhood friend and Colin's defender, not an impartial observer.

Now Thomson, Young, and two white-suited crime scene technicians beelined for the shed while Gilnockie and Alasdair beelined for Jean.

Spotting the advancing police people, Colin stopped. He put one foot behind the other as if about to spin around and run. Diana shot a level glance from Jean and Dakota to Gilnockie and Alasdair. She settled her mesh shopping bag on her left arm and took Colin's hand with her right. Victoria couldn't have claimed Albert with any more dignity.

"What's wrong with his face?" asked Dakota.

Good question. Half of Colin's face was set in handsome, symmetrical lines. The other half consisted of taut patches of scar tissue. As Diana drew him closer to the others, Jean saw that his good eye was the same startling cornflower-blue as hers. But Colin's other eye glinted dully from a nest of shattered flesh.

No telling what scars laced the body beneath clothing that Jean now saw was too large, the coat hanging off his shoulders, the trouser legs sagging over scuffed military boots. He'd lost weight. A long grueling hospital stay would do that. As for the cause… "He was hurt in the war," Jean whispered, but Dakota, staring in horrified fascination, didn't respond.

Neither did Diana. Anyone else would have looked frumpy with a scarf wrapped around her head, but on Diana, the scarf made a fashion statement. Her complexion would have abashed a rose. The words "beauty" and "beast" materialized in the back of Jean's mind, and guiltily she dismissed them.

Gilnockie stepped forward, greeted Diana, and introduced himself and Alasdair to Colin, who said nothing. A slight breeze riffled the red hackle on the bonnet pushed forward over his forehead. *Black Watch.* Another distinguished regiment.

The side and back of his head were also scarred, so that the crew-cut dark hair grew in patches above a pristine but achingly vulnerable nape. His hands knotted at his sides and his entire body seemed to shrink, coiling like a compressed spring, poised for fight or flight. Oh yes, he was a reclamation project. In spades. Was that why Fergie thought Colin wasn't good for his daughter? Was the broken man asking, or was Diana offering, too much?

Jean thought of him standing outside the house last night.

He'd thought Jean in her window was Diana. Some people might interpret that sort of thing as stalking, but not Diana.

Gilnockie said, "We've been hoping to have a word with you both," which was a typical Gilnockian understatement.

Alasdair's sharp gaze moved from face to face, ending at Jean's. His eyebrow shivered, almost infinitesimally, not at any beasts or beauties but at her little shadow. "Hello there, Dakota. You'd like to be getting on back to the house, I reckon. It's going on for noon. Diana…"

"Luncheon will be served at one," said Diana, her rasped red lips smiling imperturbably. She relinquished Colin's arm and extended one handle of her mesh bag, revealing, yes, potatoes and other edibles. "Dakota, can you help me carry the shopping?"

"Thanks for coming with me," Jean said to the child. "I'll see you later."

Shrugging—inscrutable were the ways of adults—Dakota took the proffered handle and walked off beside Diana, the bag hanging lopsided between them. "What's for lunch?"

"Mrs. Finlay's laid on a mulligatawny soup. Do you know what that is?" The two figures, one tall, one short, disappeared into the garden.

Alasdair's and Gilnockie's heads turned in unison, from Diana back to Colin.

"Would you be so good as to walk back to the house with me, Mr. Urquhart?" Gilnockie and his long shadow gestured toward the beach. "Let's go this way, shall we?"

To see, Jean added silently to herself, how Colin reacts when he passes the site of the murder. In medieval times the authorities might have had all the suspects lay hands on the body, to see if it started bleeding again at the touch of the murderer.

Colin cast a quick glance toward Thomson, who offered a gesture that was part greeting, part reassurance. He cast a slower one at the crime scene techs easing the dirk into a plastic bag, then set off down the brae. Young fell in behind Gilnockie and his—well, not prisoner, person of interest—and with a nod of satisfaction rather than encouragement followed.

Exhaling as the pressure, not to mention the heat, went out of her chest, Jean turned to Alasdair.

A tiny crack or two opened in his countenance, the every-day personality shifting beneath the police carapace. "Well done Jean, finding the dirk."

"Not really. It was Dakota who pointed it out to me. Y'all would have worked your way up here eventually, on your way to the lighthouse."

"Eventually, aye, though likely we'd have had rain or a blow or something of the sort first. We'd have had our wedding as well, Gilnockie's team dusting the aisle behind us."

Laughing, if shamefacedly, she bumped up against his side. "Here I thought you hadn't noticed the proximity of the crime to the wedding."

"I'd have made a piss-poor detective observing that little." His fierce mock frown moderated into a smile. "Just now Patrick's having his crew dredge the water off the beach and scour the rocks on the hillside. We've, he's found no evidence beyond a few scuff marks in the shingle and footprints on the path. Looks to be one set stood for a time at the head of the brae, whilst other sets ran on by. The weight's on the toes," he explained, "that means running. They're all boots or shoes with treaded soles, like everyone's wearing these days. Sorry to be letting the time get away, but…"

"Someone needs to keep the investigation moving along."

"Patrick's keeping it moving, it's just that his head's some-where else. Young let slip that he's retiring this spring."

"And she's planning to take his place?" Jean asked.

"She'll be a sergeant a long while yet. Those rough edges

need smoothing. I had a word with Patrick about the scene with Tina MacLeod, and he had a word in Young's ear."

"And now she's pegged you as a busybody and tattletale."

"Oh aye, she'll have done that, right enough." Alasdair's grim smile indicated his lack of concern for Young's opinion.

The sea shone the brilliant lapis lazuli of Diana's Egyptian necklace. Waves swelled, surged forward, tripped and fell into froth, receded and swelled again, with a slow rolling thrum like the heartbeat of the Earth itself. Jean felt her own rough edges starting to smooth—and chill seeping into her body. More food, especially spicy soup, sounded like a great idea. "We have just enough time to check out the chapel again before we go to the house. I know you want to sit in on Colin Urquhart's interview. And Diana's."

"As do you."

"If you can get me in there, great." Jean went on, "Did Fergie make his statement this morning, before we got to the incident room?"

"Aye, he did that. Patrick's saying there's nothing there to be going on with."

Well no, not if you don't ask the right questions. Jean opened her mouth to tell Alasdair about her odyssey through Fergie's computer, then shut it again. Better to work up to that.

Shoulder to shoulder, they turned away from the sea toward the shed, where Thomson had assumed his best parade-rest position. "What happened to Urquhart?" Alasdair asked.

"Roadside bomb in Iraq," replied Thomson. "There were four men in a lorry carrying supplies from the quartermaster's depot. He was the one in charge, and the only one made it out."

"That's a shame," Jean said, inadequately. How many Scottish soldiers had come home with post-traumatic stress, or shell shock, or whatever the horrors of war were called in their eras? Dealing with that made dealing with an allergy to ghosts a piece of cake.

Judging by Alasdair's dour expression, he remembered police colleagues suffering in a similar way, not just from the effects of combat, but from the effects of surviving. And she'd once thought *he* was a reclamation project. "Is Urquhart having counseling?"

"Aye, he goes away to Inverness once a month for a session. It helps, I'm thinking, though not so much as Diana's helping." This time Thomson didn't add anything about her good heart, since Jean and Alasdair had seen for themselves that more than her heart was involved. His lopsided smile, embarrassed and rueful at once, pleaded for tolerance. "Colin's needing a job, a steady routine, but they're few and far between."

"Right." Alasdair eyed the knife in the technician's hand. "It's got blood on its blade, has it? Let's be hoping it's got fingerprints as well."

"Aye, sir," said Thomson, as though that was an order he had to fulfill.

Jean and Alasdair walked on up the garden path, the primrose path, and not for the first time, Jean thought. By the time they turned down the tree-lined alley toward the new church, she'd told him everything she knew and most of what she thought: Dakota and her allergy, and how neither of her parents had alibis for the time of the murder, and how she'd seen a dark figure in coat and hat at the gate, and there was Urquhart in his regimental bonnet.

She and Alasdair should work on learning to mind-meld. That would save a lot of jawboning. Taking a deep breath of the crisp air, she went on. If it wasn't Urquhart Dakota had seen going through the gate, then who else was wandering around the estate in the dark? There was more than one kind of shimmery fabric in the world. Like a raincoat, although

Diana and Pritchard's raincoats were yellow. What if the initials didn't stand for "Colin Urquhart" but were text-speak for "see you"? What if they meant someone was trying to frame Colin, or lure Diana out of the house by using his initials? What, for that matter, if the raincoat with the card in the pocket wasn't even hers?

Alasdair walked along, taking it all in, gears meshing, grinding, meshing again.

"Still, you saw Diana and Colin," Jean said. "That answers our questions about the relationship and probably explains where Diana was yesterday afternoon, why she missed the Krums' arrival and looked so flushed when she got there."

"Likely she and Colin were at the lighthouse at three, not killing Greg on the beach."

"Yeah, but poor Fergie when he hears that alibi."

This time Alasdair's frown was perfectly genuine.

Then there was what Scott and Pritchard had said, and finding Fergie's virtual fingerprints on the Internet, and how a motive connected to the exceedingly lucrative art and antiquities trade was perhaps coagulating from the mist, and what "something else," in addition to the Fairy Flagon, was Fergie planning to reveal, anyway?

Alasdair's frown deepened and his steps faltered. Before Jean could slow her own, he stepped out again, marching like a soldier. You followed the investigative path to the end, wherever it led. They'd both done that in their previous lives, despite knowing how stiff a price such ends demanded.

"I think Pritchard has a thing for Diana, too," Jean said, "which is why he was dissing Colin last night. But then, Scott's comment was—not the sort of thing you'd say. You've got me spoiled, you know. I forget how crass some guys, some people, can be."

Alasdair's frown moderated, without comment.

"But then, like I thought when I saw that photo of Greg with another woman, jealousy makes a good motive, too."

"It does that, aye. Any strong passion makes a motive. Love become hate or fear makes a grand motive. Indifference, no."

"I can't see Tina coming all the way here just to kill Greg."

"Something might could have happened once they reached the U.K., but no, I cannot see premeditation. Even though she's not told all she knows, not by a long chalk."

"Protecting Greg, I bet."

"Oh aye. And protecting herself as well."

The bell tower, the slate roof, the delicate buttresses and finials, the lancet windows of St. Columcille's appeared through the trees. The small building looked like a stone wedding cake, set in a circle of mulched flowerbeds and shrubbery borders. A driveway emerged from the trees to sweep past the building. Sighting along it, Jean could just make out several of the whitewashed buildings in the village. "Come summer time, Fergie must have half the people in Kinlochroy taking care of the gardens. One of the costs of the heritage business."

"The heritage business," Alasdair said, "generates jobs for the locals. The old laird—the old, old laird, Norman the Red MacDonald…"

"Must have been a real carrot-top," said Jean.

"…likely had this chapel built as make-work for his tenants. More credit to him, when other lairds were turfing them out in favor of sheep, sheep turning a more handsome profit than people."

"There's a passion for you. Greed."

"Oh aye. Though I'm never saying Fergie's greedy keeping Dunasheen afloat."

"No way, no how."

"I'd not be surprised if Fergie was planning to sell off a

family mathom or two. There are few stately homeowners who've not had to sacrifice the odd Rembrandt—not that Fergie's found any Rembrandts, more's the pity. His uncle already sold off most of the farming and hunting land. Good job his grandfather rented the place out to a Glasgow millionaire in the twenties, else it would have no heating, no plumbing, no electric flex. Could be Pritchard was dealing with Krum on Fergie's instructions."

"Well, yeah," Jean said. "Sorry. It's not like I'm *trying* to implicate Fergie."

"No need apologizing."

They stopped beside the church, Jean admiring the play of light and shadow in the intricately carved dark gray stone. "So maybe Greg was here to buy. Maybe Scott's here to buy. And Fergie finds it all kind of embarrassing, so is not telling us. Yet, anyway."

"And Greg was not telling us, but went blethering on about the genealogy, Tormod MacLeod, the 1822 murder, seeing as how his business with Fergie was none of ours. Then."

"Speaking of jealousy as a motive, the master mason was jealous and so forth, but who did kill Seonaid? And why? And yes, I know you said we already had one case, but, darn it, I want to know what happened. If nothing else, that story brought Greg here as much as his business did."

"Oh aye," was all Alasdair replied, his tone dropping from analytical to pensive.

Together they peered through the tall, pointed windows of the chapel. There were the wooden pews incised with leaves and tendrils, the decorative vaulting, the white-draped altar that they'd inspected with Fergie last night—before he went back to the house and they went on to the old church, the old castle, and a new crime.

Then they'd talked about flowers, candles, menus, ritual, and music. Now Jean stood outside the tiny porch and noticed how the chapel's front door faced a break in the trees, providing a glimpse of the gable end of the old church and the sea. This new church sat at the center of a sundial, in a way. If she didn't know how recent it was, she'd suspect that it, too, had been sited on some prehistoric place of power.

The 1822 laird, Norman MacDonald, had intended to build a folly, a mock ruin, an elaborate joke. If one of the stonemasons had murdered his wife, then he'd probably felt the place was folly indeed, in another meaning entirely.

Behind her back, Alasdair rattled the door. "It's locked."

"Well, yes. Can't you just see the place littered with empty liquor bottles and used condoms? Assuming anyone from Kinlochroy would be that crass, never mind what I just said about most guys."

"I'm not minding it, no. But look here."

She turned around into the shadow of the porch, and followed Alasdair's forefinger to the iron latch and lock of the door. Several scratches glinted dully in the metal. "Looks like someone was trying to pick the lock. Recently. Was it like that yesterday?"

"I've got no idea. Fergie was leading the way with the key. Half a tick, whilst I check the vestry door." He hurried away around the building.

Jean trailed behind, then stopped. What was that beside the gnarled roots of a huge tree on the far side of the driveway? Several modest sculptures—an angel, St. Francis, Buddha—rose from the herbaceous borders, but this was different. Another of Fergie's whimsical touches, such as a ceramic fairy house shaped like a toadstool?

A few paces carried her into chill dappled shadow beneath the heavy branches. No, the mound was a miniature round-shouldered tombstone, perhaps six inches of it protruding from leaf mold and lichen. Jean bent to brush away the debris, first from the stone, then from her gloves, still expecting

to see another joke. Here lies the eight-track tape, perhaps. If
nothing else, this might be the grave of a pet.

The weathered letters didn't read *Fido* or *Felix*. They read,
A stranger known but to God. Rest in peace.

It was a grave, all right. Of a human being. But Rab had
said there were no graves near the new church.

A prickle emanated from the roots of her hair, danced
across her nape, and slipped down her back like an invisible icicle. A faint disturbance in the Force, a fragile qualm,
a whiff of the paranormal. Slight as it was, it was still more
than she'd sensed at the old church, site of a famous mass
murder. But Rab had said Seonaid was found dead at the
house, not here.

The prickle had nothing to do with the grave. Slowly Jean
looked around. The chapel and its grounds were so quiet she
heard a car engine and birds calling in the distance, and up
close the slow friction of leaf on leaf as subtle drafts played
through the woods. Or was that a draft? Yet again she heard
footsteps. It used to be that lairds would hire a hermit to live
in their gardens. Maybe Fergie, having one of those already,
had hired a Bigfoot.

Silence. Jean stood up. "Alasdair?"

The church bell rang, its bright, clear note launching a
couple of gulls, squawking in surprise, from the roof into
the sky. Again it rang, and a third time, sending a subliminal
reverberation less through Jean's ears than her sixth sense.

She ran toward the chapel. "Alasdair?"

The small arched door stood open. Jean stepped into a tiny
room furnished with table, chair, a line of coat hooks, a couple
of shelves holding candlesticks and vases. You couldn't leave
prayer or hymn books out here in the damp and cold, they'd
be worm fodder. At least the place didn't have too strong a
wet-dog smell…

Whoa. She slumped against the table, the prickle at her neck and back thickening into lead shielding. *Seonaid?*

Yes. Through the door from the main part of the church walked Seonaid MacDonald, in her green dress and ringlets as solid, as real, as colorful as any living soul—except for her gaze still fixed on another world. A sunlit world, its radiance shimmering in her blue eyes as though on the surface of the sea. Her complexion might be cool and white, but her pale pink lips were parted in a smile.

She passed so close that every follicle on Jean's body tightened and every hair twitched—the surface tension between realities touching as lightly as a kiss.

Jean was long past feeling afraid of these moments, not that she enjoyed them. But what she felt now wasn't fear at all, not her own, not any hanging like a sour odor around the ghost. Despite the cold weight on her shoulders, her heart was buoyed upward on the scent of spring flowers.

Seonaid glided with light but measured steps out into the afternoon. With a creak like that of rusty machinery, Jean turned her head and watched.

Seonaid cast no shadow, even though she walked through the shadow of several trees—through the shadow of the valley of death—to the stump of the marker. For a long moment she stood over the grave. And then she was gone, transported between one second and the next into another dimension.

Warmth flooded back into Jean's body. Her shoulders lifted and she straightened her spine. She shook herself the way Dougie would shake off water, spraying the room with motes of perception. If ghosts were bits of strong emotion caught in time like a fly in amber, then, unusually, Seonaid's strong emotion wasn't fear or grief, but joy. Jean felt her face relax into a smile. *Wow.*

Heavy footsteps thumped up to the inside door and Alasdair plodded into the vestry as slowly and heavily as though chill had penetrated deep into his bones. And yet he, too, was smiling. His voice brushed against the nap, wavering oddly, he said, "You saw her, then."

Jean's voice seemed to be transmitted through helium. "She brushed right by me. Can you still get that whiff of flowers?"

"Oh aye. No sackcloth and ashes for that one. Right cheery ghost, I'm thinking, for all she was murdered."

"She was murdered at the house. Here, she's happy. Why she's here, as in, on this plane of existence, though, is the question."

"She's not after revenge. Nor identification."

"No." Jean stretched, reveling in the pulse in her own body. "Did she ring the bell?"

"Aye, she did that. I was reaching beneath a pew when I heard the bell ring. By the time I'd looked up, there she was, up the aisle and away." With a stretch of his own, Alasdair peered out through the doorway. "She went outside, did she?"

"Yeah, and vanished at the grave."

"What grave?"

"I'll show you. I don't see any way it could be her own grave, but… Why were you reaching under a pew?"

"Everything's tidy inside, save for this. An empty bag of crisps." Alasdair held up a gaudy plastic bag. "The lock on this door was picked, not expertly, but effectively. I'll be having a word with Fergie about installing ones a bit more complex. And perhaps adding an alarm system, but then, there's no electricity here, he was blethering on about lamps and candles and the like yesterday."

"So someone breaks into the church, eats a snack, and then leaves again, closing the door. Fergie said he found Colin Urquhart here once, but…"

"But." The smile ebbed from Alasdair's face. "Time we were getting ourselves back to the house and having words with more than the laird."

FOURTEEN

LUNCH PASSED IN silence except for the occasional slurp and crunch. Dakota kept darting wary glances from Scott to Heather and back again. Each of them ate with head down, the better to ignore the other—and to ignore Jean and Alasdair and the inconvenient murder case—and peeled away in opposite directions the moment the last of the fruit salad with heavy cream had disappeared.

With a backward look at Jean she interpreted as *don't worry, our secret is safe,* Dakota, too, made her escape—only to be stopped in the hall by Sergeant Young, whose astringent voice ordered the entire family into the incident room. As Heather's equally astringent protestations faded into the distance, Jean said, "Gilnockie's not planning to interview all three of them at the same time, is he?"

Alasdair arranged his napkin into a linen pyramid. "I told him everything you told me is all. What he's doing with it is his own affair."

Yeah, right. Jean noted the tension at the corners of Mr. Truth, Justice, and the British Way's mouth and in the creases beside his eyes. She knew how he felt. So much for the positive effects of fresh air and exercise, not to mention that bolt of joy from, paradoxically, a ghost. It was the other ghost of Dunasheen, Rory MacLeod, who captured the mood of the place. You could scream on the way down, but it wouldn't soften your landing.

Fergie looked either at Diana at the other end of the table, or at the portrait of her mother just beyond. His expression wobbled into that of a child who'd anticipated a special holiday toy—or guests delighted with holiday festivities—but instead received a set of underwear, and dirty underwear at that. Then his chins firmed and his upper lip stiffened. "What difference does it make if they're interviewed together?"

Before Alasdair could answer, Diana said, "Separately, the interviewer can catch out any discrepancies in testimony. However, I expect it usually isn't done to interview a child without the parents present."

Not by Gilnockie, anyway. Jean didn't look at Alasdair, in case her look reminded him of an incident last August.

Diana asked, "Coffee, Jean? Alasdair? Father?"

"No thank you," all three said in unison.

She scooted back from the table and stood up. Something moved in the depths of her eyes, blue as her ancestor Seonaid's—amusement, perhaps. Or perhaps no more than an intelligent assessment of the situation. "If you'll excuse me, I'm booked for an interview myself. Alone."

Not in tandem with Colin, Jean finished for her. During his brief encounter with Gilnockie and Young before lunch, Colin had offered nothing more than the equivalent of name, rank, and serial number. Now he was on hold in the staff sitting room, Thomson in attendance, awaiting not Alasdair's pleasure but his reluctant duty. "We'll have another interview after your meal," Gilnockie had told Alasdair equably. "No need to go interrupting your holiday."

Alasdair had replied to that with body language Jean hoped Gilnockie didn't speak, but fully deserved, and in great-stone-face mode had repaired to the dining room.

"Alasdair, Jean," Fergie said, "if you'll meet me in the library at six, before we begin our New Year's Eve festivities, I'll finally be able to show you the Fairy Flagon and another artifact I think you'll find quite interesting."

Alasdair's smile and nod were stiff but gracious. He said,

"Speaking of your collections, Fergie, Jean overheard Scott Krum speaking to Pritchard about how he'd visited here in September, when you and Diana weren't home."

"Ah. Well." Blushing, Fergie looked down at his empty plate. "That's the, I mean, Emma's family's had dealings with the London branch of Scott's auction house, and he was touring about the U.K. appraising old family mathoms, so he asked if he could stop by."

No surprise Fergie used the same word Alasdair had, *mathom,* Tolkien's designation for souvenirs, gifts, the objects one generation loved that the next loathed—all the things that accumulated like lint on laundry in the back corners of any home, no matter how well maintained.

"Pritchard showed him round the place," Fergie went on, "and he offered on a few small items. Some day, when we've made a complete inventory, we might find…"

"He did not offer on the regimental dirk that's gone missing," said Alasdair, without hinting that it was missing no longer.

"I've got no clue where that got off to, or when. Scott never mentioned it. I suspect he's brought his family here on holiday looking out more items."

"You think?" Jean asked. "He was checking over that ivory-inlaid chest across from the door of the Charlie suite. The one about the size of a laundry basket."

"Was he now? The chest beside Seonaid's tapestry?" Fergie arranged several stray crumbs.

Alasdair repeated, "Seonaid's tapestry?"

"Well, technically a tapestry is woven, and this is petitpoint," Fergie said. "She was after providing employment for the village girls, and stitchery was seen as appropriate."

"I'll take a closer look." Jean knew she wasn't the only one wondering if Scott's interest extended beyond the chest to the almost two-hundred-year-old needlework.

"I expect Scott wants that portrait of Seonaid in my office. It's a David Wilkie, you know, fairly valuable, but I don't want it to leave the family. Doesn't she look like Diana, though?"

"Yes, she does," said Jean, with certainty not based only on the portrait. The only works of David Wilkie she knew off the top of her head were those depicting George IV, Georgie-Porgie, in Edinburgh in 1822, a nightmare in tartan and flesh-colored tights.

If Alasdair was seeing any nightmares at the moment, they were ones of Fergie not being as on top of the situation as he—either "he"—assumed. "Greg MacLeod was by way of being an art dealer as well."

"Oh, well," Fergie told the plate, "yes, he meant to do a bit of business whilst on holiday. He was interested in the antiquity I'll be showing you. I wonder if Scott heard about that as well."

The hall door opened and Rab stamped in as though he was knocking snow from his boots, if he'd been wearing boots instead of old athletic shoes. "I've fitted a bolt on the vestry door. Folk breaking into the chapel and leaving rubbish..." His voice trailed away into a mutter Jean translated as *this never would have happened in the old laird's day.*

"Thank you, Rab," Fergie said.

"Nancy's carried a tray up to Mrs. MacLeod," Rab went on, "and she's saying she's feeling much better, thank you, and she'll be coming down for the dinner and cabaret."

"Festivities," Fergie corrected, if in a murmur.

Rab turned to Alasdair. "The wee McCrummin lass is asking if you'll be wanting her to stand guard the night as well."

"That's for Inspector Gilnockie to say," Alasdair answered.

"Ah well, you'll be asking him, then." His beard leading, like a broom sweeping clean, Rab stomped on into the pantry.

Alasdair's hand landed on his napkin, squashing it flat. "Aye. Speaking of the chapel, and Rab as well, come to that—

he was telling us that there's no one buried there, but Jean found a headstone beneath that huge tree."

Jean added, "It says, 'A stranger known but to God.'"

"Oh, that." Fergie leaned back in his chair and folded his hands on his stomach. She expected him to begin, "Once upon a time," but what he said was, "The gardener turned up a human skeleton round and about 1885, some poor chap buried in a shallow grave not so long before."

"Any associated artifacts?" asked Alasdair.

"Bits of cloth, the odd buckle and button, a few coins, an old bonnet tucked up with sprigs of juniper, or so the story goes. The minister in Kinlochroy was the traditional sort, and wouldn't have the bones in the churchyard, since he had no way of knowing the man's religious views. So my great-grandfather, the laird, had them reburied where they were found, installed a marker, and that was that."

"A shame there was no one to do a forensics workup," said Jean, envisioning Seonaid's ghost vanishing at the grave.

"My great-grandfather had photos taken. Brenda at the local Heritage Museum's got them on file, if you'd like to see them. And the buttons and all as well."

"I'd like to see them, aye," Alasdair said.

"Because you don't know what's important," said Fergie with an *I get it!* smile.

Alasdair's smile was much more wry. "You never ken what's important in a murder investigation, no. Although I'm thinking the odds of your unknown body being important to either today's murder or the one in 1822 aren't so good."

"Rab gave us one version of what happened in 1822," said Jean. "What's the official one?"

"Tormod MacLeod was an apprentice stonemason working on the chapel," Fergie said. "His carvings were finer than his master's. The master schemed to get rid of him, putting it about that he was having an illicit affair with the laird's wife, Seonaid."

Alasdair asked, "Were they having an affair, then?"

Fergie shrugged. "The laird believed they were. He was twice her age, and had served with the Cameron Highlanders against Napoleon and been badly injured at Waterloo. Quite spoiled his looks. His disposition, they say, was never good."

The more things changed, Jean thought, the more they stayed the same. But if Fergie drew any connection with Colin Urquhart, he showed no sign of it.

The pantry door opened and Nancy shot into the room. "You're still sitting about, are you? You'll not mind me clearing away?" Without waiting for an answer, she started collecting plates.

"But his first wife had died childless," Fergie went on, "and he needed an heir. So he married the local beauty—a fisherman's daughter, or so the story goes."

"Not a love match, then. And I bet she already knew Tormod." Jean imagined young Seonaid dazzled by the laird's attentions, and her family urging her to better them all by making such an advantageous match. "Sounds like a cautionary tale for Jane Austen, about the dangers of letting your head rule your heart."

"If the story is true," Fergie said, "then Seonaid's heart won out and she went on with young Tormod after her son was born."

Alasdair asked, "Who killed her, then? The laird himself, out of jealousy?"

"Sounds like the plot of *Othello,* with Othello strangling Desdemona because of Iago's lies," Jean said. "Except I gather the master mason's story wasn't entirely a lie."

Two plates clashed together in Nancy's hands, making a sound not unlike that of the bell at the chapel. "Stories get twisted round in the telling. Chinese whispers. That's the way of these things."

"Undoubtedly so, but there's a fair amount of documentation," Fergie told her. "Old Norman was named 'the Red' because of his temper—he had dark hair, before it went gray. I'm never pleased at possibly having a murderer in the family tree, mind you."

"Didna fash Greg MacLeod, did it? Coming all this way looking out such a story, imagine that! Though I reckon he had other reasons for coming, poking and prying just like the polis." And Nancy popped back through the swinging door like a cuckoo back into its clock.

"The poor soul hardly had time to poke and pry," said Fergie to the slow swing of the door. "And if my ancestor murdered Seonaid, then Greg's didn't."

Jean silently repeated Miranda's mantra: *The staff sees all, knows all, and is likely to tell all unless you make it worth their while not to.*

Fergie shrugged. "Rab and Nancy have been here so long I suspect they were born in the attics. When I was a child her brother would show me all the little hidden places, until he was obliged to find work elsewhere—haven't seen him for donkey's years, he's too successful for the likes of Kinlochroy now, sends Nancy tidy sums. In any event, you can't blame Rab and Nancy for being a bit possessive."

The kink in Alasdair's right eyebrow attested that yes, he could blame them. He said, "More people than the Finlays work here, you were saying."

"Yes, God knows there are cleaners, gardeners, tradesmen of all descriptions. No stonemasons like Tormod MacLeod. Though we've just thrown up another murderer, more's the pity. A genuine murderer, this time round."

"I reckon Tormod was transported rather than hanged,"

said Alasdair, "because the local jury knew he wasn't guilty of murder."

"Even as the laird insisted that he be disappeared. Hustled off to an emigrant ship heading Down Under, in other words, a pretty grim fate in those days, but hardly worse than death." Jean imagined the echo of Greg's voice, like an antipodean banshee. "If Seonaid died from following her heart, that takes her story out of an Austen drawing room, into, oh, a Thomas Hardy dungeon. You know, life's a bitch and then you die."

"Was there any question about the bairn's paternity?" Alasdair asked.

"None," answered Fergie. "Norman acknowledged him as his son and heir. Short of doing a DNA test, and that would involve digging up Seonaid…"

"Is she in the churchyard in Kinlochroy?" Jean asked.

"Why yes, where else would she be?" replied Fergie.

"Was Greg asking you about all this?" Alasdair went on.

"He mentioned his MacLeod ancestry is all. It was Tina going on about Tormod and Greg's—well, she said 'obsession' with Dunasheen, but that's a wife." Fergie gazed again at Emma's painted features. "Greg was in too much of a hurry just then. We agreed to have us a chin-wag that evening is all, and off he went, down the stairs just as I went into my office, out the front door and away."

Out the… Jean jolted into an upright and locked position. "You heard him go out the front door? But we saw him leaving the house through the courtyard gate."

"Oh aye." Alasdair leaned forward.

"That's right, you saw him at the courtyard gate." Fergie's features pursed in pursuit of memory. "No, I didn't hear the door open and shut at all. I heard Greg walking down the stairs, then saw him going through the kitchen yard and into the back garden gate. But he couldn't have gone through the garden, could he, not and met up with you on the castle path."

Jean's memory bubbled up like a mud pit and belched what Fergie had said the day before. "That's why you said it was odd he'd gone that way. And you said he'd stayed in his room just long enough to get his hat. But he wasn't wearing a hat."

"He wasn't?" Fergie grimaced in bewilderment. "The man I saw was wearing one of those slouch hats with the wide brim, the sort you associate with Australians. I thought it was Greg, but then, I only saw his back, the hat and a heavy anorak."

"Anoraks are usually nylon, aren't they? Waterproofed. Sort of shiny," Jean murmured, even as all three sets of eyes widened and batted stares back and forth.

It was Alasdair who put the vital question into words. "If that was not Greg crossing the yard, then who was it?"

"And did Dakota Krum see the same man when she and her family were driving up the driveway? He would have had just enough time to run up from the beach, I bet—if that was the murderer, which isn't a given. I should have asked her to define 'hat,' but I saw Colin Urquhart wearing a hood, a sweatshirt beneath a coat, probably not an anorak. And then we saw him with his bonnet, and, well…" The images winged across Jean's mind and winked out. "Damn."

"Eh?" asked Fergie, his eyes growing positively bulbous with alarm. "Urquhart?"

"We met up with him by the old church just before noon," Alasdair said. "Thomson's saying he's the sole survivor of a bomb in Iraq. Could be that's what he was telling you, Fergie, about men in his vicinity dying nasty deaths."

"Oh. I didn't know. That's why he's—poor chap, he could play the Phantom of the Opera without makeup." Fergie sagged, then sat up again. "I'm sorry the man's not right in the head, but still, what he said is a threat of sorts. He's a suspect, isn't he, Alasdair?"

"Aye." Alasdair pushed back from the table. "Sounds to

be our list of suspects is longer than we've been thinking. I'd best report to Gilnockie."

Our. We. And he didn't mean Jean, who popped up beside him. Despite the spicy sting of the soup in her throat and its warm glow in her stomach, a nap was the last thing on her mind. Forward momentum, she exhorted herself, knowing by Alasdair's keen expression he needed no exhortation.

Leaving Fergie staring out the window with the same expression as his ancestors searching the horizon for a Viking sail, Alasdair paced down the hall and pushed open the door to the old kitchen.

Jean shut the door as he cut through the technological and conversational buzz and caught Gilnockie's eye. With a jerk of his head, he summoned his colleague to a brief conference beside the fireplace and the bulletin board, which now displayed not only the grim sequence of photos but notes and a list of names. Did that list already include the person—just because Fergie said "he" didn't mean it was a man—with the hat?

Dakota, wilted as a flower without water, sat between her parents and facing Sergeant Young. This time there was no accommodating cushion and cup of tea, although Scott's thunderous and Heather's sarcastic expressions suggested a cup of hemlock would do the trick. Young made notations on a pad of paper, her curled lip repelling both thunder and sarcasm.

Figuring it was better to claim a spot than ask for it, especially since Gilnockie seemed to accept her as an extension of Alasdair—his left hand, not his right—Jean pulled a plastic chair into the conversational perimeter, and sat down just as Gilnockie resumed his seat at the table. Alasdair circled like a plane looking for a landing strip, pulled another chair forward, and settled down beside Jean.

"Mr. Krum," said Gilnockie. "Do you own any hats?"

Scott stared. "Hats? Yeah, I've got a stocking cap, and some gimme caps…"

"What?" demanded Young.

"Baseball caps with company logos," Scott explained.

Heather rolled her eyes, perhaps at both Young's question and Scott's low-class headgear.

"Is that all?" asked Gilnockie.

"I might have an old cowboy hat someone gave me. I don't know. They're all in the hall closet back home. Why?"

Heather adjusted the cuticle of a fingernail long and shiny as a talon. "I have a sun hat and one of those Scarlett O'Hara things I wore at a wedding. Tacky, but what can you do, the bride calls the shots."

Gilnockie asked Dakota, "The man you saw at the garden gate last night. What sort of hat was he wearing?"

"Kind of like Indian Jones's hat, except with a wider, you know…" Dakota's limp fingers circled her head.

"Brim," said Heather. "And I guess the ghost had a hat too, huh?"

"No," Dakota said, her voice dropping to a whisper. "The ghost wasn't wearing a hat."

Scott shifted forward in his chair, as though ready to launch himself across the table. Young's body tensed even further. But all Scott said was, "Inspector Gilnockie, I have to apologize for taking up your time with this ghost business. She's a very imaginative child. We're working with her to get that under control."

Heather snorted. Jean wanted to knock her head against Scott's, all the better to adjust their attitudes. *Don't patronize her. Be glad you have a creative child.*

She had no idea what Dakota was thinking. The child fled, slipping from her chair, making tracks for the door, and plunking herself down on the step just inside.

"If you're finished with us…" Heather began.

"Not quite." Gilnockie reached into the breast pocket of

his coat, pulled out a plastic bag holding a small white square, and set it on the table.

"It's a business card," said Scott.

Gilnockie turned it over.

Heather asked, "So?"

"You've not seen this before, then?"

Both Scott and Heather shook their heads, Heather adding, "Well, there's a dish of them in the room, but without any clues on the back. I guess that note is a clue?"

"Thank you very much," said Gilnockie. "If we need anything else, we'll contact you. I hope your business with Lord Dunasheen goes satisfactorily."

"Fat chance, now," Scott murmured, but he bared his teeth in a facsimile of a smile. "Thanks."

"We're leaving Saturday morning," Heather stated. "We have to get back to Glasgow for our flight home. The kid's got to go to school. I have a business to run."

Gilnockie's smile was genuine. "I hope you'll not be obliged to change your plans, Mrs. Krum."

Great, Jean thought. There was another complication. What if Tina and the Krums couldn't vacate their rooms on Saturday morning, even though Michael and Rebecca, Miranda, and Hugh were all scheduled to arrive Saturday afternoon? At least Alasdair's mother was staying with friends in the village. Not that a wedding, and a second wedding at that, took precedence over murder.

Expelling a long breath, Jean appealed to the ceiling for patience—as quickly as possible!—and settled back in her chair for the next round.

FIFTEEN

GILNOCKIE WAITED UNTIL the nuclear—as in fissionable—family Krum had left the room and Young started drumming her pen on the table. Finally, he restored the bag to his pocket and said, "Well now. The forensics boffins are having a go at the knife, thanks to you for recovering it, Miss Fairbairn.

"Dakota saw it before I did."

Young looked at Jean as though suddenly noticing she was there. Her belligerent gaze moved on to Alasdair, who met it both imperturbably and implacably, and then back to her notebook.

"No matter," said Gilnockie. "A preliminary blood test's indicating that the regimental dirk is the murder weapon, though other tests are showing only indecipherable fingerprints. No surprise there, it was a cold, dreich afternoon, and folk were wearing gloves."

"If the murderer was wearing gloves, then there's blood on them," said Alasdair.

"Oh aye, there is that. We've found multiple prints on the other dirk and both sheaths—Mrs. Finlay's quite right, she's not had the time to clean them." Gilnockie looked up at the ceiling, either collecting his thoughts or, like Jean, appealing to the Almighty. "Neither Mr. nor Mrs. Krum has a proper alibi, and Mr. Krum already had some knowledge of these parts, though he's saying he's never heard of Greg MacLeod."

Young's lips went from a curl to a clamp. "They're not shy of a bob or two," she said under her breath, letting the implications—avarice, underhanded dealings—dangle provocatively.

"Aye," Gilnockie said, without grasping the bait. "At the time of the murder, Lionel Pritchard was driving back from a day out in Portree. Or so he's saying. I'm having someone there retrace his steps. Perhaps he's negotiating with dealers such as Krum and MacLeod on his own, but we've got no evidence of that."

"Just yet," said Young.

"Rab Finlay returned here from the pub before the MacLeods arrived, and he and Mrs. Finlay set to preparing the evening meal. Their telly was tuned to a film, and they heard nothing 'til Lord Dunasheen gave the alarm."

Then how, Jean asked herself, did Nancy know about Greg and Tormod...oh. Nancy had ever-so-helpfully kept Tina company over breakfast.

"What of the note on the business card?" asked Alasdair.

"As yet no one's admitted to recognizing it. Nor has it any useful prints." Gilnockie actually steepled his fingers à la Sherlock Holmes. His austere face fit the part. If you melted his ice, you'd get a puddle of fresh water.

"Tina MacLeod." The name squeezed from Young's mouth like toothpaste from a tube.

"We'll be questioning her again, now that we've got ourselves another possible suspect, Lord Dunasheen's stranger. Who could have been Mr. Krum, although if the young lass saw the same man outside the gate, then it wasn't him at all but someone from the village, like as not, though we'll be keeping our options open."

Jean didn't offer any thoughts on Australian mafiosos and the sign of the Red Kangaroo. "Tina and Greg didn't have any enemies. For what that's worth."

Fortunately, no one told her what that was worth.

"Lord Dunasheen has no alibi for the time of the murder," said Gilnockie, and quickly, to Alasdair, "I'm taking into account what Miss Fairbairn here noticed, that he was not breathing hard when she told him of the incident. We've not spoken with Miss MacDonald yet. However…ah. Bang on time."

The door opened and Sanjay Thomson ushered Colin Urquhart now wearing a tattered pair of sneakers, down the steps.

Young turned to another page. "Killed the man in a fit of madness, likely doesn't even remember doing it. And dropped the knife on his way back to the light—"

"Presumption of innocence," Gilnockie interrupted, his voice firm but quiet.

Alasdair said, "There's motive even in madness, Sergeant," and leaned back as Thomson pulled up a chair for Colin and then retired to the door.

With Diana in charge, Colin, and Thomson, too, had no doubt been properly fed. Whether it was the distraction of his digestive process, Thomson's presence, or both, Colin's thin shoulders beneath the nylon patches of an oversized military sweater were now more slumped than braced. But those blue eyes—or eye, rather—still looked with exaggerated caution from face to face.

"How can I help with your investigation, Inspector Gilnockie?" Colin's voice was deeper than Jean expected, emanating from his throat as though from a deep well. An ancient sacred well, perhaps, where petitioners even today left scraps of cloth along with their prayers.

"Where were you yesterday afternoon between three and four o'clock?" Gilnockie asked.

"I wasn't killing Aussie visitors," Colin replied, and, to Young, "If I had done, I'd have taken the knife to Keppoch Point and chucked it over the cliff into the sea, not left it lying about the old graveyard."

Young's mouth went so tight she looked like a centenarian with no teeth. Trying to do the right thing and make no further remarks, no doubt. Jean knew the feeling.

"Where were you when the visitor was killed, then?" asked Gilnockie.

"At the lighthouse. Watching the birds. Reading a book. I don't know."

"On your own?"

Colin's contorted face was neither smiling nor frowning. He peered down at his hands, with their long fingers and the veins blue through the pale skin seeming too delicate to lift a weapon, never mind use it. "On my own."

If Colin had been alone at the time of the murder, Jean asked herself, then where was Diana? Admittedly the question placed him between the devil and the deep blue sea, but surely facing Fergie's wrath was better than implicating Diana in a murder.

"Do you know where Diana was just then?" Alasdair asked.

"No."

"Were you by way of having an appointment at the old church at three?"

"No."

Once again Gilnockie produced the plastic bag with the business card. "What's this, then, signed with your initials?"

Colin read the card. "I never wrote that. It's not my handwriting."

At Gilnockie's gesture, Young turned the pad of paper to a new page and shoved it across the table. Gilnockie offered Colin a pen from his own pocket. "Write something, please."

Colin's back was starting to stiffen and his shoulders coil. If he'd had a pressure gauge, it would be inching upward. After a long moment, he set pen to paper and wrote out two lines, then threw the pen down like a live grenade.

Gilnockie and Young almost bumped heads over the pad.

"My love is like a red, red rose that sweetly blooms in June."
Those weren't quite the words of Burns's poem, but close.
They seemed incongruous in Gilnockie's dusty voice.

Alasdair reached past Jean, picked up the pad, and held
it so she could see it, too. No, the jagged black letters on the
card looked nothing like these, round and yet cramped, like
the mouth of the man in the famous painting of "The Scream."

Jean slid the pad across the table to Young, who reposi-
tioned it between her hands.

"Well then," Gilnockie said, "Lord Dunasheen is telling
us you threatened him."

Colin's head, bent to consider a small ink stain on his forefinger, jerked up. "Why would I be doing that?"

"Because he's unhappy with your relationship with his
daughter."

"Oh aye." His forefinger curled into his palm with the
others. "He's thinking I'm a good-for-nothing layabout with
designs on his daughter. Well, Diana's an adult, and a clever
one at that, capable of making her own decisions. I never
threatened the man."

Alasdair explained, "You were telling him that men in
your vicinity tended to die."

"They do." A wave of tension ran through Colin's body.
"I remember now, it was when Fergus was turfing me out of
the wee church, in all Christian charity, right? That's what
I was telling him, aye, by way of truth in advertising, not
threatening, not at all."

Gilnockie's smooth forehead puckered, very gently, perhaps sympathizing with Colin and yet wondering what he was
capable of. At least the younger man wasn't trying to hide his
animosity. "Did you know the MacLeods at all?"

"The murdered man and his wife? No. I didn't even know
their names 'til Diana told me."

"When did she do that?"

"She rang me last night."

"Do you know the Krums at all?"

"The Americans?" Colin asked. "No."

"Have you seen a man, a stranger, wearing a hat with a wide brim?"

"Most folk here are strangers to me, Inspector."

Gilnockie conceded that with a nod. "How do you get on with Mr. and Mrs. Finlay and Mr. Pritchard?"

"Sanjay told you about the pub, Rab and Lionel and two pensioners taking the piss. I overreacted, I'll be owning to that. But they had no call jabbing sticks through the bars of my cage, eh?" Colin laughed, a sound like saw teeth snagging on hard wood.

Gilnockie began, "I'm sorry—"

"Oh aye, everyone's sorry. I'm hearing the wee fiddles playing sad music. If you've finished patronizing me..."

Gilnockie's voice was calm, his gaze level. "Mr. Urquhart, I am sorry."

Jean thought of the old church, ancient stones settled solidly in the earth, roofed by the eternal sky, all passion spent. She glanced at Alasdair to see his head tilted pensively. He, too, sensed the wavelets of tranquility emanating from Gilnockie as surely as he scented damp ashes on the chill draft from the fireplace. Serenity was a valuable skill for a cop. And an unusual one. Jean looked back at Gilnockie, crossing Young's nonplused gaze on the way.

Colin took an audible breath and his fingers splayed out again. Oblivious to his power, Gilnockie gestured toward the door. "P.C. Thomson."

"Aye, sir?" Thomson wended his way between the tables and the technicians.

"Where's Diana MacDonald? She agreed to an interview at half past one."

"She's in the kitchen, sir. She's asking if you'd mind speaking to her there, the cooking wants seeing to."

Frowning, Young opened her mouth. But Gilnockie spoke first. "Aye, we'll come along to the kitchen, no worries." Rising gracefully, he started for the door.

Everyone started for the door, even Colin. Once the procession made it to the hall, though, Thomson intercepted him and drew his attention to a series of Victorian prints depicting kilted Highlanders with their clan tartans and clan botanical badges. Prickly thistle represented Scotland itself, Jean noticed, and Stewart, family of kings and scoundrels. Cameron was oak, deep roots, wide-ranging branches, leaves curving in simple elegance.

The sunlight glowing through the deep-set windows of the new kitchen was already taking on the sheen of late afternoon. A row of herbs along one sill seemed to stretch eager leaves toward the light, and the lemon-yellow tile with its colorful Spanish/Italian border magnified it. More windows framed the door into the kitchen yard, next to a row of hooks draped with raincoats, hats, scarves, and umbrellas.

Like a star in the spotlight, Diana stood at the central counter. Her subdued sweater and pants outfit was eclipsed by a high apron of such bleached purity her fair face seemed almost tanned. A red ribbon tied back her hair. Her hand snicked a long chef's knife up and down so briskly it seemed to be moving by itself, producing small cubes of potato.

Gilnockie gestured Young to a Swedish table and chairs sitting beside a Swedish sideboard complete with a large flatscreen television and various DVD and control boxes. A perk from Fergie, Jean wondered, or a gift from Nancy's successful brother?

"Miss MacDonald," began Gilnockie.

"Inspector Gilnockie," Diana returned. "Nancy's helping Rab and my father do up the Great Hall for the evening function, and I'm helping her by preparing the vegetables. I'm at your disposal, even so."

"Where were you when you heard that Mr. MacLeod had been killed?" Gilnockie asked.

She blinked, apparently not expecting that question. "I came back downstairs after showing the Krums to their suite and my father told me the news."

"How long had you been in the house before the Krums arrived?"

"Only long enough to freshen up. I'd taken the dogs for a walk and lost track of time, so found myself in a wee bit of a hurry." Her eyes turned toward Jean even as the knife moved on to a rutabaga. "I'm sorry you had to answer the door."

"No problem," said Jean, without adding it had given her evidence to share. "When did the dogs get away from you?"

The knife stopped, then started again. "It was you who let them into the house as well, then. They were wet and chilled, poor beasts, and ran off without waiting for me."

"Waiting for you doing what?" Gilnockie asked.

"I stopped in at the lighthouse."

Young's pen thunked the page as solidly as Diana's knife hit the cutting board, probably exclamation-pointing that she'd just contradicted Colin's testimony.

Alasdair and Gilnockie nodded in perfect unison, but it was Gilnockie who spoke. "Was Colin Urquhart there at the time?"

"Yes, he was." The faintest whiff of steam moved over the limpid pools of Diana's eyes. *Once those icy ones melt,* Jean thought.

Alasdair came around on another tack. "What dealings have you had with Scott Krum?"

"I'd never met the man. He visited her in September, whilst father and I were away, and Lionel dealt with him. He offered to buy four porcelain figurines, several pieces of my grandmother's jewelry, and the Wilkie portrait of Seonaid MacDonald. Lionel, on our behalf, reached a bargain on all but the portrait. I have no doubt he had himself a look round then, and is having himself another one now."

The knife rose and fell so fast its blade flashed like a strobe. A bit of rutabaga launched itself into the air and landed beside Jean's foot. She picked it up.

Pulling forward a beet, Diana started reducing it to more small cubes.

"Do you trust Mr. Pritchard?" Gilnockie asked.

Diana's hands stopped moving. She looked up, her gaze sharp as the knife, almost defiant. "Not entirely, no. We can't afford to pay him the salary he believes he deserves, and I suspect he may be creaming off some of the accounts or even selling small items from the lumber rooms. Even if we could pay him, he'd continue to see his position here as no more than a job. It's my father and I who are invested in this business. In this estate. In each other."

"Quite so." Alasdair took a step forward. "Were you or your father dealing with Greg MacLeod as well? Was he planning on having a look round, the better to make offers of his own? He was meaning to walk out to the old church, likely meeting someone there. Had he said anything about buying one or more of the grave slabs for his museum of religion?"

"Ooh, there's a thought," Jean said from the corner of her mouth.

Just as the side of Alasdair's mouth tightened in both acknowledgment and doubt, a telephone rang. Not the rotary-dial implement that looked like Darth Vader's helmet, so big it occupied its own table, but a cell phone trilling ABBA's "Take a Chance on Me."

Her sallow complexion reddening, Young whipped her phone from her pocket and answered it by spitting her name like an epithet. She listened to the faint electronic voice, said, "Aye. Cheers," and switched off.

Realizing that every face in the room was turned toward her, she mumbled, "Inverness, saying they've got the boots, and the photos of the prints from the beach, and the mud samples and all the rest. Urquhart's boots will be arriving soon. They'll be in touch."

"Very good then," said Gilnockie, and turned back to Diana.

SIXTEEN

DIANA'S GAZE FELL to the board and the knife. She cut a few more bits from the beet.

"Your dealings with Greg MacLeod," Alasdair reminded her.

"I would not be surprised," she answered, "if Mr. MacLeod saw Dunasheen as a cut-rate shopping mall, but I know nothing of his plans. I knew him only from his e-mails asking about our history and then booking a room."

Once again Gilnockie pulled the business card in its plastic bag from his pocket, and laid it on the counter, first one side up, then the other. "Have you seen this before?"

Diana wiped her sleeve across her forehead. Granted, Jean thought, the blazing overhead lights and the huge Aga stove warmed the room, but seeing Diana sweat was like, well, like seeing her in a passionate embrace with Colin. "Where did you find that?" she asked.

"I found it," said Jean.

"In the pocket of your raincoat," Gilnockie added.

"Then someone placed it there," replied Diana. "That's not Colin's handwriting. If he wanted to speak with me, he'd ring me. And in any event, we didn't meet at the church at three."

Young muttered something, the words unintelligible, the tone skeptical.

A scowl flew across Diana's face like the bird's shadow had flown across Jean's. She gestured toward Young with the knife, the beet juice on its blade thin and watery. In spite of herself, Jean saw the dirk striking upward into Greg MacLeod's chest. *Blood is thicker than water.*

Gilnockie asked, "You're saying that someone might be stitching you up for the murder?"

The knife swung toward him. "Or someone might aim to put Colin in the frame."

"You're thinking of Pritchard, are you?" Alasdair asked.

Without answering, Diana went back to the beet, cutting so briskly that several small red cubes rolled like dice onto the counter.

Young spoke up. "Why don't you just sack the man?"

"Who else would do the job, then?" Diana answered. "My father's already doing the work of three. As am I."

Jean thought again of devils and deep blue seas. And of Fergie, a well-meaning soul if ever there was one. Diana's fourth job was watching out for him. Jean hazarded, "Maybe the CU on the card is an e-mail or texting abbreviation, meaning 'see you.' Maybe someone was trying to lure Diana out of the house by sending her a fake note from Colin. Maybe that particular raincoat isn't Diana's. There are two more hanging over there by the door."

With a quick dart of blue in Jean's direction, Diana responded to her cue. "Many people in these parts have yellow raincoats. Last month Lionel Pritchard and I accidentally swapped ours—we're much the same size. Rab's there is quite large, and Nancy's has a floral lining."

"The coat was too big for me, but not big enough to have been Rab's or Fergie's. And it had a plain fabric lining." *And it smelled good,* Jean added to herself.

Gilnockie said to Young, "Sergeant, bring the raincoat hanging in the cloak room, please."

Young threw down her pen and sidled away crab-wise. In the moment the door was open, Jean heard Pritchard's oily voice. "…move the man on, P.C. Thomson."

"I canna be doing that, sir," replied Thomson, "Inspector Gilnockie asked Mr. Urquhart to stop here."

Diana scraped her handiwork into piles, wiped off the knife, and rinsed her hands. Taking off her apron, she said, "I believe that was Pritchard going into my father's office, where he does the accounts. Shouldn't you be questioning him about that note?"

Instead of asking, "Who's in charge here, anyway?" Gilnockie said, "Aye," and started for the door.

Jean realized she was still holding the cold, wet cube of rutabaga. Setting it down on the table brought her within range of the row of cookbooks beside the television. No, none of them were by the cooking-school maven they'd encountered in August. No omens there.

Alasdair held the door for her, his expression, if not icy, not warm either, but carefully neutral.

They followed Gilnockie down the corridor and around the corner. Diana peeled off the procession when they passed Thomson and Colin. The clan print hanging between them was, appropriately, "MacLeod," a tartan-clad figure encircled by sprigs of juniper and a scattering of dark berries. *Juniper,* Jean thought. She'd just heard that, and not in reference to gin and tonic...

Colin lurched into Gilnockie's face. "Leave her. She's done nothing wrong."

Gilnockie acknowledged him with a polite nod, but he didn't break pace.

Diana set her hand on Colin's arm and said something in his ear. His eye expanded and then shut and pain washed over his face. "If only you'd told me—" he began, before she shushed him.

Did he mean, *If only we'd synchronized our stories, we'd not have contradicted each other about your being at the lighthouse?* And yet, if either Colin or Diana was the killer, surely he or she would have made a potion of synchronizing stories.

Judging by the Alasdair-like crevice between Thomson's black eyebrows, he was thinking the same thing.

In Fergie's study, Pritchard was seated at the computer, a spreadsheet displayed on the screen before him. He spun around when Gilnockie and Alasdair walked in, Jean forming a hypotenuse at their backs. "What's this?"

Alasdair batted a glance over his shoulder and Jean returned it. Yes, it could have been Pritchard who'd looked up Greg MacLeod on the Internet.

Gilnockie was tracking a different trail. Without speaking, he presented Pritchard with the evidence-bagged business card, first the front, then the back.

Pritchard's shoe-button eyes hardened and his narrow moustache writhed. "What of it?"

"It was found in the pocket of your raincoat," Gilnockie told him, fudging for effect.

"Oh, I very much doubt that."

"Are you accusing me of framing you, Mr. Pritchard?"

Pritchard's lipless mouth opened and shut, emitting something between a snort and a hiss. He snapped back around to the computer. "If you'll excuse me, I have work to do."

Alasdair seized a paper lying next to the keyboard. "You wrote this, did you?" Craning her neck, Jean saw a list of expenses—food, cleaning supplies, repairs—written in smooth, small handwriting, the occasional lower loop protruding like a mocking tongue.

"Yes," said Pritchard.

In other words, that wasn't his writing on the card, either. But didn't its presence in his pocket indicate that he'd had an appointment at the church? With Greg? What would the call record on his phone reveal—one to or from Greg at just about three P.M.? Just because he said he'd been in Portree didn't mean he actually was.

"Mr. Pritchard. Were you after doing business with Greg MacLeod behind your employer's back?" Anyone else's voice, even Alasdair's, would hold a subtle menace. If Gilnockie's held anything, it was disappointment at the human condition. "Have you done business with Mr. Krum behind your employer's back?"

Pritchard's hand tightened on the mouse. "You've got no evidence to back up either charge."

"That's our job, looking out evidence. In the meantime, I'm wondering if you intended switching your raincoat for Miss MacDonald's. Seems a simple-minded way of stitching someone up, though, either her or Mr. Urquhart."

"What the hell are you going on about?" Pritchard spun the desk chair around, using its momentum to propel him to his feet. The scent of after-shave or cologne, one hinting at damp sweat socks and musk-ox breath, surged from his wool jacket and then dissipated.

Colin shouldered into the room. "You bastard. You've been watching Diana. You've been making suggestive remarks. Planning on having yourself a posh wife, were you? And an estate to plunder as well? But she's too clever by half for the likes of you."

Jean took a giant step into the corner as Thomson dragged Colin back to the door and handed him over to Diana. The chatelaine of Dunasheen was actually starting to look frazzled—one golden lock of hair escaped its ribbon and dangled beside her no longer ivory-pale but pastry-pasty cheek.

"Is that true, Miss MacDonald?" Gilnockie asked. "Has Mr. Pritchard been paying you unwelcome attentions?"

"It depends on your definition of 'attentions.' He's always polite." But an edged undertone in Diana's voice belied her words—*as well it should,* Jean thought, remembering

Pritchard's snigger—even as a flash of steel in her eyes asked Gilnockie to back off. Then she herself backed off, murmuring to Colin, "They're sorting it. Leave it, please."

He shuddered as though every muscle in his body clenched and then, as though to his direct, conscious command, loosened.

And here came Young, carrying a yellow raincoat over her arm. Without any such niceties as "pardon me," she elbowed past Colin and Diana and handed Gilnockie the coat. Everyone leaned forward as he held it up. Inside the lining of the collar was sewn a neat label: "Diana MacDonald."

Gilnockie turned out the pockets, finding nothing but a few dried shreds of vegetation, a flower picked in the summer, perhaps, and a lump of tissue stained with pink lipstick. Then he lifted the lining of the coat to his face and inhaled. "The fabric's smelling of your perfume, Miss MacDonald."

Diana's smile was narrow as a needle. "It's my coat, then, isn't it? But we've come back round to the start—I've never before seen that note."

Jean said, "That's the coat I borrowed last night, the one with the card in the pocket. I guess that's the one that was hanging wet on the hook by the back door when Alasdair and I heard Tina screaming from the beach."

"No way of knowing otherwise, not now," said Alasdair.

Gilnockie handed Diana her coat, retrieved the business card in its bag, and took Pritchard's elbow. "Sergeant, let's be getting Mr. Pritchard here back to the incident room."

"Hang on," protested Pritchard. "We've just established…"

"…who owns the raincoat is all. Now I'm after discussing your dealings with Mr. Krum and Mr. MacLeod."

Pritchard shot a venomous glance toward Diana. "So that's it. If you can't put me in the frame one way, you'll find another." And, his glare shifting toward Gilnockie, "I've told you, I was in Portree when MacLeod was killed. I never met the man. And I had no dealings with Krum that Fergus wasn't a party to."

"We'll be seeing about that." Young took Pritchard's other elbow and steered him down the corridor, snapping as she passed, "You, Urquhart, don't be leaving the place, eh?"

Colin half-smiled at that, probably having no intention of abandoning Diana to be bothered and beset at Dunasheen. Together they retreated, Thomson behind them like a sheep dog poised to direct any strays. Diana could no longer pretend to the local constable that there was nothing between her and Colin, but the moment of truth with Fergie was yet to come.

In the suddenly quiet room, the hum of the computer sounded like a hornet's nest. Alasdair saved and closed out Pritchard's program, then looked slowly around the room. Fergie's room.

Jean's brain felt like a pillow squashed flat in a sleepless night. Sighing, she looked up at the chubby orange face of Ganesh, who was supposed to avert bad luck—although what was going on here wasn't luck at all, but human choices. She suggested, without much conviction, "Maybe the card's been in Diana's pocket for a month and has nothing to do with the murder."

"It would be a bit more ragged, then. This one's only stained with damp." Alasdair leaned over the desk, eyed the Excalibur letter opener, and delicately, as though sifting through eggshells, moved the papers around. Picking one up, he stared at it, handed it to Jean, and turned to face the window.

On a notepaper headed *From Fergus's desk* was written a recipe for steak pie. Dripping or butter. Stewing beef, diced. Onion. Puff pastry. Heat the dripping, toss the meat in seasoned flour, and brown all over...a tiny bolt of lightning shot through her, making her hand clench on the paper. The letters were as jagged as a stock market summary, similar to those on the back of the card. Similar, but not identical—they were not pressed as heavily into the paper, and they slanted more strongly to the right. "Is this Fergie's handwriting?" Jean asked Alasdair.

"Writing changes," he said to the sky above the shadowed kitchen yard. "I've not had anything but e-mails from him for donkey's years."

"It's a recipe. It could be Diana's or Nancy's." She put the paper back on the desk and scanned the others, but saw nothing else handwritten, just several signatures at the bottom of letters and printed application forms. Fergie's *Dunasheen* resembled a squashed thistle, a bit spiky, yes, as though his rounded body and low-key personality had to break out somewhere. Still…her mini lightning bolt fizzled into ashes. "He couldn't have killed Greg."

"I know!" Alasdair's expression split the difference between irritated and frustrated.

Yeah, frustration and irritation were going around, like a rash. "Even if Fergie wrote the note on the card, it doesn't mean—"

"He's telling Patrick he's never before seen that card."

"Oh. Well, then, maybe Greg himself wrote it. Tina must have…"

"…a sample of his handwriting."

Of course Alasdair would have the same idea. They needed to convince Tina to trust them with the full story, whatever the full story was. "Although," Jean said, "even if Greg did write the note, who did he send it ahead to? It didn't crawl into Diana's pocket by itself."

"Just now," said Alasdair, "I'd credit Fergie's fairies and Greg's ancestral spirits with the entire plot."

Jean shot Seonaid an accusatory look. *Who walked into you at the garden gate last night?* Seonaid looked back—or beyond, as the case might be—offering no more helping hands. "We're not getting any testimony from her short of a séance, and maybe not even then."

"Please do not give Fergie any such idea." Alasdair turned toward the door just as regular footsteps heralded the arrival of P.C. Thomson.

"Colin's helping Diana in the kitchen," he reported. "He'll do for now. Inspector Gilnockie's setting me to asking round the village, seeing who was out and about yesterday afternoon. Other than me, that is."

Alasdair nodded. "If you'll hang on a tick, we'll come along and ask a few questions as well. The daylight's getting away, and," he added to Jean, "Tina's not."

Getting away. What a concept. "Great idea. Let's get our coats."

Leaving Thomson waiting in the front porch, they jog-trotted up the stairs, pausing very briefly at the tripping stane and the tremor of Seonaid's incorporeal being.

While Alasdair unlocked the door of the Charlie suite, Jean took a second look at Seonaid's tapestry. The colors were faded and the human shapes, folk-arty primitive, were rather lost amid exuberant trees, tumultuous waves, and fanciful ruins…no. Those ruins weren't fanciful at all, but were those of old Dunasheen, rendered by the authoritative hand of someone who knew them well. Was that a tiny figure plummeting from the tower? The thread was a bit frayed.

Unfrayed, in the foreground, stood Fionn, the once-mighty Irish warrior with his battered armor and gray beard, and Grainne, his much younger betrothed, with flowing red hair, and Diarmuid, Fionn's follower, tall, muscular, and suitably noble-browed. She was offering Diarmuid a cup of love potion, magicking him into eloping with her.

Interesting, how Seonaid had chosen to illustrate that particular moment of the legend, not Grainne and Diarmuid's subsequent adventures or his death at Fionn's hands. Interesting that she'd chosen that legend at all. Had she seen herself as Grainne—or as Isolde, in a related story—living a tale of high romance, of a passion so strong it swept all before it and therefore justified everything from ambiguity to outright sin? But Grainne had survived to tell her tale. Seonaid had not. Neither had Rory, for that matter.

Jean ran her fingertips down the decorative border of the tapestry, feeling the soft nubble of stitches and stirring up several dust motes. She'd have to ask Rebecca to lay her hands on it, see if she sensed any lingering emotion, be it joy or melancholy or…what did teenage Seonaid feel as she stitched the tapestry? Destiny unfurling and tragedy looming? Or had she merely been caught by the high romance of the era—ruined castles, brooding hillsides, strong emotion—oblivious to playing with forces beyond her control?

Diana knew what she'd taken on with Colin. She was stitching together a human being, not a myth whose knots had been loosened by time and repetition.

The tapestry rippled and one end flapped in the draft escaping the open door of the Charlie suite. "Well then," Alasdair called, "your moggie's made—"

A woman's cry of terror sliced the stillness like the sudden slash of a razor blade, sharp and short. A heavy thud seemed to come from everywhere at once, their own room, the turnpike stair, the vacant, secret corners of the house.

This time Jean didn't have to stop and ask. *Tina!*

SEVENTEEN

JEAN'S HEART JOLTED into her throat, then dropped into her stomach. The murderer, he'd gotten to her, too—a kitchen knife, a letter opener, no need for a antique dirk... Alasdair shot out of their room, slammed the door, locked it, ran for the stairs with Jean on his heels.

Feet up, she ordered herself. *Feet down. Breathe.*

Doors crashed, footsteps pounded, dogs barked, their frenzy muffled by stone walls. A voice echoed up the stairwell, W.P.C. McCrummin shouting, "She's gone out the window!"

"Out the window?" demanded Alasdair.

He and Jean rushed back down the stairs—no stane, no Seonaid, no time—and met McCrummin at the landing. Every freckle on her face bounced in agitation, her expressions flipping from alarm to bafflement, from chagrin to anger. "I was reading a magazine in the sitting room. She said she was having a nap and went into the bedroom. Not half an hour on, she screamed. I went running in. She'd tied her linens to the window frame and crawled out the window and she fell."

Jean gave her head a quick shake, rearranging her preconceptions. Not an attack. An escape.

"Stupid woman, that's the sort of thing only works in films." Alasdair led the two women jostling down to the ground floor. "Famous last words, eh? Tina's not getting away, I was saying. Bloody hell!"

Outside, in the cold sunlight, Jean, Alasdair, and McCrummin converged with six or seven people. Between their shifting bodies a life-sized doll lay crumpled on the gravel of the parking area—feet in brown boots and legs in brown pants lying akimbo, the leopard-skin coat like a pile of rags, one hand pitifully small and white, palm up, red-painted nails torn, arm twisted backward at an unnatural angle. The blond curls flopped like old straw, leaking crimson.

Jean saw Greg lying on the beach, blood trailing away toward the sea like an element seeking its primeval origins. Tina's face, too, was turned away, toward the garden wall.

Thomson knelt beside her, one hand tucked between her curls and her collar. "She's breathing. I saw her falling, I couldna catch her, she came down that fast."

"If you'd tried catching her, lad," Alasdair said, each word a pellet of sleet, "you'd be lying there as well."

McCrummin knelt beside Thomson, her hand on his forearm, although Jean couldn't tell who was steadying whom. Police radios staticked and phones chirped. Gilnockie and Young pelted through the front door. Young, carrying a first-aid kit, skidded to her knees beside Thomson and McCrummin. Gilnockie stopped below the windows of the library, the dim shape of the Christmas tree arching over his head.

His eyes closed. His lips moved silently. Going over procedures, Jean thought. And then, when he looked up and made the sign of the cross—forehead, breast, shoulders—she realized he'd been praying. For Tina's recovery, no doubt, but also for explanations. More power to him.

Fergie thudded out onto the gravel, Rab and Nancy just behind. "What's happened now?" he asked, and answered his own question. "Oh. No. No."

Diana and Colin stepped out of the house behind him, hands clasped tightly, her face filled with dismay, his with stubborn pride. Fergie glanced at them, away, and then back, in a classic double-take. Spinning around, he reeled toward

Tina, shaking his head and wringing his hands as though trying to stop events from running through his fingers.

Alasdair stopped Fergie's reel with a hand on his shoulder, so firm his fingers made dents in Fergie's sweater. Not a Vulcan nerve-pinch, as much as Fergie might like to be anesthetized right now. The gesture was the British, *buck up, mustn't complain, get on with it,* lacking only the cup of tea and the biscuit.

The Finlays stood close together, Nancy's red mouth turned down, Rab's eyebrows beetling. "No good," he said. "No good's coming of it all—bleeding Aussies, should've stayed home, got no call turning up here."

"Rab!" Nancy's voice snapped like a whip. "We canna sort things to suit ourselves. Have a care for Fergus and puir wee Di."

Rab looked down at his legs and feet, like tree stumps, and thrust his hands into his pockets.

Inside, the dogs barked. Pritchard's voice angrily shushed them. Where were the Krums? Probably in the village. Their car was still parked by the garden wall.

Jean realized she was standing with her hands pressed flat against her chest, holding her heart in place, while temblors ran through her limbs and mulligatawny soup roiled in her stomach. She turned her eyes to the sky, to the bare branches of the trees, to the windows of the Queen suite, two glass panels pushed out, one gaping open. A long, thick, white strip of fabric was knotted around the stone separating the two, and now swayed gently as a hangman's rope. Had Tina been able to grasp the linen at all? Had she fallen straight from the windowsill? With the high ceilings of the ground floor, she had fallen twenty or twenty-five feet. Even Skye's springy soil had proved no cushion.

Above that window, the bay window of the Charlie suite angled gracefully out from the facade. Dougie's small gray shape sat against the glass, looking down curiously. Something hung from his mouth that was too small to be a mouse. That's right, Alasdair had said something about *her* cat. He was *her* cat when he decided to, say, lick the butter dish.

Right now, he was welcome to butter dishes, pillows, whatever.

Dr. Irvine came running up the driveway, every limb pumping, his bag swinging. Gasping for breath, he shouldered through the crowd and knelt beside Tina.

And somewhere a phone rang, bleat-bleat, bleat-bleat… Alasdair jumped, plunged his hand into his pocket, glanced at the phone's tiny display. "Miranda. Fine timing."

"Here." Jean took the phone, warm from its nest near Alasdair's body, and held it to her ear. "Hello, Miranda."

"Good afternoon to you," returned Miranda. "How's the latest case coming along?"

"Funny you should ask." Plodding back to the shelter of the porch, Jean filled her in and reached a full stop. No more words. No more ideas. Just get on with it, keep on keeping on.

"Well then," Miranda said, with her usual discretion offering no suggestions. "I do not know if this is helping you, but I've heard from an acquaintance at the New South Wales MacLeod society. He knows—knew—Greg MacLeod, as Greg was using their records to research an ancestor, stonemason named Tormod who left Skye for Sydney in 1822. That's the one he was going on about, is it?"

"Yes, it is," said Jean. "Greg said he'd been transported for murder, although we've learned since that the story isn't quite that straightforward."

"It's not that, no. The society chap is saying Tormod wasn't a convict at all; he was a soldier, sent to guard the prisoners in the penal colony."

"A soldier?" Yes, taking the king's shilling, joining up, was as good a way to get out of town and start over gain as any. So why had Greg blithely claimed a convict ancestor? Because it made a better story for his customers? As Jean herself had said, being a descendant of one of the early convicts had become trendy, Down Under. Many of them had done little more than steal a loaf of bread, whereas some of their soldier-guards had been brutal, even sadistic. "Nothing like a little historical editing to fit your prejudices. The prisoners are the stuff of romance now. Whatever happened to the appeal of a man in a uniform?"

"It's not gone away," said Miranda. "Not if the look in your eye when you see the sentries outside the Castle's any indication."

Jean tried to smile at that, but the corners of her mouth seemed tacked in place.

"It was later on in life," Miranda went on, "that Tormod went back to working in stone, overseeing some of the work on Government House, for example. Emigrating likely worked out better for him and his Aussie family than biding in Skye."

"It's all a matter of perspective," Jean said. A police van rolled around the side of the building. Two constables leaped out and removed a stretcher from the back. She hoped it wasn't the same stretcher that they'd used to carry Greg's body up from the beach, but then, Tina could hardly complain, not after her particular version of a self-inflicted wound. "Thanks, Miranda. Every little bit of information helps."

"You're welcome. I'll soon be away with Duncan for the Hogmanay celebrations. If there's anything else, leave a message."

"If there's anything else?" Jean quelled the caustic giggle welling up in her throat. That's no doubt what Fergie was thinking. *If there's anything else, just shoot me.*

"Then try having yourself a good one, auld lang syne and all."

"We'll try. I'll keep you posted. Happy New Year to you too." Jean snapped the phone shut.

Under Irvine's direction, the police people placed Tina on the stretcher and the stretcher in the back of the van. He scrambled in after her. The nearest full-service hospital would be in Portree. If her injuries were bad enough, she'd be taken by air ambulance to Inverness or Glasgow. They wouldn't be interviewing her again any time soon. If ever.

She must have been terrified, to go out the window like that.

The van drove away. A glint of sun ricocheted from its back window and smacked Jean in the face. She receded into the entrance hall and stood beside the brass-bound kist, watching each face as everyone trudged past. No one looked guilty, no one looked pleased, every expression betrayed some variety of shock or distress.

"You're quite sure Tina was alone when she fell?" Jean asked McCrummin.

"Aye, she was that, she was not pushed, if that's what you're thinking."

"I'm thinking she was threatened, although probably not by an actual person, in person—unless there a secret panel in the fireplace or something."

A queasy half-smile tilted one side of McCrummin's mouth. "You're joking."

Not entirely, but Jean let McCrummin go on her way. From afar rose the bay of the reporters at the front gate, scenting more blood.

With one long, lost look over his shoulder, then another after Diana and Colin, Fergie marched rather than walked around the corner toward his office. Rab and Nancy, sharing more or less the same frown, went the same route. Gilnockie stopped Young in the doorway. "Where's Pritchard?"

Young's mouth opened and shut and she cast a swift glance around. "He followed us from the incident room."

"I heard him shouting at the dogs a few minutes ago," Jean said.

"Find the man," Gilnockie ordered, and Young vanished down the corridor.

Alasdair walked into the entrance hall beside Thomson, who said to Gilnockie, "That's me away, then, sir."

Distractedly, Gilnockie assented, then drifted after Young toward the incident room.

Alasdair took the cell phone from Jean's hand. "Let's have us a look at Tina's things. Sanjay, we'll catch you up in the village."

"Aye, sir." Thomson said, and closed the door behind him.

Alone again. For what that was worth. Each foot heavy as clay, Jean walked up the stairs beside Alasdair and told him what Miranda had said.

He considered, every line in his face flexing and then loosing—she could almost hear him ordering himself, *Focus, man, focus*. "Interesting. With nothing left for him here, and Norman set on revenge, Tormod went to be a sodger, to paraphrase Burns."

"You don't suppose Fergie really is descended from Tormod the mason rather than Norman the laird, do you? I mean, Fergie said Norman accepted Seonaid's son as his. Even if someone could prove otherwise, and that's not likely, would there be any legal ramifications?" Jean started up the second-floor corridor. "If there's an illegitimate birth, then the title and property would revert to, I don't know, the descendants of some cousin of old Red Norman's. Red Norman. Makes him sound like a communist rather than a minor aristocrat."

Alasdair managed a scorched snicker. "In other words, did Fergie or Diana murder Greg meaning to prevent him claiming the title and the estate? Or is Lionel Pritchard, say, the secret heir, aiming to come into his own? Jean, your mind can be positively Byzantine at times."

"You say that like it's a bad thing," she replied. "And yes, you're right, that's too complicated a scenario. But there's a lot about Greg we don't know."

"And Tina as well." Alasdair paused below another Fergie MacDonald creation, a version of da Vinci's *Last Supper.* Here the central figure was the Sphinx. His companions were Easter Island statues, a chubby, smiling Buddha, an Aztec in full feather, and the March Hare. The tablecloth was MacDonald tartan, scattered with candy wrappers and greasy newspapers wrapping fish and chips. Through the arches in the background gleamed the rings of Saturn, crossed by human footprints.

"And then there's Fergie's mind. Makes yours look…" Alasdair's voice ran down and out.

"Normal," concluded Jean. "Extra normal."

The door of the Queen suite stood ajar, presumably the way McCrummin had left it when she ran out. Jean pushed it open.

The Queen suite wasn't as spacious as the Charlie, but it was appointed as nicely, with amenities ranging from fresh, colorful fabrics to chipped bric-a-brac. If you were going to be under house arrest, Jean thought, this was the way to go. Then again, with the way Tina had gone, maybe not.

Together they quartered the sitting room, noting a ceramic dish holding MacDonald business cards, a set of golf clubs propped in the corner, a copy of *Country Life* lying in front of a wingback chair. Alasdair inspected the dishcloth-shrouded contents of a tea tray. "Tina's not touched her lunch."

"I bet she told Nancy she was feeling better and she'd be down for dinner just to get rid of her," Jean said.

"I'll accept that wager," said a slick male voice.

Jean and Alasdair whirled toward the bedroom doorway. Lionel Pritchard emerged, a smug smile attached as firmly to his face as his moustache. He held out a piece of paper. "You're looking for this, I expect."

Alasdair's narrow-eyed glare would have frozen anyone else in his tracks, but it slipped off Pritchard's smirk and shattered on the threadbare rug. He snatched the paper from Pritchard's hand. Jean leaned in to look.

The printed itinerary gave flight numbers and times from Townsville through Brisbane and Kuala Lumpur to London. Across the bottom, in black, jagged letters like motes of Klingonese, were handwritten the words, "Here you are, Tina. The holiday of a lifetime. Don't worry packing your nighties, LOL. CU. Greg."

Laughing Out Loud. See You. That answered that question. Tina had said that Greg used his phone to text, but she'd lied about recognizing the writing on the card. So who had he written to? And had the card been enough to set the appointment, so that his phone call was irrelevant?

Alasdair's face petrified. Barely moving his lips, he told Pritchard, "You wasted no time getting here, did you? Where did you find this?"

"In the pocket of Tina's suitcase. Or the suitcase filled with women's clothing and cosmetics. I know you detectives like things to be properly witnessed." Pritchard's smirk spread into a moist, wolfish grin. His other hand rose from his side. "And this was in the man's suitcase."

Alasdair seized the large brown envelope from Pritchard's fingers. The mailing label on the outside was that of Dunasheen Castle, addressed to Greg MacLeod on Ross River Road, Townsville, QLD, Australia. Inside were a letter printed on ordinary white paper and a receipt for a Hogmanay package. Jean's brows rose at the price—she knew she and Alasdair were getting a deal, but what a deal it was. The least they could do was earn their room, board, and double round of festivities by lifting the ten-ton block of murder from Fergie's back.

Alasdair read the letter aloud. "October Seventeenth. My dear Mr. MacLeod, my daughter and I will be delighted to welcome you and your wife to Dunasheen Castle for Hogmanay. It will also be a great pleasure to display the Crusader Coffer with an eye to your possible purchase. Safe journey. Sincerely yours, Fergus MacDonald. P.S. Enclosed are several business cards for your friends and business associates."

"Crusader Coffer?" Jean repeated. "Not that kist in the entrance hall, that's medieval or even younger. The chest across from our door is Middle Eastern, but it's too new to be crusader-era, probably not even a hundred years old." Not that that had stopped Scott Krum from giving it the onceover, she added silently. And then, "Oh, Fergie means—"

Alasdair shot a warning glance across her bow and she snapped her mouth shut on the rest of her sentence: *The artifact that he's been teasing us with for two days now.*

Pritchard's black eyes switched from face to face. "Just as I told you, I didn't write the note on the back of that card. It was MacLeod. He had his eye on one of Fergus's special treasures."

"And you nipped up here quick as may be," said Lesley Young from the outer door, "while Mrs. MacLeod was likely dying on the ground outside, more concerned with saving your own skin, eh?"

Pritchard spread his arms wide. His motion released another wave of sweaty, musk-ox aroma. "It's a fair cop."

"Here!" Young snapped her fingers as though she was summoning a waiter, and W.P.C. McCrummin stepped up to the door. "Take Mr. Pritchard downstairs. Have a care, he's slippy one."

"I'd never slip away from a woman in uniform," he said. "Orla, wasn't it?"

McCrummin's freckles hardened. "Come along, sir," she said between her teeth, and escorted Pritchard into the hall and away.

Jean stared after him, imagining him getting his comeuppance when Gilnockie arrested him for murder. *If,* not *when,* she corrected herself. *You had to follow the investigation where it led.*

Young grabbed for the papers in Alasdair's hands, saying "Police procedure, sir. Inspector Gilnockie's asked me to secure the scene."

Alasdair let the papers go rather than have them torn in half, but this time his glare hit home. Young ducked, held the papers defensively before her chest, and retreated.

Jean didn't waste her breath pointing out that Gilnockie would just as soon have Alasdair inside as outside the scene. With a grimace she didn't care if Young interpreted as a smile or not, she backpedaled toward the door and down the hall, up the stairs and to their own room, feeling Alasdair's chilly breath on the back of her neck the entire way.

Again he unlocked the door, door-locking being a nicety that hadn't occurred to McCrummin as she ran out of the Queen suite. But another distaff police person was on Jean's mind. "How dare Young throw your own line about police procedure back in your face? Does she have the social skills of a turnip or what?"

"Law enforcement's not about social skills," Alasdair returned.

"The heck it isn't! What about catching more flies with honey and all that?"

"Is that how I went catching you, then, with honey? I do not think so."

"You caught me with something like whiskey, sharp at first, but smooth going down."

"Right." Alasdair opened the door and stood with his hand

on the old-fashioned latch, the crevice between his eyebrows closer to a crevasse. "Greg wrote the card. Likely he sent it to the killer."

"Who then put the card in Diana's pocket? Why? To implicate her? To implicate Colin?"

He growled, "Assuming Diana herself's not implicated."

"Yes, let's assume that," Jean told him. "And what the hell is up with Fergie and this Crusader Coffer…" She suddenly saw past Alasdair into the sitting room. Bits of white and blue fluff lay on the rug, drifting in the sneaky little drafts playing along the floor. "That's right. Dougie."

Alasdair looked around. "Oh aye, your moggie's made a mess of something. Feathers?"

"I bet he killed one of those stuffed birds." Jean followed the trail into the bedroom. "Funny, though, the feather bits are only the two colors…oh boy."

They'd had a visitor at some point over the last couple of hours, one who had probably placed on top of the bed the dusty old hat box that was now lying beside it, surrounded by macerated blue and white feathers.

"Dougie?" Jean called. "Here, kitty, kitty!"

Of the two rounded lumps beneath the bed, one, she saw, was a cracked commode, called in her part of the world a thunder jug. The other lump opened its golden eyes. *You rang?*

That white bit at the tasseled edge of the rug wasn't a bit of feather but a business card. She picked it up. *Fergus MacDonald and Diana MacDonald…* She flipped it over. "'I found them. Here you are. F.M.' Fergie found what?"

Alasdair knelt beside the hatbox, shoving aside a striped lid and streamers of torn tissue paper. "A mouse once gnawed himself a wee hole here, after a nesting place. He left enough scent to attract Dougie's attentions. And then…aha. Here we are." He held up two tam o'shanters, their badges tarnished, their hackles reduced to fragile spines.

"Dougie!" Jean exclaimed. "Those are Fergie's bonnets!"

"One Cameron Highlanders—that's Fergie Mor's. My dad's is identical. The other is Royal Scots. Pontius Pilate's guard, Fergie's fond of saying. It's this chap's dirk killed Greg. That's why Fergie looked them out—he's taken to heart that bit about not knowing what's important.... What's this?" Alasdair probed delicately at the interior of one bonnet, producing a crinkle and a musty smell.

Pressing up against his side, Jean saw that the band of the bonnet was lined with newspaper, a deep yellowish-brown with decay. "Nothing like a do-it-yourself repair job."

Alasdair managed to pull one edge of the paper from behind the sweat-stained band without it disintegrating in his hand. It was the top of a page, the name of the newspaper making a faint track like an antidiluvian fossil's: *Townsville Bulletin.* Just below Jean could barely make out the beginning of a headline. "Australian troops advance..."

She looked at Alasdair just as he looked at her, wild surmise flying from mind to mind and back like a boomerang. Jean said, "We've got to take that photo down from the dining room wall and see if the dirk guy's name is on the back. No, you don't know what's important, and by this time..."

"I'm thinking there's nothing that's not to do with the murder."

Hastily they gathered up the remains of the hackles, piled them, the bonnets, the scrap of newspaper, and the tissue back into the box. They affixed the lid and shut the lot in the wardrobe. "Get your coat," Alasdair said, "and we'll have a look at the photo on our way out. Respecting you, my lad, scolding's no good, is it?"

Dougie blinked and yawned.

"What a mighty hunter," said Jean. "You went after a mouse and landed two birds."

The clock in the sitting room struck two-thirty as they walked out the door, leading Jean to ponder relativity, how the last twenty-four hours had lasted a week, whereas her average day at the office lasted about five minutes.

And there was some sort of spectral relativity as well, she thought when they stepped past the tripping stane on the turnpike stair. She was getting so used to walking through Seonaid's paranormal resonance that she no longer noticed it any more than she noticed the pink feather boa on the suit of armor or the mistletoe hanging from the archway.

The ground floor was eerily quiet, considering the number of people who were tucked away in various corners of the house. The dining room table was set with the tree-people candlesticks ranged along a boxwood garland, and with all the surgically gleaming cutlery and gold-rimmed dishes and crystal of a posh, traditional party. Now each side of the table sported three chairs. Rab and Nancy had taken Tina at her word, then, and set a place for her too.

Jean looked toward the swinging door into the pantry. It shivered a bit, leaking bits of dialog, Rab's gruff lilt rising and falling in counterpoint to what sounded like Clint Eastwood's gruffer drawl.

Alasdair lifted the photo of the three soldiers down from the wall, and, using the tip of the corkscrew lying ready on the sideboard, pried off the backing. He and Jean touched heads over the faded words written on the back in a mashed-thistle hand similar to Fergie's own.

Allan Cameron, Fergus MacDonald, Kenneth MacLeod. 1944.

EIGHTEEN

JEAN CLOSED HER eyes and opened them again, but the words didn't change. "Kenneth MacLeod."

"So it says." Alasdair's sturdy forefinger touched the letters as though to make sure. "Greg's brother's name is Kenneth."

"Well yeah, but a lot of people are named MacLeod. Michel Campbell-Reid told me once that there are so many little boys here on Skye named Donnie MacLeod that teachers assign them middle initials according to when they enrolled. Donnie A. MacLeod, Donnie B. MacLeod, you know."

"We're past finding coincidences." He turned the photo over. The yellowed face of his own father looked up at him, gaze even, mouth firm—Allan had been the beta model of Alasdair's Ice Prince. But Alasdair was focused on Kenneth. "This chap's the right age to be Greg's father."

"Kenneth senior, sure. But wouldn't an Aussie join one of the Anzac regiments?"

"Fergie's saying his dad and Kenneth were at school together. He likely joined up here."

"So in the thirties young Aussies were sent 'home,' for some extra polish? I bet Kenneth was tickled to meet someone from his family's ancestral stomping grounds." Beneath the photographic tarnish, Kenneth's blunt, square face, compressed in a frown, revealed nothing more than a vague similarity to Greg. If this is Greg's father, then he wasn't just getting newspapers from home, he obviously went back and engendered at least two kids. "How old was Greg, do you know? Over sixty? Didn't Fergie say this Kenneth was killed in the war?"

"Which war? I'm thinking the Royal Scots served in Korea as well."

"Ah, yeah, that would do it."

From the kitchen came the sound of gunshots and sirens and a whirring that was probably a food processor. The aroma of onions sizzling in butter wafted through the air and Jean's mouth watered.

Unmoved—impressive, how men could disconnect stomach from brain—Alasdair tucked the disassembled frame into the sideboard and started for the door. The delectable odor followed them down the hall to the incident room, where Gilnockie and Young were, judging by her frustrated and his aloof expressions, still struggling to climb the greased pole of Pritchard. Instead of joining in, Alasdair beckoned Gilnockie to the door.

Gilnockie turned the photo over and back again while Alasdair explained, and at last summarized in his own words, "So the man might have been killed with his own father's dirk? That's no coincidence, that's a bit personal."

Murder is always personal. But Jean knew what Gilnockie meant, clan feuds, arguments festering for centuries. "We already know that Greg came here for more than genealogical research."

"And Tina will not be answering questions, not just yet," concluded Alasdair. "What's her condition?"

"Not so serious as it first appeared. Broken arm and a mild concussion." Gilnockie eyed the photo again, the three faces preserved in time. "I'll have my folk contact Greg and Tina's family in Australia, see if we can make any sense of this."

Yes, let the official forces do it, Jean thought. She wouldn't be able to raise Miranda now anyway, not with the full spate of Hogmanay under way in Edinburgh.

Gilnockie stopped to deliver the photo and instructions to a minion before returning to the table where Pritchard was ignoring Young's belligerent gaze.

"You didn't," Jean told Alasdair, "suggest that he question Fergie again."

"No. I reckon that job's on my head. Every time I think we've moved the investigation away from Fergie it circles back round again."

"If not to Fergie then to Diana, whose job one is protecting him and Dunasheen." Jean pretended not to see Alasdair wince at that.

They walked down the corridor past the clan prints to Fergie's office and found the door shut. Music penetrated the dense wooden panels, Hugh Munro's fiddle tracing the clear melody and the grace notes of "Peace and Plenty." In spite of herself, Jean smiled, comforted.

Alasdair raised his hand to knock, then, with his own smile of more rue than comfort, let it drop. "Here's us away to the village. Fergie will keep."

They wended their way to the entrance hall, and were donning their coats when Diana passed along the corridor carrying a tray of glasses toward the Great Hall, her face set in a stern "the show must go on" expression. Close behind her came Colin toting an armload of logs, his face unreadable. Neither acknowledged Jean and Alasdair's presence. Neither Jean nor Alasdair asked for acknowledgment.

They were several steps into the thin, chill sunlight, when the phone rang in Alasdair's pocket. Checking the screen, he answered, "Hello, Rebecca," then responded to her greeting with, "Night's falling, the murderer's still at large, we're in it up to the oxters. And you? Ah, good to hear things are going to plan in town. Here's Jean."

Making a face at him, Jean took the phone. "Hey, Rebecca.

Never mind the bit about being in it up to the armpits, I think we're in it up to our chins."

Rebecca said, "I hope your 'it' is the wedding. Favors, flowers, toasts, you know, all the happiest day of your life stresses?"

"Not exactly," replied Jean, and added to herself, *Buck up, mustn't complain.*

Discreetly, Rebecca moved on. "Michael says you're interested in the Bible History Research Society, something to do with your investigation."

"Well, not the BHRS specifically, but our Aussie victim's relation to it."

Alasdair looked around from his perusal of land, sea, sky, and the elliptical, golden-ivory face of a rising room. Jean tilted the phone so he, too, could hear Rebecca's digitized voice.

"That's what we were thinking," Rebecca said. "I've just now seen a press release from the BHRS, announcing the purchase of an inscription with Pontius Pilate's name, only the second one ever found."

"Really!" Jean's antennae twitched like Dougie's whiskers.

"Except this one's complete. It says Pilate is a procurator, which is what Tacitus calls him and what we were all taught in Sunday school, not a prefect, like the 1961 inscription does. Six of one, half a dozen of the other, in terms of his political functions, but an interesting discrepancy."

"It sure is. And the BHRS purchased this darn near priceless item from…"

"…Australian antiquities dealer Greg MacLeod, who meant to display it in his new museum. The deal went down a couple of months ago, but the BHRS is saying they've just now had the inscription authenticated, not that they're normally believing in authenticating mechanisms such as peer review."

"They never let geologists analyze what was supposed to be a bit of petrified wood from Noah's Ark," said Jean.

"Nope. However, this time they're saying they've dated bits of dust and debris in the interstices of the inscription to the Roman Era and Palestine."

"Really?"

"I'm guessing they've released the news because of Greg's death, either hoping to piggyback on the publicity or as a tribute. Hard to tell without tapping their phones."

Alasdair angled his own phone closer to his mouth. "Where'd Greg come by such a thing?"

"He said it was discovered in the Holy Land by a family member who'd done a tour of duty there. It's a small piece of basalt, chipped off a larger monument, a dedication of some sort. The Roman equivalent of 'Pontius Pilate was here.' Is that sensible to you?"

"Kenneth," said Alasdair. "Greg's father. If I'm remembering aright, the Royal Scots served in Palestine just before the war."

"When trade in antiquities was legal under the British mandate," Rebecca added.

Jean shook her head as again shapes fell through her vision, this time imaginary ones, tiny bits like the flecks of color in a kaleidoscope, not the definitive form of Kenneth MacLeod's dirk lying against a tombstone dedicated to a crusader.

Crusaders also brought home souvenirs. "Fergie was saying there used to be a Pilate inscription here at Dunasheen."

"Was he?" asked Alasdair.

"It was at dinner last night. You were talking to Irvine."

Rebecca's voice said, "An inscription at Dunasheen? How many Pilate inscriptions are floating around, anyway"

"Good question." Jean stared unfocussed toward the facade of the house—someone had removed Tina's makeshift rope from the window. Alasdair stared unfocussed at the gravel beneath his feet.

Then Rebecca said, "That's given you food for thought. Speaking of food, we're not going out into the madness tonight; Michael's sister and her family are coming to us. Four children, that's madness enough."

Jean pulled up her train of thought and changed tracks. This might be her first Hogmanay—she'd just missed last year's—but she knew the vocabulary. "You never let Michael first-foot, do you? He's too fair."

"He's usually bad luck," joked Rebecca. "No, Maddy's husband is our first-foot, he's black Welsh and will do nicely. Besides, he always brings a single malt to die for."

"Please don't. Happy New Year, and see you Saturday," Jean said, reminding herself, when, not if.

Alasdair muttered something appropriate, and restored the now-mute phone to his pocket. His gaze, wider rather than narrower than usual, met Jean's. "The thot's plickening," she told him, shook out her tongue and tried again. "The plots thickening."

"It was quite thick enough to begin."

They started down the driveway, Jean lifting her feet, throwing her shoulders back, raising her chin. The cobalt blue of the sky was now diluted, washed with fragile shades of peach, plum, and pink. Darkness gathered in the north and east, but far to the southwest the setting sun painted skeins of cloud with gold dust and cast glimmering gauze over the jagged edge of the Black Cuillins. The cold air was scented with peat smoke, silvery-gray strands rising vertically from a dozen village chimneys and dissipating into the dusk. "It's a pretty evening. Early, but pretty."

Alasdair's face tilted upward in agreement, and the light eased the whetted angles of his features—until they neared Dunasheen's wrought-iron gates. Then he saw the two media vans parked outside, and the camera-carrying figures camped around them. Most of the reporters had hared off after Tina, then, as well as back to civilization for the holiday. Still, his features hardened again.

Snapping to attention, two constables opened the gates wide enough for Alasdair and Jean to slip through. The waiting reporters surged forward. "Inspector Cameron, Inspector Cameron, how are you getting on with this new case?"

Great. He hadn't been retired long enough to fall off the media event horizon.

"It's not my case," he replied, pushing through.

"It's Miss Fairbairn, isn't it? Are you assisting the police in this case as well?"

There was someone with much too good a memory. With her best inscrutable smile, making no eye contact, Jean dodged the extended microphones and lengthened her stride to match Alasdair's, past several rundown cottages that had once housed estate workers and onto the main—and pretty much only—street of Kinlochroy.

The white-stuccoed, gray-slated buildings had a pared-down look, square and plain, with narrow eaves like spinsters pulling in their skirts. Even the signs marking several shops and a couple of guesthouses were simple wooden boards, not a one of them swinging dramatically out over the street. In the summer, flowerpots and window boxes might brighten the village, but not now. And perhaps not ever. The place seemed to Jean to be modest and tidy not just from an urge to cleanliness but from the need to use up and wear out, to make do and mend.

A child crossed the street without bothering to look, a video game bleeping in her hand. Two more whizzed by on skateboards. An elderly couple left the Co-op grocery store, carrier bags swinging. Small cars were parked along—and on—the sidewalks. Boats bobbed in the harbor, a bulbous

GPS unit squatting atop every superstructure, just as every rooftop boasted an antenna or satellite dish.

The town's war memorial was a granite Celtic cross. In the fading light, Jean could barely read the names carved into the main plinth, dating from 1914–18, let alone those from 1939–45. The latter list had been embossed on a bronze plaque and affixed to the base of the cross when World War I, The War to End All Wars, didn't.

"There's a fair puckle of MacLeods and MacDonalds," said Alasdair. "No surprise there. The lads from these small towns joined up together and died together. There's no place in the U.K. that did not lose the flower of its youth."

That was unusually poetic for him. But then, Jean, too, could almost hear distant pipes playing the lament, "The Flowers o' the Forest," for soldiers of more than the twentieth century who had never returned home. She could definitely hear the grating shriek of gulls scavenging along the waterfront and whirling overhead in an airborne scrum.

Shivering, she turned back toward the windows of the town, some dark behind their lace curtains while others glowed with warmth. "Over here," she said, and led Alasdair to the door she'd spotted yesterday, across the street from the Flora MacDonald pub.

This sign read *Kinlochroy Bookshop and Café*. One of the windowpanes displayed not only posters of local events, but also a blue Tourist Information sticker and a computer-printed notice: *Heritage Museum*. The moment Jean stepped inside, her glasses steamed up, leaving her to smell books, coffee, and scones, and hear a mellow voice singing Burns' "Green Grow the Rushes, O."

"Time for a snack," she told Alasdair as her vision cleared. "Dinner's late and we'll be up until midnight or past."

"Oh aye, that we will." He stepped briskly across to a counter displaying trays of pastry and sandwiches and consulted with the teenage lass behind it.

Several tables and chairs were grouped at the front of the shop. One was occupied by two older ladies chatting quietly over a pot of tea. Three young men sat around another, their outdoor garments, muddy rucksacks, and spread of soup, sandwiches, scones, and soft drinks declaring them to be hikers momentarily gone to ground.

Opposite the café counter stood a second one, this in the style of a library circulation desk. A rack of ghost stories, Dunasheen guidebooks, and various tourist pamphlets propped up one side, no doubt the collection that had drawn Dakota's attention yesterday. On a counter behind the desk sat a framed black and white photo, a soldier wearing full kit, from hackle to kilt, beside a woman dressed in the extravagance of an Indian wedding outfit—embroidered veil, jewelry, flowers, sari in elaborate folds. By comparison, a Western white wedding seemed plain and dull as a saltine.

Beyond the desk stood shelves teeming with books new and old, a display case, and a table topped by two computers. The woman bending over one looked up, dark eyes sparking at the sight of customers. Thick black curls sprang from her high forehead and her comfortably upholstered figure was draped by a flower-embroidered cardigan and a denim skirt, its hem hanging above fuzzy wool socks and sneakers. Her golden complexion plumped above the dazzling white crescent of a smile. "Good afternoon. Can I help you?"

Jean returned the smile in kind. "Hello. We're ah…" *Investigating a murder* might be a bit abrupt. "We're interested in your Heritage Museum."

"Yon case of odds and ends is it, though we've got census records and the like on file. Looking out your genealogy, are you?"

"Well, not ours specifically. I'm Jean Fairbairn and that's my fiancé, Alasdair Cameron. We're staying at the castle."

The woman stepped forward. "It's yourselves, is it then? Sanjay was saying you'd be stopping in. I'm Brenda O'Donnell, his aunt."

"I see the resemblance," Jean told Brenda, and with relief that P.C. Thomson had already covered the preliminaries. "He's a fine young man. You must be very proud of him."

"He'll do," Brenda said, her beam belying the neutrality of her words. Then she sobered. "He's telling me the puir murdered man was Greg MacLeod, and now his wife's been carried away to hospital."

"I'm afraid so, yes."

Alasdair paced across the polished wooden floor, his hands holding a tray rattling with metal pots and earthenware dishes, his features set inquisitively. Jean made introductions and Brenda swept the tray from his grasp, placing it on the table closest to the bookshelves. "Here you are. I'll sit with you, shall I?"

"Please," said Alasdair, and with his courtliest manners seated both women before sitting himself.

He'd chosen a cheese scone and a piece of millionaire's shortbread. As though butter and sugar-rich shortbread alone wasn't enough, some fertile Scottish mind—or tongue—had come up with the idea of embellishing hearty slabs of it with layers of caramel and chocolate. "Feeling your sweet tooth?" Jean murmured, and poured tea steaming into a pair of cups.

He doctored his with milk. "You're the one saying the climate justifies sugar and fat."

"The climate's good for Mum's curries as well," said Brenda. "But you're here asking about the puir murdered man, eh? He e-mailed me about the story of Tormod MacLeod and Seonaid MacDonald, Thomson that was."

"Your family's related to Seonaid?" Jean asked.

"Ah, everyone's related to everyone here."

And worldwide, just not quite so intimately. Around a toothsome morsel of scone Jean went on, "You told him the story, then, of Tormod being transported?"

"Tormod emigrated, no doubt of that, but likely he left of his own will after the scandal, the murder and all. Seems to be the story's changed round a bit in the telling."

"Most do, being stories." Alasdair bit into a piece of shortbread without needing to add, *And Greg knew it before ever coming here.*

His mouth being immobilized with caramel, Jean asked the next question. "Was Greg interested in anything beyond Tormod's story?"

"After that first message, he never spoke of it again, mostly asking the history of the house and the estate, how Fergie and Diana are getting on, that sort of thing. Making up his mind whether to visit, I'm thinking."

The parallel furrows along the tops of Alasdair's brows indicated he was thinking, too, and not necessarily about one of Fergie's sketches for sale at the book counter, of Diana as Titania, queen of Faerie. Clearing his mouth with a swig of tea, he asked, "Did Greg and his wife stop in here yesterday?"

"No, like as not they went straight on to the castle."

"And how are Fergie and Diana getting on, then?"

"Well now." Brenda leaned across the table, dropping her voice. "It's been said at the pub they're near skint, looking to sell more than a few valuables after the bank and Inland Revenue come howling like a wolf pack at the door. Look at the laird who was after selling off the Cuillins themselves so as to repair the castle's roof, and the one near Inverness selling his castle for a golf course and luxury time-shares. How the mighty have fallen, you could be saying, but I'll not. The lairds are ordinary folk like us anymore. Even the royals with their divorces, though they're not half wealthy, still."

"Tradition and economics make uneasy bedfellows." Jean thought of the application forms on Fergie's desk. A lot of other historic properties competed for available funding and corporate grants.

Alasdair muttered something about either historic Scotland or hysteric Scotland.

"Top off your cups?" Brenda hoisted the metal pot and poured tea, black as cola but twice as fragrant.

Jean ate a bite of the shortbread and floated away on the sugar rush.

"Have you seen any other strangers in town the last day or so?" asked Alasdair. "Other than the reporters."

"The reporters have been thick as midges, aye, but yesterday there was only the American family, the parents like film stars, ever so smart, and the child with the big eyes like a creature in a Disney film. Was I hearing the father right, he called her Dakota?"

"Aye, that's her name," said Alasdair.

"Fancy that." Shaking her head, Brenda went on, "Mind you, I'm here in the shop all day. Sanjay, now…"

"He's on it," Jean reassured her. Mulling over the art of naming children, she drained her tea and with her forefinger blotted up the last pastry crumbs.

Brenda pushed back from the table. "You're wanting a keek at the heritage display, are you? We've got nothing of Tormod's, but there's a miniature of Norman the Red as a child." She walked them to the long, glass-topped case.

On a blue fabric background lay a small copy of the Wilkie portrait of Seonaid. Beside it lay a miniature of a child about Dakota's age, his face propped like an egg on an intricately folded neckcloth and dark jacket. The tiny oval revealed nothing more than a set of human features, no clues to personality or passions. "What happened to Norman?" Jean asked.

"All the local folk reckoned he'd murdered his wife,"

replied Brenda, "but there was no one accusing him, with him being the laird. He sent his son away to school, shut himself up in Dunasheen Castle, and spent his remaining years alone, the place going to rack and ruin about his ears. When he died it's said there was no one to follow his coffin to his grave. Not like when puir Seonaid was buried, when folk came from miles away. A sad story, from start to finish."

"I'm not sure it's finished yet," Jean said.

Alasdair inspected the other contents of the case. A series of prints and photos leading from Norman to a young Fergie, his face less round but just as mild. Other photos of boats long sunk, buildings long crumbled, fishermen, farmers, and shepherds long dead. Postcards home from the world wars. A massive iron key that probably locked a dungeon. A very nice sketch of old Dunasheen, the signature "Fer McD" looking like a wilted thistle in one corner. The obligatory item once belonging to Flora MacDonald—in this case, a scrap of fabric from her petticoat.

What the Kinlochroy Heritage Museum didn't have, Jean noted, was the obligatory lock of hair from Bonnie Prince Charlie. If you collected all the hair in Scottish museums purported to be his, there'd be enough to stuff a mattress, like combining all the bits of the True Cross scattered around the world would build a structure the size of St. Giles Cathedral in Edinburgh.

She eyed a small, soot-stained bit of stone from the old church above the sea, and a nicely carved baby gargoyle from the new chapel. "Tormod's work?"

"Who's to say?" Brenda leaned over the glass, using a corner of her cardigan to polish away a sticky fingerprint.

Tormod's work. And who's to say whether Tormod had ever tried his hand at a mock Roman inscription, for the glory of God and the chapel, for the laird's collection of relics and souvenirs, or for his own descendants, late in life?

With a quirk of his eyebrow, Spock-style, Alasdair's gaze darted toward the gargoyle and back to Jean's. Beneath his breath and over Brenda's head, he said, "Convenient, that Greg would have stone bits to sell, with a stonemason in his ancestry. Though the dirt's dated it."

Brenda straightened. "Eh?"

"Some research we're working on," Jean told her in complete honesty.

Speaking of souvenirs, above the case hung a series of products—mouse pads, key chains, T-shirts—embossed with the MacDonald and MacLeod clan crests, the seaborne galley of the former coexisting in happy commercial proximity with the bull of the latter. Jean grinned at the legend *Leod, Preod, MacLeod* arranged in an arc above the crest and motto: *Hold Fast.* And those little chicken tracks were meant to be the clan plant badge, which was...

Juniper.

Yes, Jean thought, she'd just heard "juniper." A good thing she believed in synchronicity more than coincidence, where events were grouped not by cause but by meaning.

NINETEEN

JEAN TURNED ON Brenda. "Fergie says you've got the photos of the bones found in the garden near Dunasheen chapel. And the associated artifacts."

"Oh aye, so we do." Brenda stepped over to a nearby filing cabinet and dug around in a drawer.

"Ah, that," said Alasdair. "After yet another wild goose, are you?"

"Quack," Jean replied. "Or honk, or whatever geese say. Although this time I'm hoping to find one already cooked."

"Here you are." Brenda produced an antiquated portfolio and a scruffy cardboard box that had once held candy, and handed them to Jean. "This puir soul was loved by someone. Putting a name to him would be a good deed."

The front door opened and Sanjay Thomson made his entrance, every bit of insignia on his uniform shining. The two ladies and the hikers fell abruptly silent, their faces turning toward the emblem of authority. His smile brighter than any insignia, he called, "Auntie Brenda? Oh, hullo there, Mr. Cameron, Miss Fairbairn," and everyone went back to eating and drinking.

Brenda confided, "He stops by about four o'clock, most days. A young lad's needing his provender. I'll leave you with the evidence." Returning Sanjay's smile, she conducted him to the food counter. The teenage server colored prettily and switched her body language from upright professional to girlish flirt.

Suppressing something between a chuckle and a groan,

Alasdair plucked the box from Jean's hand. "Let's have a look at the remains."

She opened the portfolio to reveal several sepia-toned photos on thick paper, closeups of a skull and long shots of an entire skeleton, pieced together in more or less anatomical fashion on a canvas cloth.

"Narrow pelvis, heavy brow ridges, strong jaw," said Alasdair. "That's a man."

"A lot of wear on the teeth," Jean said. "And some of them are missing, thought they could still be in the ground. Look, the growth fissures in the skull are shut tight. He wasn't young."

Alasdair arranged the contents of the box on the glass top of the display case. "Four good-quality brass buttons. A buckle. Two pennies with a young Queen Victoria, never so dour as the old one. Someone's cleaned these up. Not much to be done with this, though." He held a strip of dirty, moldy cloth between thumb and forefinger.

"All that's left of the man's waistcoat?' hazarded Jean. She poked at a dark mound of material that might just as well be a dead mole. "Is that the bonnet Fergie mentioned? How could they tell?"

"Likely it was spread out, then. Now it's too far gone. But this, and this as well…" Delicately he stirred what looked like several thin toothpicks, the needles from a defunct Christmas tree, and tiny spheres like wrinkled olive pits. "Sprigs of juniper, oh aye. These are the berries. And I'm thinking this here might just be a hackle."

"If this was a military tam o'shanter, not a civilian one, shouldn't there be a badge?"

"An enterprising gardener might nick himself a silver badge tarnished from a few years in the ground, knowing it would clean up nicely. Or melt down, come to that."

They looked at each other, two minds, one thought. Jean

put the thought into words. "Could this be Tormod himself? The sea lanes between here and Down Under run both ways. Most men do wear hats of some sort, in this climate, and an old military tam o'shanter would work just tine—we saw Colin wearing his this morning. Juniper's the clan badge of the MacLeods. A bit of nostalgia for the returning emigrant, tucking juniper into his bonnet? You'd expect Australian coins, but then, if Tormod came back he'd have picked up some local currency."

"Australia was a British colony, and not one that went haring off on its own, like you lot. I'm not so sure it had its own currency 'til this century."

"I bet he came back, years later, as an old man, after his Australian wife died and their children grew up. Maybe he stayed with family that was still here in Kinlochroy, and asked them to bury him where he and Seonaid had been happy, at the chapel. Maybe he just lay down and died there. Whatever, we saw Seonaid walking toward his grave."

"There's high romance for you," Alasdair said. "A Hollywood-style ending, their ghosts going into the west hand in hand."

"There's a reason Hollywood endings are so popular. Although, like I told Brenda, I'm not sure this story has ended."

"We'll never be proving any of it, not with no more evidence than these things and a ghost."

"I know. It's just an educated, maybe enlightened, guess."

"Coincidence." Alasdair looked up at the speaker embedded in the ceiling above their heads.

Jean realized that the disembodied voice was reciting "A Canadian Boat Song," the lament of the emigrant Scottish Highlander in many more countries than Canada. The words might be wistful but they carried a sting, about mountains and seas dividing, and yet the blood being strong and the heart Highland, and how in dreams we can behold the Hebrides.

With her own bittersweet smile, Jean slipped the photos back into the portfolio. Maybe death was a dream. Maybe life was. Maybe it all flowed on together, no now, no then. That would explain synchronicity, ESP, and ghosts in one fell swoop.

Here came Brenda back again, having done her bit for law enforcement and family as well. Jean looked past her to see Thomson, his hat tucked beneath his arm, raising a steaming cup toward his lips. He tossed it down what must have been an asbestos-lined throat—an inheritance from both sides of his ancestry, no doubt—and inhaled a rich, raisin-studded cake called a black bun, all the time chatting affably with the winsome lass across the counter.

"What do you make of that lot?" Brenda indicated the remnants atop the glass.

"Well now," said Alasdair, and gave Brenda their analysis of the photos and the boxed relics, if omitting the clue of the cheerful ghost.

She listened in increasing amazement and gratification, leaning forward at each sentence, until she had to take a quick step to keep from falling over. "Tormod himself, is it then?"

"Perhaps," Alasdair cautioned. "We've done no more than make a guess."

"Entire industries have been built on guesswork, inference, and extrapolation," said Jean, without giving the Bible History Research Society as an example.

Thomson ranged up beside them, not one crumb marring either his chin or his uniform, and Alasdair repeated the explanation, concluding with the same caution.

"A pity," Thomson said, "that Greg MacLeod never knew of this."

"I'd not be so sure of that," said Alasdair, and, before Thomson could ask him what he meant, went on, "What have you learned asking round the village? Any strangers about?"

Folding her arms over her embroidered flowers, Brenda settled in to examine this evidence, too.

Thomson began, "Lachie at the Co-op's saying a man with an accent—Londoner, most likely—stopped in yesterday, buying some bits and pieces as though for a picnic, though it's hardly picnicking weather. Yon hikers, now, they're young, warm-blooded, but this man was not so young."

"A picnic," said Alasdair.

Jean knew he was seeing a bag of potato chips beneath a pew in the chapel, and the lock to the vestry door picked. "Did Lachie say whether the man was wearing a hat?"

"No, why should he, most men hereabouts are wearing hats."

Not Alasdair. The perpetual motion of his brain kept his head warm. "A toe rag, perhaps? A vagrant, unemployed or not quite right in the head? Or a native son who's been working away, making a visit to the home ground? No matter—he's a potential witness to the murder."

"Or the murderer himself," said Jean, without delving into the difficulties of motivation.

"I'll be keeping a lookout," Thomson said, and went on, "Most folk hereabouts are gey predictable. Lionel Pritchard, now, he's in the pub most every day, same as Rab Finlay. But not yesterday. He's stated he was in Portree."

"Is he well liked in these parts?" asked Alasdair.

"He's not disliked, save when he's giving in to the incomer's curse, telling us we should be conducting our business the way his folk do in England. He and Rab, like chalk and cheese."

"Let me guess," said Jean. "Pritchard thinks everything should change and Rab keeps talking about how things were better in the old days."

"They were, in a way. Then, entire families were supported by the estate. Now most of the young men, like Rab's own brother-in-law, are obliged to work away. Fergus is the odd man out, coming instead of going, eh? Still, Rab's loyal to the MacDonald's, and he and Pritchard work for them, so there are times they make common cause."

Brenda called, "Cheerie-bye!" Thomson turned to wave at the older ladies, who'd gathered their shopping bags and were heading out into the night.

"Common cause, like the day Rab, Pritchard, and a couple of pensioners started fighting with Colin?" Alasdair asked.

"They didna aim at fighting," Thomson replied. "Colin stopped by the pub to buy himself a bottle of whiskey, and the pensioners took notice of him. They were going on about their own war, and, for once, how things were worse then. Pritchard's not got much use for Colin, thinks he's got his own chance with Diana." He snorted a demurral. "And Rab, he's thinking Colin's not right in the head, and is causing trouble for the family. They joined in the ragging, and Colin, well, he's thinking the best defense is offense, eh?"

"Puir lad, Colin," said Brenda. "Diana's got a good heart to take that one on. Although he's got something to offer, I'm sure."

Jean wasn't going to touch that line. "Is Fergie the only person in town not to know the, ah, full extent of their relationship?"

"I'm thinking so," Thomson said. "He's a fine man, Fergus, no airs and graces, none of this incomer rubbish like Pritchard, and he's going his best for Dunasheen, but...well, dinna go taking this wrong, but he's got his own ways of thinking and doing, and there's times he's seeing what wants seeing, and there's times he's seeing only what he's wishing to see, if you follow my meaning."

Alasdair followed his meaning just fine, Jean estimated. So did she. "And Diana?"

"She's here shopping from time to time, giving the school

prizes, having a blether at the pub," said Brenda. "Lovely girl, Diana. A bit posh for us plain folk, but polite to a fault."

Now the hikers started collecting their gear. With no customers, Brenda would want to close early, it being New Year's Eve. As quick on the uptake as ever, Thomson pressed on. "Mr. and Mrs. MacLeod likely drove straight through the town without stopping yesterday. No one's seen them at all. The Americans, the Krums, they stopped here."

"Here," said Brenda, pointing at the floor. "The father bought a book and a sweetie for the lass whilst the mother, well, I thought at first the drains were giving off a bad smell, then decided that's just her way."

"Yes," Jean said, "that's just her way."

"Yesterday," said Thomson, "they spent an hour or more in the pub—I was by way of seeing them myself when I stopped in. The father went away, and then the mother. The two Morrison lads saw Scott walking to and fro with his phone. Mairi Macaulay met the mother, Heather, outside the Co-op, thinks Heather was asking her if she'd seen Scott, but Mairi couldna quite understand the woman's lingo, and Heather couldna understand Mairi's, so they both gave it up as a bad job."

"Bottom line," said Alasdair, "is that both the parents were out and about at the time of the murder. And Dunasheen's gates were standing open then."

"Oh aye. They're always open. I didna know they would shut, to tell the truth, but Pritchard, he put his back into it. Closing the gates to the barbarians."

Jean reminded herself that she might be a journalist, but she was no barbarian. Her relief at Dakota's story about the pub being confirmed was tempered by her guilt for pumping the child to begin with.

Thomson went on, "The Krums are in the pub just now, after walking up the lane beyond old Calum's cottage for the lass to have a look at the sheep, and then back round to the harbor. They stopped in at the Co-op to buy sweets and day-old bread to feed the gulls."

Who needed a Protect and Survive surveillance system in Kinlochroy?

"Cheerie-bye!" Brenda called to the hikers, and, as the door shut behind them, "You'll be excusing me please, Mr. Cameron, Miss Fairbairn, the lass is needing help with the clearing up."

Behind the counter, the lass started from her reverie and reached for a dish cloth.

"I'd best be away to the castle," Thomson said, his dark eyes with their bright gaze targeting first Alasdair and then Jean. He touched his forefinger to the side of his nose. "Fergus is asking me to play the first foot. I'll be seeing you at the bells, then, carrying my lump of coal, my tin of short-bread, and my bottle of whiskey—Fergus has already given me them, just to make sure."

The bells of midnight. The cusp, the turning point. How many events were marked by bells—death, marriage, or no more than the passing of the hours? Jean's gaze fell on a framed print hanging on the wall, Dunasheen in the sunshine, its towers and gables rising above a lawn covered with daffodils. Spring would come, no matter what else happened. "We'll see you then."

"Thank you, constable," said Alasdair, and as Thomson walked way settling his hat on his head, "It's time we were getting back as well, Jean. Fergie's expecting us in the library at six."

"Yeah, the whole artifact and article thing is one of the reasons we're here. Exploiting history is why everyone's here, in a way." Jean didn't mention their own bottom line—speaking of the devil of wedding cancellation might make it appear.

Alasdair called to Brenda, "Thank you kindly."

"It was nice meeting you," Jean added, and braced herself for the cold and the dark outside.

Despite the dark and cold, warmth emanated from the buildings, probably the psychological effect of all the lighted windows. Night had erased the Cuillins and muted the gleam of the sea. But Dunasheen Castle glittered bravely, even stubbornly, behind its wall and beyond its naked trees.

Leaning close together, Jean and Alasdair walked across the street and looked through the front window of the pub. Yes, the Krums occupied the settle closest to the fireplace, Scott gazing into an empty beer glass as though into a crystal ball, Dakota wrapped around a paperback, Heather writing with a thick pen in a small book.

If any reporters had taken refuge there, they were gone now. A few locals sat at tables or stood at the bar, while the publican minded his post between a fence of knobby beer spigots and a wall of bottles and glasses. A pop song played in the background and leaked out onto the sidewalk, making less of an impact on the silence than the everlasting murmur of the sea.

Alasdair and Jean turned away from one of the town's sanctuaries and walked toward another, the white-painted church at the end of the street. Its windows were dark arrowheads in its pale flanks, and the array of monuments behind its surrounding wall looked in the gloom like a thicket of stone. The peaked roof of a small building rose to one side. "Fergie's family mausoleum." Alasdair's breath seeped in a sparkling cloud toward the graves and vanished.

"I guess Norman the Red and Seonaid are lying side by side. Seonaid's physical remains, at least. And their son, and his son, and so on down to Fergus Mor and his brother the laird, primly and properly arranged for eternity. Or for Judgement Day, whichever comes first." Jean caught Alasdair's quick gleam, but he didn't dispute her theology.

A door slammed, and voices echoed down the tunnel of the street. One of them spoke with a familiar accent, its flatness emphasized by its underlying whine. "...I deserve it, that's why," Heather was saying. "Journaling relieves stress. What's a good pen and a nice book, to relieve stress?"

Scott probably had an answer to that, but he didn't vocalize it. He and Heather, Dakota at their heels, passed within several yards of Alasdair and Jean.

Alasdair called, "Hullo there."

The three shapes spun around. "Whoa," said Scott with a forced laugh. "I thought for a minute we were hearing voices from beyond the grave."

"Sorry," Alasdair told them. "You're away to the house, then?"

"Yeah. The whole Hogmanay thing gets going at seven, Fergus said."

They walked away en masse, Heather adding, "About time. So far just about the only entertainment is the whole *C.S.I.: Dunasheen* thing."

"Entertaining?" demanded Scott. "There's a guy dead..."

"Too much information for the k-i-d," Heather retorted, as though Dakota couldn't spell. "You know what I mean. Cut me some slack for a change, will you?"

Maybe Heather meant *We don't know them, so they don't matter.* Jean caught Dakota's eye and smile encouragingly. Dakota smiled back, then shrank into her muffler as the group approached the gates, iron looping and swirling against the lights of the house.

But the news vans had gone, leaving a solitary constable on guard, his dark clothing shadowed so that his yellow reflective jacket seemed to be disembodied.

Heather flashed a grin. Thumbs upraised and forefingers pointed, she pretended to draw from the hip and fire shots at him. His face went from bored to deliberately blank, and he spun toward the gate. Everyone hurried through the narrow opening so quickly Heather had to break into a jog to avoid being left behind. "Thank you, constable," Alasdair enunciated, and the gate clanged shut.

The driveway ran into the deep shadow between village and house. Jean directed her steps closer to Alasdair and eyed the black bulk of the garden wall, of Pritchard's cottage, of the trees spaced across the lawn. Someone could easily be hiding there, watching them. Just because the gates were shut didn't mean the estate wasn't easily accessible.

A few paces further on, Dakota stopped dead. "Wow! How did they do that?"

Oh. Jean crawled up from the primordial sludge of her doubt and dread to see stars strewn across the sky, luminous freckles on the face of God. Some were hard points of icy light, others were smudges. Groups of stars made smears of radiance that faded near the glowing puddle of the moon— and in the west, blotted by thin streamers of cloud.

"How did who do what?" asked Scott.

"Those are special effects, right? There aren't really that many stars."

Definitely a city kid, Jean thought. "Yes, there are that many. You just can't see them when there are a lot of other lights. Street lights, lights of buildings."

"Oh. Cool." Her head tilted back, Dakota wobbled along, her mother's hand on her shoulder keeping her if not on the straight and narrow, at least on the driveway.

Scott, too, looked upward, so that when a black Lab and a white terrier rushed toward him from the darkness he almost fell over them. "Hey! Oh, hi, guys."

Rab Finlay trotted along after the dogs. "Bruce, Somerled, get back here you sons of… Hullo there. Just walking the dogs."

"Looks like they're walking you," said Heather.

"They're that eager to be off, slipped their leashes whilst I tied my trainers—the polis took my wellies, much good that'll do them, and here's me, heading for the nearest patch of glaur and ice." The dogs capered on across the lawn. "Somerled! Bruce! No free run tonight, lads, there's things doing at the house, get back here with you!"

"I hear you, pal." Scott bent his knee and lifted his foot so that a pair of polished wingtips caught the light. "I wasn't anywhere near the place when the guy, you know, but still they took my hiking boots, brand new ones. A heck of a lot warmer than these."

"I should hope so," said Heather. "They cost as much as designer pumps."

Rab's black and white beard bristled like the southbound end of a northbound badger. His eyes glinted in the shadow of his tweed cap. His silence rejecting Scott and Heather's familiarities, he hooked the dogs' leashes to their collars and continued on down the driveway.

"Why did the police take everybody's shoes?" asked Dakota.

Alasdair, who had so far borne out her estimation of his speaking habits, answered. "There were footprints near the scene of the crime, prints of shoes with treads. The boffins—the laboratory technicians—are after making a match. And matching the mud and other matter at the scene with matter caught in the treads of someone's shoes."

"The problem is, everyone wears shoes with treads these days." *Like Brenda and her comfortable sneakers,* Jean added to herself. "There must have been a dozen pairs of wellies in the cloak room, just for a start."

"Too much information," Heather said again, despite Alasdair's circumspect "matter." "Come on people, let's get dressed for whatever's going on tonight. I hope they have more of that wassail. That was good."

"It sure was," said Scott, leaping on a point of agreement. "Let's ask for the recipe."

The two adults swept Dakota across the gravel and into the porch. The door opened, emitting a burst of light, and shut again. In the darkness, the dogs woofed perfunctorily at the gate constable. The phone in Alasdair's pocket rang, and the light of the display cast a greenish, alien glow on his face. "Hullo, Hugh."

This time he angled the phone toward Jean, so she could hear Hugh's voice. No thanks to the tiny audio circuits that it came across clear as a bell, if only half as loud—he made his living as much with his voice as his musical instruments. "I've got two minutes before the taxi arrives. Three, if it's slowed down by the crowds on the High Street. But I've heard from my fiddler friend in Townsville, a quick message before going off to a New Year's barbie on the beach whilst I'm freezing my nose hairs here in Auld Reekie and Darkie."

"Any good gossip about Greg MacLeod?" Jean asked with a grin.

"She did not know him personally, but knew of him. Quite the smooth talker, she's saying, and a clever businessman, with many a scheme, resorts, apartment buildings, suburb development, a souvenir business, your art gallery and museum of religion."

Alasdair waded in. "Rebecca's saying he sold an ancient inscription to the Bible History Research Society, all the time working a deal to display it in his own museum. Eating your cake and having it as well, sounds to be."

"That's Greg," said Hugh, "or so she's saying. Always selling up the last venture and starting in again, looking out the main chance. Mind you, he's never known for churchgoing, or New Age piety, or even holding séances, nothing of the sort. It's that with war, fire, flood, economic troubles, nowadays there's muckle money in religion."

"Hence a museum of religion and an antiquities gallery under one roof." The side of Jean's face next to Alasdair's was almost warm. The other side was so cold she felt the gold studs like tiny icicles in her earlobes.

"Hope that helps," Hugh said. "Time to go singing for my supper."

"You'd sing for nothing," Jean told him. "Thanks, it does help. Happy New Year!"

"'Til Saturday," stated Hugh. "I'll not be missing out Alasdair's stag party."

Alasdair twitched, a stag party not being on his list of priorities. But before he could remonstrate, the connection went silent. He tucked the phone away.

Jean leaned away from him, feeling the chill fall on her face. "I really wish we'd gotten to know Greg. He sounds like quite a character."

"He was after the main chance, was he? So are the Krums. And Pritchard."

"An old manor house," said Jean, "filled with precious objects religious, secular, no one knows what, the owners in difficult financial straits, and a shady manager. Quite a setup."

Alasdair looked up at the glowing windows. "What was Greg wanting that someone killed him to stop him getting it? What was Tina knowing that made her risk her life escaping? Was she thinking the murderer nearby, and coming for her next?"

The light streaming from the library window wavered as Diana leaned in close to the Christmas tree. Its tiny red and green lights winked on, casting a hard-edged gleam into Alasdair's eyes.

Jean could sense his thought cycling like an electric current: *Every time I think we've moved the investigation away from Fergie it circles back round again.*

The lingering sweetness in her mouth went sour.

TWENTY

ALASDAIR CONSIDERED HIS image in the tall mirror. Jean considered him and his heather-blue tie, charcoal jacket, and tall socks with red flashes, all setting off the red and green Cameron kilt—not quite the red and green of Christmas, but then, tartan was appropriate for all seasons. "There may be something about a man in a uniform," she said, "but there's really something about a man in a kilt."

"Kilts have been uniforms. See my dad and Fergus Mor." He thrust the tiny traditional dagger, the *sgian dubh,* into the top of his sock, and double-checked the clasp on his kilt pin. "You had no call giving me an engagement gift."

She fluttered her left hand toward him. "You gave me a diamond ring. Besides, I couldn't resist that pin." A silver dragon with a sapphire eye, it was just small enough not to be gaudy, otherwise he'd never wear it.

"Bonny Jean." He took her hand, raised it to his lips, and kissed it. Above the gleam of the diamond, heat lightning flickered in the depths of his own sapphire eyes, ones more changeable than the dragon's. "That's a lovely frock you're wearing."

"Thank you, dear." Still holding his hand, Jean checked her mirrored self. Okay, she paled in magnificence next to him, the way a peahen paled next to a peacock. But still, the deep-crimson dress Miranda had talked her into buying looked good with her fair skin and auburn hair, and the necklace of chunky stones and twisted wires seemed both

antique and contemporary. She might even hold her own next
to Diana and Heather.

Her dress for the wedding waited in the wardrobe, sheathed
in plastic and anticipation. It was a lovelier frock than her first
wedding dress, which had been so stark a white she hadn't
been a blushing bride but a blanched one. She should have
taken that as an omen.

As for whether she'd be wearing her second-time-around
dress on schedule, she could use an omen, a sign, a por-
tent—if she had a magic eight-ball she'd consult that too. At
least she'd see Alasdair in his kilt tonight, even if they had
to delay—not cancel, delay—the formalities and the celebration following.

"Penny for your thoughts," said Alasdair, his fingers tightening on hers.

"I'm not going to start charging you for them now," she
replied.

"Worrying about the wedding, eh?"

"I don't want a furtive ceremony and hushed voices. I
don't want to honeymoon under a cloud. We've done a lot
of compromising, but I don't want to compromise with this.
Although we may have no choice."

"You're sounding like Nancy and her 'we canna sort things
to suit ourselves,' not Bonny Jean the stubborn."

"Stubborn, *moi?* Look who's talking," she retorted, and
the little clock on the mantel struck five-forty-five.

With a smile and a last firm squeeze of her hand, Alasdair
picked up her best beaded evening bag, just big enough for
a pen and notepad, and draped it over her shoulder. "That's
us away, then."

Having exhausted himself stalking and killing the two
hackles, Dougie now slept soundly on the French gilt chair.
"All he needs is a couple of footmen in white wigs deliver-
ing catnip," Jean said.

Alasdair's iron rod of an arm urged her out of the room and into the hall, where she eyed Seonaid's tapestry. "Is it possible to deliberately choose ghosthood over going into the west, or the night, or wherever souls go? Given my druthers, I'd rather fade out and rest in peace than spend eternity searching for something I never attained in life."

"Is it possible to choose—ghosthood, hah—for someone else, by not letting them go?"

"You're thinking of Tormod and Seonaid? Although you'd think once Tormod was gone, Seonaid would go, too."

"Habit." Alasdair tucked the room key into his sporran and they strolled off down the corridor.

"With all that Fergie and Diana have had to deal with, they might prefer us being fashionably late," Jean told him.

"I'm after having a proper chin-wag before the Krums arrive on the scene," he returned.

"Well, yes, like how you weren't far wrong guessing that Greg was after one of the crusader tombstones, when he was after something called a Crusader Coffer." Jean paused at the tripping stane, and not only because she was now wearing shoes with dizzyingly tall one-inch heels. What she felt, though, wasn't dizziness, just the delicate prickle, the cold press of something that was only abnormal, she supposed, because so few people were sensitive to it.

"You haven't heard the Green Lady, Seonaid, wailing or anything, have you?" she asked.

"Warning of disaster? If she was carrying on about Tina's falling from the window, I did not hear." With a barely perceptible shudder, Alasdair walked on down the steps, his elbow angled in Jean's direction should she trip over her own feet or feel the need to make a formal entrance on his arm. She confined herself to a light pat on the sleeve of his jacket.

They were walking through the entrance hall and its aroma of cooking food and a hint of smoke when Gilnockie and

Young rounded the corner from the back hall. "Good evening," Gilnockie said. Young exposed several teeth, then looked their finery up and down and folded her arms across her nondescript coat.

Jean and Alasdair rendered appropriate greetings, which included not commenting on how Gilnockie seemed grayer, graver, and more cadaverous than ever, as though he'd eaten nothing but ashes since his arrival at Dunasheen. "Hogmanay's under way, then," he said. "Lord Dunasheen's been kind enough to ask us to join in the festivities…"

"Used to be," muttered Young, "the lairds would be inviting their tenants."

"…but with the lab boffins in Inverness missing out their holiday, we're after doing no less. We're away to Portree just now for a teleconference. And we're hoping to interview Tina MacLeod."

"She's still in Portree, then," Alasdair said.

"Aye, the concussion's not so bad, the broken bone's a simple fracture, and there are no internal injuries. She's regained consciousness, though she's not yet coherent."

"Have you spoken with any of her and Greg's relations in Australia?"

"It's the morning of New Year's Day there, no one's answering the telephone. We'll have another go as soon as may be."

"Don't worry about tomorrow," said Jean. "It's already tomorrow in Australia."

Young turned a blank stare in her direction, then jerked back, blinking, at the electronic strains of "Take a Chance on Me." Grabbing for her phone, she retreated several steps closer to the door and mumbled her half of a conversation.

"The chap in the photo," Gilnockie went on, "looks like being Greg MacLeod's father, right enough. Lord Dunasheen did not know that, or so he's saying."

The corners of Alasdair's mouth tightened. But it was Gilnockie's job to be skeptical.

"We've not yet worked out the ramifications," Gilnockie went on, "though I doubt there are some."

I suspect there are some, Jean translated automatically, even though she was the only outlander present. "I can see Kenneth senior throwing the shrimps onto the barbie and telling his sons about Scotland, land of their forefathers. Between his ancestors and his business, Greg had plenty of motivation to come here."

"He did that." Gilnockie went on, "Lord Dunasheen tells me this Sunday is your wedding day. May I be offering you both my best wishes for a long, happy life together?"

"Thank you," said Alasdair, echoed by Jean. No need to repulse the man's courtesy by adding provisos.

"Cheers." Young snapped her phone shut and scowled down at her feet, turned somewhat pigeon-toed on the tile floor. "Portree's reporting that Pritchard's alibi is solid. He spent the day in a pub with a woman, and didn't come away 'til four, after the murder."

Oh. Damn. Jean had actually started to hope Pritchard was the guilty party. She didn't want it to be a member of the household, for Fergie's sake. Or Scott or Heather, for Dakota's sake. Or Colin, for Diana's sake. At least they had a stranger who could still qualify.

Alasdair said nothing. His face showed no expression. Beside the pleats of his kilt, his hands shut, opened, and shut again.

Gilnockie went, if possible, even more colorless. But he recovered his voice first. "Well then, I'll relieve Thomson of sitting with Pritchard. His report was right helpful, by the way. W.P.C. McCrummin and P.C. Nicolson are going round to the area B and Bs, looking out the chap from the shop in Kinlochroy."

"Here's hoping he turns out to be the chap hanging about the night of the murder," Alasdair said. "We're having an interview of sorts with Fergie just now. If there's anything…"

I think you should know, Jean finished for him.

"…I'll be in touch," Alasdair finished for himself.

Young fell into a walk toward the door. "They'll have brought the car round."

"Half a tick," Gilnockie told her, and as she opened the door, "Alasdair, I'm thinking this is not a good way to end a career, leaving a case open."

"It's early days yet, Patrick."

Yeah, it was still early. This could drag on for a long time. And Gilnockie, if anyone, knew how cases were more likely to be solved sooner rather than later, cold case dramas notwithstanding.

"Aye," said Gilnockie. *"Nil desperandum."*

Don't despair. That was the message of the evening. The cold draft from the open door rippled Alasdair's kilt and fluttered Jean's dress. She stepped backward. Gilnockie made for the door. "Good night, then," he called.

"Good night," Alasdair and Jean both returned, and hurried on into the slightly warmer air of the hallway. The front door shut behind them.

In front of them, Nancy Finlay stood outside the half-closed door of the library, her dishtowel jerking over a picture frame.

Alasdair's subtle expulsion of breath wasn't quite a "hah!" but close. Nancy was eavesdropping. Without any embarrassment, though, she looked around, said, "Good evening to you," and headed toward the kitchen.

Alasdair sent a scowl after her. Jean shook her head and shrugged—Miranda would say that eavesdropping was staff prerogative. From the narrow space between the library door and its jamb issued what Nancy had overheard, a strain of baroque music, violins soaring nervously.

And Fergie's voice, with an odd blustery resonance. "…insurance alone, if we opened every day. And we'd need extra help, more facilities, more paperwork—planning permission, licensing inspections—when we've barely got time to deal with woodworm, dry rot, damp rot. The drains. Ice buildup in the gutters. We're running has hard as we can to stay in the same place."

"But simply selling the landscape's become a cliché. And, considering the climate, an uphill job. We're obliged to position ourselves as a destination for luxury short breaks, or a stop on diaspora tours, the descendants of emigrants rediscovering their roots." Diana's voice was cool and calm as the surface of Loch Ness, mirror-flat while a primitive form glided by below.

"Greg MacLeod was on a diaspora tour, looking out his ancestors."

"He was on a buying trip as well, don't forget that."

"How could I?" asked Fergie. "Lionel's saying there's no such thing as bad publicity, but I can't agree. What sort of clientele will we attract now, I ask you?"

"And yet you've arranged for Jean to write about the Crusader Coffer and your related…" One beat, two, and Diana settled on, "…theories. What sort of clientele will you attract with those? I do so wish you'd wait until the police investigation has been finished. Circumstances are quite awkward enough without—"

"We've come too far to stop now," Fergie interrupted.

Alasdair raised his hand to knock on the door, then, no doubt realizing how clumsy their sudden appearance would be, took several catfooted steps back down the hall. He beckoned to Jean, but she hesitated—there was eavesdropping, and then there was research. Besides, this was the answer to more than what Diana and Fergie had been quibbling about on the staircase yesterday.

"We should organize concerts, then," said Diana, "in addition to weddings, dinners, receptions. Living history, study tours, boat rides and wildlife tours on the loch. Craft or cooking weekends."

"More facilities," repeated Fergie. "Extra help. Rab and Nancy aren't growing younger. Neither am I, come to that."

"Colin could help."

"Diana, please, I can't deal with Colin Urquhart, not just now."

"If you'd been willing to deal with him earlier...but no, we're not speaking of him, are we?" Diana's voice grew choppy. "You've dismissed taking out another loan to make the tenants' cottages over into holiday homes—no, no, you're quite right, we'd have only seasonal income from those. I could put it about that we're willing to lend objects to corporations who'll sponsor repairs. Many new companies build their images on heritage of some sort or another."

"Can you see Seonaid's portrait hanging in a bank in Tokyo?"

"Yes, Father, I can. Better there than on an auction block." Diana continued, "There's Pritchard's idea of selling off one square foot plots of land. We could advertise in the U.S., Canada, Australia, New Zealand. Buy a bit of the Auld Sod, call yourself a laird or lady, that sort of thing. We'd essentially be selling deckle-edged, hand-lettered certificates of purchase, suitable for framing."

Something creaked, probably a chair as Fergie sat down in it. He made a strangled sound that evolved into laughter. 'Can you see an Aussie buying enough for a campsite? Or a Yank wanting to be buried standing up in his one square foot?

Can you see a Canuck turning up with a shovel and digging up the sod to take home?"

"Have we a choice?" Diana asked, her words positively whitecapped.

Jean could see one of her own countrymen wandering around with a GPS unit and little pegs to mark out his claim, dressed in a polyester kilt and "Braveheart" T-shirt.

Behind her, Alasdair whispered not, "You were right, we should have turned up fashionably late," but, "You and your flapping ears."

"Like your ears are folded over politely?" Jean whispered back. "This is a murder case, isn't it?"

"It's not—"

"—something you want happening to your friends. I know, I get the message."

In a cascade of chimes, less-than-synchronized clocks struck all through the house. Six o'clock. They were no longer early. Jean barely had enough time to leap backward before the library door flew open and Diana shot out into the hall, the color in her compressed lips dull, the color in her cheeks high.

She didn't seem to notice that Jean and Alasdair were just standing there, rather than walking toward her. Neither did she notice Alasdair's suffused expression, which, Jean was sure, her own face replicated. "Good evening. Please go on in, Father's expecting you. I'll bring the drinks round soon as I've changed."

"Thank you," Jean said.

"Very kind of you," said Alasdair, and with a roll of his eyes—okay, she deserved that—he bowed Jean into the room and made sure the door was shut behind them.

Flames crackled in the fireplace. The Christmas tree's glitter was doubled in the window behind it. The doors between library and drawing room stood open, providing a vista ap-

propriate to *County Life* or a travelogue on the stately homes
of Britain.

Just to complete the picture, Fergie, too, was wearing a
kilt, a garment that flattered any type of male physique, from
bean pole to walrus. A man in a kilt stood tall and walked
with a certain strut.

Although when Fergie set an empty glass on the side table
and rose to his feet, he didn't strut but stood to attention. A
stiff smile was plastered on his face, which was colored even
more brightly than Diana's. Jean wasn't surprised to catch a
whiff of whiskey. Why taking a wee dram to brace yourself
up was called Dutch courage, she didn't know—it could just
as well be called Scotch courage. She hoped Fergie had had
only the one glass, that no more than his smile was plastered.

"Here we are, then," he said.

"Aye," returned Alasdair.

The shrill music of the violins swooped like songbirds
trapped beneath a high ceiling. Fergie stepped over to the
CD player nestled between skull-shaped bookends and put
the piece out of its misery, producing a silence so deep his
slight wheeze seemed loud.

Jean said, "I'm afraid our cat got into the hatbox you left
for us and tore up the hackles on the bonnets. I'm so sorry, I
know they were heirlooms."

"Hackles? Oh, yes, the old bonnets. Not to worry, Jean,
I'd not seen them for years. It was just that one of them belonged to my father's friend Kenneth MacLeod, and Inspector Gilnockie's saying it was his knife killed Greg. That Greg
was likely his son. I wondered why that name sounded so
familiar. It was you who took down the photo in the dining
room, then?"

"Aye, that was us," Alasdair answered. "The frames in
the sideboard."

"Good. I mean, good it was you. Rab was thinking Pritchard

had made off with it, or Scott Krum. The frame's an antique in its own right, a century older than the photo."

"Was it Pritchard who looked up both Krum and Greg MacLeod on the Internet?"

"I expect so," Fergie said. "Seems a bit ill-mannered, but then, Lionel's looking out for Dunasheen's well-being."

"And for his own as well?" asked Alasdair.

Fergie's gaze dropped to the stack of CDs. He chose one and inserted it into the player. "Lionel Pritchard's not the most congenial of colleagues, I'll grant you that. I'm not at all pleased with the way he looks at Diana. No surprise she mistrusts him. But he's willing to work here, his accounts are accurate to the last decimal point, and nothing's gone missing."

"That you know of," said Jean.

"Well, yes. I gather Pritchard's your prime suspect for the murder?"

"Not anymore," Alasdair said. "He's been cleared."

"I suppose I'm relieved to hear that." Absently, Fergie patted one of the skull bookends. "I don't rightly now how I feel, to tell truth. I'd rather have Pritchard turn out to be a villain than anyone else I can name. Even Colin Urquhart, for Diana's sake."

"I know how you feel. But it's going to come down to motive, what Greg wanted and what someone else didn't want him to have…" Jean looked over at Alasdair.

He was eyeing the cabinet holding the Fairy Flagon. "Was Greg after buying the Flagon? Or was he interested only in the Crusader Coffer?"

Fergie didn't ask how Alasdair knew about the latter. He didn't answer either question. He said, "Time to get the show on the road, you Yanks would say," and punched the "play" button. The Chieftains begin to sing a jolly Christmas ditty, "The St. Stephen's Day Murders."

"I'm thinking it's time to open the show, aye." Alasdair drew his camera from his sporran.

Jean pulled out her notepad, found a fresh page, and smiled with that surge of glee she always felt when the gates to something strange and perhaps wonderful swung open before her.

Fergie tweaked the linen runner on a waiting table, then turned a key in the lock of the cabinet door and, with a flourish, threw it open.

TWENTY-ONE

WE MEET AT LAST, thought Jean, and leaned in for a better look.

Fergie lifted the alabaster cup from its cavity as carefully as he'd have lifted baby Diana from her cradle. He set it on one end of the table, leaving room for a second object, and stood back. His starched smile broke into a beam that eased the grooves in his face. "You've seen it before, have you, Alasdair?"

"A long time ago, as a wee lad." Alasdair, too, tilted forward.

The lotus-shaped cup stood less than nine inches tall. Its smooth milk-and-honey flanks, glowing as if it contained an internal light, traced one sinuous curve from lip to stem to base. The handles on either side rose up and out like stylized wings. Tiny, blocky scratches imbedded with traces of black ink marred the surface sheen of one side of the bowl. Jean guessed they were hieroglyphs, but she couldn't see more than that with her naked eye. Or even with her glasses-enhanced eye. "That's a work of art, all right. It's been in your family how long?"

"My uncle invited an expert from the Museum of Antiquities in Edinburgh to have a look at it. He pronounced it an Egyptian artifact, perhaps brought here by a crusader. Or at the latest, by Norman the Red's father, a Cameron Highlander who fought Napoleon at Alexandria. Norman himself wrote of it." Fergie chuckled. "My uncle dismissed the expert's opinion, saying he knew for a fact the Flagon was given to Rory MacLeod by fairies. And the expert said, 'Then I shall accept your superior knowledge.' A diplomatic reply, if ever there was one."

Yeah, Jean thought, writing as fast as she could. "Did the expert decipher the inscription?"

"It's an ancient Egyptian prayer for the dead, the equivalent of 'rest in peace.'"

"Rory MacLeod?" asked Alasdair. "The chap who leaped from the old castle?"

"More likely his father, the old laird. The legendary Rory was the younger son, who made the mistake of falling for his older brother's wife. Falling literally, I'm afraid. Family orthodoxy has it that the Flagon belonged to the MacLeods at the old castle, the ones my own ancestors turfed out. Unless it is Napoleonic-era, in which case it's been a MacDonald relic all along. No matter."

"What matters is whether Greg MacLeod wanted it." Alasdair took a photo, considered his work in the camera's display, took another.

"He was not uninterested in it, though he never had the chance to look at it or the Coffer. No need taking photos of the Flagon, Alasdair, I'll give Jean a publicity still. Amazing antiquity, isn't it now? It evokes the alabaster jar carried by the woman in the Bible, the one who poured ointment over Jesus's head and he said she was preparing him for burial."

It would evoke that passage, Jean told herself, even if it had been made in Alexandria five minutes before a Scottish soldier went souvenir-shopping.

"Anointing him for burial." Fergie's beam radiated upward, making his eyes gleam. "That's incredibly apt. It's amazing the way things work out, eh? Makes you wonder whether there's some force causing coincidences."

Alasdair looked around at Jean. She met his gaze with a slight shake of her head. She had no idea what was coming, just that they were launching into uncharted and debatable territory.

Fergie unlocked a second cabinet and removed what looked like a gray breadbox. Although, since he strained to lift it, it was more likely a metal chest stuffed with several generations of coin collections…no. It was an oblong stone coffer, a fairy-sized sarcophagus containing not fragile bones and disintegrated wings, but a sprinkling of black dirt, gray dust, and either threads or cobwebs.

"The Crusader Coffer, I presume?" This time Jean leaned so near the stone she could smell it, cold, damp, redolent of decay and long-dead fires.

Alasdair took another picture, the flash dazzling the corner of her eye.

Fergie's expression reflected dazzlement to the point of dazed. "We found this in one of the cellars whilst laying pipes for the new kitchen. I've managed to keep it under wraps, so to speak, but it's time it made its appearance on the world stage."

"You were after selling it to Greg MacLeod?" asked Alasdair.

"Yes. He was hinting about making a grand offer, if he liked what he saw—we both knew he was talking about the Coffer. I would have hated to let it go, but then, it doesn't have the family history the Flagon does. And it might well be the most expensive, even priceless object we've got. It could be Dunasheen's salvation, no pun intended."

"Priceless?" Alasdair asked. "Pun?"

"It's an ossuary, isn't it?" asked Jean. "Without its lid. People would bury their dead, then come back later, gather the bones, put them in a chest and re-bury them."

"A Jewish burial practice at the time of Jesus," said Fergie.

Alasdair looked sharply around at him.

Jean's glee was deflating beneath an all-too-familiar

weight in the pit of her stomach. She'd hoped Fergie's odd notions would be more digestible than some of the others she'd tried to swallow this past year, but if he was heading where she thought he was heading, dyspepsia was going to be the least of her worries. "There are several famous examples from that era. One contains the heel bone of a crucified man. Others have intriguing inscriptions, although the most famous, supposedly naming Jesus and his brother James, is pretty much assumed to be a fake."

Unfazed by that caveat, Fergie switched on a lamp and angled the long side of the chest toward it. "This one's inscription is more than intriguing. Have a look."

To the accompaniment of The Chieftains' "The Rocky Road to Dublin," Jean dropped to her knees, not in prayer, but to see the gouges and scratches straggling across the face of the stone. All she could make out at first were the tiny grains of the rock, a micro-miniature field of stars. *As above, so below*—but that was a phrase from magical tradition, not Judeo-Christian.

Barely aware of Alasdair's warm breath on her ear, Jean squinted and tilted her head back and forth until at last, in the lamplight raking the side of the chest, she either saw or imagined she saw lettering, not in Hebrew or Aramaic but in Latin. "Well, it could be the INRI inscription, the words of the indictment placed above Jesus's head on the cross, telling onlookers what he was convicted of doing. Or, in his case, of claiming, according to authorities such as Pontius…" Bones rattled in the ossuary of her memory. "…Pilate."

"Eh?" Alasdair's question rippled through her hair and set her earring to swinging.

"It's Latin, *Isus Nazarenus Rex Iudaeorum*. Jesus of Nazareth, King of the Jews. At least, I think I can see *Isus Nazarenus*. I'm guessing at *Rex Iudaeorum*, because that's usually what comes next." She looked up at Fergie, hovering like a tartan-swathed blimp above a sports stadium. "If this had been found in the Holy Land, with proper provenance and documentation, and examined by scientists and peer-reviewed, then it could be an early occurrence of the INRI phrase, carved on the ossuary in the days when Christianity hadn't separated from Judaism. Or it could even be independent confirmation of the Biblical account of the crucifixion, but that's a leap. A leap of faith."

With the aid of Alasdair's large, strong hand, she regained her feet and brushed at the bits of dog hair clinging to her dress. "Even though it has no provenance, no documentation, and has never been reviewed," she went on, "I can see Greg wanting this for—for his museum."

"Ah," said Alasdair, his keen hearing picking up the chalky rattle of her memory. "But surely that's natural cracks in the stone. Your eyes, your mind, they've got a tendency to apply order to random shapes. See early astronomers thinking they were viewing canals on Mars."

Fergie's laugh split the difference between a knowing chuckle and a rapturous giggle. "Early astronomers didn't have the telescopes we have now, just as early archaeologists didn't have the microscopes and other equipment. But you haven't quite got it, Jean."

"I'm usually not quite getting it," she returned.

"What if the words carved on the chest," Fergie stated, "on the coffer—coffin, eh?—are *Isus Nazarenus Ignis Salvator.*"

Jean peered again at the scratches and gouges. "I don't see—well, Alasdair's right, you see what you want to see…" Which is what Sanjay Thomson had said about Fergie. An intelligent lad, Thomson. "*Ignis Salvator?* Fire Savior? Savior, sure—aha, that's your pun, Dunasheen's salvation. But why *fire?*"

"Therein lies a tale. Sit down, be comfortable." Fergie

gestured toward two wingback chairs beside the fireplace, their fabric faded and frayed.

Smoothing his kilt beneath him, Alasdair sat, but his body language hinted at anything but comfort—he perched on the edge of the chair like a little boy outside the principal's office. Jean sat down and, surprised to find her notepad and pencil still in her hand, scribbled an outline dense with question marks.

Fergie posed on the hearth, in front of the flaming peat, hands folded behind his back and face almost feverish—not only from strong drink or the heat of the fire. "The Crusader Coffer. Perhaps it was brought to Dunasheen by Norman the Red's father, who found it, like the Flagon, in Alexandria. Crossroads of the world, Alexandria, and famous for its catacombs, both pagan and Christian."

"True," said Jean, and wrote *listen* on her page.

"Perhaps the Coffer was brought by crusaders. Perhaps—well, this is a bit over the top..."

"Is it now?" Alasdair murmured.

"...perhaps it was left here on Skye two millennia past, by the Romans who sailed round the British Isles, the ones who left Roman coins here. They knew of Skye, Ptolemy of Alexandria wrote of it. Alexandria again, founded by Alexander, and your name's the Gaelic version of Alexander, Alasdair."

"Like as not," said Alasdair, "those coins were lost by some lad just back from a Grand Tour, no more than two centuries ago. Or it could be that your wee chest was brought here by soldiers serving in Palestine in the nineteenth or twentieth centuries."

"No provenance," Jean reiterated. "No documentation."

But Fergie was in full flow. He rocked back on his heels, kilt swaying. "You're eager to get to the crux of the matter, understandably enough. *Crux,* Latin for cross, right? This is it, then: I not only believe the chest is an ossuary of the time of Jesus, I believe that it contained relics of Jesus Christ him-self. Now, I know what you're thinking."

"No, Fergie," said Alasdair faintly, "you do not know what I'm thinking."

Jean was beginning to feel like a hostage, except she was trapped by courtesy and curiosity. With no choice but to play along, she squeaked, "Um, the, er, crux of the Christian faith is that Jesus was resurrected. There were no remains to put in an ossuary."

"Got it in one," Fergie said with a sage nod. "We know from studying the Shroud of Turin that Jesus's body discorpo-rated in a burst of energy. That's the only deduction you can make from the singe marks on the cloth. A remarkable event, one that we'd call a miracle. There's no saying how many times a similar event may have happened over the course of history, but this is the one suitably documented."

It might not be logical, Jean thought, to use the Bible to document the Bible, but logic had left the building along with Gilnockie and Young.

"The cloth that was pinned round Jesus's head is in Oviedo, Spain," Fergie said. "The bloodstains and singe marks on it correspond to those on the Shroud."

"Well, yes, they do," conceded Jean, more to Alasdair than to Fergie.

Slowly, expressionlessly, Alasdair reached out, placed the camera on the table, and let his hand fall to the arm of the chair.

"No one knows how many other cloths were in contact with his body, stained with blood and sweat, when he dis-corporated. But one thing we do know. The disciples of Jesus were eager to gather relics of his time on Earth. They would have swept the stone slab where he was laid, the stone slab where the Shroud and the Oviedo cloth were found, and saved every loose thread, every grain of dust or ash."

"And," Jean said on a long sigh, "put them in an ossuary labeled 'Jesus of Nazareth, fire savior.'"

"Yes, yes." Fergie grinned happily, his glasses glittering in the lights on the Christmas tree—or, more likely, in the lights in his eyes.

A female voice on the Chieftains album launched into "O Holy Night." Wrong season. This should all be going down at Easter. Or Pentecost, when tongues of flame, symbolizing the Holy Ghost, appeared on the heads of the Apostles.

Alasdair's own eyes went from fixed to positively glazed. "You're joking. You're having us on. You're taking the mickey on account of Jean's writing about, erm, weird stuff."

"No, not a bit of it," Fergie assured him. "I want Jean to write about the Crusader Coffer. That's a misnomer, I confess, but I had to call it something less, well, inflammatory, if you'll pardon the expression. I want Jean to write about it because it's weird. Because it's uncanny. That's the point. It proves the existence of a world beyond ours."

"Proves," Alasdair repeated, his tone dripping despair.

Jean sent him a sympathetic look, which bounced ineffectually off the side of his face. Yes, her tolerance for this sort of bafflegab was a lot higher than his—especially when the person gabbing the baffle was one of his oldest friends. She didn't feel threatened by this sort of free association, a gonzo tour of history and mythology. She enjoyed it the way Dougie enjoyed catnip. It was intoxicating, even if you did feel a bit foolish after you sobered up.

The problem, as Alasdair would quickly point out, was not realizing this sort of thing was myth. Acting on it as though it was chemistry rather than alchemy, astronomy rather than astrology. A leap of faith could just as well be a leap of folly. Or both.

Foolish. She looked up at Fergie's guileless face. Foolish fire, *ignis fatuus,* was Latin for will o' the wisp. A supernatural light leading a traveler from a sunburned land to his doom, while not saving a deeply rooted laird from his. Jean tried again. "Why is the inscription in Latin? Jesus and his followers spoke Aramaic."

"But within only a few years of his, ah, disappearance, St. Peter brought the faith to Rome."

"And the Romans wanted to get rid of this particular relic by dumping it here, at what they saw as the end of the world? Why didn't they just throw it into the ocean?"

"No, no, it's the other way round. Early believers brought it here to save it from the Roman persecutions. The foundations of Dunasheen's old church could have been laid hundred of years before those of St Ninian's church at Whithorn in Galloway."

"Which is thought to be the first Christian foundation in Scotland," said Jean.

"Exactly. Whithorn's attracted excavations, a visitor centre—loads of attention. That just goes to show how holy mysteries lead to heritage conservation. I'll not mention the worldwide interest in Rosslyn Chapel." Fergie throttled back his grin. "But then, let's not go overboard. The Coffer was brought here in the Middle Ages, I expect, along with the Flagon. No matter. Finding the Coffer is a miracle, in its own small way, for us here at Dunasheen. *Dun na sithein,* fortress of the fairies. Maybe my uncle wasn't far wrong about the provenance of the Flagon, in a way."

Alasdair's head fell forward and he covered his face with his hand.

"In a way?" Jean prompted.

"Suffice it to say now," said Fergie, "that tales of fairies are based on an ancient race of people who were driven underground. By whom?"

Jean didn't bother answering, *Celtic invaders armed with iron swords.* She clutched her own weapon, her pencil, braced for the next blow. The fire popped. A clock ticked. A peal of bells sounded from the CD, foretelling the midnight bells of New Year's Eve, soon to come.

Again Fergie rocked back on his heels. "The Ark of the Covenant supposedly held a sacred stone that fell from the sky. The sacred stone in Mecca's Kaaba fell from the sky. Tut-ankh-Amun's pectoral is centered on a scarab cut from glass formed when a meteor, a stone falling from the sky, hit the Egyptian desert. Some versions of the Holy Grail story say it's a stone that fell from the sky."

"Fergie," said Jean, "please do not tell us the Fairy Flagon is the Holy Grail."

"Oh! Do you think it might be?" Fergie replied.

Alasdair darted Jean a baleful look from between his fingers.

Fergie laughed. "Sorry, I couldn't resist a wee bit of a tease there. Of course it's not the Holy Grail. That's a legend."

"Never underestimate the power of a legend," Jean told Alasdair rather than Fergie.

Fergie was off again. "Although the shape of the Flagon's handles is suggestive, isn't it? Like wings. In Egyptian iconography, wings are protective and feathers mean truth. The feathered serpent is a major part of Mayan iconography. We talk about the winged flight of the soul. It was once customary to carve winged skulls on tombstones."

"Oh aye," said Alasdair beneath his breath. "So it was."

"Wings, angels, flight, heaven is up, hell is down. Sacred stones fall from the sky. Early figures like Krishna, Buddha, Jesus worked miracles and beat death itself. All together, there's only one logical conclusion. It's staring us in the face."

Not Alasdair's face, revealed as another work of stone when he lowered his hand and looked in appeal at Jean. She looked from the manger scene on the mantel to the dark lump of the Coffer to the pale, elegant Flagon, which seemed to glow against the dark backdrop of the bookcases.

Bookcases holding books about alien astronauts.

"You're remembering the old science fiction writer." Jean paused to clear her throat. "The writer who said that any sufficiently advanced technology would seem like magic to those less technologically advanced. Except you're not thinking magic. You're thinking miracle."

Fergie applauded. "Yes! Well done, Jean! I must say, Alasdair, you've chosen yourself a very clever lady here."

Especially when you took into account Alasdair's first wife's own capacity for bafflegab—a calculation that, judging by Alasdair's slightly crossed eyes, he was making. He opened his mouth, shook his head, closed it again, and waved his hand toward Jean. *It's all yours.*

No, it was all Fergie's. "When you look at the stars," he said, "at the vast array of the heavens, how can we be the only sentient creatures in existence? What if other cultures had head starts on ours, and explored Earth millennia ago, helping our own ancestors down from the trees and up into civilization? Fairies are racial memories of the inferior beings our ancestors once were, of the beings we can still be, whilst our deities are superior beings who came to us from the sky. There's evidence all over the world. Look at the Maya tomb clearly depicting Lord Pacal as an astronaut, for example. Look at the faces on the Easter Island statues."

Well sure, look at the way an inkblot clearly depicted your mother-in-law. Jean tried to pull Fergie back to an object more solid than ink. Or moonshine. "Greg MacLeod may never have actually seen the Coffer, but you must have sent him photos."

"Oh yes, I did, to whet his interest. He offered to pay out of his own pocket to have it tested, inside and out. We have the residue of the ages in the tracks of the inscriptions. We have blood, ashes, scraps of cloth adhering to the interior walls. A shame the lid's gone missing, but then, you have the symbol of the empty tomb, don't you? Carbon-dating, DNA tests—they can do amazing things with tiny bits of DNA."

"Like on the *C.S.I.* shows?"

"Well yes, I expect so, but I was thinking of medical equipment—Emma, mind you…" Fergie slumped, the light fading from his eyes, then pulled himself up again. "Finding DNA of Jesus Christ would set the world on its ear. Sequencing the DNA, proving it to be that of an alien—oh my. What a glorious moment in human history that would be. Proof, absolute proof."

"Of alien astronauts?"

"Yes, yes, of course. But also of life beyond this earth, beyond this reality. It would prove the truth of all the world religions in one *coup de foudre*." Pressing his lips together, perhaps to still their trembling, Fergie turned to lean his forearm on the mantelpiece and his forehead on his arm.

It wasn't done to show strong emotion, was it? Jean wondered vaguely as if Fergie was on some kind of medication—although it seemed unfair to attribute such a formidable flight of imagination to an array of chemicals, or to try and ground it with another array.

Coup de foudre. A lightning bolt from the blue. Like love at first sight, not something that had happened with her and Alasdair. Whether it had happened to Fergie and Emma didn't matter, not now.

Alasdair gazed bleakly at the silver buttons on the tails of Fergie's formal jacket. It wasn't done, either, to put your arm around an old friend suffering from lost love.

Through the heavy panels of the door came the rumble of the drinks trolley.

TWENTY-TWO

DIANA MADE HER entrance to The Chieftains' "The Mason's Apron." But blaming the convolutions of Western history on the Freemasons, Jean thought, was about the only variation on a theme—on a vastly overused and overrated theme—that Fergie hadn't played. Yet.

Diana looked from face to face to the back of Fergie's head. Her features, now lightly touched with cosmetics, set themselves sternly. "Father, Mr. Pritchard would like to see you in your office."

"Oh. Well then." Fergie straightened. When he turned back around he was smiling bravely, although the glitter in his eyes was now less gloat than grief. With an admiring glance at the Coffer and the Flagon and an affectionate pat on Diana's shoulder, he walked away down the hall.

Alasdair rested his elbows on his thighs and contemplated his clasped hands against the tartan apron of his kilt. Jean closed her notepad and tucked it back into her bag. Even though her stomach had sunk into her knees beneath the weight of Fergie's castle in the air, she managed to get to her feet and stay on them. "Beautiful dress," she told Diana. "Is it the one in your mother's portrait?"

Diana smoothed the dark green velvet panels of her skirt, her throat and head rising from the satin shawl collar like the classical burst of a goddess. "Yes, it was her favorite. If we'd buried her, we'd have buried her in it, I suppose—I do beg your pardon, that was a morbid remark."

Alasdair's gaze shot upward from beneath his eyebrows.

Good lord, Fergie had Emma cryogenically frozen, waiting for the aliens and their miracles to come back. Jean asked, half-strangled, "Your mother wasn't buried?"

"She was cremated," Diana said. "We scattered her ashes amongst the daffodils here at Dunasheen."

Alasdair closed his eyes. Swept with relief and embarrassment, Jean began, "I'm sorry, I didn't mean to pry."

"Not to worry." Diana's stern face softened into sadness. "I know what Father's been telling you. He's gone round the bend. Mother's death, and the pressures of running the estate, and, well, I tried to spare his feelings by hiding my relationship with Colin. Hindsight being what it is, we realize we've made a mistake when it's too late to mend the damage it's caused. Was it you asked for wassail? Would you prefer whiskey or something else?"

Jean detected a request to change the subject. "The Krums were asking for wassail. But I'll take some, too, thank you."

"I'll have the whiskey, cheers." Alasdair almost concealed his groan as he stood up.

Diana wielded cup and ladle, glass and bottle. "There you are."

"Thank you. Can I help in the kitchen?" Jean asked.

Turning up her lips in a smile, Diana stepped over the fireplace and grasped the poker. "Thank you, no. Since Inspector Gilnockie asked Colin to stop here tonight, he's set himself to work preparing food for the police officers in the incident, erm, old kitchen. I dare not send anyone else into the new kitchen, Rab's muttering in his beard about folk underfoot and Nancy's threatening to wallop him with her spoon. Rab, that is, though I expect Colin's on her hit list as well." She jabbed at the fire. Sparks flew. Flames leaped.

Alasdair tossed back a swig of his whiskey, the water of life. Jean could trace its path through his mouth, down into his stomach, up into his head, by his features once more becoming pliable and the sheen of steel draining from his eyes.

She gulped thirstily at her punch. The sharp, sweet spices cleared the acid from her mouth and eased her clenched stomach. Another gulp, and she was surprised to see the cup empty. Every object in the room slipped into higher resolution, even as the floor executed an infinitesimal shimmy beneath her feet. *Whoa.*

"Father and I are making contingency plans," Diana said to the images writhing in the fire, "in the event your friends arrive Saturday but Inspector Gilnockie hasn't released the Krums or re-opened the Queen suite. We'd meant to put your Mr. Munro in our single, the Robert the Bruce room, but Colin's there just now. He's still a suspect. But as ex-police, Alasdair, you know that."

"Aye." Alasdair's tone was gentle, his message not.

Diana spun around, her eyes a blue blaze. "Colin couldn't have killed Greg MacLeod. He'd never met the man. He had no motive."

Couldn't have, Jean thought, rather than *didn't?*

"You were with him at the time of the murder, then?" Alasdair asked.

"No I wasn't, more's the pity. I stopped in at the lighthouse but he wasn't there. Nor did I see him in the gardens. You could hide a small army there, even in winter."

Yeah. Jean remembered her impression that someone was following first her and Dakota, then her and Alasdair. She'd assumed it was Pritchard, but she'd been wrong many times before.

"Colin wouldn't hide from me," Diana concluded.

Not unless he was up to no good, said Alasdair's frown. He finished off the whiskey.

"Did you go by the old church?" Jean enunciated with her slightly benumbed tongue. "Did you see anyone there?"

"No. I walked through the far end of the garden. In the murk, I could barely see the church. Someone might have been standing behind the walls." Diana clanged the poker into its stand. "I didn't kill Greg. His purchase of the Coffer would have made quite a difference to our, erm, to us. I don't know where we'll find another dealer with, with less than..." She bit off her sentence.

With less than a full deck of scruples? Yes, Greg knew exactly what he'd have bought.

"Well then. I believe Scott Krum deals in art rather than antiquities, but you never know what might interest him." Diana's shoes clicked briskly across the room.

Alasdair leaped forward to open the door, but she was already through it and away. He shut it instead. The fire popped. The Chieftains fell silent. Jean realized she was still holding the cup, and put it down next to Fergie's empty glass.

"Fergie's gone daft," said Alasdair.

"Well, it is the Daft Days, not that I think he'll snap out of it at the stroke of midnight." Jean walked over to the table holding the two antiquities, antiquity being relative.

"I knew he enjoyed reading about alien astronauts and the like," Alasdair went on. "I did not know he'd launched himself into outer space. You're always reading that sort of rubbish, you're writing about it, but you're knowing what's real and what's not. Most of the time, leastways."

She could hear the wry half-smile in his voice. "At least Fergie's not wearing aluminum foil on his head to keep the aliens from reading his mind."

Glass rang, probably as Alasdair returned his tumbler to the trolley. His solid shape stepped up beside her. "You cannot write about this. He wants you to, I know that, but..."

"I'll figure out some way of presenting it in the context of, 'Hey, travelers, Dunasheen is a great place to visit.' God knows I've wanted to make fun of some of these people, but this is your Fergie Beg. There's publicity and there's public-ity." She touched the surface of the Flagon, so smoothly pol-ished it felt like cold butter. "I can't help it, Alasdair. The true believers, they get me at 'what if.'"

His forefinger flicked the alabaster, which replied with a sound between a chime and a thunk. "That's the problem. Fer-gie's not saying 'if' nearly often enough. Here's the poor sod thinking that selling the Coffer's the answer to their financial prayers. But there's no saying what hopes I'd be clinging to, if I'd lost—you." He folded her in his arm and pulled her close.

She slipped her arm around his waist, reveling in the liv-ing flesh beneath his coat. "Poor sod, yes. He's grasping at every possible straw. Well, almost. For a minute there I ex-pected him to segue into the old wheeze about the plots of the Freemasons, especially since there really is a stone mason involved with all this."

"Tormod MacLeod, aye, and his descendant going into the trade in holy relics. You were thinking earlier about Greg selling the Pilate inscription, were you?"

"Yep." Jean peered critically into the dank, scrubby inte-rior of the Coffer. "God only knows what was in here. They find so many ossuaries in the Holy Land that people uset-hem as flower pots."

This time Alasdair's finger-flick produced a dull clunk. "I'm no geologist, but that's looking to be basalt, same as the inscription, eh?"

"I'm under the impression that the most common stone in the Holy Land, that every provenanced ossuary, is limestone. You're thinking what I'm thinking, aren't you? The Flagon really did come from Egypt at some time or another, but the Coffer didn't come from anywhere. It was made here, from local stone. Just like Greg's Pilate inscription."

"One test, and Fergie's house of cards will come tumbling

down." Alasdair glanced at the painting over the mantle, Calanais beneath not a rising moon but a landing spaceship.

"People used to see angels. Now they see UFOs. Seeing is
believing, and believing is seeing. Never underestimate either
the will to believe or the will to exploit belief."

"Greg MacLeod scored a goal with the Pilate inscription,
so meant to..." Alasdair's keen blue gaze skidded back to
Jean's face. "Half a tick, now. Rebecca was saying that testing the inscription showed dust and debris from the right era."

"And if the BHRS bought the Coffer from Greg and actually tested it, they'd find the same. Probably exactly the
same. Soil samples from an archaeological dig aren't all that
hard to come by, even in Australia, not if you're a resource-
ful guy like Greg."

Alasdair's brows lofted upward even as his head canted
to the side.

"When I talked to Michael yesterday, he said Rebecca
herself had just been involved in a case at Holyrood, a collar
supposedly belonging to Mary, Queen of Scots. The collar
was genuine sixteenth-century, fine, but someone very recently sewed Mary's monogram on it, scuffed the new stitches
around to make them look worn, and then smeared them
with period dirt. But there were traces of polyester on the
actual thread."

"Ah. Clever, that."

"There's been more than one case of genuine Bible-era artifacts enhanced with inscriptions or whatever, to make them
more valuable. And forgers and fakers are learning how to
outsmart sophisticated scientific equipment."

Alasdair nodded, sorting, processing, filing.

Jean picked up her cup and Fergie's glass and headed back
to the trolley, more in the interests of tidiness than thirst. Her
buzz might be evaporating, but still, more wassail now and

she'd be under the dining room table by the end of the evening meal.

"You know," she went on, with another look at the manger scene, "by definition, faith is evidence of things unseen. I don't understand why so many people think it has to be supported by 'seen' evidence. That makes faith into a house of cards. A church of cards. You pull one out and the entire structure is worthless. If your faith is that precarious, then why bother with it at all?"

"Is that what Fergie's on about? Proving the supernatural underpinnings of religious faith and therefore proving the afterlife?"

"I'm not sure Fergie knows what he's on about. At least he's not holding Emma here as a ghost—she's not the Green Lady, Seonaid is. I don't know what Rory down at the old castle is."

"An old soul looking out a soft landing," said Alasdair.

Heavy footsteps approached and the door opened, shoved by Fergie's shoulder. He was carrying a tray piled with bits of fruit and veg on toothpicks. He set it on the trolley and stared at it, not exactly frowning, but his face so tight Jean expected it to bow into a frown at any moment.

"Lionel Pritchard?" suggested Alasdair.

"Bloody cheek!" Fergie exclaimed. "He only just handed in his resignation before I sacked him. I told him to vacate his cottage straightaway—we can settle your guests there, if necessary."

"You fired him?" Jean asked.

"He said he'd been harassed by the police, that Colin's detracting from the tone of the place and is likely the guilty party, and that Diana's a hypocrite, hoity toity to a fault but with a taste for the rough in Colin. Damn the man!" Fergie didn't specify which man. "Lionel feels he was perfectly justified in—well, I can hardly credit his confession. The neck!"

"Confession?" Jean and Alasdair said simultaneously, and

Alasdair added, sidling toward the door, "He's confessed to killing Greg, has he? The Portree alibi's a setup?"

"Ah no, no. Sorry." Fergie turned his red, indignant face toward Alasdair. "He was right chuffed to tell me he'd found that, that, damned business card, the one Greg gave or sent to someone—likely his killer, I realize that—Pritchard found it in the parking area soon after returning from Portree, and—I ask you! He realized the implications, yes, but did he take it to the police? No, he put it in the pocket of Diana's coat so she'd assume Colin was the murderer, and turn against him. Then Pritchard himself would move in for the kill. Not his words, mind you, but mine."

Jean didn't point out that no matter what Pritchard had done, Colin was still a suspect, or that everyone up to and including the local sheep had walked through the parking area potentially dropping business cards the afternoon of the murder. A break in the case—or a hairline crack—was still a break. She said, "Those initials weren't Colin's. They're shorthand for 'see you.'"

"So it seems. Now. And now we're obliged to do without a manager—economizing on his salary, that's all to the good…" Fergie sputtered out.

Alasdair fished the telephone from his sporran and punched a couple of buttons. "Well then. Pritchard and I are going to be having us a wee word about concealing police evidence. Jean struck lucky finding that card, it might have been days before Diana turned it up, if ever. Hello, Patrick, Alasdair here…" Closer to spitting than sputtering, he vanished out the door.

TWENTY-THREE

"Good man, Alasdair," Fergie said stoutly. "He'll sort things."

Jean nodded agreement, if more flabbily than stoutly, but then, positive thinking never hurt.

Chimes ranging from deep-throated to tinny resonated in the corners of the house as all the clocks struck seven. American accents wafted up the hall—Heather's snarky whine, Scott's edgy rumble, Dakota's hesitant trill.

Here they came, dressed to the nines. Scott's dark suit was impeccably tailored and color-coordinated with his shirt, just as his yellow power tie matched the handkerchief square in his pocket. Heather's dress was draped just so, clinging here, flowing there. The fabric was printed with a retro groovy psychedelic pattern, man—starbursts and daisy chains in shades of purple. Dakota wore decorative flats, a pink dress, and a sweater appliqued with cats, if not the frilly-socks-and-petticoat of a little girl, then not the mini-hooker style that Jean blamed on marketers gone wild.

"Ah, bang on time!" Finding his second or perhaps third wind, Fergie once again donned the mantle of genial host. "Come in, come in. Here's your wassail—a find tradition, wassail. And here's another tradition, the holiday boar."

Heather's eye-roll implied she'd heard that as "bore." Scott eyed Fergie's kilt with a half-concealed snicker.

Fergie went on, "In place of the boar's head that our ancestors would have had for their holiday feast, I've had Nancy make us one from half a pineapple."

Everyone leaned closer. Sure enough, the toothpicks holding morsels of fruit or olives resembled bristles rising from the half-mound of a pineapple. Two maraschino cherries and an apple slice formed a face, and a curled licorice whip a tail. Even as she handed Dakota a melon square and helped herself to a stuffed green olive, Jean imagined what Nancy—or, more likely, Rab—had said about such whimsy, especially when the holiday boar was an olde English custom, not Scottish.

She drifted away toward the tree, inhaling its head-clearing pine fragrance. The Christmas tree was another English custom late coming to Scotland. So was wassail, for that matter. Fergie's "old-fashioned" Hogmanay was as much imagination as tradition—not that there was anything wrong with that.

He carried on to the Krums about the exceptionally humorless Scottish Protestant Reformation, and how Hogmanay had become more important than Christmas, since Christmas was seen as Catholic, even pagan. Christmas Day wasn't a holiday in Scotland until the 1950s, about the time Fergie was born.

So, Jean thought, Norman the Red's folly of a chapel with its Catholic features would have brought down the disapproval of the local community within living memory, never mind in Norman's era…. She cast a sharp glance at the Coffer just as Scott strolled toward it.

Dakota hung on Fergie's every word, blinking owlishly and seizing the occasional grape from the back of the boar. "The days between Christmas and New Year's are the Daft Days, it being the time of year for role reversals, the lairds and ladies serving the tenants…" His gaze strayed to where Scott was circling the Flagon and the Coffer like a sharp scenting prey. "Excuse me, please."

"More family heirlooms, like Diana's necklace?" Scott asked as Fergie hove to beside him.

"Why yes, they are that." Fergie proceeded to deliver a sales pitch in which he confined himself to the facts, such as the facts were.

Wassail in hand, Heather sat down next to the fire. Her strappy sandals with spike heels enclosed purple toenails—from polish, Jean assumed, not the cold.

From outside the window came the emphatic slam of a car door, followed by the sounds of its engine starting up and puling away into the distance. From the corridor came Alasdair, doing his best imitation of the Sphinx. He nodded a stiff greeting to each of the Krums and joined Jean in the lee of the Christmas tree. If he noticed each set of American eyes focused on his tartan-clad nether regions—Scott skeptical, Heather intrigued, Dakota impressed—he ignored them.

"Well?" Jean asked, lowering her voice.

"I put a flea in Pritchard's ear, right enough, and had him show me where he found the card, just next a flower pot to the left of the porch."

"Out of the rain, sort of."

"Aye, but still, it had not been lying there long when he picked it up."

Nibbling a bit of pineapple off its toothpick, Dakota drifted past the tree toward the bookshelves. Heather leaned back in the chair, crossed her legs, and let her sandal dangle from her toes.

"Maybe Greg never sent or gave the card to anyone. Maybe it fell out of his own car. Although," Jean added before Alasdair could, "he had to have intended to give it to someone, to remind them of their appointment. Unless Pritchard's lying about finding it where he did."

"I'm seeing no reason for that. He's enjoying the stramash caused by one wee bit business card."

Scott said to Fergie, "Yeah, there's a lot of money in that sort of thing. The problem is…"

"Patrick," Alasdair went on, "is saying that he'll stop by the hospital soon as Tina's coherent, may or may not be returning here the night, depending."

Dakota's voice came from the far side of the Christmas tree—for a fraction Jean thought it was a robin ornament speaking. "What business card is that?"

"A bit of evidence." Alasdair peered around a tinsel-hung branch.

Dakota peered back again. "Tina. That's the Australian lady, right?"

"Right."

"Why's she in the hospital?"

It was just as well the Krums had been wandering around Kinlochroy and missed the entire episode. "There was an accident," Jean said, "and she fell, but she's going to be all right."

Her words plummeted into the room like Tina from the window. Heather said, "You told us the man had been hurt in an accident and it turned out to be..."

"Heather," said Scott.

"I'm just saying," she retorted. "What's going on here, anyway?"

"Madam," Alasdair told her, "that's what we're after finding out."

The door opened and Diana swept in. "Well now, isn't this jolly," she didn't ask but stated, with the air of Captain Picard on the bridge of the *Enterprise* saying, "Make it so."

"Is that a vintage dress?" Heather asked.

"Why yes, it is."

"Nothing like recycling other people's old stuff, is there?"

Diana's smile froze rather than faltered. "More wassail, Mrs. Krum? What are you having, Mr. Krum? Dakota?"

Dakota started to speak but Heather beat her to the draw. "No more for her. The kid's gonna spoil her dinner with that fruit stuff. Isn't it time to eat yet? All they had at the pub in the village was chips and peanuts, no Buffalo wings or regular food, you know."

Fergie didn't know—or so his blank expression attested. But he rallied quickly. "Yes, yes, let's go on to the dining room. I'm sure Nancy's almost ready to serve the starter course."

With one last look into the Coffer, annotated by a slow nod, Scott rounded up his womenfolk and followed Diana toward the dining room.

Fergie stayed behind to stow the Coffer and the Flagon in their cabinets. Locking the doors and slipping the key into the breast pocket of his jacket, he turned to Jean and Alasdair and said, "Well then. All might not be lost after all."

"Did Krum have himself a look at the Coffer when he visited last autumn?" asked Alasdair.

"No, he wasn't familiar with either it or the Flagon. Or so he said," Fergie added, his hand raised in a placatory gesture. "I know, I know, if Pritchard did show Krum the Coffer when he was here, then maybe he wanted it badly enough to bump off, to rub out—" Jean heard the quotation marks in his voice "—a rival from Down Under. Pity, that. If the two men had started bidding against each other—but no, no, mustn't be greedy. A man's life has been lost. Dinner?"

"We'll be along straightaway," Alasdair told him, and, after Fergie had made his exit, "Greg was a freelancer. Krum works for an auction house."

"Yep," said Jean, starting for the door, "Scott would need more than Fergie's 'what-ifs' to justify buying the Coffer. He'd need tests."

They dodged as Rab plunged through the doorway like a wild boar on his way to a china shop. Despite his barrel chest and short legs, his suit was as well cut as Scott's, even though its rusty blackness evoked mortuaries rather than art auction houses. "We've seen the back of Pritchard, have we?"

"Aye, that we have," said Alasdair.

"Good riddance. We've got more than enough incomers as

it is." Rab shut the doors between the library and the drawing room, switched off the lights and the CD player, then seized the drinks trolley and with many a clink and gurgle charged back through the doorway and trundled off in the direction of the Great Hall.

"What was I saying about the hospitality business and strange bedfellows?" Jean asked as she and Alasdair proceeded to the dining room.

He opened the door, releasing a warm gust of air and multiple luscious smells, and said nothing about Rab. He said nothing about anything, even as he seated Jean at the table and took his own seat beside Dakota. Tina's chair had once again vanished.

Fergie and Diana began batting the conversational shuttlecock up and down the table. Rab reappeared to wield the corkscrew and fill the wine goblets, heavy glasses etched with age as well as designs. Nancy trekked back and forth between table and kitchen, carrying plates and bowls in dish-towel-protected hands. Tonight her ruffled apron covered black silk pants and a silver lamé tunic that complemented her rhinestone earrings and her gray hair, which was adorned by a sprig of holly.

Jean didn't know whether it was Diana's vegetable-carving abilities or Nancy's culinary talents, but even the usually humble neep bree, or turnip soup, was delicious. Probably each bowl contained the equivalent of a stick of butter, but what the heck, it was New Year's Eve. The end of another year. The end of the most remarkable year of her life.

Fergie said, "Hogmanay stems from ancient rituals and customs determined by the working of the land and the passing of the seasons."

"Such pagan customs lingered here in the western isles," said Diana.

Heather sucked in her soup. "This is turnip? You're kidding."

Nancy swept it with the next course, haggis rounds on diced potato. "What?" asked Dakota.

"Boiled guts," Scott told her, and excavated his potato from beneath the brownish, browned patty without touching it.

Considering the tarted-up stunt-cooked haggis—haggis pakora, haggis wonton—Jean had recently encountered, Nancy's no-frills version of the national dish was tasty indeed. And not because Rab kept cruising by topping off every glass except Dakota's and, Jean noted, Diana's.

The child looked from Jean to Alasdair and back as though assessing the prospect of such elderly people holding a wedding. Or maybe her thoughtful looks indicated a siblinghood of the ghost-allergic, one with its own passwords and secret handshakes. Maybe she was simply bemused by the stately home lifestyle, since her gaze rested on Rab and Nancy as long as they were in the room.

Fergie began recounting the legend of Rory MacLeod, his lady love, the vengeful sword, the leap from the tower into death and a local, at least, fame.

"Mom," Dakota said, making the one-syllable word into two, "we haven't been to the old castle yet."

"And we're not going," Heather returned. "It's dangerous."

"We'll walk down the path toward it," suggested Scott. "You know, far enough to take a photo."

With a heavy sigh, Dakota's gaze fell to her boiled guts.

Jean offered Scott a narrow-eyed look. He and Heather did not have proper alibis for the time of Greg's murder. What they had was a motive of sorts, competition for the artifacts needed to support a high-maintenance lifestyle. He'd parked the car near the place Pritchard had found the card. When he'd brought in the luggage, his muddy boots left prints on the tile floor of the entrance hall… Well, Gilnockie and Young were teleconferencing over the preliminary crime scene reports right this minute. Maybe they'd match tread and mud.

At Fergie's signal, Rab stepped up to the sideboard and sacrificed yet another bottle of wine on the altar of conviviality. Jean turned her studious gaze to him.

Pritchard's alibi might depend on the testimony of his female friend, but he also had the backup accounts of other pubgoers. Rab and Nancy, though... Well, Jean reminded herself, first Thomson had seen Rab in the pub, then Fergie had seen both him and Nancy in the kitchen, cooking dinner.

The heritage industry wasn't Rab's thing, any more than incomers were his thing, but how did that translate into a motive for murder? Diana was right—why would she, or Nancy or Rab, or even Colin, the collateral suspect, murder their golden goose? Fergie could still auction off the Coffer, but most buyers would ask questions. Even the BHRS needed their pump primed by Greg's archaeological dirt, and they were more credulous than curious.

Rab whisked away her empty plate and Jean tuned back in to hear Alasdair making a few remarks about his own childhood holidays in Fort William. Fergie contributed an account of a London Christmas. Jean offered several snack-sized tidbits of historical gossip. Dakota asked about the progress of the murder investigation, and was quelled right smartly by her parents.

Nancy delivered salmon in pastry, lamb bundles and vegetables and sauces, and eventually a dessert of Tipsy Laird, layers of cake and custard laced with sherry and topped with cream. Dakota took one bite and made a face.

Jean was not a fan of sherry, either, although it was palatable when spiked with sugar and cream. Nibbling, she wondered whether Nancy could cook anything that didn't include some variety of full-fat milk product.

Heather scarfed the lot, laughing merrily, while Scott egged her on with double-entendres. Fergie smiled on them all, benignly if a bit out of focus, embodying the laird who was tipsy.

Although, Jean thought when she followed Diana's example and stood up, she should speak for herself. This time the walls shimmied, so that the faces of all the warriors seemed to nod and wink.

Alasdair glided around the table to take her arm. "You've got no head for drink, have you now," he murmured.

"I know, I'm a disgrace to my Celtic ancestry," she replied, and stepped gingerly into the corridor.

W.P.C. McCrummin and an unidentified male colleague stood outside the old kitchen, sipping from mugs. Playing the role of tenants, Jean supposed, although their roles wouldn't be reversed—laird, lady, tenant, servant, or local hermit, a murderer was a murderer was a…

No more alcohol, she informed herself, and let Alasdair's firm grasp guide her back down the corridor to where Fergie had thrown open the doors of the Great Hall.

This was Jean's favorite room of the house, from the intricate plaster whorls of the high ceiling, one pendant dangling an iron lantern, past the silky wood railing of the musician's gallery and an array of banners that Fergie had bought from a movie prop company, to the somewhat threadbare Hunting MacDonald tartan carpet that matched the backs and seats of several chairs. Here was where the wedding reception would be held. Was scheduled to be held.

Tonight a massive Yule log burned in an even more massive fireplace, beneath a plaster MacDonald crest, the galley sailing a sea that looked like soot-stained billows of whipped cream. The pungent odor of juniper overwhelmed that of smoke and furniture polish—burning juniper on New Year's Eve being another good luck custom, not a slap at the MacLeods.

"Whoa," said Dakota. "Cool! It's like a princess's palace!"

Heather leaned against Scott with a grope, a giggle, and a *nyahh!* glance toward Diana, who ignored them. Thank goodness the Krums turned goofy, not even more combative, when they'd been drinking. Jean even forgave Heather for asking Alasdair, "So what do you have on beneath your kilt, huh?"

Smiling thinly, he replied, "And what are you wearing beneath your dress, Mrs. Krum?"

"Wouldn't you like to know?" she replied with another giggle.

"Liqueur?" Fergie made his approach to the trolley, intent on observing a very genuine and much-honored Scottish tradition, that of sliding well lubricated into the new year.

Jean took a glass of fizzy water with a slice of lemon. So did Alasdair, designating himself the resident adult—as though Diana wasn't already playing that part. Fergie tuned a radio to dance music, accordions pumping and fiddles flying, and organized word games and charades. Soon he no longer looked as though he was blowing air into a balloon with a hole in it. Even Diana acted as mistress of the revels with more than good grace, with actual laughter.

Rab drifted in, collected empty glasses, drifted out again, the roll in his step indicating he was observing liquid tradition himself. Nancy placed platters of digestive biscuits and cheeses on the refectory table and guessed at a few riddles. A throbbing soprano on the radio sang Burns' "Ca the Yowes to the Knowes," leading to Fergie's exposition on Scots dialect. Scott and Heather tried a few impromptu dance steps and Dakota inspected the cinematic banners—the raven of Odin, Cernunnos with his horns, the White Horse of Rohan and the White Tree of Gondor from *The Lord of the Rings*. "Cool," she said again, and grabbed a chocolate cookie.

Every now and then, Jean noticed, Alasdair retired into his own thoughts, no doubt trying to wrestle a solution not only to murder but to Fergie's dilemma by sheer will and brain power. Every now and then she faded out, too, as though the signal on her mental radio station momentarily weakened.

It wasn't that she was exerting brain power. She'd done that. Now she was tired and her stomach slightly queasy, not only from the rich food and drink but also from digesting Fergie's pie in the sky. The gaiety began to seem forced, as though everyone was waiting for something—for Gilnockie to appear and call them all together with his solution to the case, for Alasdair to leap forward and finger the culprit... Well, duh, they were waiting for midnight. The witching hour.

She caught a movement in the musician's gallery and looked sharply up. But no, her thumbs weren't pricking and nothing wicked stood there, not even Seonaid. Colin leaned on the railing, smiling wistfully down at Diana—until he realized Jean had seen him and faded back into the shadows.

Neither of them had alibis for the time of Greg's murder, either. That they'd admitted to having no alibis was surely a point in their favor. On the other hand, Colin had said he was at the lighthouse and Diana had said he wasn't, so who was telling the truth? And never mind Young's overzealous persecution, she had a point—what if Colin had for some reason flipped out, just as he had in the pub—he'd have to have taken the regimental dirk, though...

Alasdair considered the polyester zebra skin draped over a chair, a fabric carrot glued in its mouth. Jean couldn't speak for him, but she was reminded of Tina and her leopard-skin coat and her dead husband, the symbolic ghost at the feast.

Fergie checked his pocket watch—Jean expected him to launch into "I'm late, I'm late," but no, his ears weren't long enough—and began to explain the custom of first-footing. A dark-haired man arriving first in the new year was good luck, a fair-haired one was bad luck, and how this custom came about was anyone's guess, except it was an old one perhaps dating back to the Viking raids—Vikings, blond, right?

And not to worry, P.C. Thomson, the darkest-haired man in the area, would be doing the honors in just seven, six, five...

From the house came a cacophony of chimes. From the radio came a peal of bells. "Happy New Year!" exclaimed Fergie, positively glowing with bonhomie and booze, and launched into a chorus of "Auld Lang Syne."

His surprisingly strong, mellifluous voice was interrupted by the ring of the doorbell in the far reaches of the house. In the further reaches of the house, the dogs began to bark.

"Come along now, step lively!" Fergie led the procession into the entrance hall and paused dramatically, his hand on the door handle. Diana guarded the rear. Rab, Nancy, Colin, and the two constables gathered in the hall.

The doorbell rang again. The door rattled beneath several strong blows. And suddenly Jean felt a qualm. "Don't open the door," she wanted to call, but no, that was silly, it was only Sanjay Thomson bearing gifts.

Fergie threw the door open. A gust of icy air fluttered Heather's dress and Scott's tie, and they shrank together, Dakota caught between.

The man who stood on the doorstep had a square, blunt, deeply furrowed face, tanned into leather by years of sunburn. Uneven strands of blond hair streaked with gray shifted uneasily above a wide forehead and bloodshot gray eyes. He huddled into his quilted coat, one hand grasping the handle of a small suitcase.

Even Diana stared. The color drained from Fergie's face with an almost audible gurgle.

The stranger's lips parted over crowded teeth and the light caught silvery whisker-stubble on his block of a jaw. "Sorry. It's a bad time, I know, but I've just arrived in the U.K. I'm Kenneth MacLeod."

Jean felt her own jaw drop down to her chest and static explode in her brain. Kenneth MacLeod. Not Allan and Fergie

Mor's old colleague… Alasdair pushed his way to the front of the pack, his severe expression good as a warrant card for claiming precedence. "You're Greg's brother."

"Yeah, I'm Greg's brother. Tina rang me, told me what happened. Now she's gone down as well."

"I'm afraid so. Your sister-in-law is in hospital…"

"Sister-in-law?" Kenneth repeated, with a guffaw that came close to being a sob. "No, mate, she's my wife. And I've come to take her home."

TWENTY-FOUR

AFTER A LONG moment tingling with chill, Fergie choked out, "You'd best come in, then. I'm Fergus MacDonald."

Everyone took two or three paces back as Kenneth stepped over the threshold.

Before Fergie could shut the door, Sanjay Thomson came loping out of the—what had happened to the clear night? The murk had returned, veiling the stars and casting the grounds into impenetrable shadow. "He stopped in at the police house. I've brought him up to date. Sorry, I meant to arrive first, but he got ahead of me on the drive."

"No worries," said Fergie, as blatant a social lie as Jean had ever heard, and the door slammed.

Alasdair squared his shoulders. In his best cool and correct voice, like dry ice, he told the Krums, "The party's over. If you'd be so good as to go to your room."

Heather and Scott stared in bleary bewilderment but for once said nothing. Steering Dakota before them, they headed upstairs. "But Mom…" The child's thin voice receded onto the second floor.

"Tea, please, Nancy," Alasdair ordered, and pulled the phone from his sporran. "Mr. MacLeod, I'm Detective Chief Inspector Alasdair Cameron, retired. Step this way, please."

Kenneth looked around suspiciously, but trudged along without speaking. So did Jean, following the men to the incident room. Behind her Diana issued further decrees: "Colin, Rab, and I will tidy up the Great Hall whilst Nancy makes the tea. Father…"

Phosphorescent computer screens glowed like Scrooge's ghosts between the dusty vaults and the ashy hearth of the old kitchen. Jean sat down, if not out of the way then not obtrusively in it. Removing her glasses, she massaged their imprint in her nose and temples and thought, *January first. Never Day. Ne'er Day.*

Thomson's blurry image placed the first-foot gifts, a bottle of whiskey, a tin of shortbread, a tissue-wrapped lump of coal, on a nearby table. Luck, bad or good, was no more than superstition, than happenstance, and yet coincidences happened and events made tangled webs… She resumed her glasses in time to see Thomson, smooth as a maitre d', extract Kenneth's suitcase from a hand reddened by both sun and cold and point the man to a chair.

Tossing his coat aside to reveal a frayed sweater, the source of the faint wet-sheep aroma annotating his aura of stale sweat and old fry-ups, Kenneth thumped down. "Let's get on with it, okay?"

Alasdair's unhurried but intense tones into his phone were doubtless directed at Gilnockie. "Aye, I'll have Thomson witness and record—she is, is she? We'll come round the morn, then."

Nancy appeared with steaming mugs of tea and the remains of the post-dinner biscuits and cheese rearranged on a smaller plate. Whatever pleasure she'd taken in the Hogmanay games had soured, and she considered Kenneth with a dour stare he returned twice over. "You favor your brother, not quite two peas in a pod, but close. You'll have eaten, I reckon, though I might could be heating the dinner leavings."

"No, thanks just the same," Kenneth replied, even as he accepted a cup and cradled it between his hands. "I've eaten airline stuff 'til my gut's turned up. Kuala Lumpur's the best connection, but the tucker's nothing but chook-food and fruit."

When Tormod MacLeod went out to Australia from Skye

in 1822, he traveled in a wooden cockleshell eating half-rotten food for months on end. As recently as Jean's parents' generation, if you emigrated to the other side of the world, you were gone for good, almost as though you'd died. Even if an aging Tormod had returned to Scotland, to the dark and bloody ground of his lost love, his journey hadn't lasted only a few hours. But Kenneth...

"Nancy," asked Alasdair, "how do you know what Greg looked like?"

"Ah," she said, "well now, there was a photo on Mrs. MacLeod's mobile—she's still Mrs. MacLeod, isn't she?—she showed me whilst we were having us a blether over breakfast, though, come to think it, likely the photo was of you..." She peered more closely at Kenneth, frowned, shook her head, and backed toward the door. "That's me away, then."

Alasdair watched her until she left the room, expression intended to be unreadable, even if to Jean it was an open book—wheels turning, gears meshing, not a speck of rust in the works, no matter how reluctantly activated.

"Tina told you she was Greg's wife, did she?" asked Kenneth.

Jean looked around. "He called her 'the wife.' We assumed the rest. Sometimes you don't ask the right questions. Sometimes you don't know you should be asking questions." Ignoring the sugar bowl, and milk pitcher, she gulped at her unsweetened black tea. The clear, hot, mildly acrid liquid cleared away the gunk packing the crevices of her mind—rich food, excess drink, the long, demanding day—although the shock at the front door had already knocked some of her wits back into her.

Thomson stepped forward, punching buttons not on his cell phone but on a tiny digital recorder. He gave the time, place, Alasdair's name and Kenneth's, and placed the recorder on the table. "Here you are, sir."

Alasdair added milk and sugar to his tea, drank, and only then turned to Kenneth. "P.C. Thomson will have told you that Tina's in hospital in Portree. She fell from her bedroom window whilst climbing out, she was that anxious to leave the house. She suffered a broken arm and a concussion. Inspector Gilnockie's just telling me she's sensible again. We'll be interviewing her tomorrow morn. You're welcome to drive with us, though I reckon you've got a car."

"Yeah, I've got a car. Flew to Inverness and hired one." Kenneth looked anywhere but at Alasdair's face—around the room, up, down, sideways.

Alasdair cut to the chase. "Greg and your wife ran away together."

"Yeah. Couldn't settle, either of them. I thought she was settled okay with the kids, but then they grew up and left home and she went all restless again. And Greg'd go from scheme to scheme like he was pure grifter. Dunvegan—that's our place, cane farm, been in the family three generations—that was never good enough for him. A bit of a spiv, I'm afraid, even if he's my brother. Was my brother."

"Did he ever speak of your ancestor, Tormod MacLeod?"

"The stonemason? Yeah, that was one of Greg's crappy ideas, tracing the family back to Skye and finding Tormod's grave—the bloke came back here as an old man, but there's no grave registered. What the hell does stuff like that matter? Look ahead, I say, never mind about what's left behind."

You could never look ahead to a fresh, new future unstained by the past, Jean thought. Even Greg and Kenneth's grandfather had named his farm after Skye's Dunvegan, MacLeod Central.

"Greg's six years younger than me. He's been a thorn in my hide all his life. I had to look after him when our dad died in Korea. Now that he's done more than well for himself, he's acting like he has to look after me." Kenneth gazed so intently at the fireplace that Jean glanced around. But nothing moved in the cavernous darkness. He was still avoiding the keen blue gaze of his questioner.

Who summarized, "Greg was restless, as was Tina."

"Tina," Kenneth said, and Jean could almost see her materializing on the hearth. "She left me a letter, said she wasn't getting any younger and if she was ever going to run mad, now was the time. Said she was sorry it had to be Greg. I reckon, though, that keeping it all in the family's not such a bad thing. You know what you're getting, then. You know what you're losing."

"Were you surprised learning there was something between them?" Thomson asked.

Kenneth thrust his cup toward Jean. *Oh.* He wanted her to refill it. That told her something about his relationship with Tina right there. But without comment, she poured.

"Ta," he said. "Greg always flirted with her. He'd flirt with anything in skirts. She knew that, but she'd still flirt back. And now this. He was away again, he was always away somewhere, business, pleasure, all one to him. This time when he asked her to go along, she said yes. Probably surprised the hell out of him. Probably surprised her that he'd take her. But he showed her a good time, I'm sure of that. An eye for detail, and too clever by half, that's Greg. That was Greg."

"You never had a good relationship with your brother?" asked Alasdair.

"It wasn't a bad one. We're just not—well, we look alike is all. Tina likes to say one of us was left on Mum's doorstep by fairies, that we're not actually related. We are, though. Greg and Tina knew how I'd feel about them spitting the dummy, but they did it anyway."

"Spitting the dummy?" Thomson asked.

"Yanking the pin. Getting sick of it all."

"How are you feeling, then?" asked Alasdair. "Angry? Jealous?"

"Goes without saying, mate. How'd you feel if your…sorry, didn't catch the name, missus."

He assumed she wouldn't be there if she weren't connected to Alasdair. For once, an assumption was right. "Jean Fairbairn," she answered.

With a thin, lopsided smile of apology toward her, Alasdair went on, "So you followed Greg and Tina here. Why?"

"To bring her home, like I said. Now she's had her fling, I thought she might settled down."

"Were you planning on taking Greg back as well?"

Kenneth's face creased as though straining to see something not quite in focus. "I just want things back how they were. Tina's got her shoes and her artsy-fartsy projects, but she's a good mum to the kids and the grandkids. I've seen families break up because one or two people played the fool. I don't want that."

"You can't have things back the way they were. Greg's dead." Now it was Alasdair who sounded like Nancy and her fatalistic retorts to Rab's nostalgia.

"Yeah. Tina phoned and said he was dead. Said he'd been murdered, though I kept hoping that was just her usual carry-on." Kenneth's sigh of weariness seemed to well up from his toes. He rested his elbow on the table and his face on his hand with its ragged cuticles and dirty nails. Muffled, he concluded, "I'd just phoned him. He said they'd got to Dunasheen and he was off to meet someone over a deal. Said part of it would interest me. I wasn't interested in much he did, I'll say that. Except for Tina, of course. Said he'd phone back, we'd have a talk, work things out. Suppose he never had time."

Alasdair's deceptively cool gaze met Jean's. Greg had been

talking to his brother outside the courtyard. Civil wars, clan feuds—brother against brother could be the worst sort of conflict.

"Did you know your father's old regimental dirk was here at Dunasheen?" Alasdair asked.

Kenneth shook his head, letting his hand fall heavily away from his face. "I'd seen it in photos of him, but that's all we had of him, old photos."

"His bonnet's here as well," said Alasdair. "His regimental hat, a tam o'shanter, a beret."

Kenneth didn't reply. But then, Jean thought, he'd said himself he didn't care about souvenirs of the dead. All he wanted was peace, quiet, and to tend his sugar cane Down Under. Not that she knew Down Under—red dirt, and eucalyptus trees, and the unrelenting sun that had taken its toll of his...

Lower face. His forehead was several shades paler. So were the tops of his ears. The classic image of the Australian outdoorsman or soldier included a wide-brimmed hat.

Jean sat up straight. Not all webs were tangled. A quick slash of Alasdair's favorite weapon, Occam's razor—the concept that the simplest explanation was the true one—cut away many a knot. Why should there be two men, both a stranger and Kenneth? Maybe there was only one, the murderer, whose motive was jealousy and revenge, never mind his mild words.

She glanced down at Kenneth's suitcase, then up at Alasdair, drawing his gaze back to her. *Hat,* she mouthed, and mimed the shape of a broad brim around her head.

He nodded in grim comprehension. "Ask Fergie to stop in, would you please, Thomson? And Nancy."

Nancy? thought Jean.

Thomson handed the task off to McCrummin and returned to his position beside the table. Alasdair turned back to Kenneth. "Mr. MacLeod, I could be getting myself a warrant to

check over your luggage, but we'd moving things on if you'd
agree without a fuss."

Again Kenneth rubbed his hand over his face. "Go on
then, mate."

As bright-eyed and bushy-tailed as ever—nothing like a
police classroom on his own doorstep—Thomson leaped on
the suitcase, spun it around, flipped it open. Resting on top,
stuffed with wadded garments, was a floppy, wide-brimmed
canvas hat, sun-faded, sweat-stained, dust-sprinkled.

Thomson's nod held an element of surprise. Placing the hat
on the table, he delved further into the suitcase and turned up
a used brown envelope, Kenneth's address cancelled out with
a stroke of a pen. From inside he drew a printout of Fergie's
map on the Dunasheen website.

"Your passport, please?" Alasdair asked.

Reaching into his shirt pocket, Kenneth produced the navy
blue booklet of a passport and handed it over.

"Thank you." Alasdair flipped it open. "You arrived at
Heathrow airport December the twenty-eighth, did you?
When Mrs. MacLeod rang you with the news of her husb—
of Greg's death, you were already in the U.K. Just because the
phone's got an Australian number's not meaning the phone's
in Australia."

Kenneth's bloodshot eyes stared dully ahead.

"P.C. Thomson," said Alasdair, "I reckon Lachie from the
Co-op's still out and about, with Hogmanay and all. If you'd
go asking him if he's met this man before…"

"But Lachie said the man was a Londoner," Thomson protested.

"I once told a couple of my nephews," Jean said, "that
a cartoon koala bear was speaking Cockney, the accent of
London's East Enders. Then I realized my mistake. A koala,
Australia, duh. Lachie didn't have that much of a clue. He
heard the flat vowels, the twang, and gathered the man wasn't

a local, but then assumed he was from the south of Hadrian's Wall, not south of the equator."

Fergie marched down the steps into the room. "Alasdair? Sanjay?"

"Sanjay?" Kenneth echoed faintly.

Alasdair asked Fergie, "The man you saw walking through the kitchen yard, the one you thought was Greg. Was he wearing a coat like this?" He pointed to Kenneth's bulbous coat, a drab, dark, gray-green polyester shiny with cheap waterproofing. Dropped suddenly into winter, Kenneth might have bought the first coat he'd come to in the first shop he passed in the U.K.

"Yes, yes, it was. And the hat on the table there, that's the one he was wearing. I saw you, then, Mr. MacLeod? And the American lass, Dakota, she saw you as well—this must mean… Oh." Catching on, Fergie stepped back and stage-whispered to Alasdair, "But he's Greg's brother!"

Alasdair made a down-boy gesture just as Nancy, Rab on her heels and McCrummin just behind, walked back into the room. "Aye?" Nancy asked, pointedly wiping her hands on a dishtowel.

Alasdair's gesture changed direction and indicated Kenneth. "Nancy, tell me again where you saw this man's face."

"On Tina's mobile," she repeated.

"Aye, Greg's mobile, that Tina was using, had several photos of family members. Small ones, none too clear. I'm asking if you've seen this man before, in the flesh. Wearing that hat."

Ahhh, Jean told herself. That's where Alasdair was going. The windows of the new kitchen overlooked the yard, just like the windows of Fergie's office.

Nancy's colorless eyes flicked from Kenneth to Rab—his forehead crumpled and his eyes scrunched, leading Jean to conclude he was hiding a scowl behind his beard—and then back to Alasdair. "Well then, I was thinking it was Greg I caught a glimpse of in the kitchen yard. Are you telling me it wasn't him at all?"

"It wasn't him at all."

Fergie overrode Alasdair's follow-up question, which would probably have been, *Why did you not say so to begin with?* by asking Kenneth, "You haven't just arrived in the U.K., have you? You've been here since…"

The murder. The words hung in the air like a bad smell. Even the appearance of Diana in the open doorway, an apron wrapped around her green dress and Colin a shadow in the corridor behind her, didn't provide any fresh air.

Alasdair reclaimed command by lowering, not raising, his voice. "You bought food at the Co-op. You wandered about the area. You broke into the chapel and spent the night—there's a sleeping bag or blanket in you car, I reckon. Where is it? In the village park by the harbor?"

"Yeah," said Kenneth. "That's right."

"Why'd you come to P.C. Thomson? Because the chapel's locked up now? Because Lachie or someone else told you of Tina's fall?"

"I'm tired, all right? It's a bloody mess and I'm tired of it all."

No kidding, thought Jean.

Kenneth's chin tilted defensively even as his eyes sagged with weariness and grief. "Yeah, I followed them to the U.K. Just missed them in London, but got here first. I saw them driving in the gate, laughing together. I saw them unpacking the car. I told Greg in that last phone call that I was here as well, that we were going to have it out—talking, that's all. I never meant it to get rough. He's my brother, after all."

"Even though Tina phoned you," Alasdair went on, "she did not know where you were. Not 'til Nancy identified Kenneth's photo as Greg, and told Tina she'd seen him in the kitchen yard. That must have given Tina a horrible shock. She went frantic to get herself away. She thought you'd killed Greg and were coming for her."

"I hung round, trying to get a word with her, just the two of us. But no. You lot had her locked away in the house." Kenneth's jaw tightened. "How could she think I'd touch either of them?"

No one answered. No one could answer.

Maybe back home, Kenneth had a reputation as a violent man. Maybe here, Tina had felt so much guilt, especially after Greg's death, that she made an assumption. Or...Jean told herself yet again that she didn't have enough straw to make one brick, let alone a wall of them.

Alasdair's face was hard enough to have been built of bricks. "Where were you when Greg was killed, then?"

"Filthy weather here, cold, wet, dark—I don't blame old Tormod for leaving."

"There was more to his leaving than the climate. Where were you—"

"I went out into the garden," Kenneth replied, his hoarse voice sharpening. "That's where I stopped and phoned Greg. Someone was walking ahead of me, and I thought it was him, but I couldn't hear him except on the mobile."

Jean sensed the flap of several pairs of ears. Alasdair went into his patented looming position, never mind that he was sitting down—head lowered, shoulders coiled, spine extended. He was on a roll. If he sent everyone away he'd give Kenneth a chance to think about his answers. "Someone was walking ahead of you?"

"Yeah. When I came out onto the headland, I saw him, bloke in a camouflage coat and a regimental hat like my father's. Except his had a red flash, and my dad's was white, near as I can tell from a black and white photo."

A low gasp and murmur ran through the watchers. Fergie went more or less onto his toes, his body following his eyebrows into the stratosphere. As one, Rab and Nancy backed away.

"I saw him squatting beside that green shed," said Kenneth. "Looked like he was scraping moss off a heap of stones. He saw me, I'm pretty sure of that."

Alasdair did not look around, although his back-of-the-neck sensors were no doubt registering Diana's presence, not because she was moving or breathing but because she was not. As for Colin...

Colin was the one who had lied. He had not been at the lighthouse at the time of the murder. An eddy in the watchers was Thomson loping up the steps and out the door. "Eh, Colin, wait up."

Alasdair's sharp gesture sent the male constable in pursuit. Then he asked Kenneth, "Did you see the chap's face? Did you see where he went?"

"No. I ducked back into the trees, didn't want him to see me. I'd just got to the new church when I heard Tina screeching. I'd know her voice anywhere, like a galah with a carpet-snake round its nest. But by the time I got back to the headland—that garden's a bloody maze...I don't know." Kenneth slumped down again, rubbing his face with his grimy hands. "I got to the edge of the headland and saw the flashlights on the beach. Saw what the flashlights were aimed at. Tina was gabbling at some bloke—guess it was you, Cameron. You were looking after her. She didn't need me. She'd made it clear she didn't need me."

Thomson's voice echoed along the corridor. "Colin!"

This time Alasdair did look around, grimaced in frustration—even he couldn't be in two places at once—and turned back to his antipodean bird in the hand. "It was you standing just where the path down to the beach begins, was it?"

Kenneth tucked his mud-caked, low-cut boots further beneath his chair. "I never went past the top of the track. I never went onto the beach. I didn't kill Greg."

Jean sensed the infinitesimal breeze of several pent-up breaths released at once, including her own. Far away, a door slammed with a report like that of a shotgun.

Diana stood petrified, her face whiter than her apron. Fergie might have adopted a martial posture entering the arena, but now he walked like a ballet dancer out of it, delicately, on his toes. He wrapped his arm around Diana's shoulders and guided her away. If he said to her, "I told you so," Jean didn't hear. But how unlike Fergie it would be, to gloat over his enemy's defeat.

Assuming Colin had been his enemy. Assuming Kenneth's evidence was Colin's defeat. She and Alasdair and everyone else, for that matter, had manufactured a lot of assumptions recently, to say nothing of leaping to an array of conclusions, and most of them had been mistaken.

Occam's razor was all well and good, but if Kenneth had not played Cain to his brother's Abel, if Colin or someone else had killed Greg, then she could no longer pretend that the murderer was not someone belonging, however temporarily, to Dunasheen.

Nancy and Rab stood close together, his scowl eased into neutrality, her neutrality tightening into a glower that hit every face in the room in turn. Alasdair met her gaze with an almost audible clang. "Thank you, Nancy, Rab. I'm thinking it's time to be calling it a night."

"Easy for you to be saying," said Nancy. "I'll be tidying up 'til the wee hours."

And Alasdair wouldn't? But all he said was, "It's already the wee hours." Turning to McCrummin, he ordered, "We'll be keeping Mr. MacLeod's things. Catalog every piece."

"Aye, sir," she said, and picked up the passport.

Thomson shouldered past the Finlays, his own glower one of chagrin edged by worry. "Sorry, sir. Colin's got away from me.

With a muttered curse, Alasdair ran for the door.

TWENTY-FIVE

JEAN LEVERED HERSELF to her feet and propelled herself into a walk. She didn't notice until she stood beside Alasdair in the entrance hall that Kenneth had lumbered along behind her.

Thomson offered no excuses such as, *It's dark out there.* He simply opened the door again and peered out into the night.

The air filtering in seemed even colder than it had been earlier, with a raw edge. Her skin shrinking beneath the fabric of the dress, Jean tried visualizing August in Texas, vast parking lots radiating heat like pancake griddles and furtive breezes hot as gusts from a blow dryer. All that did was raise goosebumps on her arms.

Beyond the lights of the house the world had disappeared under a pall of darkness, which suddenly lurched closer...oh. Someone had turned off the lights on the Christmas tree in the library window. The rest of Creation still existed—someone who had obviously indulged in his first-foot beverage sent up a celebratory shout from the village.

The second constable materialized from the murk and jog-trotted onto the porch, his rapid breath steaming upward and mingling with the mist condensing from the air. "He's either gone to ground or still running, though I couldna hear his steps."

"He's got no coat," said Thomson. "His jacket's hanging in the cloak room. And he's wearing Rab's old trainers, a size or more too large. But he's familiar with the gardens and the woods."

"P.C. Nicolson, is it?" Alasdair asked the other constable. And, without waiting for an answer, "Have a look at the lighthouse, in the event he's gone there. Has he a vehicle?"

"An old banger," said Thomson.

"Watch that as well, then. And issue a bulletin." Alasdair made an abrupt about-face and showed no surprise whatsoever in finding himself nose-to-nose with Kenneth. "Thomson, have you a room at the police house for Mr. MacLeod?"

"Oh aye. The lock-up makes a fine guest room, long as I'm not actually locking the door. Lest you're wanting me to go locking the door." Thomson's dark eyes assessed Kenneth's bulldog face but drew no perceptible conclusions.

"No need," Kenneth said. "I'm tired of hiding. I want this over with."

"As do we." Alasdair didn't bother defining his "we." "P.C. Thomson will be taking your boots for testing. He'll lend you a pair of trainers."

"Fine, mate. Anything. You've got a shower, have you?" he asked Thomson.

"Aye, sir. No worries. I've got clean pajamas as well. And an extra coat, if you're all right walking a wee while in your sweater." Thomson herded Kenneth toward the door.

The Aussie stopped on the threshold. "I'm sorry about all this, Inspector Cameron. I should have come forward soon as I arrived, or soon as Tina rang me about Greg, but Greg was always the one in trouble while I kept my head down, and..."

"Good night," Alasdair told him, and shut the door.

His fingers still grasping the handle, he let his forehead fall against the wooden planks. For a moment Jean thought he was going to hammer on the door with his skull. But no, that would have been too dramatic. He stood immobile. The pleats of his kilt swayed and then settled above the braw Cameron calves. The epaulettes on the broad Cameron shoulders rose and fell.

He wouldn't let anyone but her see him in such a pose. She set her hand on his sleeve and squeezed the cloth until she could feel his arm beneath, and sense the now-familiar but never-taken-for-granted hum of his body. If together, they didn't make more than the sum of their parts, then what was the point of the relationship, let alone marriage?

The tiny hairs in her ear canal twitched to a low murmuring wail, almost a voice but not quite. "The wind's picking up," she said.

"That's never the wind." Alasdair looked up and around. "That's Seonaid playing the Dunasheen *glaistig*. Is she predicting good news or bad?"

The cry twined down the staircase, a vine of sound. Drawn upward, Jean and Alasdair passed the dark hallway of the second floor—no sound came from the Wallace suite and the door of the Queen suite was locked tight—and paused at the tripping stane.

The air on the staircase was so cold it sizzled. The wail rose and fell and died into an elemental resonance, no longer sound at all. As Seonaid had died, there on the staircase, the breath of life squeezed out of her. Here she'd known fear and grief. At the chapel, she'd known joy, foolish as it might have been.

Sleet gathered in the creases bracketing Alasdair's lips. Clearing his throat and taking Jean's hand, he walked on up the stairs, down the corridor, and through the door to their own sanctuary. "Get on to bed. I'm looking to have a word with Fergie or Diana." And he was gone again, her knight errant riding back into the lists.

Don't think about it, any of it, Jean ordered herself. But she thought about all of it while she washed, put on her pajamas, shoved Dougie out of the center of the bed, and climbed under the covers. The little cat placed his paw on her arm and fixed her with his calm golden gaze. The rumble of a purr came from his throat, echoing a soft brushing noise from the window. Snow. Colin was outside, shivering, alone.

The door opened and shut and the key turned. Alasdair plodded into the bedroom, shedding his jacket and unbuckling his kilt. "Diana's locked herself in her room. Fergie's locked himself in his office and is listening to monks chanting. I'd suggest sleeping whilst we can. It's already tomorrow."

"The tomorrow we were worried about, yeah."

Even after Alasdair washed, changed, and climbed in beside her, making a cat sandwich, Jean still failed to not think about it.

By his breathing she knew he wasn't asleep, either, even though he lay still as a tomb effigy. A knight carved on a grave slab overlooking the Outer Hebrides, a grave slab that was broken into a hundred pieces that Jean was trying frantically to reassemble, while Alasdair stood chanting with the other monks in the tiny stone-built chapel—religious figures were often ghosts, perhaps because of the spiritual dimensions of their lives—her dream shifted and she saw Dunasheen as Elsinore above the sea, and Diana holding aloft Tormod's skull. "Alas poor Rory, I knew him well." And there was Hamlet himself, sensing a presence behind Seonaid's tapestry, killing a bristle-bearded Polonius with his father's regimental dirk...

Jean awoke abruptly to something poking her in the side. Alasdair?

Dougie had somehow swapped his velvet paws for iron prods, and was kneading her ribcage. The moment her eyelids flickered he meowed. The clock in the next room struck six. At least three more hours of darkness yet to come. What was the matter with the dang cat, anyway?

Alasdair shifted and his breath caught. Subtly but distinctly came the sound of a door shutting, and footsteps, and something falling to the floor accompanied by a muffled curse.

Jean sat up, shedding Dougie—someone was in their living room...

"Someone's in the Queen suite." Throwing back the comforter—Dougie's indignant meow came from beneath the cloth—Alasdair leaped out of the bed and seized his bathrobe.

Oh. The wooden floor transmitted sound much better than the thick stone walls. Jean jumped up, grabbed her robe, and hopped along behind Alasdair, cramming her sock-clad feet into her slippers.

Walking into the corridor was like walking into the Ice Age, the air dank with the dying breaths of mammoths and cave bears. Shoulder to shoulder, Jean and Alasdair crept toward the dimly lit staircase, Jean cursing herself for not having brought a flashlight upstairs. Not that anything lurked in the corners that hadn't been there in the daylight. The ivory-inlaid chest was still an inlaid chest. The suit of armor was still armor.

Yeah, she'd been trying that ploy for years. It might have worked if not for her allergy to the unseen.

They passed by the unseen on the staircase, and crept up the second-floor corridor, and stopped at the now partially open door of the Queen suite. Inside, floorboards creaked and a light flared and faded—someone else hadn't forgotten a flashlight.

Alasdair reached into his pocket with one hand and shoved the door with the other. A shadowy figure swung a beam of light toward the door and the room disappeared in a flash of brilliance.

Wincing, Jean realized that Alasdair was armed with the camera.

He stepped into the room. Another flash, and the shadowed figure reeled back and emitted a yelp of pain. Alasdair didn't say, "Come out with your hands up." He said, "Lost your way, did you, under the influence of the evening's drinks?" and switched on the lights.

Jean squinted. Scott Krum wore a velour robe over silk pajamas. His razor-cut hair was disheveled and his finicky goatee was smudged by new whiskers. With a grimace of pain, he lowered both his flashlight and the hand he'd raised to shield his face. "Oh. Hi."

"How'd you get in here?" With his other hand, Alasdair raised his phone and set it to record.

"It's an old Chubb lock, easy to pick with a nail file. Heather's got an arsenal of nail files."

"Why'd you break in?"

"Would you believe me if I said I was looking for items for the auction house?"

"No." Alasdair took a step forward. "You could be doing that in the daylight, with Fergie's permission, in rooms of the house not sealed by the police."

Jean stayed by the door, her toes curled, her arms locked, trying to quell the tiny shivers that crawled like insects through her muscles.

"All right, all right." Scott turned off the flashlight, rubbed his temples, and grimaced again. "I couldn't sleep. I got to thinking that maybe Greg had printed out one of my e-mails and how that wouldn't look good, with him being murdered and everything."

Alasdair said, "What's not looking good is you breaking and entering. It's you lying to Gilnockie about knowing Greg."

"Oh no, no, I didn't *know* him, we'd just e-mailed each other a few times. We had a mutual friend, a dealer in Chicago, and he told Greg I'd been to Dunasheen, and so, you know, Greg was pumping me for information."

"About the Crusader Coffer?"

"Oh, man." Scott shook his head and then groaned, as

though his brain had ricocheted off the sides of his skull. "I'm not touching that. Religious stuff is too political. There's too much skullduggery. Diana's Egyptian necklace, those Chinese snuff bottles, the Wilkie portrait—I could do something with those."

So much for Fergie's Plan B, Jean told herself. She hoped he had a Plan C that didn't involve any ambiguous artifacts.

"What was Greg asking you about, then?" Alasdair took another step forward.

Scott stepped back and collided with a chair, which went down with a crash. Moaning, he kneaded his scalp. "Give me a break, I've got a headache that would knock over a horse."

"What was Greg asking you about?"

"The terrain and the gardens," said Scott. "Whether the house is in good repair. What sort of collections Fergie has. What he and Diana are like. Couldn't help him there, I never met them, just Pritchard. Hey, is it true Fergus sent Pritchard packing?"

Jean heard footsteps on the staircase, and not Seonaid in her ephemeral slippers.

Alasdair demanded, "Did Greg ask you anything at all about the Crusader Coffer? Did he mention Tormod MacLeod at all?"

"I never heard of the Coffer until tonight. I never heard of that other guy, period."

P.C. Nicolson appeared in the doorway, both face and uniform wrinkled by a long night's doze in a chair. "Is there a problem, sir?"

"Oh aye," Alasdair replied. "Take this man to his room and make sure he stays there the night."

Nicolson reached toward Scott, who fended him off. "I get it already. Busted. I'll go quietly."

Alasdair waited while Nicolson reinstalled Scott in his room and found a chair to collapse into. Then he switched off the lights in the Queen suite and shut the door. "I'd be obliged if you'd keep an eye on this door as well, constable," he said, and let Jean pull him toward the staircase.

When they were tucked back into their own bed, pressed together like chilled slabs of meat in a butcher's window—thank goodness for Dougie serving as foot-warmer—she asked, "Does Scott know that what you got on the phone and the camera isn't necessarily admissible evidence?"

"He knows I'm no longer a cop, or should do, if he's been paying attention."

"By the time that occurs to him maybe we'll have more evidence."

"Right." The glow of the bedside clock reflected in Alasdair's eyes like starlight on twin icebergs. "Gilnockie had all the rooms searched, not just the Queen Suite, and Greg and Tina's luggage as well. There's no correspondence. Krum's hoisted himself with his own petard."

"Nothing like a little alcoholic remorse to muddle your thought processes," Jean suggested. "Though if he was lying about what Greg asked him, you'd think he'd come up with something more creative than a description of the estate and the collections."

"Aye," said Alasdair.

"Do you think he killed Greg? It's possible he had the dirk…oh!" Jean exclaimed—it wasn't exactly *a coup de foudre,* but she'd taken any inspiration she could get. "What if Greg himself had the dirk? That would eliminate the need for either Colin or Scott to have sneaked it out earlier. Maybe Fergie pointed it out to him when he and Tina arrived."

"You're forgetting, Fergie did not know our fathers' friend was Kenneth MacLeod, let alone that Kenneth was Greg's father. Or so he's saying." Alasdair jerked fretfully, the starched pillowcase rustling beneath his head. "If Greg had the dirk on him, that's bringing us back round to unpremeditated murder, an argument gone wrong. A brother out for revenge. We've got to have a word with Colin, see if his testimony agrees with Kenneth's. Damn the man for running."

"Yeah, well, he's twitchy. That doesn't mean he's guilty."

"Someone's guilty." Alasdair's hand lay heavy on her flank, the fingers rising and falling as if typing a police report. Or arranging pieces of a puzzle, several of which were missing. Slowly his body warmed. He was no effigy, he was a man, her man, an ex-cop who couldn't get away from copping any more than she could get away from academicizing.

She couldn't stay awake, but she couldn't sleep, either. She dozed and woke, heard Alasdair breathing deeply and evenly, and dozed again, seeing a succession of images rather than real dreams—Scott Krum's face stark and startled in the light of the camera, Dakota insisting she'd seen a ghost in the glare of the headlights—I'll have to tell her she saw Kenneth, Jean thought. And that the ghost she did see, Seonaid, was perhaps running toward him, Tormod's descendant...

Jean opened her eyes to see the room filled with a thin silvery light, sunshine veiled by clouds sparkling with ice crystals. Alasdair sat on the edge of the bed staring dully at his kilt and jacket hanging from the handle of the wardrobe. Dougie sat on the foot of the bed having his morning bath, each lick loud in a silence deep as that of the MacDonald mausoleum.

Jean and Alasdair washed and dressed. Halfway downstairs, he detoured for a word with Nicolson. If anyone deserved coffee, Jean thought, Nicolson did. But it was like the flight attendant's instructions on an airplane—if you didn't apply your own oxygen mask first, you weren't going to be helping anyone else with theirs.

The dining room stood empty, the expanse of the table swept clean and polished into a mirror. "Nancy? Rab?" Alasdair pushed through the pantry door and a minute later called, "Everyone's still sleeping. Let's be making our own breakfast."

The cheery lemon-yellow kitchen shone, light and bright, despite the wan morning. And clean, too. No wonder Nancy wasn't up yet. She'd probably been up until four A.M. scrubbing the tiles with a toothbrush. Even the remotes for the television and its related systems were lined up like soldiers on parade.

Alasdair pulled bread out of the breadbox and removed the lid from the butter dish. Jean pounced on the sleek stainless-steel coffee maker that ground its own beans. So where were the beans? Not in the first two cabinets, not in a tier of drawers, not in the plastic garbage bin set into its own alcove beneath the counter and emitting a faint vapor of meat scraps, fish scales, and dog food. "Surely Gilnockie had the rubbish bins in the kitchen yard searched for the killer's gloves."

"Aye, that he did. No joy."

"Why'd the killer ditch the gloves but not the knife? Ah, here we go, coffee beans. Or do you want tea?"

"Either's fine."

She inhaled deeply, the aroma not only helping to wake her up but overriding the garbage bin's reminder that all flesh must pass. "Alasdair, what sort of alibis do Rab and Nancy have for the time of the murder? I mean, they told Gilnockie they were here in the kitchen, but did Fergie or anyone see them?"

Frowning, searching his data-storage banks, Alasdair slipped the bread into the toaster oven. "Fergie welcomed Greg and Tina, then went straight to his office and sat there with his papers and his music 'til he heard you calling. That's when he came into the kitchen. If one of the Finlays is the killer, then the other's either covering or denying, eh?"

"You expect to go out on a limb for your spouse."

"There are those who'd be chuffed sawing it off beneath him. Or her."

"True." Bracing herself on the edge of the counter, Jean

watched the black elixir stream down into the coffeepot and told herself to be patient, that drinking straight from the nozzle would be counter-productive...there. A cup, coffee, milk—the morning was looking better.

She and Alasdair sat down at the table and the door opened. Fergie peered around its edge like a groundhog on February second. "I thought I smelled coffee. Lovely. How'd our ancestors ever get up and going of a morning without coffee or tea, I ask you?"

Alasdair's glance at Jean intersected hers at him. Here was their chance to add that last straw to Fergie's burden. Better them than anyone else, though—even Gilnockie's gentle touch could only go so far.

Fergie sat down with coffee and toast. "I'll have Nancy organize a fry-up soon as may be. Comfort food."

Jean's stomach was uneasy enough without filling it with bacon, sausage, eggs, and bread drenched in salty grease. She managed something noncommittal.

What Alasdair had no stomach for was waffle, friend or no old friend. "Did you know, Fergie, that you had Greg's father's dirk hanging in your front hall?"

"No," Fergie replied, it apparently not occurring to him he'd already answered that question.

"Good job you looked out into the kitchen yard just as Kenneth walked by."

"I looked out because I heard a thump, probably the garden gate swinging shut. But Kenneth said he wasn't the first person through. He said someone was ahead of him. Colin."

"He was saying he saw Colin at the crusader stones. That it was Colin walking ahead of him is by way of being circumstantial, leastways 'til we've talked to Colin."

Fergie smeared butter and strawberry jam, red as blood, onto his toast. Instead of coming into sharper focus he seemed to be blearing out. "Colin. My daughter's likely in love with a murderer."

"Not necessarily," said Alasdair.

"The Krums will be giving Dunasheen a low rating on Internet travel sites."

Jean said, "Not necessarily."

"Scott Krum's not interested in the Coffer, said that sort of thing's too controversial. But—" Fergie set one of his chins, "—controversy sells, I learned that working in public relations. Someone else will buy it."

"Jean's friend Rebecca," Alasdair articulated slowly, "was just telling us someone's bought an inscription mentioning Pontius Pilate."

"Have they, now?"

Jean's turn. "Was it Norman who said there was an inscription here at Dunasheen with Pontius Pilate's name on it?"

"Yes, yes, he did, just a quick reference in passing. If it's still here, though, we've yet to turn it up. The inscription, not the reference."

Alasdair said, "We're thinking it's the same inscription. It was Greg selling it. By cheating."

"Cheating" was close enough. "He might have smeared the inscription with dirt and pollen and so forth from an archaeological excavation of the right period. He might have intended to do the same with the inscription on the Coffer. As it is, though, even simple tests, well…" Jean's voice ran down. She drained her coffee, which now left an acid taste in her throat, milk or no milk.

"Greg had the Pilate inscription? You mean Tormod took it to Australia with him?" Fergie looked from face to face, butter knife upraised.

"Apparently so, aye," said Alasdair. "As a souvenir, or a sample of his work—we'll never be knowing for sure. Just as we'll never be knowing for sure whether those bones turned up by the chapel are his."

"Tormod's bones? The ones by the chapel?"

Having run more than a few academic committee meetings, Jean quickly herded this particular cat back onto topic—in another minute Fergie would be sitting on the garden wall yowling. "The carvings that Tormod was making in the chapel, so fine the master mason was jealous. The ones that Nancy called pernickety. They weren't, by any chance, a sequence depicting the last hours of Jesus Christ? The stations of the cross, they'd say in a Catholic church. The sort of church Norman was trying to evoke but that people in this area would have called 'papish.'"

Fergie hadn't yet blinked. "Well now, that's right impressive, your deducing that."

"Greg's inscription called Pilate a procurator. A genuine one found in 1961 called him a prefect. If Greg's inscription was carved by Tormod for Norman's folly, it would be in the old style."

Fergie's stare moved from Jean to Alasdair. With a sickly grimace—tag-teaming the man was the equivalent of using a kitten as a kickball—Alasdair explained, "This sort of historical puzzle's her field."

"Oh yeah, if I had a family crest the motto would be 'what if.'" Without waiting for further commentary, Jean plunged on. "What if Norman planned a set of stations of the cross but then cancelled it, either bowing to local feeling or not wanting Tormod's work in his chapel after the scandal surrounding Seonaig? Tormod carried away a small piece of the first station, where Jesus is condemned to death by Pilate. A piece of the last station, a miniature sarcophagus, ended up in the cellar. You recognized it for what it was, a symbol of the empty tomb and the Resurrection."

"Yes. I recognized it. I just never connected the dots, did

?" Fergie's knife clinked against the plate. His first chin
sagged over his second. "There's so much evidence for alien
visitation, I was hoping I'd found the truth of the matter is
all. Hoping I'd found proof."

"Right." Alasdair's chair squealed over the tile and he
snapped to his feet. Briefly he rested his hand on Fergie's
shoulder—*steady on*. "This is us, then, away to Portree—
here are pieces of the murder investigation still missing."

"Yes. That has to take precedence." Fergie looked up, at-
tempting a brave smile even though his eyes were so dull they
might have been painted on his glasses. "And your wedding's
the day after tomorrow."

"Yes, it is." Jean bent to give Fergie a quick hug while
Alasdair poured the last of the coffee into a clean mug. His
other hand pulled the phone from his pocket and thumbed
a number. "Thomson, we'll be passing the police house in a
quarter of an hour... Ah, good man. Cheers."

"He's got Kenneth ready to go?" Jean asked, then reeled
back from the door as it opened, almost hitting her in the face.

Every hair on Nancy's head was lacquered into submission,
and her red lips were indented into her seamed cheeks like
puncture wounds. She'd dispatch a mouse without compunc-
tion, but a human being? Alasdair had once said something
about killers of his acquaintance. Jean now had a few killers
in her album of acquaintances, too, and not one of them had
worn identification.

Darting a glance around the kitchen, Nancy demanded,
"The coffeepot's all right for you, is it? The toaster? Ah, Fergus. Good morning."

Stiffly, Fergie sat up. "Bacon, please, Nancy. Sausage,
eggs, tomatoes, mushrooms, beans. The lot. I'll have a word
with the Krums. Yesterday they expected pastries."

Alasdair and Jean escaped into the hall, Jean telling herself everyone to his own way of dealing with stress. If bacon

fat worked, fine. Right now she herself would have fallen gleefully on a chocolate cake, preferably with vanilla-bean ice cream.

In the entrance hall, the Krums were exiting the staircase followed by a rumpled Nicolson. He fell on the proffered cup of coffee like a dog on a bone. "Cheers, sir. Very kind of you."

Either Heather was flushed or had applied too much blusher, while Scott was almost as disheveled as Nicolson, with the addition of a distinct hound-dog droop. "Morning," he said.

Heather kept on walking, with no more than a perfunctory "Hi."

Dakota looked up from struggling with the zipper on her pink hoodie sweatshirt, dark eyes lusterless with sleep. "Are you gonna be around this morning?"

"We're away to have a word with Mrs. MacLeod in Portree," Alasdair replied.

"Oh. Okay. When you get back—"

"Dakota," called Heather. "Come on. Breakfast. Maybe they'll have some real cereal today, not that porridge stuff."

"I could sure use a double espresso," Scott said, "but guess Nancy's batter acid will do."

"Talk to you later," Dakota told Jean, and trotted off after her parents, if not without a backward look utterly devoid of drowsiness.

Jean watched her little disciple disappear around the corner. What did Dakota want from her that she could possibly provide?—well, other than solving the murder and clearing the air. That was still in her and Alasdair's grasp.

The two dogs burst through the entrance hall toward the front door, nails clattering on the tiles like sleet on a window, Rab in cursing, heavy-footed pursuit. Jean dodged up the stairs.

January first. New Year's Day. Ne'er Day. The year was

nder way. The first day of the rest of her life, of everyone's
ves, begun with business left from the old.

"Jean?" called Alasdair from around the curve of the steps,
nd she picked up her feet and her pace as well.

TWENTY-SIX

THOMSON WAS JUST slamming the driver's-side door of hi
boxy vehicle when Alasdair braked beside it. In the passer
ger seat, pulling the seat belt around his shoulders, sat Ken
neth MacLeod. The younger Kenneth MacLeod, who ha
inherited more than he wanted from the past he disdained.

"So much for letting him drive himself." Jean hunkere
down in her seat, waiting for the car's heating system to sto
blowing frigid air.

"One suspect on walkabout is quite enough." Returnin
Thomson's salute, Alasdair accelerated through the deserte
streets of Kinlochroy. The village looked even plainer in th
anemic light, which was filtered not through leaden cloud
that threatened serious snowfall but through a fragile icy haz

The road wound over hill and down dale, also deserte
except for sheep peering incuriously, jaws moving, at th
passersby. The cars seemed to be moving in a bubble su
rounded by mist, one that opened over road signs, sheep, th
occasional farm and frequent ruined houses, then swept on
leaving sheep and ruins to fade into nothingness.

Even after they came to the intersection at Dunvegan—
the original Dunvegan—and turned into the two lanes of th
main road, drifts of snow filled hollows and lay against bou
ders, making the harsh moorland look as though it had bee
dusted with powdered sugar. Rough terrain, this. Jean wor
dered how many years of backbreaking labor it had taken t
create Dunasheen's garden acres.

"Maybe," she thought aloud, "I heard Kenneth's steps i

the garden while I was walking with Dakota. Just because I saw Pritchard watching Diana doesn't mean it was him."

Alasdair gazed straight ahead, hands steady on the steering wheel. "Could Kenneth have kept ahead of you, not knowing the gardens?"

"Good question." A lot of good questions bumped and caromed like billiard balls across the table of her mind, but she didn't try taking any other shots.

Before long their bubble of visibility included more houses, small businesses, and finally the semicircular sweep of Portree's waterfront, lined with houses painted in bright colors. The gray water of the harbor heaved up and wallowed down and every now and then belched a whitecap. Jean knew the feeling—that was the way her stomach had felt listening to Fergie construct his dream-castle on custard.

Among the buildings climbing the slope behind the waterfront stood the small hospital. What the building lacked in geographic distinction—no turrets, no crow-stepped gables, no stag's antlers over its entrance—it no doubt made up for with mod cons like plumbing and electrical systems.

Jean and Alasdair walked into the antiseptic-tinged interior to find Gilnockie waiting by the reception desk. With his washed-out complexion and austere features, Jean couldn't help but envision a vampire being released after successfully completing a blood-addiction program.

"Good morning," he said.

"Good morning," Alasdair returned, and quickly acquainted Gilnockie with the latest developments, including the incident of the American antiques dealer in the nighttime. "Kenneth had a strong motive to go killing Greg, and looks to be he had the opportunity, but he's only got the weapon if Greg had it with him—Jean's thought of that angle."

Jean met Gilnockie's grave nod of acknowledgment with a cramped smile.

"'Til we find Colin… Ah, here's Thomson and Mr. Mac-Leod."

Gilnockie greeted Thomson and introduced himself to Kenneth, who seemed no less worn this morning than he had last night, square face drooping into a trapezoid and steps dragging.

"Mrs. MacLeod's just this way." Gilnockie conducted Kenneth, Jean, and Alasdair, Thomson just behind, along a corridor into a room that could have served as a dictionary definition of clean and neat. To the right of the door, Sergeant Young sat with her legs twined, ankles locked, hands clasped, narrow face with its insectivore eyes revealing no expression.

Only one of the room's two beds was occupied. Tina was propped against pillows, her arm and shoulder in a sling. Without makeup, she looked neither older nor younger, just more vulnerable. The skin beneath her eyes was tissue-thin and faintly purple, the bones of her face seemed delicate as a bird's, her brassy curls lay muted and limp. Her pale lips moved, emitting a wisp of sound. "Ken."

"Teen," he returned, his voice no stronger than hers.

"You followed us." If Tina noticed the others clustered near the doorway, she gave no sign.

Ken sank down on a plastic chair beside the bed. "Yeah, I followed you."

A quizzical look passed over her features. "How'd you get here?"

"Airlines, Teen. Kuala Lumpur, London, Inverness. A hired car."

She closed her eyes, and for a moment Jean thought she'd fallen asleep. Then her lashes fluttered and her lips moved again. "I'm sorry, Ken."

"So'm I." He looked down at his hands spread on his knees, knuckles like knots.

"Why work so hard, day after day? Why deny yourself some pleasure in life? You've been pinching every penny when there's no need."

"No good throwing out things that might be useful. No good buying new things when the old work just as well. That's why we've got no need to scrimp and save. No need to take Greg's charity."

Beside Jean, Alasdair shifted his weight. There was the discussion-cum-argument that served as Ken and Tina's refrain, just as the conflict between faith and fact was their own.

Ken said, "Greg had glamour. Greg had conversation. Greg made money fast and spent it faster. I'm a cane cocky. But Teen, I'm your husband. Dunvegan's your home."

She didn't reply.

"What were you going to do, after—after you and Greg got home again?"

"Thought maybe I'd go to Brisbane or Sydney, somewhere I could be someone else."

"You've bushed the marriage, then? You want a divorce?"

Again her eyes closed. "Ken. Where'd you come from?"

"Home," he said. "Got a last-minute ticket, cheap. I could have used the money to fix the harvester."

Jean winced at that. But then, most men had moments of tone-deafness at their significant other's melody.

"I knew it was you." Tina looked up. "That Finlay woman said she'd seen you. She couldn't leave me alone. Kept on asking questions like a cop. Why was Greg killed, was I scared the guy would get me too."

Neither the two cops to one side of the door, nor the ex-cop and his caboose on the other, said anything, although Jean knew she wasn't alone in scheduling another conversation

with Nancy. Curiosity attracted the attention of the authorities—no one knew that better than she did.

"How could you think I'd hurt you?" His voice rising, Ken
leaned forward, pulling at Tina's blanket. "How could you
think I'd hurt Greg? It's your own guilt. And shame."

"Guilt. Shame. Yeah, that's you, Ken, always passing judgment, always angry. I could never say a word that didn't of-
fend you."

"I don't understand you, Teen. I've never understood you."
Ken fell back into the chair.

Okay, so they weren't going to witness a scene of tender
reconciliation. The wounds ran too deep, and Greg's ghost
grinned at the bedside.

Gilnockie's stance contained such a depth of quietude that
beside him Alasdair looked fidgety. Jean regretted her vampire simile—Gilnockie's supernatural calm ran the other way,
toward the angels.

He stepped forward. Some detectives would have berated
Tina for her earlier lies, or at least for her unhelpful answers,
no doubt intended to muddy the true nature of her relationship
with Greg. Gilnockie merely asked again, "Mrs. MacLeod,
was Greg saying anything about meeting someone at Dunasheen just after your arrival?"

She blinked up at him. "Have we met?"

"Begging your pardon, madam. Patrick Gilnockie, Detective Chief Inspector, Northern Constabulary. Detective
Sergeant Les—"

"Oh, Lesley's been a big help to me, explaining about
Dunasheen and Skye."

Every eye glanced toward Young. She shrugged, shoulders jerking up and down. "She's after asking the same thing
over and over again. Concussion, they're saying. We've been
sorting it."

"Well done, Sergeant," said Gilnockie.

"Greg," Tina said. Every eye turned back to her. "He hardly ever talked about his investments and stuff. It was all boring anyway. Not like the time he went to a party with movie stars. I could have looked at those pix on his mobile over and over again."

"What sort of investments?" asked Alasdair, unimpressed by movie stars. "Art and artifacts, such as the inscription he sold to the Bible History Research Society?"

"Overpriced junk," Ken muttered.

Tina said, "If someone's willing to pay, then they're not overpriced, that's what Greg said. Like those units along the river, the ones he went in for with the developer. Over the top prices and people queuing up to pay."

"Spoiled the view," said Ken. "People don't need half-million-dollar units. Or any more developments, let alone all the resorts Greg put money in. Yeppoon, Cairns—the man didn't recognize his own home, not anymore."

"Who cares what people need? Greg never forced anyone to pay for a unit or a bit of artwork. He built resorts because he was mad about golf, reckoned he was going to play St. Andrews—classic course, he said, using up rough beachfront. He went on about golf and resorts the way he went on about the flipping family tree and tracking down old Tormod."

"He knew Tormod wasn't a convict," Alasdair said.

"Yeah, he was a soldier, they reckon. Didn't matter to me one way or the other. Same with Greg and Ken's dad. He was water under the bridge even when Ken and I got married, but Greg couldn't let it alone."

"Dad never had much use for us," muttered Ken. "Wanted to see the world. Greg's like him, even though I got the name."

"Did Greg know Fergus MacDonald had your father's regimental dirk?" Gilnockie asked.

Ken shook his head. Tina said, "He was meeting up with— that's what you asked, isn't it? Who Greg was meeting?"

"Aye, that's what I was asking," said Gilnockie.

"He said Dunasheen's manager offered him the dirk for a
good price. He said he meant to do a bigger deal than that, but
because the dirk belonged to the family..." Tina frowned as
though chasing a memory. "Maybe he went to talk to the manager. I don't know. I was in the loo and he shouted through
the door that he was off, he'd be seeing me for drinks and
dinner. But when I saw him again, he was—dead." Her face
collapsed on itself, shattering the illusion of youth. Her free
hand, its nail polish chipped, clenched on the blanket.

Kenneth took it between his own, cradling it like a naked
chick just out of the egg. "I'm here, Teen."

Gilnockie looked at Alasdair. Alasdair looked at Jean. Jean
tilted her head in bewilderment. Greg was meeting Pritchard.
Well yes, Pritchard had admitted planting Greg's card noting
the appointment in Diana's raincoat, but Pritchard himself
hadn't been at Dunasheen at the time of Greg's arrival, let
alone his murder. Unless he'd set up an alibi the way a movie
director would set up a scene.

Unless, Jean thought again, just as Thomson stepped aside,
admitting two more constables, one male and one female.
Portree, collectively.

"We'll be taking statements from the both of them," Gilnockie said to the newcomers. And, lowering his voice to a
dry whisper, "Don't go telling them more than that we're not
releasing Greg's body just yet. The boffins have finished with
it, but 'til Kenneth's been cleared, well..."

Kenneth and Tina were bent together, saying nothing.
Probably with no need to say anything, when so much had
already been said.

Leaving Young to deal with the MacLeods and Portree,
Gilnockie mobilized his forces, led them out of the room and
down the corridor, and stopped just inside the main door.
"The crime scene reports have just arrived. Soon as we've

taken the statements, we're away to the police station for a detailed look. Suffice it to be saying now, nothing's showing bloodstains."

"It was going on for a mizzly day," said Alasdair. "Everyone was wearing a raincoat."

"We weren't. But then—" Jean visualized the coats, umbrellas and other protective gear hanging in the cloak room and the kitchen. "We're not locals outside every day, expecting a mizzle and dressing accordingly."

Gilnockie continued, "With the beach being shingle, not sand, there were only a few prints."

"Someone stood about at the top of the path leading down from the church," said Alasdair.

"Aye. Now that the boffins have photos of Kenneth's boots, they're thinking they've got a match."

Thomson nodded. "So he was saying last night."

"There were other prints overlying those, though," Gilnockie added, "all jumbled, someone running, most likely, and the path right slippy."

"Kenneth was saying he saw Colin walking toward the beach. If he came back running…" Leaving the implication lying on the polished linoleum floor like a body on a morgue tray, Alasdair went on, "Greg was asking Krum about the terrain round Dunasheen, the state of the castle and the collections, the personalities of the MacDonalds. Your aunt, Thomson, she mentioned the sale of the castle near Inverness, how it's gone for a golf course and luxury time-shares."

"I'm hearing luxury hotel," said Gilnockie, "but that's as may be. You're wondering if Greg was after investing in the estate as a whole, not just buying an artifact or two."

"Aye. I'm thinking Greg was using his knowledge of Tormod to be getting his foot in Dunasheen's door. To be looking it over as a potential investment."

"He wouldn't have a problem selling the Crusader Coffer

to the BHRS," said Jean. "But re-developing the entire area
or even buying Dunasheen outright? We overheard Fergie
and Diana talking, they're in bad shape financially, grasping
at straws..." *And how,* she added to herself. "But they never
once mentioned the possibility of selling the place."

"Maybe Greg hadn't yet offered to buy it. First the dirk,
then the Coffer, perhaps, then after he'd taken Fergie's measure, and inspected the house and the landscape, then he'd
move in." Alasdair's eyes lifted to the scene beyond the glass
doors, at the light bleached of color like a faded photograph.

"But someone killed him first," said Gilnockie. "Why? To
stop him from making an offer? If Mr. MacDonald was not
wanting to sell up, he had only to refuse."

No one said anything about Greg making an offer Fergie
couldn't refuse, Jean thought, but then, what kind of offer
could that have been?

"With respect to Greg having an appointment with
Pritchard," Gilnockie went on, "we'll be double-checking
the statements of the folk in the pub."

Jean raised her hand. "But what if the manager Greg was
going to see..."

"...was not Pritchard?" Alasdair finished for her.

Yeah, he'd be, if not ahead of her, at least with her. "What
if someone else got onto Fergie's computer, checked out Greg,
and e-mailed him?"

"Anyone, Colin, Rab, Nancy, Diana, could have set up an
appointment either using Pritchard's name or claiming to be
the manager."

"Quite right," said Gilnockie.

"The problem is, it wasn't 'til Jean and I took the photo
down from the wall anyone knew the significance of the
dirk. Or so we've been thinking," Alasdair amended. "Much
easier for someone in the household, including Pritchard, to
have sussed it out."

"Not Colin, then," Thomson murmured beneath his breath. "Though Diana, now…"

Every face puckered in thought. Finally, Gilnockie said, "We're getting a good ways ahead of ourselves. Colin needs finding and interviewing. And Scott Krum as well. I'm not happy with the Finlays' role in all this. Nor with Diana's and Fergus's."

"The MacDonalds are not concealing evidence," Alasdair said, adding quickly, "In my professional opinion."

"I've got a deal of respect for your professional opinion," Gilnockie told him. "Off you go, back to Dunasheen, continue with your researches."

"Right," Alasdair said on a breath that just might have been a sigh, while Jean, thinking a hysterical laugh would disturb the peace of the hospital, confined her reply to a nod.

"P.C. Thomson, soon as I've looked over the crime scene reports and taken the MacLeods' statements, you can go carrying copies back to Kinlochroy with you. Then you, McCrummin, and Nicolson, begin another sweep of the area. If nothing breaks by sunset, I'll be calling out the crime scene team again tomorrow. They likely missed something at the scene or in the house."

Jean saw that the clock on the wall behind Gilnockie's back showed noon-forty-five. Less than three hours until sunset. And then tomorrow, and the day after that…

Gilnockie turned back toward Tina's room. "Well then. We'll be joining you at Dunasheen presently, Alasdair, Jean. P.C. Thomson, if you'd be so good as to wait outside Tina's room."

"Aye, sir." Thomson marched off down the hall.

"Later, Patrick." Alasdair opened the door for Jean and she stepped out into the chill. A couple of snowflakes drifted down onto her glasses, leaving tiny wet dots. No problem—she wasn't seeing too clearly anyway.

Once back in the car, she again hunkered down into her coat. Her brain hunkered, too, not cold but sore as though it had been used as a punching bag. She didn't want any of these people to be the murderer. But one of them was.

TWENTY-SEVEN

WORDLESSLY, ALASDAIR DROVE around Portree's main square. A few people were out and about, despite the late night and the cold day. One older couple laid a single red rose at the base of the war memorial, a chunky base with a slender shaft not nearly as well proportioned as the monument in Kinlochroy. But the plaques holding the names of the dead were what it was all about, Jean told herself. They should include the names of men like Colin.

There was St. Columba's Church, where she and Alasdair had stopped on their way to Dunasheen on Tuesday, or last year, whenever it had been, to finalize wedding plans with Reverend Elphinstone. Then she'd been almost giggling with delight at the reverend's name, Scottish standard though it was, and all the way to Dunasheen had batted jokes and literary references toward Alasdair. He'd batted them back, a few "yes, dear" smiles notwithstanding.

Today his profile against the frosty mist revealed no humor, no accommodation, just a grim expressionlessness. No need to share her thoughts with him now. No need for him to eke out a few for her. They were of as like a mind today as they ever had been, or were ever likely to be.

Their entire relationship had been rocky. No surprise their wedding, too, was traveling a rough road. It wasn't a matter of getting to the church on time. It was a matter of getting there at all. And even if they did get there, if the proper, time-honored words were actually said, like an incantation, then…what? Would that exorcize the malice that had been shadowing them?

Her breath casting thin sheets of fog on her window, she wondered whether the Krums' holiday was serving its purpose. Could that marriage be saved? Probably not, no more than her and Alasdair's first marriages could have been saved. And what about the MacLeods' marriage?

What didn't kill you either made you stronger, or it left you disgusted with the whole thing and ready to bail.

The miles passed, a flurry of snowflakes blew across the windshield, and once again they were in Dunvegan, passing another Celtic-cross war memorial. Here, too, people were out and about and a shop or two had opened for business regardless of the holiday. Light glowed in the conservatory windows of a small hotel, revealing people seated at tables, utensils flashing. *Lunch,* Jean thought. Hunger trumped unease every time.

"I could do with a cuppa." Alasdair guided the car into the hotel's parking area.

Within minutes they were seated in the warm, slightly steamy, conservatory, tucking into plates of fragrant curried chicken and rice that were hot in more than one meaning of the word.

Spices and sweet, milky tea—Jean's stomach relaxed a bit, even if her brain still hurt. She gazed past several hanging ferns interspersed with hanging Christmas cards and through the plate-glass window, feeling as though she was on display in a department store as little match girls peered in from the cold…

She sat up so abruptly her spine bounced off the chair spindles. Out of the shop just across the road walked a familiar figure, a slender young man in a camouflage coat and a bonnet sporting a wilted red hackle. "Alasdair…"

"I see him." Alasdair already had the phone in his hand.

Colin's ravaged face looked right and left. But he didn't hurry across the road. He turned back to the door of the shop.

Between a swinging ice cream sign and a newspaper rack glided a lissome figure in a lilac tweed coat. Once again Diana's golden hair was partially concealed by a colorful scarf. Once again she wasn't fooling anyone—the driver of a passing van leaned on his horn in approval. Her glare after him should have caused all four tires to go flat. Whether Colin glared, Jean couldn't tell. He handed Diana down the steps of the shop as though he was handing the Queen herself from her fairy-tale coach.

"Thomson," Alasdair said into his phone. "Where are you? Good. Colin Urquhart's in Dunvegan, with Diana MacDonald at the wee shop across from the MacLeod Arms Hotel... aye. Just now."

Colin wasn't acting like a fugitive. Instead of slinking away—*you didn't see me, I wasn't here*—he stood on the sidewalk talking to Diana. Jean tried to interpret their body language, the tight gestures, the tense stances, the way Diana's gloved hand jiggled a plastic bag against her leg. They weren't exactly exchanging recipes.

Thrusting the phone into his pocket, Alasdair headed for the door. Jean leaped to her feet. An orange-striped all-terrain vehicle spun around the corner and skidded to a stop. Colin whirled, Diana extended her hand, Thomson jumped out of his car. Colin whirled the other way, saw Alasdair sprinting across the road toward him, and stopped. He didn't raise his hands in surrender, but made more of a blessing-the-multitudes gesticulation, hands out, palms down.

Jean only realized that she, too, had bolted out of the hotel when a voice said in her ear, "Excuse me, madam, you've not settled for your meals."

"Oh." Jean looked around to see the proprietor, a dark green apron wrapped around his ample midsection, his coloring revealing that he not only came from south of Hadrian's Wall but also from east of the Bosporus. She reached into her bag. "Sorry."

Alasdair pretty much picked up Colin and Diana by the scruffs of their necks and dragged them toward the hotel. Thomson vaulted back into his car and ran it into a parking place, then beat Alasdair and his captives to the door.

Sizing up the situation, the proprietor handed Jean back her twenty-pound note, scooted another table up to the one where they'd been sitting and added chairs. "Tea, is it? Sandwiches? Right you are." The other patrons went back to their meals, pretending nothing had happened.

Alasdair seated Diana and Colin with their faces toward the window, the light revealing their expressions. Her cheeks were more than rosy, they were the color of ripe cherries, more from embarrassment than from the cold, Jean estimated. Colin's blue eye was less the color of cornflowers than of the Atlantic shipping lanes far from land. "I was an idiot to go running," he said.

"Aye, you were that," said Alasdair. "And you, Diana, did you let him in through the cloak room after Thomson and Nicolson lost him? He did not leave the house wearing his coat and bonnet."

Thomson laid a file folder on the table, then quickly moved it aside as the proprietor distributed metal pitchers and ceramic teacups. As soon as he'd retired out of earshot, Diana set her single, sculpted chin the way Fergie had set one of his flaccid ones that morning. "Yes, I helped him. He didn't kill Greg. Give me one reason for him to have killed Greg."

Alasdair did just that. "If you and Fergie sold up and moved away, then he'd lose you, eh?"

"What?" Diana exclaimed.

Biting her tongue, Jean busied herself pouring tea. Not one face was softened by the steam wavering above the cups.

"Was Greg offering to invest in Dunasheen?" Alasdair asked. "Was he offering to buy it outright and make it over into a luxury hotel with a golf course?"

"Good heavens, no. He only ever asked about the Coffer and his ancestor Tormod."

Thomson whipped out a pen and began taking notes on the back of the folder.

"He only ever asked *you*," said Alasdair, to which Diana could only nod. "He asked about his father's dirk as well, did he?"

"No." This time Diana annotated her negative with a shake of her head that set her blond locks dancing. "No one knew about that until Greg was murdered with it."

Alasdair turned to Colin. "You were telling us you were at the lighthouse at the time of Greg's murder. Why were you lying?"

"It could be Kenneth lying," said Diana.

Alasdair shot her a withering look and she shrank back. Jean pushed the milk and sugar toward her.

"Colin?" asked Alasdair.

The young man leaned forward, fixing Alasdair with a gaze like unexploded ordnance. "I often stopped by the church, thinking of this and that. Thinking of how religion's supposed to bring you peace and comfort, but so often brings the opposite. I was standing there when someone in a yellow raincoat left the garden path, looked about the headland, then walked down to the beach."

"He saw you?" asked Thomson.

"No, I was behind the wall."

Alasdair asked, "Who was it?"

"Maybe Pritchard, maybe Fergie, maybe Rab. It wasn't Diana, I'd have recognized her walk. It didn't matter to me, not then." Colin swigged his tea, but even the undamaged side of his face remained twisted and tense. "I was thinking that the chaps buried beneath the stones, they were comforted, so I went to cleaning away a bit of the lichen. Then I sensed a man in a dark green coat watching me from the garden."

"Kenneth," said Diana.

Colin shrugged agreement. "I didn't know who he was, what he wanted. But soon as I saw him, he ran back into the garden and away."

Alasdair nodded and Thomson wrote, both of them registering the accuracy of Ken's testimony, although Jean knew there were often slips between the alibi and the lip.

"Then I heard raised voices from the beach. I thought maybe Pritchard was harassing some poor soul of a hiker—he never had much truck with the concept of right-of-way—so I walked down the path…" His hands around his cup tightened, the bones standing out beneath the fragile skin, and his body was racked with a shudder.

Jean glanced up to see the proprietor's wary eye moving from Colin's trembling form to Thomson's uniformed gravity to Alasdair's great stone face. He set down plates of sandwiches and backed away slowly.

Diana's even gaze encompassed both representatives of the law. "Colin only remembered what happened last night, when he saw Kenneth again. I was driving him to Portree, thinking he might feel safer talking to the authorities there, away from Dunasheen. We stopped here for sandwiches and drinks."

Alasdair once again cut to the chase. "What happened, then, Wednesday sunset, on the beach?"

"A man in a yellow raincoat," said Colin, the words sieved through his teeth. "A man in a red jacket. He laughed. The other one shouted. He had a knife. There was a flash of red sunlight, and then the knife was red, and the man in the red jacket fell down."

Gently Diana removed Colin's hands from the teacup, which was now rattling in its saucer, and held them in her own. "It wasn't your fault. You had nothing to do with it," she told him, not in the indulgent tone one would use with a child, but matter-of-factly. In the same tone she told Alasdair, "He blanked it out. He genuinely thought he'd spent the afternoon at the lighthouse, as he would usually do. After a time he went on to the village shop, heard of the murder, and was concerned about me. He knew something was wrong, yes, but…"

"There's always something wrong," Colin said.

A shadow and a threat in his mind, Jean thought, paraphrasing Tolkien.

"Colin," asked Thomson, "do you know who murdered Greg MacLeod?"

"I thought it was Pritchard, he's bloody-minded enough."

Alasdair said, "If his alibi's no good, then…"

"It's good," Thomson said. "They told me at Portree station, a dozen folk saw him at the pub that afternoon. Took notice of him, rather, him never being known for couthiness."

"Ah." Alasdair shoved the sandwiches across the table. "The ones you bought at the shop will keep. Eat."

Diana released Colin's shaking hands. He began dismembering the bread and cheese. "I'm sorry I didn't see who it was. It wasn't Diana. It couldn't have been Fergie, she's saying."

"I'm not saying that because he's my father," Diana added, taking a firm bite of her own sandwich. "You've cleared him, I believe."

"Then, unless…" Alasdair paused. Jean knew what he was thinking—*unless Colin is giving us the runaround. Unless Diana is lying in her pearl-like teeth.* "Unless we've got some other stranger hanging about, it was Rab or Nancy killed Greg."

Thomson tapped on the file folder. "I've got the reports on the footprints and all here, sir. And something else, as per that stranger in the village. Aye, we're knowing now who it was, who he is, it's Kenneth MacLeod, but still."

Four sets of eyes turned toward him.

"I was blethering with my Auntie Brenda as to who Lachie's stranger could be. You yourself, Mr. Cameron, were saying it was perhaps a local lad who'd been working away."

"Fergie'd been telling us about Nancy's brother having to leave to find work," Jean said.

Diana nodded. "Jimmie's done well for himself. He's sent Nancy and Rab gift cards and all—the telly in the kitchen, that's the latest. And Nancy's earrings. My mum's diamonds are half the size."

Oh. Jean poured herself another cup of tea, to drown her chagrin. If Diana had been wearing those earrings, she would never have assumed they were rhinestones. What you believed was what you got.

Alasdair turned back to Thomson. "Go on."

"Auntie Brenda's not heard of him in donkey's years. Just on principle, I asked Portree to check up on him. Turns out Jimmie's living in a bed-sit in Birmingham and has not got a bean. If Nancy was not sending him money, he'd be living on the dole. Neither she nor Rab has any other family, Auntie's saying. He tapped the pen on the file folder. "If they're not getting their money from Jimmie, well then, where's it coming from?"

Jean stopped stirring her tea. She saw a family walk in the door and take off their coats. She heard a car horn honk briefly, in greeting rather than anger, and a sheep baa. She saw Alasdair's lips tighten in a thin smile. *Aha!* "Fergie was telling us, Diana, that there's nothing gone missing from the house. So far as he knows."

"So far as either of us knows, yes. Only God knows what's been stored in lumber rooms and dark corners. We can't make a proper inventory and keep the place running at the same time."

"You were saying you suspected Pritchard of cooking the books or making off with the odd item. What of the Finlays, either with or without Pritchard's collusion?"

Her features went from puzzled to indignant, but not, Jean thought, at Alasdair's question. "Father trusts them. He's known them since he was a boy. They've lived at Dunasheen all their lives, working for my great-uncle, then for us. Pritchard was bitter about that, come to think of it, said more than once that Father trusted them over him. He must have suspected something."

"What I'm suspecting," said Alasdair, "is that it's no matter of God knowing what's in the attics and all, when Rab and Nancy know. And they're likely knowing whose dirk was hanging in the hall as well."

"When Greg booked his and Tina's holiday," said Jean, "one or the other of the Finlays contacted him, claiming to be Dunasheen's manager and offering him the dirk. Thinking they were speaking for Fergie, Greg told them the dirk was all well and good, but he was also looking the place over for a golf course or resort or whatever. And then Fergie started talking abut a big sale. He meant the Coffer, but…"

Diana arranged knife, fork, and spoon like bars on a graph. "The Finlays have had their opinions on our plans. They're entitled to those."

"If Dunasheen was sold, refitted, repurposed further than it already has been, would they be entitled to stay on?" asked Colin.

"Greg would want a younger, hipper staff," Jean pointed out. "One that didn't grouse about paying guests."

"And even if the Finlays weren't sent packing by a new owner," said Alasdair, "that new owner'd be making proper inventories and clearing out the lumber rooms. No more nicking the odd item and selling it on. I reckon Rab and Nancy have been doing that for a good many years."

Diana was looking less like a blushing rose and more like the Snow Queen.

Thomson added, "Nancy's by way of taking things as they come, but Rab, no, he's fussed. He was in the pub Wednesday talking about happy days with the old laird, when they were not obliged to suck up to strangers. And the Krums sitting in the window just then, though I'm thinking they didna understand all he was saying."

Well no, Jean thought, the Krums hadn't been marinating in Scottish accents like she had.

"Rab Finlay." Alasdair's hands remained clasped on the table, but his tone was enough of a pointing finger. "He made an appointment with Greg, to show him the gravestones—and the dirk—and likely telling him he could organize a word with Fergie about the estate itself. But Rab was meaning instead to take Greg's measure as a threat."

"Meaning to kill him?" The faint sheen of bronze, his genetic tan, was ebbing from Thomson's face, but he didn't shy away from the facts.

"That's a question for the jury, not for us."

Jean could see the scene, Rab grim and tense, and Greg's ready laugh inadvertently pushing Rab over the edge.

"Rab and Nancy know we're struggling to make a go of the place," said Diana. "We might have taken Greg's offer, if with some plan to stay on as managers ourselves."

"Someone did kill Greg to stop him from getting something," Jean said. "To stop him from getting Dunasheen itself. Rab didn't kill the goose laying the golden eggs. He killed the man who would deprive them of the goose, the eggs, and the nest, too."

"Rab came away from the pub in good time to be meeting Greg," said Thomson. "I saw him myself, stopping for a word with the American lass, Dakota—she'd dropped a scrap of paper, I'm thinking—and then buttoning his coat and pulling on his gloves."

Alasdair picked up the story. "His mind muddled by beer or whiskey…"

Scotch courage, Jean thought.

"…Rab went walking through the kitchen yard into the gardens. If Fergie'd seen him, he'd have thought nothing of it. Rab's job was to go walking about the place. Save Kenneth was just behind him. And Rab did not know that."

"It was Rab I saw, then. I should have known, his raincoat's big as a tent. But it was gey murky with the mizzle and…" Colin choked. Again, Diana took his hand.

"Rab took the knife but left the sheath," Jean suggested, "so Fergie or Diana wouldn't notice it was gone. He didn't throw it into the sea—it had belonged to Fergus Mor in the good old days, and it would be worth a bundle to a collector of military memorabilia. He intended to retrieve it, clean it, and put it back in the sheath. But Diana did notice. So did Dakota."

"I reckon," said Colin faintly, "Rab never thought it all out, not like that. Likely he found himself standing on the beach holding a bloody knife and the man's body…"

Diana's fingers knotted with his. "That's why Nancy was slow to say she saw Kenneth in the yard. Whether or not she knew that Rab intended to meet Greg, let alone kill him, by the time she was interviewed she knew what he'd done. And she was dealing with it, as she's always dealt. Practical. Pragmatic."

"Nancy befriended Tina," Jean said, "to find out how much Tina knew about Greg meeting Rab. She might even have planted the suggestion that Tina let herself down from the window to escape the murderer, hoping she'd fall—but that's going out on a limb."

Alasdair said, "I'll get onto Gilnockie. We'll be needing

a show of force when we go confronting Rab. And hard evidence, more than all this supposition, sensible as it is."

"More than any statement I could be making, eh?" Colin asked.

No one answered. Alasdair reached for his phone. "The crime scene reporters, Thomson. What have you got there?"

Thomson was staring bleakly off into the distance, probably watching a turret of his childhood castle subside into the sea—how often had Nancy given him and the other village lads cookies... Jerked back to the present, he flipped open the folder. "Aye. The reports. What footprints we've got aren't at all definitive, save there are muckle ones of large boots, and Rab's are the largest."

"His job is walking around the estate," Jean reminded him.

"Aye, but when the boffins went comparing prints to boots, Rab's were the only ones that were clean. Everyone else's had some muck in the treads, but not his."

"Nancy's cleaned them, then," Diana said. "She had ample time to clean them."

"That's all well and good, but it's still no more than circumstantial." Alasdair punched buttons on the phone. Thomson considered another page of the report. Diana wilted against Colin's shoulder and no doubt considered the ramifications. Dunasheen left without any staff at all, for one.

Jean remembered Rab standing beside Greg's body, saying, "No good will come of that." No wonder he'd spoken with such conviction, and resentment as well, with Greg's blood staining his boots. But then, she, Alasdair, and Thomson might have traces of Greg's blood on their footwear. If Nancy had just left well enough alone Rab could have claimed that he, too, had picked up blood droplets when he came to move the body. And the same would go for droplets on his...

"Raincoat," Jean said. "Rab was wearing a raincoat and gloves when he left the pub, right?"

"Right," said Thomson.

"And he was wearing his raincoat when you saw him, Colin?"

"Right," Colin said.

"But when he came down to the beach with Irvine, he wasn't wearing a raincoat. He left it at the house so Nancy could clean it off, too. And he wasn't wearing gloves, either. He dumped them somewhere."

"Patrick," Alasdair said into the phone. "We're needing you at Dunasheen soon as may be—the reports, Thomson, aye, reinforcements—you're on your way, then? Good."

Just below the crisp notes of Alasdair's voice, Jean heard something else, a rattle of bones in the wardrobe of her mind, or the clatter of billiard balls across it—traditionally billiard balls were bone-ivory… She focused on a Christmas card hanging between Colin and Diana, one depicting a traditional robin-redbreast. And her mouth went dry.

Last night, Dakota Krum had been standing on the other side of the Christmas tree, just beyond a robin ornament, while Jean and Alasdair discussed Pritchard and the business card. Dakota had asked about it. Ever since then, the child had been looking at them as though trying to make up her mind to say something. As though deciding whether to crawl out once again on the limb of witness, when her first foray out there had left her hanging on by her fingernails.

"Sanjay," Jean said, hearing her own voice go sharp. "Rab was in the pub Wednesday afternoon at the same time as the Krums?"

"Aye. Well, the mother and the father were coming and going, but the lass was sitting there with her book."

"She dropped her bookmark or something and Rab picked it up as he was leaving. Or did *he* drop a scrap of paper, and *she* picked it up?"

Thomson frowned. "Maybe it was the other way round,

aye, Rab dropping a bittie white scrap from his pocket as he went pulling out his gloves, and her handing it to him. I didna know I was playing witness, or I'd have had a closer look."

Focus, woman, focus! Jean said slowly, meticulously, "What if it was Greg's business card that fell from Rab's pocket, just as it did again, later on, in the parking area? What if Dakota saw it? Gilnockie asked her parents about the card, not her. Last night, though, she asked Alasdair and me about it."

Every eye around the table, from Thomson's dark brown through Alasdair's, Colin's, and Diana's shades and temperatures of blue, snapped toward Jean and widened.

"Rab does not know the results of the tests on the boots," said Alasdair. "He does not know that we've found the truth of his and Nancy's embezzling, or that we've found Colin, come to that, and that Colin saw the murder. He's likely thinking the only evidence we have against him is his having that card in his pocket—when he's made a formal statement he knew nothing about it."

Horror oozed like cold jelly down Jean's back. "In other words, what if Rab thinks Dakota's testimony is the only thing that can put him in jail?"

"Who'd go harming a child?" asked Colin.

"A man," Alasdair answered, "who's already killed."

After a long moment in which the words fibrillated above the table, Diana ventured, "Her mum and dad have never left her alone."

"Yeah, when she wanted to walk in the garden they asked me to go with her." Jean's horror ebbed on a long breath. *It's all right...*

The phone, still in Alasdair's hand, rang. He jabbed at it. "Fergie?"

Fergie's voice emanated from the tiny speaker, whetted by agitation. "The dogs, they've found a pair of bloody gloves just outside the courtyard—Alasdair, what if they broke loose from Diana on Wednesday because they, well, animals have ESP, you know—they sensed the murder, and they scented the killer's gloves and found them and brought them back here." He gulped. "Alasdair, they're Rab Finlay's gloves, fleece-lined leather, Nancy's brother sent them."

"Fergie," Alasdair demanded. "Where's the lass, Dakota?"

"Odd you should ask. Her parents went upstairs and she was sitting here in the library—I saw her not half an hour ago—but she's not here now. I don't know where she's gone."

Jean's horror came roaring back like a tsunami, swamping her every sense. *Dakota!*

Alasdair was on his feet, waving the others toward the door. She stumbled after him, then spun around and threw her twenty-pound note back down onto the table.

"Find her," Alasdair was saying. "Get McCrummin from the incident room—Nicolson's off duty, damn and blast—find Rab and Nancy as well. Here's Jean."

Thrusting the phone into Jean's hands, Alasdair threw open the door of their car and had the engine started before she'd scrambled in beside him.

From the phone in her hand came Fergie's breathless voice, "Nancy's upstairs, Rab's round the back… Is it Rab, then? How could—oh God, when I came into the kitchen to get help with Greg he was just taking off his coat, breathing hard—I thought he'd just come from the pub—oh God, it was Rab, wasn't it? Oh God."

And the phone went dead.

TWENTY-EIGHT

JEAN LET GO of the phone, hung onto her seat belt with both hands, and watched with slitted eyes and gritted teeth as the mist-covered landscape sped by on either side of the car. Thank goodness it was Alasdair driving, hands locked on the wheel and eyes hotter and brighter than the headlights he'd switched on.

Thomson's vehicle and then Diana's followed close behind. The one time Jean glanced in the side mirror she saw them rising and falling along the narrow, winding, bumpy road like ships on an angry sea. She winced, swallowed a rush of nausea, and didn't look again.

Ahead, a sheep stood on the very edge of the pavement. Alasdair hit the horn, a bleat like that of a super-charged goat split the air, and the sheep looked around. The passing car almost shaved him more closely than the best shearer and he scrambled away.

The sparkle in the sunlight was fading, and the light itself growing gray and dull. How did people live in this part of the world before artificial light? Jean wondered. They must have developed huge eyes, like amphibians living in caverns.

And she wondered what they'd find back at Dunasheen—surely not bodies scattered all over, like in the last scene of *Hamlet*. Please, no, no more bodies. "Fergie just dropped the phone is all," she said.

"Right." The dashboard lights sketched Alasdair's features in harsh shadow and shine.

Suddenly the houses of Kinlochroy leaped from the gloom.

Two or three people watched slack-jawed from the sidewalk and a couple of others lifted their window curtains as the cars sped through the village and, brakes squealing, stopped in front of Dunasheen's gates.

They were closed. And, Alasdair and Jean discovered when they bailed out of the car and pushed at them, locked. Thomson ran up and trained his flashlight on the black iron-work, revealing a massive padlock and a length of even more massive chain.

Where were Scott Krum's lockpicking skills when you needed them?

Here came Diana, Colin at her side. "Father told Pritchard, and Rab as well, to lock the gates if there's no constable on duty."

Colin threw his weight against them. They rattled as for-lornly as the shackles on transported prisoners. Beyond the iron tracery, through the darkening, thickening mist, the house seemed no more than dense shadow, not showing even the one lighted window of a Gothic novel.

Alasdair went right, to where the wall enclosing Duna-sheen ended at the sea strand. Colin went left, toward the driveway leading back to the chapel. Thomson said, "I ra-dioed Orla…"

"Who?" asked Diana.

"W.P.C. McCrummin when she's at home."

She wasn't at home, thought Jean. She'd been called out on a murder case.

"She's saying the generator packed up," Thomson went on. "Fergus's phone is a portable with a base unit, eh? That's why he was cut off, I reckon."

I hope, Jean thought for everyone.

"Orla's got a torch, she's searching the place for Dakota and for Fergus as well. Have you got a key to the gate, Diana?"

"I went off without one, they're huge, Victorian slabs…

Half a tick. Your aunt's got one on display. I'll knock her up."
Diana sprinted into the village, her hair streaming back from
her face so that she looked like a ship's figurehead.

"Right." Stowing his flashlight in his jacket, using the
decorative curlicues as foot and hand holds, Thomson clam-
bered up the gate, straddled the top, and dropped down on
the far side. "Haven't done that since I was a lad," he said and
raced up the driveway.

Jean, the fifth wheel, stood alone in the dusk. Her own
breath wasn't just visible, it was audible in the sudden silence... Footsteps scrabbled along the shore. Far away, like
the report of a gun, a door slammed. Alasdair reappeared
inside the gate just as Diana pelted back from the village.
"Brenda answered my knock straightaway, she's coming as
well, here you are."

Diana handed the massive, ornate key through the bars of
the gate to Alasdair. Metal scraped metal. The chain rattled
to the ground. Skreeling, the gates swung back.

Diana and Jean jostled each other through the opening and
hustled up the driveway behind Alasdair—the house loomed
ahead, every window a blot of nothingness—someone bolted
from the shadow of the trees—oh, it was Colin, breathing
hard, stumbling, and yet outpacing Alasdair to the front door.
Which was also locked, but this time Diana had a key.

The wooden panels flew back against the wall. "Father!"
shouted Diana.

"He said he was in the library." Jean charged off across the
entrance hall. There was just enough light that she avoided
barking her shins on the kist or caroming off the corner into
the corridor.

The door to the drawing room was closed, the one to the
library open. The Christmas tree blocked most of the—hardly
light, more of a phosphorescent glow—leaking through the

all windows. The pale stone of the fireplace gleamed like a spectral trilithon. Something moved…

Two shapes hurtled out of the shadows and Jean reeled back against someone too slender to be Alasdair. The dogs barked and leaped and shed, doing their best "Timmy's down the well" routine.

Diana dropped to her knees beside the mounded form sprawled across a chair. "Father? Father!"

"I'll fetch Dr. Irvine." Colin said, and his steps thumped away down the hall accompanied by the patter of furry feet.

"Di," said Fergie's wheezing, whispery voice. "There's my wee lass."

A bolt of lightning bounced through the door, and another one, and the lights flashed off the glass doors of the bookshelves and bits of tinsel on the tree—Thomson and McCrummin, with beautiful police-issue flashlights the size of truncheons. Thomson said, "The incident room door was unlocked—Orla's not yet found the lass…"

"Her mum and dad didna answer my knocking 'til I'd pounded my knuckles raw," said McCrummin, "and even then would not open the door, just shouted, right shirty at first, saying the lass's not with them, she was told off to sit here in the library…"

"Is that Fergus?" Thomson asked.

Alasdair leaned over the chair to support Fergie's head and shoulders while Diana kneaded his hands. Even in the dubious light Jean could see the color and texture of his face, like sour bread dough. Despite the icebox-chill of the room, beads of sweat trickled down the furrows of his jowls.

"Is he injured?" asked McCrummin, reaching for the radio riding her shoulder.

Diana's voice caught and cracked. "It's his heart. All this has been too much for him."

Jean wasn't placing any bets on her own heart right then. It was bouncing up and down between her throat and her chest like a paddle ball. She grabbed a floppy cushion and a lap blanket from another chair, then helped Alasdair place the cushion beneath Fergie's head and Diana arrange the blanket over him.

McCrummin retired to the hall, exchanging mutters with a staticky voice—*ambulance, Dunasheen.*

Been there, Jean thought. *Done that.* Déjà vu *all over again.*

"I'm perfectly fit," Fergie said slowly, his words slurred "Just had a bit of turn realizing Rab was, well—the gloves are there on the table, Alasdair, Sanjay."

Thomson concentrated his light on something that looked like a squashed squid, two leather gloves crumpled together, fingers stiffened with rust-brown stains.

"Where's Rab?" asked Alasdair. "Where's Nancy?"

Fergie licked his gray lips. "The lights were dimming and blinking. He went to see to the generator."

Thomson muttered, "The power plant, aye, in the west tower," and slipped out the door. From the hall came his voice "They're in the library, Auntie. Irvine's where? Ah, good…"

Brenda O'Donnell ran into the room, fell to her knees beside Diana, and opened a bag. "I've got hot tea and cold compresses, whichever you're needing."

"Nancy's in the attics," Fergie wheezed, "took a big torch with her, there's no lights there in any event. The lass, Dakota. She was sitting here, reading. I walked by and saw her then I walked by and she wasn't here at all."

Jean looked frantically around, but saw no notes, no maps—*she went thataway*—only a book lying on the table beside the chair. The cover of *Mysterious Castles of Scotland* still sported a price tag reading "Kinlochroy Heritage Museum."

Dakota had wanted to come to Scotland, Scott had said for ghosts and castles…

Two pairs of feet pounded down the hall and Heather burst through the doorway. "Where is she? Where's my baby?"

Scott pounded behind her. "We told her to stay here. We just went back upstairs for a few minutes, didn't mean to fall asleep..."

Jean assessed the state of their clothes, disheveled, their hair, mussed, and their faces, flushed. Heather's glasses skewed across her nose. She and Scott had been groping each other during the party last night, in a confirmative marital way, of course. But alcohol subverted male performance—or so Jean had heard. Maybe that's why Scott had defaulted to business concerns in the middle of the night, trying to save some face. Maybe he and Heather had retired upstairs to take care of other unfinished business, leaving Dakota safe and sound here in the library.

If you couldn't be safe in a library, where could you be safe?

Alasdair was saying, "She's wandering about the house having a look at Fergie's whimsies, I reckon—there are torches in the cloak room..."

"Torches?" demanded Heather. "You're going to have travel agents marching up to the gates waving torches when we get done with you, you got that? One-star reviews on every Internet..."

"Dakota!" Scott bellowed, and charged back out into the hall.

"Dakota!" Heather shrilled, if not beside him, then not far behind. Their cries resounded through the house, setting the dogs to barking again.

"And they do not know the half of it." Alasdair turned back to Fergie. "Was Greg MacLeod offering to invest in Dunasheen, build a golf course, convert the place into luxury condos? Was he offering to buy the place, lock, stock, and barrel?"

"No, he was…" Fergie's eyes goggled. "Was *that* what he meant by making a grand offer, not for the Coffer, for the estate itself? No, no, I'd only sell up over my dead body!"

That won't be necessary, Jean beamed toward him. Nor had it been necessary making Greg into a dead body, never mind how desperate Rab was to stop the march of—if not progress, at least change.

Alasdair's face in the failing light glinted like an ice sculpture. "Rab. Nancy. Perhaps she was offering to show Dakota the attics. No good going with strangers, the lass is too canny for that, but Nancy's no stranger."

"Neither is Rab," Jean replied.

But Alasdair was already out the door, saying, "You're with me, McCrummin."

Brenda's round face registered first concern, then confusion, then concern again, but she said nothing, only wiped Fergie's face with a soft cloth.

"I'll stay with Father." Diana smoothed Fergie's gray ponytail on the cushion.

His lips crimped in a crooked smile. "Di, I'm sorry about Colin, you, he, have my blessing…"

"Hush," said Diana, her voice now calm as a mill pond. "We'll deal with that later."

At some point, Jean thought, Diana had looked at Dunasheen, at Fergie, and at Colin. She'd thought, "This will never do," and taken them all in a firm hand. But Diana couldn't help find Dakota. She couldn't apprehend Rab and Nancy, not now… Jean twitched left, jerked right, then gave it up and ran after Alasdair.

She skimmed the corner into the entrance hall. The front door stood open on a rectangle of smeared landscape and the feeble glow that was Kinlochroy. Shouts, barks, and footsteps echoed down the densely shadowed coil of the turnpike stair. If they'd all been running in a clump they'd be imitating the

Keystone Kops, but no, they'd fanned out, and she'd been left alone in the dark. Setting her jaw, she grasped the cold, slightly prickly rope handrail with both hands, felt for each misshapen step, and repeated her mantra: *Nothing is here that isn't here in the light.*

But there was plenty that was there in the light.

Like the door to the second floor. A dim light washed over the steps, then faded as Jean worked her way further upward into the chill, the cold, the icy air—a tremor surged from her hand up her arm and amassed on her shoulders. *Seonaid.*

Shadow upon shadow, shape upon darkness—the ringlets, the dress, the shawl—an otherworldly light in two staring eyes. A faint rustling sound…oh. That was the draft from the open front door moving Seonaid's tapestry, nothing paranormal about that, the tapestry was cloth and thread and depicted Old Dunasheen as a backdrop for dramatic events.

Old Dunasheen. Dakota was reading *Mysterious Castles of Scotland.* Dakota had wanted to go out to the old castle. Without lights, she couldn't read about it, so she'd gone to see it. She wasn't lacking courage, to go out there in the dark, alone.

Jean prayed that she was alone.

She turned her back on Seonaid's ghost, shrugging away the cold fairy fingertips brushing the nape of her neck. She felt her way down the stairs, then picked up speed into the back corridor, only to stop abruptly at the library door. "Diana, Brenda, how's he doing?"

"He'll be right as rain." Diana's voice in the darkness brooked no debate.

Again Jean accelerated, shouting back over her shoulder, "I think Dakota's gone out to the old castle. Tell the others—wait, I've got the phone."

She patted herself down as she fumbled along the corridor. No, she didn't have the phone. It must have slipped off her lap in the car and was now between the seats, probably ringing

its little electrodes out. She'd lose valuable time going back
outside and searching for it.

She was in the cloak room. Where was the cabinet? There
Gloves. Scarf. The cold cylinder of a flashlight. In the sudden, bright beam she scanned the hooks on the wall—was
Diana's raincoat gone? Dakota's own coat would have been
in her room.

Jean scooted out the door, down the steps, and across the
courtyard. After the gloom of the house, the light outside
seemed bright. She partly ran, partly stumbled down the
path—heather roots like grasping hands, boulders like trolls
crouched, ready to spring forward—the walls of Old Dunasheen materialized from the mist before her as the walls of
New Dunasheen faded into the mist behind her. The sky and
the horizon, a very close horizon, blurred into one uncanny
gleam tinted the pink of blood-tinged water and the gold of
a dying fire. Sunset, and a hint of smoke hanging in the tur-
gid air. She imagined the old church burning, the cries of
the wounded and dying, the indifferent calls of seabirds…

She really was hearing voices, Irvine's perhaps, from the
front of the house, and in the distance the rising and falling
bleat of at least two sirens closing in on Kinlochroy.

Her shoes thudded on the damp planks of the footbridge
Was that a light behind the enceinte wall? Two days ago, two
sunsets past, she and Alasdair had seen Greg's red jacket van
ish behind that wall.

"Dakota!" she shouted. Then her already ragged breath
caught in her throat—she'd just given herself away. But
she didn't know whether Rab was here, too. Alasdair and
Thomson could already have him in custody. "Where are
you, Dakota?"

Jean fought her way up the path leading past the enceinte
into the keep, splashing through ice-rimmed, peaty puddles
feeling her coat catch on brambles and weather-roughened

rims of stone. Unless it was being caught by bony fingertips reaching through time and space.

She'd never before met a ghost with substance. Then she'd met Seonaid. Seonaid, who'd stitched Rory MacLeod's falling body.

She stepped between two bulwarks of stone, through the gaping gateway into the cage of the tower. Her light flashed across gouges, hollows, lumps of brush, dragging shadows behind it. "Dakota!"

A rustling noise might be a bird disturbed on its nest. But no bird would have said, in a small, trembling voice, "Here, I'm here."

TWENTY-NINE

HER VOICE CAME from the dungeon, the cellar—Jean couldn't remember now what Alasdair had called it. But she remembered where it was, behind a buttress and down a set of steps subsiding into bedrock. Tucked in beneath the weight of the tower's remaining walls.

"Sit tight, Dakota. I'm coming." The beam of her flashlight probing ahead of her—tumbled cobblestones, mud, lichen—Jean started down the steps one at a time, her left hand braced against the cold grit of the wall.

The doorway was still mostly rectangular. Beyond it, her puny light no more than pricked the darkness. The stench of mold, mildew, and decay clotted in her nostrils and her throat. Every nerve in her body thrilled. The hair on the back of her neck squirmed. She forced herself to walk on. "Dakota?"

A sudden light blasted her eyes and she recoiled, her arm across her face.

Rab Finlay said, "I'm telling you, no guid will come of this, any of it."

Squinting, Jean peered over her sleeve. There, on a stone that might once have been a headsman's block, sat Rab. His cap was pulled down low over his eyes. His beard stuck out in a dozen directions. One gnarled hand held an industrial-strength flashlight. The other rested a kitchen knife, also industrial-strength, on the knee of his yellow raincoat.

The meager light revealed the chamber as a nasty hole in the ground, the flip side of a hobbit hole. No, the rough vault of the ceiling wasn't sinking any lower. Jean tried to look into every muck-filled corner without taking her eyes off Rab…

There. Dakota crouched behind a low stone partition, her knees drawn up to her chest beneath a too-large raincoat and her eyes gleaming with tears. Why hadn't she run? *Oh.* She wouldn't make it to the door any faster than Rab would. *Check.* Time to throw a second pawn into the game. Maybe a knight, leaping at odd angles. Not quite an all-powerful Queen.

Jean tried a step outside Rab's spotlight. The glare didn't follow her.

One slow step at a time, she sidled toward Dakota and took the child's hand in her own. The chill in Dakota's flesh struck right through her glove even as her senses warmed to an all-too-brief whiff of Diana's perfume trapped in the lining of the coat.

"I wanted to see the old castle," Dakota said, words staccato. "Mom says we're leaving, like, first thing tomorrow morning, but Dad didn't have time to bring me down here like he said."

"That's okay," Jean told her.

"It was almost light for a few minutes, but when I got here it was dark again. And *he* followed me. *He* scared me. So I tried to hide, but he found me."

Scared. Oh yeah. Good thing Dakota had found a narrow space where Rab couldn't quite get at her. He could get at Jean, though.

Skin crawling, heart palpitating, she looked around. But while Rab was sitting on his rock like a cat at a mouse hole, he didn't move. Perhaps he was crushed by the weight of his own thoughts. The vestiges of conscience. The enormity of what he'd done. Or perhaps he was simply immobilized by sobriety. They still had a chance…

"No guid will come of this," he said.

No shit, Sherlock. Jean pulled Dakota to her feet.

"Everything was all right 'til the auld laird died. Then Fergie Beg and wee Diana came. They're family, they had no call opening the place to incomers, outlanders, foreigners, the lot of them poking and prying." Now the glare of Rab's light turned toward Dakota and Jean. "The lass there, she was by way of telling Fergie about the Aussie's card and all. Should have minded her own business."

"I didn't tell anyone you dropped the card and I gave it back to you," Dakota said. "I didn't even know it was important until last night. I told about seeing the ghost on the driveway, you know, and they made fun of me, even though that turned out to be important."

Jean pulled her one stiff step closer to the door. "That's okay. We figured it out anyway. As for ghosts…"

"There's one here. I saw him falling. I yelled, I guess. And then *he* came running. I couldn't always understand what he was saying, just that I shouldn't be here, Mom and Dad and the Australian lady, we should go back where we came from and stop making trouble. He's got that knife and he doesn't like me very much and he scared me, you know?" Dakota's voice climbed into a higher register.

"I know." The hair on the back of Jean's neck was doing a snake-dance, like medieval villagers circling a bonfire on the Winter Solstice, welcoming the return of the light… Medieval. Rory MacLeod falling. Jean pulled Dakota another step.

"We canna help it. We canna sort things to suit ourselves." Rab's voice rose, too—he was imitating Nancy. Then his words plummeted downward, reverberating in the tiny chamber. In a dark crevice, something stirred in response. "Rubbish, woman. Stuff and nonsense. We're never helpless. I'm proving that to you. I'm proving it to Fergie and Diana and the polis."

He was working himself up. His next thought would be, *In for a lamb, in for a sheep.* In for an Aussie, in for two Americans.

Jean eased Dakota further toward the doorway. Leaning close to the child's ear, she whispered, "Alasdair's seen the man falling from the tower, too. But I haven't. Can you call him, do you think, so I can see him, too?"

Dakota nodded, her eyes reflecting one tiny gleam of light. She took another step without Jean's urging. Jean turned them both toward the door even as she kept her face pointed at Rab. His eyes glittered beneath the bill of his cap. The knife glittered in his hand.

Now! Jean yanked Dakota through the doorway, but it was her own foot that snagged and stumbled, and the child's hand that steadied her and the child's momentum that propelled them up the rough steps, out of the dungeon, the cellar, the hole, out of the darkness into open air. Jean swept her flashlight around the enclosing walls—the gateway out of the keep, where the hell was the gateway?—there!

Their footsteps echoed. So did a scrape, a bird disturbed or a pebble beneath someone's foot. The entire Northern Constabulary, right down to the janitors, could have besieged the castle in the time she'd spent underground. But Jean wasn't going to stop dead—the operative word being "dead"—and wait for a possibly nonexistent cavalry to arrive.

Flashlight flaring, Rab burst out of the dungeon doorway like a grizzly bear from its den.

Jean released Dakota's hand and shoved her toward the gateway—you don't have to outrun the bear, just outrun your companion—Rab's steps thudded closer and she sensed the sharp blade at her back—at least Greg had been stabbed in the chest, he'd faced his killer...

Not now, chattered the teeth of her brain. *Not now, I'm getting married!*

Caught between fire and sword, Jean's nervous system convulsed. Even as she lurched over brush and stone, her mind, her senses, screamed: *Jump! Leap! Take the plunge!*

And in front of her Dakota darted a frantic look upward. "The ghost, he was there. He jumped, he fell…"

The invisible weight, the weight of the invisible, dropped like armor onto Jean's shoulders and she gasped. Through her vision swooped a bird, no, a falling body—fluttering fabric, limbs pumping, mouth open on a wail of surrender as much as despair, a perceptible howl that cut the dark mist like the slash of a dagger.

Rab looked up, stopped, spun, cried out in horror. Rory fell right through him, knocking him off balance so that Rab tripped over his own feet and toppled to the ground.

Jean and Dakota collided, clutched at each other, staggered backward. For what seemed like a long, long moment but was probably no more than a split second, the ghost of the fallen man and the living flesh of a man whose mind had fallen lay tangled together, yellow raincoat against rough plaid, Rab's mouth gaping like a cavern in a thicket, Rory's eyes focused on a dimension above below beyond.

Then Rab lay there alone. Flailing and cursing, he pulled himself to his feet.

Jean pushed Dakota over the threshold and out of the keep. Beyond the enceinte wall lights sprang up, distorted eerily by the mist. Footsteps converged on the gateway. A woman's acid-etched voice said, "Stop just there. Drop the knife."

Lesley Young stood between the two bulwarks of stone, flashlight in one hand, gun in the other, both pointed steadily at Rab. He crouched, head swinging back and forth, scowling. One beat, two, and his fingers opened. The knife clattered onto the muddy cobbles.

Young stepped forward and with a well-placed kick sent it flying into the shadows.

People boiled into the keep—fluorescent jackets, stark white faces, voices shouting. There was Heather, crying, her makeup leaving streaks on her cheeks, and Scott, stunned. They fell on Dakota and crushed her in a double embrace.

"Good job," said Patrick Gilnockie's dry voice, "that Rab tripped and fell just there." He walked on past Jean before she had a chance to reply, not that she had a reply to make.

And there was Alasdair, his arm pulling her so tightly against his side she felt his heart hammering behind his ribs. His grit-on-velvet voice said, "I'm here. I'm here."

The tension seeped down Jean's body and out through her toes. She fastened her arm around Alasdair's waist and hung on as her mind drifted into the sparkling mist...

The sparkles steadied. Flashlights focused. The uniformed scrum eddied and revealed Rab standing handcuffed. D.C.I. Gilnockie stood over him, the archangel over the beast. "Rab Finlay, I arrest you in connection with the murder of Greg MacLeod. You do not have to say anything, but it may harm your defense if you do not mention, when questioned, something which you later rely on in court. Anything you do say may be given in evidence."

Rab growled unintelligibly. The uniforms hustled him away, followed by the multilegged knot that was Heather, Scott, and Dakota. The child glanced back at Jean, tautness ebbing from her features, exhilaration flowing into them. Her small face split into a broad grin. Then the Krums, too, were gone, no more than lights and footsteps receding across the footbridge and the mist.

Which seemed to be thinning. Or else, Jean thought, her eyes were clearing. She let Alasdair's strong arm propel her through the gateway and down the slope to the bridge. Even though the sun was long set and night fallen, she could make out the ocean waves rolling forward one by one, as they always had, as they always would.

His voice barely louder than the swish and thrum of the sea, Alasdair said, "Brenda ran up to the attics, telling us where you'd gone."

"Clever deduction," said another, familiar voice, "that the lass had gone to see the old castle." Ah. Sanjay Thomson was walking right behind them, followed by Young and Gilnockie.

"With Jean," said Alasdair, "it was by way of being a flash of intuition."

Smiling, Jean asked, "How's Fergie?"

"He'll do, Irvine's saying. A night in hospital, two at the most."

"We've got Nancy," said Thomson. "Orla's handcuffed her to her own cooker. She's not blaming Rab. She's saying it could not be helped, circumstances conspired, and all that."

"Right," Jean said. They followed the path up the brae and stopped. Dunasheen, windows gleaming, fairy lights glistening, rose ahead of them, an oasis in the midst of darkness and despair. "Who fixed the generator?"

"Colin," replied Thomson, "keeping himself busy."

Gilnockie edged past them, telling Young at his side, "Urquhart saw the murder. That's why he ran."

"He should have come forward," she said. "We'll do him for perverting the course of justice."

Gilnockie's voice sank into its supernal serenity. "You were seeing how confused Mrs. MacLeod was after her concussion. Could be Urquhart's seeing a murder concussed his mind, being a blow upon a bruise, in a way."

"Ah." Young's voice indicated a thoughtful rather than an accusing frown, but with her back turned and retreating up the path, Jean couldn't tell.

Thomson fell into step behind Young and Gilnockie, Alasdair and Jean behind him. Alasdair asked Jean, voice now soft and smooth, "How'd you get Rory to appear on cue?"

"Do you remember how, soon after we first met, we were

acked into a corner and a ghost staged a timely distraction? Maybe two people having an allergic reaction, and a crisis blooming—ghosts are emotional resonances, after all—and you know, sometimes things are more than the sum of their parts, so there are times even people who don't normally have allergies… Well, we called him, I guess. It's Duna-heen, *Dun na sithein,* fortress of the fairies, and the ghosts have substance here."

Alasdair chuckled. "That's the sort of lucid explanation I'd be expecting from you, Jean."

The tall, lean shape that was Thomson half turned toward them. "Mind you, odd things are always happening. They could be our small minds connecting with the larger one. There's a reason folk believe in sacred places, landscapes, holy relics, eh? Mind your step, the gravel's slippy."

Jean smiled—the lad's hearing was as finely tuned as his brain—and considered Alasdair's minimalist features in the courtyard lights. *So there.* Ultimately you believed because you chose to believe. Ultimately you made your choices based on your beliefs.

His gaze rolled from Thomson's back to Jean's face. Shaking his head and returning her smile, he locked his arm even more securely around her shoulders, and they walked back into the house.

THIRTY

JEAN GAZED OVER the railing of the minstrel's gallery, if not in command, then at least in appreciation of all she surveyed.

Below her lay the Great Hall of Dunasheen Castle. Sunlight streamed in the tall windows, making the gold thread in the banners sparkle. The long refectory table was set with glasses and plates, trays of nibbles, and a wedding cake, its three tiers of chocolatey goodness embellished with red strawberries, red raspberries, and a few strategically placed red flowers.

"Only you could get that all the way here from Edinburgh in perfect shape," Jean said.

Miranda Capaldi smiled her best Mona Lisa smile and did not disagree. In her pale aqua silk suit and pearls, she displayed her usual understated elegance, acting as Jean's maid of honor without overshadowing her. She'd even reduced her crest of golden-red hair to a smooth cap of ash-blond.

Jean hoped she looked as good in her long silk suit shimmering teal, green, and blue, and her gold Claddagh jewelry, variations on the theme of two hands holding a heart. Miranda was in charge of Alasdair's wedding ring, a gold band incised with Celtic interlace. Knowing Alasdair, he'd glued Jean's matching ring to Fergie's hand.

The laird and best man had returned from the hospital late yesterday, Irvine in attendance, in good time to stage a stag party for Alasdair at one end of the house while Diana staged a hen party for Jean—and why wasn't it a doe party?—at the other. A few drinks, a few jokes, ribald and otherwise, were sufficient to mark the occasion, considering.

"Well then," said Miranda with a delicate arch of her eyebrow. "The butler did it."

"Rab wasn't exactly the butler, but yeah, he did it. Ironic, that if Fergie hadn't been going on about a big sale that would save them all…"

"Meaning the Coffer, not the Estate," said Miranda.

"Yes, but Rab didn't know that. He thought Fergie was going to sell Dunasheen. And he knew a clever businessman like Greg wouldn't buy the place without evaluating its contents and auditing the books, at the very least."

"Rab and Nancy could no longer be creaming off the goods, then."

"A new owner would change everything, and if Rab was afraid of anything, it was change." Jean shook her head. "If Fergie hadn't been so sure he'd had something valuable in Tormod's little sarcophagus, then Rab wouldn't have murdered Tormod's descendant."

"If," Miranda repeated. "There's no way of knowing."

There was knowing, and there was perceiving. Jean looked back down into the Hall to see Diana tweaking the Christmas holly and ivy along the fireplace and brushing away an invisible speck of ash remaining from the Yule log. No need, the happy couple had decreed, to bring in fresh, off-season flowers when the place was already spruced up—literally, when it came to the Christmas tree.

Ken MacLeod would have approved of that frugality. But he and Tina had started for Australia this morning. What happened once they got there—other than the formal disposition of Greg's ashes—was beyond Jean's brief.

So was wallowing in what-might-have-beens.

She summoned a smile. "It was nice of so many people

from the village to help turn the guest rooms over and fix things for the wedding."

"Everyone loves a party." Miranda did not add that the party would soon be over, leaving the MacDonalds and their neighbors to pick up the pieces. But then, there were pieces to pick up. At least the last of the second wave of reporters had receded, following the action to the legal edifices of Portree and beyond.

Brenda O'Donnell bustled into the Hall with another platter of edibles, this one decorated with sugar doves. In her polka-dotted best dress she looked like an ambulatory bedspread. Next to her, Diana in her soft, spring-green wool dress and jacket appeared even more chic than usual. The Egyptian necklace would have complemented the color of Jean's dress, but Diana wasn't wearing it. Touching, the way the real beauties dialed themselves back in honor of the bride.

Bride. That's me. Jean forced a deep breath into her chest and noted that Miranda and Diana wore the same perfume. Jean had actually remembered to dab some behind her ears and on the pulse point at her throat, a light floral fragrance symbolizing the rising of her sap into, among other places, her cheeks, which were now two little furnaces heating the rims of her glasses. Prickles of anxiety and delight ran up and down her limbs. *Don't lock your knees,* she reminded herself, and did a couple of bends for practice.

"Is living in Scotland what you were expecting, then?" asked Miranda.

"Didn't you ask me that mere hours before I met Alasdair? In the same paragraph as something about romantic fantasy?"

"All I'm remembering is you claiming to be a hard-bitten cynic."

Jean laughed. "Heck, no. It's merciful fantasy that keeps you going. Scotland, writing, *The Lord of the Rings,* marriage. Speaking of marriage…"

Miranda's significant other, Duncan Kerr, strolled into the Hall. With his sleek silver hair, beautifully groomed moustache, and striped suit befitting a corporate lawyer, he looked positively Viennese, too smooth, too refined, to be Scottish.

"Marriage?" Miranda's eye tracked Duncan's progress around the room. "We'll be watching how you and Alasdair make a go of it."

"Yeah, I know. If it ain't broke, don't fix it."

And there was Scottish refinement, needing no fixing whatsoever—Alasdair in his kilt and jacket, a red rose sweetly blooming in January pinned to his lapel. Beside him walked his mother, so small her tartan sash fell almost to the hem of her dress. When she grew up, Jean wanted to be like Rhona Cameron. She exuded Alasdair's intelligence and gravity, but had a tart tongue of her own and a crown of unabashedly red hair that made her almost look younger than her son.

Diana asked Rhona, "What have you got there?"

The foreshortened Mrs. Cameron—the one and only Mrs. Cameron—lifted a bonnet emblazoned with a silver crest and blue hackle. "It's Allan's. I was thinking Fergie'd enjoy seeing it, since Fergus Mor's was destroyed. Or so you were saying, Alasdair."

Not mentioning Dougie, *Jean's* cat, Alasdair took the bonnet and settled it on his blond hair tipped with gray. There was the something old, and the something blue, and the something borrowed. Jean herself must be the something new.

With an open, unconstrained laugh, Alasdair took off the bonnet and set it on the table. "You'd best be getting me to the altar, Mum."

"Oh aye," replied Rhona, "it's time Jean was making an honest man of you." And they strolled from the room.

Smiling—her face was going to hurt from smiling before the day was over—Jean and Miranda made their way down the turnpike stair. Down, not up past the tripping stane, never mind that Jean hadn't sensed Seonaid's ghost since the two of them together, the quick and the dead, realized where Dakota had gone.

Jean missed her little doppelganger. By now she was back home, surrounded by familiar things, anticipating returning to her school and her friends. With a tale to tell, which, unlike many tales, would of necessity shrink in the telling.

Dakota had left Jean her copy of *Mysterious Castles of Scotland,* inscribing it *To my friend Jean. Happy wedding. xoxo,* the "i's" in "friend" and "wedding" dotted with tiny hearts. In time, Jean hoped, Dakota's tiny, cautious handwriting would expand to fill the space it deserved.

As for Scott and Heather, well, maybe they had mellowed a bit after their scare. Heather had thanked everyone politely and rescinded her threat to post one-star reviews of Dunasheen. Scott had apologized for the episode of the Queen suite even as he handed out business cards. He'd driven his family away not into the sunset but into the sunrise, Dakota waving through the back window until they'd vanished down the drive.

Now the driveway glistened like jet beyond the open front door, where Fergie and Patrick Gilnockie stood in quiet conversation. Jean pulled up beside them while Miranda continued discreetly on around the corner, murmuring about collecting coats.

Gilnockie said, "I've had a word with Alasdair, but just so you're knowing, Jean, Rab's not confessed. Nancy's made a statement, though, and Fergus, and we've got Dakota Krum's statement and yours as well, agreeing as to what he said at the old castle. We've found traces of blood in the stitching of his raincoat as well, despite Nancy cleaning it."

Beside the crisp pleats of his kilt Fergie held a sturdy walking stick, its brass handle shaped like a sea serpent. His eyes shone as brightly as his polished glasses, and the white rosebud decorating his lapel had nothing on his complexion, pale but fresh. "I can't believe I never suspected Rab and Nancy of, well, of anything. Alasdair even asked me if any items had gone missing."

"They betrayed your trust, Fergie." Jean set her hand on his arm. It was rock-steady.

"Nancy admitted to reading your mail and spying on your guests," Gilnockie went on. "In her and Rab's own best interests, they're saying."

"They deserved to participate in the profits," said Fergie. "Apparently they felt they weren't meant to participate in the risks as well."

"Quite so," Gilnockie agreed. "I'm thinking Rab was seeing his chance to dispose not only of Greg MacLeod but also, with the coincidence of the texting 'CU' on Greg's card, of Colin Urquhart. He went accidentally dropping the card in the pub, when the lass picked it up, but like as not he went dropping it deliberately in the car park. He was right baffled when it turned up in Diana's pocket, but then, Pritchard…"

"…also wanted to scapegoat Colin. That's my own fault." Fergie shook his head. "Well, I hope I'm making it up to the lad. I've hired him as manager. He repaired the generator, he's got a good head for figures, and with Diana, well, he'll be all right, in time."

Maybe there would be another wedding, also in time, Jean thought. "You're going to be all right, too, Fergie. You'll make a go of Dunasheen."

He set both his chins and his shoulders as well. "Yes, I will. We will. Diana's agreed to sell her Egyptian necklace, and we're looking into a loan arrangement for Seonaid's portrait. I'll be donating the Crusader Coffer to Brenda's museum—it's an interesting artifact in its own right, eh, Jean?"

"Yes, it is."

"I'll offer the area round the chapel as an archaeological

field school, hoping we can establish the bones as Tormod's. The old church deserves an excavation as well."

"It does that." Gilnockie turned to Jean. "Again, my best wishes to you and Alasdair on your marriage."

"Thank you. And good wishes to you on your retirement. I guess you'll be limbering up a fishing pole or chasing golf balls, not criminals."

The peaceful depths of his smile, the sort that passed all understanding, made Miranda's look agitated. "No. I'll be joining the community at Moray Abbey, to try my vocation as a Benedictine."

Jean stared. D.C.I. Gilnockie was going to enter a monastery? Well if that didn't—explain a lot. Again she stammered her good wishes.

"I'll be praying for the souls of Tormod, Rory, and Seonaid," he said to her and Fergie both. "Perhaps all they've ever wanted was acknowledgement. That's what most folk are wanting, acknowledgment. And I'll be praying for the Finlays as well." Still smiling, he walked away into the sunlight that had transformed Skye's Calvinist gray to ecumenical color.

"Here I thought Alasdair and I were making a commitment," Jean said as Gilnockie's attenuated shape dwindled down the driveway.

"It takes all kinds, and thank goodness for that." Fergie cocked his head to the side. "Was he implying he believed in our local ghosts and spirits?"

"If you believe in the Holy Ghost, then…"

Miranda swept down the hall, Diana and Brenda just behind. "It's time, Jean."

If impending execution concentrated the mind, then impending marriage concentrated the heart. Jean's shimmied up and down her chest—*ooooh*—and again she flexed her knees.

Fergie set off into the cold if brilliant day. Miranda draped Jean's coat over her shoulders. Brenda handed her a nosegay of roses wrapped with tartan ribbon, slightly larger than the one Miranda already held. Adjusting her diamond ring so that it caught the sunlight and sent flashes of rainbow across the old stone walls, Jean began her last journey as a single, independent, lonely entity.

She glanced back at the house to see the two dogs, brushed to within an inch of their lives, sitting in the drawing room window. In the beetling window of the Charlie suite sat Dougie, ears pricked like the famous Egyptian statue of Bastet.

Fergie walked along, swinging his walking stick rather than leaning on it, every inch the dapper laird. "The family cradle's all right for the Campbell-Reids' bairn, is it now?"

"Rebecca and Michael said she slept all night. Good vibes, I'm sure."

Beyond the garden wall, the chapel bell rang merrily. Diana opened the gate. Brenda closed it. Funny, Jean wasn't cold at all. In fact, she was contemplating grabbing a bit of ice from a nearby birdbath and rubbing it over her face—or even dropping it down the back of her neck—when they emerged from the woods to see the chapel in all its intricate glory rising before them.

A few people moved through the porch into the building. The open door emitted the sound of a jig or reel played on a harp, happy, resilient music.

Michael stood to one side, his bagpipes beneath his arm, the drones lying against his shoulder sporting tartan ribbons on the ends. He, too, made a handsome picture in kilt and jacket, and his Alasdair-blue eyes danced. "Here she is," he called to his other half.

Rebecca strolled across the grass, her long tartan skirt flowing behind her, reminding Jean of Seonaid's ghost. She'd been happy here, if guilty as well. Maybe now, after all these years, she'd found peace. Maybe Gilnockie was right, and recognition had eased the ghosts of Dunasheen into eternal rest.

"Look what I found by the little gravestone beneath the tree. Alasdair's impressed." Rebecca crossed Fergie's palm with a gold coin. There was no need, and no time, for her to explain how she, too, had paranormal abilities, her small mind connecting with the larger one...

Oh. Jean, Brenda, Miranda, and Diana all bent forward as Fergie brushed a few remaining grains of dirt from the coin. One gleaming side read "Sydney Mint, Australia, One Sovereign." The other displayed the sober, proper profile of Queen Victoria. "It's been working its way through the soil all these years," Jean said.

"If the bones aren't Tormod's," said Fergie, "then how... well, later, eh? When we're not hastening to the wedding." He tucked the coin away in his sporran and hurried to the vestry door.

Rebecca raised a camera and took photos of Jean and her entourage arriving in the porch, where Orla McCrummin stood holding six-month-old Linda Campbell-Reid. They were both dressed in frilly party frocks, although Orla was standing on her own feet, elevated in high-heeled shoes. Linda's bright eyes took in every color, every movement, and her soft, toothless mouth opened in a laugh. The scent of baby powder emanating from her blanket mitigated the porch's aura of musty stone.

Beside Orla hovered Sanjay Thomson, smiling and nodding. Brenda adjusted one of his buttons, more out of affection than need—his kilt was perfectly arranged and pinned with a miniature sword.

The door opened again, revealing Dr. Irvine's shock of white hair. "Is everything a go?"

"It's a go," said Jean, even as her voice caught in her throat and her knees wobbled. *This is it. A leap of folly and a leap of faith.*

Irvine flung open the door. Diana took Jean's and Miranda's coats. With a whispered, "Keep your pecker up," Miranda glided down the aisle and the audience rose.

Hugh Munro sat to one side of the chancel cradling his small Celtic harp. His bald head with its fringe of white hair glowed in the golden light of candles and sunshine both. His round cheeks above their fringe of white beard swelled in a grin. His fingertips stroked the strings and the graceful notes of "Peace and Plenty" filled the room and spilled out onto the lawn.

"Go on," said Michael, and quelled a squeak from his pipes. "In just a few moments I'll be piping you back down the aisle a married woman."

Marriage, a state of grace...

Far, far away, at the end of the aisle, the blocky, bespectacled figure of Reverend Elphinstone led Fergie and Alasdair out of the vestry. Alasdair took up his stance at the altar step and looked Jean straight in the eye.

Alasdair. Her lodestone. Jean walked herself past all the smiling faces and put her hand in his. His warm, sensitive, capable fingers enclosed her chilly ones. His blue eyes sparked. The curve of his lips moved and he whispered, "Bonny Jean."

Dizzy, and yet never more steady, Jean looked toward Elphinstone. His voice rose and fell like the pulse of the sea, and the words flew into her heart and nestled there.

"O God, who hast consecrated the state of Matrimony to such an excellent mystery...look mercifully upon these thy servants."

Amen, Jean thought. *Amen.*

* * * * *

ABOUT THE AUTHOR

LILLIAN STEWART CARL has published multiple novels and multiple short stories in multiple genres, with plots based on myth, history, and archaeology.

The Blue Hackle is her seventeenth novel, the fifth book in the Jean Fairbairn/Alasdair Cameron mystery series, after *The Secret Portrait, The Murder Hole, The Burning Glass,* and *The Charm Stone.* Most of her novels are in print, and all of them are also available in various electronic formats.

Three of her twenty-five published short stories have been reprinted in *The World's Finest Crime and Mystery* anthologies. All are available in electronic formats, and all but one in two print collections, *Along the Rim of Time* and *The Muse and Other Stories of History, Mystery, and Myth.*

She is also the co-editor (with John Helfers) of the Hugo award–nominated *The Vorkosigan Companion,* a retrospective on the work of science fiction author Lois McMaster Bujold.

Lillian lives in North Texas, in a book-lined cloister cleverly disguised as a tract house.

Her website is http://www.lillianstewartcarl.com.

REQUEST YOUR FREE BOOKS!

2 FREE NOVELS
PLUS 2 FREE GIFTS!

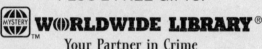

W RLDWIDE LIBRARY®

Your Partner in Crime

YES! Please send me 2 FREE novels from the Worldwide Library® series and my 2 FREE gifts (gifts are worth about $10). After receiving them, if I don't wish to receive any more books, I can return the shipping statement marked "cancel." If I don't cancel, I will receive 4 brand-new novels every month and be billed just $5.49 per book in the U.S. or $6.24 per book in Canada. That's a savings of at least 31% off the cover price. It's quite a bargain! Shipping and handling is just 50¢ per book in the U.S. and 75¢ per book in Canada.* I understand that accepting the 2 free books and gifts places me under no obligation to buy anything. I can always return a shipment and cancel at any time. Even if I never buy another book, the two free books and gifts are mine to keep forever.

414/424 WDN F4WY

Name	(PLEASE PRINT)	
Address		Apt. #
City	State/Prov.	Zip/Postal Code

Signature (if under 18, a parent or guardian must sign)

Mail to the Harlequin® Reader Service:
IN U.S.A.: P.O. Box 1867, Buffalo, NY 14240-1867
IN CANADA: P.O. Box 609, Fort Erie, Ontario L2A 5X3

Want to try two free books from another line?
Call 1-800-873-8635 or visit www.ReaderService.com.

* Terms and prices subject to change without notice. Prices do not include applicable taxes. Sales tax applicable in N.Y. Canadian residents will be charged applicable taxes. Offer not valid in Quebec. This offer is limited to one order per household. Not valid for current subscribers to the Worldwide Library series. All orders subject to credit approval. Credit or debit balances in a customer's account(s) may be offset by any other outstanding balance owed by or to the customer. Please allow 4 to 6 weeks for delivery. Offer available while quantities last.

Your Privacy—The Harlequin® Reader Service is committed to protecting your privacy. Our Privacy Policy is available online at www.ReaderService.com or upon request from the Harlequin Reader Service.

We make a portion of our mailing list available to reputable third parties that offer products we believe may interest you. If you prefer that we not exchange your name with third parties, or if you wish to clarify or modify your communication preferences, please visit us at www.ReaderService.com/consumerchoice or write to us at Harlequin Reader Service Preference Service, P.O. Box 9062, Buffalo, NY 14269. Include your complete name and address.

WWL13R